PRAISE FOR STEPHEN ARYAN

"Packing in an epic's worth of action and feeling, this thought-provoking fantasy argues that even the most vicious monster battles are less harrowing than the struggles within men's souls. This is a knockout."
Publishers Weekly, Starred Review

"A tremendous sword & sorcery romp with a lot of heart and plenty to say. I really enjoyed this book."
Peter McLean, author of Priest of Bones

"Stephen Aryan puts the epic into Epic Fantasy."
Den Patrick, author of The Boy with the Porcelain Blade

"Aryan's battle scenes are visceral masterpieces that transport the reader deep into the melee."
Taran Matharu, author of the Summoner series

"Sparkling action sequences punctuate keen dialogue and a journey full of colour and interest... Compelling, consuming and a novel in which no character can be considered supporting cast... Bring on the sequel."
James Barclay, author of The Chronicles of the Raven

"Fast-paced and action-packed, steeped in plots and schemes – a great fantasy tale."
Ed Cox, author of The Relic Guild Trilogy

Stephen Aryan

THE COWARD

ANGRY ROBOT

ANGRY ROBOT
An imprint of Watkins Media Ltd

Unit 11, Shepperton House
89 Shepperton Road
London N1 3DF
UK

angryrobotbooks.com
twitter.com/angryrobotbooks
Kell-ing Yourself

An Angry Robot paperback original, 2021

Cover by Kieryn Tyler
Edited by Eleanor Teasdale
Map by Tom Parker
Set in Meridien

ISBN 978 0 85766 888 2
Ebook ISBN 978 0 85766 889 9

Printed and bound in the United Kingdom by TJ Books Ltd.

9 8 7 6 5 4 3 2 1

For all of those who have served, past or present, in the armed forces

Five Kingdoms

PART ONE
The Legend Rides Out

CHAPTER 1

Twelve rode forth, twelve answered the call,
Eleven heroes and a boy of no deeds at all.
One rode home, one brave lad,
Who saved the world from eternal darkness.

EXCERPT FROM THE SAGA OF KELL KRESSIA
BY THE BARD PAX MEDINA

Kell Kressia, slayer of the Ice Lich and saviour of the Five Kingdoms, tripped on a rake and fell into a pile of horse shit. With a vicious curse he scrambled to his feet, trying to brush the moist steaming turds off his clothing. Instead he managed to smear it down the front of his shirt and trousers.

"Fuck! Shit!"

His old nag, Droga, snickered as Kell stumbled towards the rain barrel. Pulling off his soiled shirt he filled a bucket and sluiced himself off before scrubbing his trousers and hands. Damp scraggly bits of hair clung to his face. His beard itched and a cool wind touched his bare skin making him shiver. The sun should have been baking today but the good Shepherd, in his infinite wisdom, had decided to thwart him and every other farmer with bad weather. If it didn't improve over the next few weeks it would mean another poor crop and more empty stomachs.

People were already struggling after last year's meagre harvest.

Not for the first time Kell wished he had someone to help him with the farm. It wasn't a big holding, enough for him to make a living, but working alone meant it was a lot of hard work and long hours.

Just once he'd like to come home and find someone waiting for him at the front door. Maybe they'd lit the fire or heated some water for a bath. Or maybe they'd made a nice stew for dinner. Someone to trim his beard and warm the bed.

Before his fantasy went any further he walked back up the hill to his empty little house. With a sigh Kell pulled on a fresh shirt, rolled up his sleeves and returned to work in the fields. His vegetables usually grew well by themselves but he was hoping the horse shit would give them a boost.

"I should sell you to the Choate," he said to Droga, while collecting turds. "They drink horse blood, you know."

Droga said nothing. He just dropped another huge steaming pile and went back to chewing grass. Kell laughed and patted the old horse with affection.

By the time his chores were done for the day it was getting late. The market would be closing soon and the streets would be quiet which he preferred. In search of a meal cooked by someone else for a change he hurried into town.

Honaje was a good place to live because of the lake, the dense forests and the rich black soil. There was always plenty of work so that meant a fair amount of money flowing in and out of town. It also helped that King Bledsoe, who was a sneaky old bastard, kept carving up parts of his territory and selling them off. He even gave some bits away for free, out of the goodness of his heart. Scrubland and rocky holdings on hillsides that most people couldn't farm. And yet the settlers were smart and somehow always made it work, raising hardy sheep or goats. And in return, for his apparent kindness, once a year the wily King sent the taxman to visit.

The narrow-faced collector, Obbrum, always arrived at the same time and yet every year people were surprised to see him. Kell had paid the local Manx to hex Obbrum and make his cock drop off, but so far it hadn't worked. Then again, perhaps it had. The only thing that seemed to give the taxman any pleasure was taking money from other people. He probably hadn't used his cock in years.

As Kell walked down the main street everyone waved or said hello. It always startled him that they all knew who he was, and what he'd done, but he knew nothing about them as individuals. Complete strangers would greet him as if they were old friends, shake his hand and pat him on the back. The physical contact was always jarring and he did his best to avoid it.

As he skirted the edge of town Kell waved to those that greeted him, but didn't stop to exchange small talk with anyone. He never remembered their names as he spent as little time as possible in town and there were too many new faces to keep track.

Despite his infrequent visits Kell noticed there had been significant changes over the last few years. There were a lot more visitors from across the Five Kingdoms. Those in the rugged north were suffering where the weather was cooler and the land more barren. Traders from far and wide, even pasty Corvanese, were now bringing in more fruit and vegetables from across the Narrow Sea. There was always a stream of travellers passing through town either heading west to the capital, Thune, or east to Lorzi, the Holy City and beyond to the coast.

As he entered the market Kell's nose was assaulted by a range of smells. Questionable meat, combined with heady spices and medicinal herbs, created a blend that wasn't appealing. Normally the market would be full of noise and people, but at this hour it was quiet and felt abandoned. He'd timed it perfectly.

At the centre of the market most of the stalls were packing up for the day, but Dos Mohan was still there, sharpening his razor on a leather strop. All of the awnings were white or yellow to ward off the sun, but the barber's was dyed in the traditional pale blue. A thick wooden pole, as wide as Kell's leg and as tall as a man, stood at the front of the tent. It was painted in hoops of red and white to announce Mohan's honourable profession.

Mohan was at least sixty years old so the intricate blue tattoos on his arms and cheeks had faded over the years. The designs were also partially hidden by the wrinkles on his weathered face. He'd been living in Honaje almost ten years so Kell considered him a local despite being one of the vicious Choate. In the past they'd rarely ventured outside their territory, but in the last thirty years they'd begun to explore the lands of their neighbours.

"Ah, here he is, the big hero man," said Mohan, showing off huge white teeth. The barber insisted it was because he scrubbed them every day, but Kell was convinced they were painted wood.

"You need a shave? A haircut? You have a bad tooth?"

"Just a shave, if you have time?" asked Kell.

"For you, I always have time," said Mohan, slapping the padded chair.

As Mohan pulled on his short white apron Kell tried to get comfortable. Putting his trust in someone was difficult, especially when they wielded a razor, but over the years he'd found a strange kinship with the barber. In their own way they were both outsiders who people smiled at in public but talked about behind closed doors. They'd struck up a peculiar friendship and Mohan was among a handful of people that he trusted in town.

"Your hair is dry and coarse like a horse brush," said Mohan, rubbing Kell's scalp. "Do you want me to cut it? Put on some resin?"

"Maybe next time. I don't want to keep you from getting home. I know it upsets your wife when you're late."

"You're a good man," said the barber, starting to trim his beard. If the barber was late home Mohan's wife would spit at Kell in the street as she'd done two months ago. She'd also hissed something at him in her own language. Although the Choate was reluctant to speak about his life or homeland, he was happy to teach Kell his native language. Learning a few words at a time Kell had picked up a rudimentary grasp of the Choate tongue. Every time he saw Mohan's wife she cursed him for something. Last time it had been something to do with a ruined meal.

Mohan had customers in his chair from across the Five Kingdoms. Many came just to say they'd seen a Choate up close without being stabbed in the face. As a whole, Mohan's people had a fairly aggressive reputation and with good reason. There was a long history of feuds between them and the neighbouring kingdoms. It was only a hundred years ago that an uneasy form of peace had been established. Most people thought they were savages who lived in mud huts, but then again, most people were idiots. While customers sat in the barber's chair, nervous and scared, they talked and Mohan listened. The barber often knew what was happening before anyone else, including the town Chief.

"I heard some worrying news," said Mohan.

"Famine?"

"No, but there's been trouble in the north. Fights breaking out over food and merchants being robbed on the road. If the weather doesn't change, then it may come to that. Have you noticed how cold it's been?"

"Too cold," said Kell. His crops were at least two months behind where they should be. It was the second year in a row of mild winters and cool summers which meant low yields. "Trouble is on the way."

"Yes, it is," said the barber, as his scissors flashed around Kell's chin. "There, neat again."

Kell opened his eyes and peered into the battered old mirror beside the chair. His scraggly beard was gone. Mohan had turned it into something neat that emphasised his broad jaw. Staring into his pale blue eyes Kell wished his nose wasn't quite so wide. His hair was still a mess, but it would have to do. He didn't want the barber to be late. Mohan clucked his tongue and tied back Kell's hair without being asked, gathering it up with a piece of leather cord.

"Now, you look like a hero," he said, winking at Kell in the mirror. It was at that moment Kell noticed Mohan was holding a metal spike in one hand. "Let me look at your teeth," said the barber with a grin.

"No, that's fine," said Kell, trying to get up but the Choate pressed him back into the chair. Despite working all day on the farm he wasn't nearly as strong as the old barber.

"This won't hurt," promised Mohan, which was a lie. It always hurt when he stabbed Kell's teeth with a steel spike, but apparently it was for his own good. "Open."

Realising he wasn't going to get away, Kell opened his mouth and Mohan peered in. "Ugh," he said, wincing at the smell. "Trapped meat," he said, poking at one tooth until he dislodged something. "Apple peel," he said, stabbing another tooth and hooking out something else. "I don't even know what this is," he added, holding up a chunk of something to the fading light. After stabbing Kell in the mouth a few more times he finally seemed satisfied. "It's better now, yes?"

Kell didn't want to admit it but the ache was gone from that annoying bit of apple. "Yes. How much?"

"For you, big hero, three dinars," said Mohan. Kell dropped four dinars in the brass dish at the bottom of the striped pole. Mohan heard the clink of the coins and offered him a big smile.

"You're most generous," he said.

"Shepherd's blessing upon your house," said Kell. Before the barber tried to check him for lice he hurried out of the tent towards his favourite tavern, the Dancing Cricket.

It was still early in the evening but unfortunately the main room was already packed, with only a few spare tables. In the far corner was a raised stage for performers which was empty tonight.

Noticing a free table close to the fire, Kell squeezed past chairs and sat down, taking a moment to enjoy the heat on his back. Normally at this time of year the fireplace would be cold and every window thrown open, but not tonight. Not until the weather improved.

Everyone in the room knew Kell but they left him alone. Even after all this time he was still getting used to being around large groups. Sometimes the smells and particularly the noise were overwhelming. By focusing on his breathing, the anxiety began to ebb away until he felt almost normal again.

Despite his unease, sometimes it was nice to be in a room

with others and feel as if he was part of the community. Working alone on the farm all day meant he didn't see many people and occasionally it was lonely. He'd grown comfortable with solitude and preferred it, but Kell never wanted to feel isolated.

After ordering a mug of ale he paid for the cook's special, a spicy chicken stew. The price was eye-wateringly high, and he doubted there would be much meat in his bowl, but this was a rare treat. While waiting for his food Kell eavesdropped on conversations. As expected, most of the talk was about the weather or taxes.

When the food arrived the stew was tangy and delicious. The vegetables were crisp, if a little shrivelled, and he didn't see much meat, but at least there was plenty of rice to fill him up. The cook's husband was a lucky man. To come home to such a meal every night would be a real blessing from the Shepherd. Despite keeping to himself, a shadow fell across Kell's table.

"Are you him?" asked a buxom merchant. She was Corvanese with pink skin and yellow hair, which had been rare ten years ago. More ships were crossing the Narrow Sea all the time. "Are you Kell Kressia?"

"I am." She wore a black tricorn hat marked with five blue ribbons. That meant she was allowed to trade across all Five Kingdoms, including the Holy City.

"Is that your sword, Slayer?" she asked, gesturing towards the silver blade above the fireplace. Its surface seemed to shimmer in the firelight. Everyone else pretended not to notice the excited merchant. This wasn't the first time someone from out of town had reacted like this.

"Yes, that's it," said Kell.

"It's a pleasure. A real pleasure," said the woman, her eyes wide with delight. "My name is Rowaz tan Nadia."

Kell forced a smile even though he was starting to feel anxious. People were beginning to stare. He could feel their eyes on him like ants crawling across his skin. He needed her to sit down and leave him alone.

"Can I join you for a drink?" asked Nadia. "I'll pay, of course," she volunteered.

Kell shook his head, despite the offer of a free drink. It was always the same. They asked the same questions without fail. What did the Ice Lich look like? Did he really cut off her head with one blow? What happened to the heroes? Are their bodies really still up there on the ice?

To them it was nothing more than an exciting story, but he'd lived through the events in the bard's saga. Digging up the past always left him feeling uneasy and bitter. They had been rich and famous warriors that people still adored despite being dead for ten years. As the only survivor he'd come home to a fanfare but little else for his efforts. There'd been no reward. No riches. Not even a reprieve from his taxes.

"I don't think that's a good idea," said Kell, not wanting to indulge Nadia's curiosity. More heads were turning in his direction and now three merchants were standing beside his table. The other two were a local apprentice and another Corvanese with only two ribbons.

"Please, we just want the real story. We've heard it from the bards, but they always embellish it."

More people were taking note of their conversation. Without being asked, Nadia sat down and before Kell could protest her two friends followed suit. One placed a mug of beer in front of him.

"We just want the truth," said the apprentice. People went back to their own business and Kell felt some of his nervous energy drain away.

Kell shook his head. "You don't want that."

Nobody wanted the truth about what had happened. They all said it but the truth was ugly. It was a knotted web of grey decisions, not black and white. People wanted neat and simple but life was a convoluted path of decisions that no one could predict.

If he told Nadia that he'd been kicked out of the army at seventeen because he was tired of following orders she'd tell him it was fate. Otherwise he wouldn't have been at home to hear about the call to arms.

When the weather changed, the dwellers beyond the Frozen Circle, the Frostrunner clans, sent an emissary south to meet with the five Kings. There hadn't been such a conclave in hundreds of years. Normally the clans had no reason to leave their homeland on the ice, but even they were struggling to survive. Ten years ago the Frostrunners had been starving to death along with everyone else.

The five kings came to an agreement and called upon their best. The bravest and greatest warriors. Lowbren One Eye, Cardeas the Bold, Droshalla the Beautiful, Bron the Mighty and others. A total of eleven heroes that everyone knew and loved. Kell, like every other teenager, had idolised them.

How quickly that had changed.

They might have been warriors with famous names, but they weren't heroes. After days in the saddle they'd moaned about sore arses like everyone else. No one wanted to hear about that. Or how their mighty leader, Cardeas, had a bad belly and got a run of the shits for three days.

"Tell us about the heroes," said the apprentice, startling Kell from his reverie.

"No, tell us about the Ice Lich. Did she really turn the weather sour? Was it worse than now?" said the other merchant.

"I don't want to talk about it," said Kell, sliding the untouched beer across the table. He didn't want to go back there in his mind. Kell was about to get up from the table when Nadia's question caught him by surprise.

"When were you most afraid?"

Anger flooded Kell's mind and he sank back into his chair.

According to the Medina saga his worst moment had come when he'd battled the Ice Lich. The truth was far more shocking and that part of the story hadn't made it into the bard's tale.

"Fine. I'll tell you the real story," said Kell. "It was the day Bron the Mighty collapsed..."

CHAPTER 2

Across the Narrow Sea the ice would creep,
The cold would spread and all would perish.
But no aid came from overseas, no heroes and no hope,
The Five Kingdoms stood alone.

Excerpt from the Saga of Kell Kressia
by the Bard Pax Medina

"I was a fool. I was just a boy of seventeen and I hadn't been chosen. But that didn't stop me."

When news reached Honaje about the gathering of heroes Kell knew it was his chance. It was the opportunity he'd been waiting for to prove his worth.

The heroes were rich men. They were always paid well for their efforts and Kell had no doubt they would receive a hefty reward after completing this latest quest. It made sense. After all, they were the ones facing the dangers that others shied away from. While his mother appreciated an extra pair of hands and a strong back on the farm, Kell was confident he could do more for her by going with the heroes. Once he became as rich and famous as them, he could hire people to farm the land while his mother merely supervised.

"The heroes didn't want me to go with them. I had to prove my worth."

When shouting and kicking him in the arse hadn't worked they'd given him all of the worst jobs. They were determined to break his spirit and make him go home. Every night Kell had carried water, fed and watered the horses, cleaned their armour, polished their weapons, foraged for herbs and mushrooms, even dug the shit-pit night after night. But he'd endured it all, never once refusing a task. The only time he'd said no was to Umbra the Quick. One night Umbra had offered to put in a good word with their leader, Cardeas, if he could bugger Kell.

Eventually the heroes realised Kell wasn't going to give up so they'd agreed he could go with them. There were many days after that Kell wished he hadn't been so stubborn.

Looking back he knew his reasons for going had not been selfless. Part of him had genuinely wanted to ease his mother's burden. The main reason was that he wanted to be just like his heroes; rich and adored. Theirs was a charmed and easy life. As ever, the truth was not so simple.

Many of the heroes had families they rarely saw more than a couple of times a year. Children, who mostly grew up without their fathers as they were constantly away in service of their King and country. After only a day or two on the road with them Kell began to differentiate between myth and the men.

Although the stories told about them were generally true, they often left out many details. Lowbren and Pragor had problems staying sober and were always a little drunk. If they didn't get a drink every day they would begin to shake, sweat and lose control of their bodies. Umbra regularly snorted snuff laced with something that kept him calm as he had violent mood swings.

All of the heroes, without fail, had nightmares. They would cry out in the night, screaming and begging forgiveness from the dead who continued to haunt them. It didn't matter that the people they'd killed had been enemies at the time, or that their cause was just. The weight of their actions was a constant burden.

Whenever they passed through a village or town on their way north the heroes became different people. They were friendly, larger than life characters. Away from prying eyes they were often sullen, haunted by the past and worried about the future. Kell saw both sides and over time his opinion of them began to change.

"By the time we reached the ice fields more than half of the heroes were already dead. We'd had no choice but to abandon their bodies. We couldn't bury them, so they were left for the scavengers." Kell stared at each merchant in turn, noting their excitement in spite of what he'd just told them. "It wasn't long after we'd left Kursen behind to die. All of us were exhausted beyond anything we'd imagined. The wind was howling but there was no shelter. Everyone was injured, but we had no choice, so we kept going. I didn't know it then, but several of the *heroes*," Kell said with a sneer, "had already sustained wounds that would eventually kill them.

"The cold, it went so deep you felt it in your bones. Day after day of unrelenting ice and snow with no reprieve. After a while, feeling cold became a good sign. It was when you started to feel warm that it became dangerous. That night we made camp beside the ice fields. Normally there was banter, but not that night or any night thereafter. That was when Bron collapsed."

Bron the Mighty was a mountain of a man, almost as wide as he was tall. Bron was the physical embodiment of power and endurance. His homeland, Kinnan, was a rugged country where all of its people were hardy and used to working outdoors. Bron was something else. Born into poverty he'd raised himself up until he'd become famous across the Five Kingdoms for his legendary feats of strength.

When the others faltered because they were tired, Bron kept going, but not before mocking them. When they lacked the strength he called them weak. And when they complained about their wounds he laughed in their faces.

"I'll never forget the sound Bron made as he fell over. If one of the others had done it, he would have said they sounded like a little girl. He whimpered and then mewled in pain like a child. At first we couldn't find what was wrong with him, but then we discovered the infected wound on his arm. He must have been ignoring it for days. The skin was so hot and swollen and he cried out at even the slightest movement. The only way to save him was to cut off his arm but no one was trained for it. They were fighters not healers. We didn't even have a saw and there was no fire to seal the wound."

Kell glanced at the merchants and saw the colour drain from the apprentice's face. The other two were pale as well but it was too late to stop. They'd asked for the unbridled truth.

"They'd been careful about rationing whisky but that night most of what was left went into Bron. He was drunk and yet still delirious with pain. He was just too big. We couldn't numb him properly."

Everyone tried to hold him down but for once his great strength became a curse. He thrashed about making it a hundred times worse. He cursed and spat, swore and even bit one of the others.

"I tried to hold onto one of his legs but he kept kicking me. It took forever for the sword to cut through his flesh. And the blood. There was so much. I didn't think it was possible. It was a blessing when he finally blacked out. We did the best we could, binding the wound, but it was a poor job and we all knew it.

"No one knew if they had caught the infection in time. In better circumstances, with a real healer, Bron might have had a chance of surviving. It was clear from their expressions that no one expected him to survive the night.

"Bron was many things, but without question he was the toughest of the heroes. If even he could die then the odds of anyone else surviving were slim and they all knew it. I saw it then. The loss of hope. All of them were afraid. All of them knew they were going to die."

The merchants weren't smiling now. The apprentice looked as if she was about to be sick. Nadia and the other merchant sat with their mouths hanging open. A pool of silence was spreading around Kell's table, but he doubted they'd noticed the glares directed at them.

"I was so tired, freezing cold and desperate for sleep, but throughout the night Bron screamed in pain. Eventually, despite the noise, I passed out from exhaustion. At some point I woke with a start but at first I couldn't work out why. It was the silence. Bron had stopped crying and I assumed the worst, but the irony was that he had survived but two others didn't make it to morning." Kell laughed, startling the others.

"It's funny, I can't even remember the order that they died in after that. I just know that one man froze to death in his tent and another was dragged away by something, probably a maglau. We found a piece of his leg and a couple of fingers, but we didn't search very far. There was no point.

"That was moment when I was most afraid. Because, only then, did I realise what had been obvious from the start. I'd idolised the heroes. I thought of them as invulnerable mythical figures, but the awful truth was they were just men. They could die just like everyone else. And if they could die then I had no chance at all. Death had been a constant companion on that journey, but never had it felt so close than in that moment." Kell stared at Nadia and saw his fear from that time reflected in her eyes.

The excitement of meeting him had been wiped from their faces. In its place was horror at his story and regret at having come into this particular tavern and having approached his table. After tonight they'd never listen to another retelling of the Medina saga in the same way. When people spoke about the heroes, or him, they would flinch or quickly change the subject. Right now Kell suspected they were wishing they'd never met him.

There was more. So much more he could have told them about the heroes. About how all but one of them were awful people, about the kind of things they said when no one was around. But Kell had sworn an oath to his King to keep the worst of it a secret. To protect their legacy, to preserve the memories for their families, and to protect the Five Kingdoms.

A horrible prolonged silence had settled on his table.

"The weather," blurted Nadia, startling the others.

"What about it?" asked Kell.

"It's turning again."

"It's just a bad season, that's all. People were starving ten years ago," said Kell, even though he clearly remembered his earlier conversation with Dos Mohan.

"Isn't this how it started, with one bad season?" asked Nadia.

"Yes," admitted Kell.

"Then what if the Ice Lich has come back?" asked the other merchant.

"She can't come back," said Kell, gesturing at his sword above the fireplace. "I cut off her head. Nothing can come back from that."

"But what if there's a new menace in the north? What if the Ice Lich had a child?" she asked.

Whether it was just a bad couple of seasons or something else it didn't really matter to him. Whatever was happening it had nothing to do with Kell any longer. He'd done more than his share and now he was just a farmer. It was up to someone else to deal with it this time.

"Leave him be," said someone as the merchants launched into another line of questioning.

Without saying another word Kell turned his back on the three merchants and headed for home.

Five days later he returned to the tavern to find a summons waiting for him from King Bledsoe. The letter was brief, requesting his immediate presence regarding a matter of grave importance. He was to bring his famous sword and warm clothing for a long journey.

Kell tossed the letter on the fire, had one drink and then returned home to bed, confident that everything would look better in the morning.

CHAPTER 3

And at the end the Ice Lich begged for mercy,
But Kell had none for all that it had wrought.
And with one mighty blow from Slayer,
He severed the Lich's head from its shoulders.

EXCERPT FROM THE SAGA OF KELL KRESSIA
BY THE BARD PAX MEDINA

Two weeks went by and life in Honaje stayed much the same. Despite poor weather Kell worked daily on his farm doing his best to coax the crops to grow. Taking a day off was rare but unless the weather improved, there would soon be nothing to fill his hours.

On the fifteenth day after receiving the King's letter he finished all his chores in the morning and went fishing in the afternoon for his supper. That day the good Shepherd smiled on him as he caught six fish in the first hour. Further out on the lake he could see the town's fishermen at work with their nets. As long as he didn't get in their way they wouldn't bother him. Did they ever feel lonely spending so much time on the water by themselves?

Before it started to turn dark he rowed back to shore with a dozen fish. Ten were salted and cured for the larder. The other two he cooked with a few scrawny potatoes dipped in butter, chives and garlic. All day the only people he'd seen were at a distance across the lake and he'd not spoken to anyone for almost a week.

In need of company, and perhaps a drink or two, he took another trip to the Dancing Cricket. As soon as he set foot inside, Kell knew it was a mistake. Every eye in the room turned towards him and all conversation stopped. Kell searched the crowd, trying to identify the cause of their alarm. His answer came in the form of two warriors dressed in blue and white padded armour. Stitched across the back of their gambesons was a familiar crest; the blue-tipped eagle of King Bledsoe of Algany.

A third warrior wore black armour edged in silver and even had a steel breastplate which was rare given the cost. Two of the warriors carried spears and daggers but the one in black had a sword on her hip, another sign of considerable wealth.

Even though his stomach began to churn, Kell casually approached the bar. The eerie silence in the room continued. He could feel people watching as he sat on a stool and ordered a drink. It was only when one of the King's warriors turned to face the room that conversation started up again. The babble of voices swept over Kell like the tide. After days of not speaking to another person it seemed loud but for once it was a welcome sound. Anything was better than the silence on his farm where the only voices were ghosts rattling around inside his skull.

"I am Captain Semira of the Raven," said the warrior, sitting down next to him. Kell was surprised that someone of her status would come in person. There were twelve members of the Raven, the King's elite, and they rarely left his side. He guessed her presence was a meant as a sign of respect from the King, but from Semira's expression she clearly thought this task was beneath her.

Semira's black hair was cut short into a bob. Her face wasn't particularly memorable but her eyes were a rare green. The deep notches between her eyebrows indicated a serious nature.

"Buy you a drink?" he offered, knowing that she would refuse.

"We need to leave as soon as you're ready," she said. Kell pretended not to have heard, earning a frown. "We have horses standing by," said Semira.

"Off you go then," he said, sipping his ale.

"Did you not receive a missive from the King?" she asked.

So far he'd received four letters delivered to his door. He hadn't opened any of them after the first. They'd all gone on the fire.

"No. Nothing. Why?" asked Kell with a glance at the barman, Torb. All post in the village was delivered to the Dancing Cricket and Torb knew everyone's business. Normally post wouldn't be delivered to a person's door but everyone recognised the royal seal. Every few days Kell had returned from the fields to find a new letter awaiting him on his doorstep. There was only one way they'd got there.

Kell stared daggers at Torb, urging him to mind his own business. The barman wisely went elsewhere to serve another customer.

"A letter was sent," insisted the Captain. "Several, in fact."

"Well, I never saw them," said Kell, getting ready to leave. The Captain put a hand on his arm and he idly glanced at her.

"This is important," insisted Semira.

"I'm sure it's a matter of life or death, but I'm just a simple farmer."

"I order–"

"You can't give me orders," snapped Kell, slamming his mug on the bar. He let the anger trickle away and took a deep breath. A few people in the room had noticed his outburst and were closely watching the conversation. "I'm not in the army anymore. So why don't you sod off back to the capital."

Captain Semira gave him a vicious smile showing teeth that would make Dos Mohan proud.

Semira produced a sealed letter which she dropped on the bar in front of him. He didn't need to read it. The wax seal was enough to tell him who it was from. It would be the same as the others. A plea to an old hero for help. Hadn't he given enough already?

Behind Kell the room had fallen silent as everyone waited for his response. Seeing no way out he tore open the letter and read its contents as if for the first time.

"Horses are standing by," said Captain Semira, knowing that he was trapped. "You've been formally summoned to visit the King. Either you can come peacefully, or I'll knock you out and hogtie you to the saddle. It's up to you, but choose quickly as I'm losing patience."

The look in her eye told him she was serious. Kell turned to face the room and several locals stood up to show their support. Although he often struggled with names and faces these were not people that he would ever forget.

Among the dozen were Allanah and her husband Ram who owned the farm down the road from his plot. In Kell's absence they had cared for his mother and had run the farm when she'd become sick. Daucus, the local Manx, had tended to his mother, day and night, never once asking for money for the expensive herbs that numbed the pain. Although never a true believer in the Shepherd, Kell's mother had been devout and Sister Gail had often called in to see her. Normally the stout priestess had a kind smile but now she looked ready to chew rocks and spit out sand.

If he decided to fight they would side with him.

"Stay out of this," said Semira, warning the entire room. The King's warriors were severely outnumbered but she showed no fear. The other two looked worried but she was confident no one would actually move against her. To make her point Semira drew her sword but held it down at her side. "This is the King's business. Go back to your drinks."

The dozen individuals on their feet ignored her, looking instead to Kell for direction. A smile tugged at the corners of his mouth. He was touched by their loyalty after all this time. Those who'd been here ten years ago had seen what the journey had done to him. The scars on the outside had faded but those within had never really healed.

"If you don't come with me today, the next time I visit I'll bring more soldiers," said Captain Semira. "Who knows how many of your neighbours could be injured or even killed. Is that what you want?"

"I'll go with you," said Kell. There was already enough blood on his hands. "But I have a farm to run. Crops and animals that need tending."

"We'll take care of it, won't we?" said Allanah to her husband. Ram nodded, although his eyes never strayed from the King's warriors. Both of them were beginning to sweat under his glare.

"You'd best pack a bag," said Semira, sheathing her sword. As Kell turned towards the door the Captain's voice rang out. "Aren't you forgetting something?"

"Like what?"

Her stare was incredulous. When she realised he wasn't pretending, Semira pointed towards the fireplace.

It took Kell a moment to notice his famous sword hanging above the mantelpiece. He saw it so often it had become just another decoration. The only time the sword came into focus was when someone asked to hear the story. It was all part of another life and a different version of him. A façade created by the Medina saga.

Torb retrieved Slayer and reverentially carried it across the room. Kell snatched it from his hands and was about to storm out when he found the door blocked by one of the warriors.

"Radek will make sure you don't get lost on the way home," said Semira. Radek moved to one side, letting Kell out the door, but then fell in two steps behind.

The short walk home felt like a special one. Perhaps it would be his last as a free man. Perhaps he'd never see Honaje again. Perhaps he wouldn't survive the day. It was a sobering thought, but it also made him think about everything he would miss about his home.

Radek stayed outside but he made sure the front door stayed open, propping it ajar with his foot. As Kell glanced around his small house, gathering together what he'd need for the journey, he found himself thinking about the past.

What would have happened if he hadn't chased after the heroes? Maybe if he'd stayed home he would have found a good woman, settled down and had a family. A boy and a girl who might chase chickens in the yard, splash through puddles in the rain, fall asleep on his chest at night. That didn't sound so bad. He was still fairly young. There was plenty of time, at least there had been before today.

"Do you ever wonder where your life would be if you'd taken a different road?" he asked Radek. The warrior said nothing. He just stared at Kell with suspicion.

Kell dismissed him from his mind as he stuffed warm clothing into a knapsack. He added his spare pair of boots, some shirts, a woollen cap and his old worn pair of gloves.

He left behind a few personal items as they'd be of no use on his journey. A curio he'd found in the field that looked like a chicken bone but was made of metal. A sparkly piece of stone he'd found on the ice beyond the Frozen Circle. A rusted axe that he'd been told had belonged to his father. The small pieces of armour he'd salvaged from the heroes. He left all of these and other items in the trunk beneath his bed.

He made a point of packing his cooking knife, his special flask, a paring blade which he sometimes used to shave, a whetstone and his trusty old dagger. Radek must have seen the glint of metal as he shifted in the doorway but didn't complain. Kell left his bow and arrows where they were. It felt strange to be wearing a sword on his back again. He would have to get used to the weight.

He'd spent many years living in this house and was disheartened by how little time it took to gather his important belongings.

With a wave at his old nag, Kell walked back to the main street where Captain Semira waited beside four sturdy horses. A small crowd had gathered outside the Dancing Cricket to see him off. The last time he'd ridden through Honaje they had lined the streets, cheering his name. Today they were deathly silent as if he was being led away for his execution.

Semira impatiently gestured at the spare horse, keen to be on their way. As Kell mounted he wondered if he would ever see his home again. All of his dreams about the future had been snatched away. With the weight of a sword on his back and warriors beside him in the saddle, Kell knew that he was reverting to his old self. It was not a pleasant feeling.

It had been ten years since his last visit to the capital city, Thune, and in the interim much had changed. Even at a distance he could see more tall buildings than he remembered rising above the surrounding stone wall. Pointed spires, bulbous domes and blocky slabs, all of them made from identical silver-white stone which reflected sunlight.

Built on five hills, only a fraction of the city could be seen from this far away. The bulk of it was in the valley below where the network of sloping streets twisted around like tangled pieces of string. It was common for visitors to become lost in the Warren which is why most stayed on the widest and busiest streets.

Another new addition was what looked like a shanty town that had sprouted up outside the east gate. As the sea of flapping canvas and striped awnings came into focus Kell realised it was a vast market bustling with activity. The main road had been left untouched but on either side a network of pathways ran between stalls which were flooded with people from the Five Kingdoms.

Kell saw several people dash across the east road to get from one side of the market to the other. They ducked around traffic coming in and out of the city with practised ease so as not to stop the flow of carts and riders. Occasionally a wagon driver would shout or curse at them for startling his horses but no one paid them any attention.

As they drew closer to the city the smell of it all began to overpower Kell. Living in the countryside he didn't really notice how other people smelled. Everyone spent a lot of time outdoors, and even working on a farm he bathed regularly. At home the air was fresh and uncluttered, but here there were so many people crammed together it created an intense stench of warm bodies and sweat.

Other smells were also fighting for dominance. Garlic bulbs hanging from stalls, fish and blue crab brought in from the coast, and the reek of cows and sheep in pens. Somewhere in the heady mix he detected the sickly sweet aroma of shisha. Small clouds of blue smoke drifted up from tea dens where men and women would be lounging on cushions sucking on hookahs. It seemed as if some things never changed. Ten years ago there had been talk of King Bledsoe banning the practice but in all that time it clearly hadn't progressed.

Kell's nose began to run and he sneezed four times in a row. Pressing a finger to the side of his left nostril he snorted to clear his right. "How can you stand the smell?" he asked.

Semira said nothing but her expression was one of distaste. The decision to let the market thrive didn't sit well with her. As Kell rode past the stalls several people glanced at him but there were no signs of recognition. Right now he was just a country bumpkin being escorted into the city by the King's warriors. With such an escort they probably thought that he was a criminal. With a grin he waved at the crowd to show them he wasn't tied to the saddle. A few people raised eyebrows but it was clear no one recognised him.

When a teenage boy ran alongside Kell's horse, shoving a clutch of plums towards him, one of the riders tried to chase him away.

"Good price. Good price for fresh fruit," chirruped the boy, dodging Semira's boot.

Kell smiled benevolently down at the boy, flicked him a dinar for the plums. It was far more than it was worth and the boy stared at him with wide eyes.

Despite being escorted by one of the Raven there was a short delay at the east gate. A Scith merchant with heavily-laden donkeys was flapping a document in the air while the uniformed official endured his rant in silence. Eventually the tirade came to an end leaving the man gasping for air. Kell didn't hear the reply but the merchant visibly paled. His posture changed, his gestures became smaller and his tone of voice more wheedling. An agreement was reached as the merchant passed through the gate accompanied by a pair of warriors. Perhaps the merchant's reputation was also not what it once was.

There was a moment of shade as they passed through the tunnel before emerging back into dull sunlight, as he moved from one world into another. Outside the city he could see and feel the sky. It was endless wash of blue with drifting grey clouds. Here it was reduced to a narrow, pathetic thing. A strip that he glimpsed between the sloping rooftops that bent towards each other across the street. On all sides he was surrounded by buildings, a seemingly endless number of people, and a cacophony of sound. All of his senses were overloaded. The natural world slipped away and was replaced with one made of stone. Even the ground beneath his horse's hooves was cobbled, no longer the soft brown earth of the countryside.

"This way," said Captain Semira. She directed him away from the east road and its crowds for which he was grateful. Leading their horses in single file they headed south and west towards the palace which sat at the top of the southernmost hill. Staying at this height the roads were fairly level which made it easier for the horses. It appeared to be a kind gesture to spare the animals and avoid battling through the crowds but Kell wondered. The Captain didn't strike him as a warm and cuddly person who cared about horses.

Semira and the other warriors were unusually alert. Their eyes constantly roaming for signs of danger and Radek jumped when an alley cat sprinted across their path. Kell raised an eyebrow but said nothing as he soaked up some of their tension. He didn't think his life was in danger but clearly there was more going on than he'd been told.

They encountered few people on the quiet roads and when the gates of the palace came into view the three warriors heaved a collective sigh of relief. Kell had a brief glimpse of the black iron gates before he was hustled inside, their horses were led away to the stables and he was rushed across the courtyard.

"Not a word," said Semira, even going so far as to put a finger to her lips.

She took the lead, guiding him down narrow servants' corridors and up twisting staircases. They saw many servants in white and blue palace uniforms but all of them had somewhere to be. None spared him more than a glance and no one showed any signs of recognition. But all of them were familiar with the Captain as she received curt nods adding to his impression of her stiffness.

Finally they arrived at a large bedroom where he was told to wait. Kell noticed she locked the door, leaving him with little to do but inspect his surroundings.

The room was dominated by an ancient hardwood four-poster bed that was so high, almost level with his chest, that it came with a set of moveable stairs. Thick red curtains edged in gold thread hung from all four corners and the sheets were so soft Kell wondered if they were made from silk. Even the walls were covered with soft red material that hung in peculiar layered folds presumably to muffle sounds. A huge mirror on one wall reflected light from outside which made the room unpleasantly warm. All of it was undoubtedly expensive making him feel even more like an outsider. Even the washbasin was made from delicate porcelain. He'd have to be careful not to break it.

The door flew open and a rotund man with wavy blond hair and a foppish demeanour sauntered in. He was wearing rouge on his cheeks and smelled of peaches.

"My, you're certainly rugged," he said, throwing open the window. A meagre breeze wafted in barely stirring the curtains. "Has anyone come by to measure you?"

"Measure me?"

"Of course not. It's always left up to me. No one ever thinks that poor old Darzi might have other business. Very well. Stand there, arms out," said Darzi.

"What is this for?"

Darzi stared as if he was an inbred. "You can't go before the King dressed like that. Arms out!" he said, holding up a knotted piece of string.

Kell did as he was told, as the faster this was done the sooner the annoying man would leave. Darzi made a few quick measurements across his arms, shoulders and down the back of his legs. He clucked his tongue and muttered to himself all the while.

"Hmm, it won't be perfect but I think I have something. Wait here," he said, disappearing in a cloud of perfume. Almost as soon as he'd left, the bedroom door flew open again. A sturdy matron with arms like tree trunks and a face like a cow's backside stumped into the room. In one hand she held a dry sponge and in the other a block of soap.

"Bath time," she slurred, making Kell recoil in horror. "Follow." She left the door open as she disappeared through it, but he could hear her thunderous footsteps receding down the corridor. Poking his head out the door he saw her waiting at the end of the hallway. She pointed one paw at another room and he slowly crept towards it, afraid of what awaited him inside. Mercifully it was just a bath full of steaming water. Beside it sat a stack of clean towels. More water was being heated in a huge copper cauldron beside the tub.

"You get in. I wash," said the servant.

"I can wash myself," he said, snatching the soap and sponge from her. The woman laughed, a low dirty sound, before shuffling away. Kell went inside and closed the door, even going so far as to bar it with a chair, just in case.

The water was a little too hot but he didn't complain as he was still a bit saddle-sore. He'd bathed the day before setting off for the capital so it wasn't as if he stank. No doubt it wasn't up to the high standards of the King's court. This was another reason he hated the city. The concealing layers of paint smeared across faces. The tight elaborate clothing with scratchy collars and dainty food that was neither tasty nor filling. It was all so fake. Finery that served no purpose. Underneath it all they were just like him. They pretended otherwise but they all sat down to take a shit. Even the King put his trousers on one leg at a time.

Kell scrubbed himself all over with the sponge then soaked for a while to ease his aching muscles. When the water began to cool he wrapped himself securely in one of the towels and cautiously opened the door. Expecting to see the burly servant leering at him he was surprised to find a familiar face instead.

"It's been a long time," said Lukas, the King's Steward.

Even though it had been ten years Kell thought the man looked no different. Tall like all Hundarians, Lukas's black hair and neat moustache showed no signs of grey although he must have been at least fifty. With few lines on his face he could be easily mistaken for a much younger man. It was the eyes that gave him away. Over the last twenty-five years of serving King Bledsoe he'd seen a great deal and it had left its mark. The pinch between his eyebrows never faded even as he offered Kell a friendly smile.

A shrewd man in the King's court was not uncommon but Lukas kept the rest on their toes. If not for him the King wouldn't be as prosperous or well loved.

"You look well," said Kell. "How is the family?" he asked, unable to remember if the Steward had any children.

"My wife and three children are in good health," said Lukas with a wry smile. He knew Kell had no idea. "Come," he said, gesturing down the corridor.

Several different sets of clothes awaited Kell on his bed in a variety of outlandish colours. Not even the Shepherd could force him to wear mustard trousers. Five itchy-looking white shirts had been folded over the back of a chair and four pairs of stout black boots were lined up in a row.

Sensing his distrust of bright colours Lukas selected a modest grey jacket with blue trim and matching trousers. Kell thought they would be too small to squeeze his arse into but he was willing to give it a try. Lukas waited in the corridor until he was dressed, then returned with a barber carrying an assortment of scissors and combs.

"Leave the beard," said Kell, taking a seat. The woman actually glanced at Lukas before agreeing. A tense silence filled the room.

"Don't you want to know what this about?" asked the Steward.

"No," said Kell. "I want to know why your thugs threatened to kill my neighbours if I didn't come with them."

"They shouldn't have done that, but I did want them to impress upon you the importance of the situation. Letters were sent."

"I never saw them," said Kell, averting his eyes. "Why? What's happened?"

"You know as well as I that the weather is changing."

"The cold will pass. It's just a couple of bad seasons."

Lukas was already shaking his head. "Last year the Frostrunner clans sent an envoy."

The seed of fear in his stomach sprouted limbs and the cold began to spread. Lukas's voice cut through the air like a knife. "Something has taken up residence in the Ice Lich's castle. The ice-dwellers sent a dozen people to investigate and a dozen heads came back on a sled. The danger is real."

CHAPTER 4

When mankind trembled in the dark,
The Shepherd brought fire and with it light.
But His greatest gifts were the twelve pillars of faith,
Which saved our souls from eternal darkness.

Excerpt from the sacred Book of the Shepherd

Reverend Mother Britak, high priest of the Shepherd, gazed down at the small idol she'd prayed towards for forty years and raised a questioning eyebrow.

"Really?" she muttered. "Now?"

Lately, the easing of her worries that came from prayer had been evading her. The quiet voice inside had fallen silent. She was confident this was merely another test of her faith. Comfort was a luxury and that way led to sloth and laziness. She would remain true to the path.

With a grunt of effort she stood up and her back cracked alarmingly. After stretching her hands above her head she twisted her neck to loosen the muscles. Next she worked on her shoulders, running through a series of stretching exercises to wake up her ageing joints. There was nothing she could do about her sagging flesh, nor the increasing number of purple veins she could see under the skin, but she was determined not to end up like her predecessors, hump backed or bedridden. Her duties required her to be active. She would not retire. Sloth led to the softening of the mind and a rapid plummet towards the shores of death. She would fight it every step of the way with every tool she could muster.

After half an hour of stretching she had worked up a light sweat. With no time for a bath she sponged herself down with a damp cloth and then anointed her skin with lavender scented holy oil.

Stepping out of her private chapel she was greeted with a picture of order. Everything in her reception room was exactly where it should be. From her vestments hung in the wardrobe, to every cup, book and pen on her desk. She insisted on such consistency and was known for being a stickler for the rules. Britak didn't care what others said behind her back, as long they didn't know the truth. Of late she'd realised her mind had begun to wander. Sometimes it was difficult to find the right words and from time to time she mislaid an item. Forcing such rigid consistency into the areas of her life that could be controlled made it much easier to conceal the problem.

Despite her station, the reception room was modest, barely ten paces wide in each direction. The grey stone walls were bare, apart from faded tapestries, and beneath her feet the cool tiles were the colour of faded lemons. The wooden table and desk were cheap and plainly made, without any adornment, as were the two sturdy hardwood chairs. The only real luxury she allowed herself, given her advancing years, was a single cushion to pad her rear. Over time that too had diminished in size making it difficult for her to sit for very long without it becoming uncomfortable. The cushion was a concession but she was confident the Shepherd would forgive her for such a small indulgence.

Someone had already been in and thrown back the thick purple curtains. They kept out the heat in summer and trapped the warmth in winter when the snow piled up outside. She'd begun to hate the onset of winter as the cold sunk into her bones and didn't leave until the middle of spring.

The view outside her window was one she'd seen countless times and yet never grew tired of studying. The Holy City of Lorzi was a Kingdom unto itself. A shining beacon of hope in a land rife with greed, lust and sloth. Although it was the smallest of the Five Kingdoms she would argue that it had the most power and influence. People flocked to its streets to see the ancient buildings and holy sites. It was here that the first brave settlers had landed from the old world. Little was known about the old country except that it had become a place rampant with destruction. It was also here that her ancestors had built the first church dedicated to the Shepherd.

As a young girl she'd run through the streets of Lorzi with dreams of growing up to be a merchant or captain of her own ship. Instead, as the third child and an unwanted surprise thanks to her careless parents, she'd been sent to a convent at an early age. Britak had not grown up to become a leader of industry, but as the Reverend Mother her power extended far beyond that of a merchant or ship's captain.

Staring over the city her eyes were inevitably drawn to the majestic cathedral in which she spent an inordinate amount of time. Its immense blue dome stood higher than all the other buildings and its shining white walls gleamed in the morning light. The only other building that could compete in terms of grandiose stature was the palace of King Roebus. Britak could grudgingly admit to herself, although not to anyone else, it had taken her breath away the first time she'd seen it as a child. Now such overt displays of wealth made her furious. To waste money on something as excessive as gold leaf decoration set her teeth on edge. The only reason to have large and colourful decorations was to celebrate the glory of the Shepherd, everything else was a frivolous waste. Even the vast mural upon the inside of the cathedral's dome had been completed with simple oil paints. Its majesty came from venerating the Shepherd, not its substance.

Purity, sobriety and thrift were the three cornerstones of her faith. The twelve pillars of the Shepherd had brought progress but she demanded more of herself and her people. She tolerated no deviations in any of her priests and was doing her utmost to bring that message to the people.

Sallie, the doe-eyed initiate she'd been cursed with as a personal assistant, stood waiting by the door.

"Good morning, Reverend Mother," she said with a bob of her head. In her hands she held a wooden tray upon which rested a bowl of porridge, a pot of tea, a single slice of lemon and one hard-boiled egg.

"Set it on the table, child," said Britak. The girl had all the initiative of a potato. Unless told exactly what to do she would just stand around staring at the walls. It wasn't completely her fault. Both her parents had the wit of a boiled cabbage so it had been inevitable that Sallie would be a dullard.

After Britak had eaten breakfast the girl helped her dress, first in a plain white robe and then the tools of her office. The golden stole. A golden edged shawl and her biretta. The crosier stayed where it was for now. Although she wasn't required to take it out with her, Britak had been using it more in the last two years to assist with her walking. It felt good to have something upon which to rest some of her weight. Each day she spent a long time on her feet and despite her age was rarely offered a chair. It would be seen as an indulgence and besides, in her mind, sitting was only for eating or writing.

Once she was dressed, the girl scurried away leaving Britak to enjoy a final moment of quiet before the inevitable rush and noise. All too soon there was a knock on the door announcing that her escort had arrived.

Six burly priests in unadorned white hooded robes waited outside her door. All of them were armed with a wooden baton which hung on a plain rope belt around their waists. Such precautions for her safety had not been necessary in the past but recently the respect for her office, among some of the population, had faded somewhat. Some even refused to step aside when they saw her walking through the streets. Her escort was there to persuade them to make way.

Taking up her crosier Britak set off at a steady pace through the corridors of the rectory. In the past she would have walked as fast as possible but she no longer had the stamina.

The first thing Britak saw when she set foot outside was the seagulls. They looked harmless enough, wheeling about overhead on a westerly breeze, but she'd seen what their shit did to buildings over time. If it were up to her she'd have every one of the vicious little beasts shot. Unfortunately her personal wishes were irrelevant. All animals had been made by the Shepherd and were therefore blessed, no matter how noisy and destructive. But if just one more of them crapped on her she'd take steps to make sure it never happened again.

"Are you ready, Reverend Mother?" asked one of her escort. The question sounded innocent enough but she heard a hint of concern. She'd been staring up at the sky for a while, lost in thought. They probably thought she was going senile. "I was just saying a prayer of thanks for another glorious day. Lead on," she said. The fact that it was slightly overcast didn't matter. The priest nodded and pushed open the front gate.

With three guards on either side she began the familiar walk through the city to the palace. The narrow winding streets in the outer district brought back a host of memories from her childhood. Stringy green vines with small purple flowers had spread across the tops and down the sides of many walls. The light fragrance brought a faint smile to her weathered face as did the faint squeal of children at play. She heard the rapid patter of tiny feet and her guards tensed but she wasn't concerned. Six screaming children raced past, totally ignorant of her, wrapped up in an adventure of their own.

Children were wonderful. At such a young age their minds were open and they were excited by everything. They were like dry sponges ready to be filled with water, or something even more nourishing: faith.

It was the perfect time to teach them about the glory of the Shepherd and get them into the habit of attending church. Their

faith would flourish and in time they would hopefully pass it
on to their own children. King Roebus was still fighting her on
mandatory school lessons about the Shepherd but she would wear
him down.

Once every child in the Holy City had been put on the right
path she would see about spreading it further into Algany and
beyond. King Bledsoe was vehemently against the idea, but he
wouldn't live forever and she already had people working on his
daughter, the Princess Sigrid. She wouldn't be the one that sat on
the throne but it would be her hand that guided the nation. The
princess was too strong-willed to be dominated by any man.

As her escort directed her through the city Britak imagined what
could be achieved when the Five Kingdoms were all marching
in the same direction. She would cast out the cults that were
sprouting up like mushrooms and strenuously urge non-believers
to return to the fold. It might not be a future she lived to see,
but her successors would ensure that the plan continued in her
absence.

"Bless you, Reverend Mother," said a homely merchant in a
grey tricorn hat. The woman's voice brought Britak back to the
present. She absently noticed they were already passing through
the heart of the city. At this early hour of the morning shops were
just setting up and the streets were quiet. Those with stalls outside
showed a meagre array of fruit and vegetables and what was on
offer was shrivelled or small. Another poor harvest meant that it
was beginning to bite everywhere. There were more beggars in
the street than last year, some of them children, and every day it
seemed to be getting worse.

The merchant who had called out was loading her wagon with
sacks of rice but she'd paused to doff her hat.

Britak raised her right hand and made the sweeping gesture of
the crook in the air. "Bless you, my child," she said, offering a wan
smile. The woman was fat around the waist, which meant she
was a glutton, and the broken veins on her nose spoke of a love of
harsh alcohol, but such blessings from strangers were uncommon

these days. The woman's spine straightened at Britak's words and her smile widened showing a set of crooked teeth. A lost cause but perhaps not. Perhaps a blessing from the Reverend Mother would urge her to return to church. No doubt this was another small test meant to erode her faith but Britak wasn't fazed in the slightest. Over the years she'd come across far worse candidates who had found their way back.

Britak doggedly marched on, noting with annoyance the number of people who saw her coming and said nothing. Most simply went about their business but one or two turned away, showing her their back which was a grave insult given her station.

She felt the mounting rage of her escort. All of them now had their batons in hand and their hoods pushed back so that everyone could see their grim expressions. People noticed the change and began to move out of the way but Britak was still concerned what might happen if anyone was too slow.

"Stay calm," she muttered, noting the white knuckles and grinding teeth of the priest on her immediate left. Only a month ago Tallon had nearly beaten a man to death for spitting in her direction. Britak thought it had been accidental rather than malicious but Tallon had not. Thankfully the man in question had lived, although he would forever walk with a limp and now had to wear an eyepatch. According to King Roebus the severity of the punishment did not fit the crime. The incident had also forced her to concede on a few issues in recent months. Her time of contrition was over and she couldn't afford another outburst like that.

Thankfully she arrived at the palace gates without any violence and there she was handed over to the Baru, the King's personal guard. Quick and deadly, the hundred Baru were a breed apart from other warriors. Some claimed they were trained together from birth but Britak knew it wasn't quite that long. The thing she liked about them the most, other than their silence, was the respect they showed her.

The leader of her escort tried to set the pace but she merely gave the man a look and he slowed down. Britak kept her eyes forward, doing her best to ignore the repugnant displays of vanity hanging on the walls.

The huge paintings were an historic reminder that Roebus was descended from a line of gawping weak-chinned fools who thought it was noble to have themselves painted beside the corpses of dead animals. There was much to be said for honouring those who came before. After all, the present was built upon their shoulders, but this gallery of freaks merely demonstrated what Britak had always known. King Roebus was an idiot. There was a certain slyness to him, but he was indulgent and therefore could be manipulated through his appetites.

As Reverend Mother she barely had to wait before the herald announced her. The King, a short weak-chinned, portly and balding man in his middling years, was lounging on the throne. Beside him on a much smaller chair was a petite woman with raven dark hair and dark skin from Algany. She was at least twenty years the King's junior and if not for the delicate crown on her head she could be mistaken for his daughter.

"Ah, Reverend Mother, a pleasure to see you as always," said the King. "Punctual as ever."

Her station protected her from the need to bow or curtsey to the King and she wasn't about to honour his vacant new wife.

She waited for the guards to leave the throne room before replying. "We need to talk."

"Are you not going to ask about my health?" said the King, feigning offence. "Or offer me a blessing?"

Britak took a deep breath and leaned more heavily on her crook. It was going to be one of those meetings. "Why doesn't she curtsey?" asked the vapid Queen, turning to her husband. "Shouldn't she curtsey or bow?"

Mercifully the King already had two sons from his first wife so he was not reliant on breeding with such poor stock. Nevertheless she noticed a certain flush to the girl's cheeks and suspected her belly would begin to swell in the next month or two. Hopefully she wouldn't need the King to explain why it was happening.

"The Shepherd's blessings be upon your house, your children and all of your family," said Britak, interrupting the King's explanation of why she didn't genuflect.

"Well, that's just not fair," said the Queen, petulantly crossing her arms.

The King rolled his eyes and sighed, saving Britak the effort. "How about you run along and see if the kitchen has any of those biscuits that you like," he suggested. The Queen's eyes lit up, making Britak reconsider the rounding of the girl's face. It was probably a result of eating too much. The Queen scampered away like an unruly child, holding up her dress so that she could run faster.

"I have news," offered the King, by way of apology. Normally they did this dance for a long time before finally getting down to business. Perhaps his young wife was exhausting him more than she realised. "King Bledsoe of Algany summoned Kell Kressia to the palace."

"For what reason?"

"He believes the poor weather is a result of a new evil in the north."

"Again?" said Britak, not even pretending to hide her scorn. "Doesn't the man have any original ideas?"

"He's convinced it's real. Another emissary from the Frostrunner clans came south with the news."

"They're godless heathens. They can't be trusted," she said, shaking her head in disappointment. She knew Roebus was slow but hadn't thought him a complete idiot.

Ten years ago King Bledsoe had managed to convince the four Kings that the danger was supernatural in nature. It was blasphemy of the worst kind. Britak knew there were dark forces in the world but they were of the spirit and the mind. She'd spoken to dozens of condemned criminals before they were executed. Some of them claimed to hear voices, but they were nothing more than by-products of a sick mind. It was mercy to end the suffering of such people.

Only the gullible believed in magic and the supernatural. It was nothing more than sleight of hand contrived from ridiculous superstition. She'd done her best to stamp down on it but in some places they still had Manx, so-called wise-men and women, who granted favours in return for money. It pained her that such con-artists still existed, robbing people of their money.

The story from ten years ago was just another elaborate scam that had been politically motivated. A gathering of heroes had been sent and, miraculously, it was one of Bledsoe's people who was the only survivor. Apparently the rest had all died but Britak suspected Kell had murdered them.

"The weather has changed for the worse," said King Roebus.

"It's just a couple of bad years, nothing more," said Britak. "Just as it was ten years ago. I've seen this sort of thing happen before. Next year, or the one after, there will be a bountiful harvest. The Shepherd will provide."

"What about the stories?"

"The Ice Lich is a wicked tale designed for misbehaving children. There's no such thing as magic or the supernatural." As Reverend Mother she'd been having this argument for decades. Across the years a few people had claimed to have powers but when put to the test they never yielded any measurable results, even when strenuously questioned by her inquisitors.

"Witchcraft. Magic. Pagan gods. They're all fantastic distractions from the one true faith."

"I knew you'd get back to that, Britak," said the King.

"You shall address me as Reverend Mother."

Roebus raised in an eyebrow. "In which case you shall address me as Your Majesty, or Highness."

"No man or woman is higher than any other. We are all equal," she pointed out.

"Even you?"

"Yes, even me," she said, shifting her feet to try and restore circulation. Pride was a grave sin and she did her best to avoid it. "I'm no better than anyone else."

The King's expression softened. "Would you like to sit down, Reverend Mother?" he asked, gesturing at one of the chairs against the wall.

"No, thank you. Now, what are you going to do about King Bledsoe?" she said. She would not accept pity from anyone.

"Nothing. What can I do?"

Britak realised she would have to guide him towards what was obvious. "Tell me, did King Bledsoe's popularity increase after his champion returned home?"

"Of course. It was all the people wanted to talk about across the Five Kingdoms. Bledsoe was seen as a hero as well. He practically doubled the size of his army overnight with recruits."

"And what do you think will happen this time?" she asked, forcing herself to be patient.

"I thought you didn't believe."

"I don't, but some people do. All Kell has to do is travel to the Frozen North, camp on the ice for a week and then return home after apparently vanquishing this new evil. Next year when the weather improves, everyone will attribute it to him."

Realisation slowly blossomed behind the King's eyes. "Bledsoe will be unstoppable. He could become High King!"

It was a far-fetched idea that had yet to become a reality. Some believed that one of the five kings would eventually usurp the others. As king of the Holy City, Roebus had imagined himself inhabiting that position. It was a dream that Britak had allowed to flourish in his mind over the years.

"It's possible," she conceded. "His army will grow and his popularity will soar again. But, by admitting he believes in this new evil, he will also be proclaiming his lack of faith."

"Who cares about that?"

"You should," said Britak, through clenched teeth. "If you publicly denounce his claim and assert your belief in the Shepherd, the people would see you as an example to follow."

"While also filling your churches with more bodies," said the King, reminding her that he wasn't completely stupid.

"That is true, but more people coming into the Holy City, for any reason, would also fill your coffers which have been suffering of late." A great many merchants visited but the majority of them travelled onwards to other kingdoms or across the Narrow Sea. Food prices were starting to rise across the Five Kingdoms. The number of pilgrims visiting the Holy City had also significant decreased in the last fifteen years.

"It's an interesting idea," said the King after a long pause. That meant he liked the idea but wasn't ready to agree. He would pretend to consider it for a few days before asking her to visit again so that they could plan what happened next.

"There's still the issue of Kell," she said. "Every day he's out there it benefits King Bledsoe while spreading more lies about the supernatural. That damages the Holy City which in turn damages you. Kell needs to be stopped."

"What exactly are you suggesting?" asked Roebus, lowering his voice as though someone was listening.

"I'll leave the details up to you," said Britak. This wasn't the first time they'd had this kind of conversation. "He's a known drunkard. Such indulgences are dangerous sins."

She said no more and let the King fill in the gaps. He nodded thoughtfully. "I have someone in mind."

"Let nature run its course. A good harvest will follow poor, of that I have no doubt. Hold firm to your belief and you will be rewarded by the Shepherd."

"Of course," said Roebus, but his voice had developed a whine. "It seems a little extreme."

Britak counted to ten in her head before speaking to keep her temper in check. She'd shouted at him in the past and had learned it didn't work. He needed to be gently coerced into making difficult decisions while being exposed to the painful alternatives if he failed to act. "Then do nothing and see what happens. Bledsoe's popularity will increase, as will his power, and the Holy City will become a crumbling ruin."

It would never get that far but fear was a powerful motivator. She wanted to press him about the schools but now wasn't the time. He couldn't focus on making more than one big decision at once.

Britak recognised the expression of pained resignation on his face. He would do it even though some part of him thought that it was wrong. She would pay penance for both of them until her guilt was assuaged, but the sacrifice of one life would reap vast rewards for them both in years to come.

Leaving the King to mull over his decision she marched out of the throne room. Britak was almost at the front door of the palace when she heard a familiar girly shriek echoing down the corridor.

"Wait here," she said, gesturing at her escort. One of them was about to argue when she simply raised an eyebrow.

He bobbed his head and stepped back, giving her space.

A short walk down a narrow servants' corridor brought her to a preparation room where one of the kitchen staff was decorating a cake. Beside the servant stood the Queen eating icing from the bowl. Somehow she had already managed to daub the pink mixture across her face and down the front of her expensive dress. Cackling with delight she gobbled up more of the pink goo, her eyes rolling back with pleasure.

As a result the servant saw her first, making a deep curtsey before Britak dismissed her with a flick of her hand.

"But we've not finished," complained the Queen, as the servant scurried away.

"I think you've had quite enough," said Britak, pushing the door closed. When she turned around the gormless expression had drained off the Queen's face making her almost unrecognisable. Even her posture became straight and elegant. "Report," said Britak.

"The King is still undecided about the schools," said the Queen.

"Then you need to be more persuasive."

"I'm doing my best, Reverend Mother."

"Clearly you're not."

The Queen rolled her eyes. "If my hands weren't tied from playing an idiot all day, I might be able to—"

"I don't want to hear excuses," said Britak, cutting her off. "A lot of time and effort was expended to put you in this position. Someone with any semblance of intelligence would never have been allowed to get this close to the King. Use your other assets to persuade him," she said, gesturing at the Queen's shapely figure. As Reverend Mother she'd been celibate for decades but she understood the power of lust. "Get it done."

"Yes, Reverend Mother," said the Queen, making a deep curtsey.

"But first, make sure Roebus sends someone to deal with Kell Kressia. I won't stand for his continued blasphemy."

"It will be done. I promise."

"I want the matter resolved by the time I get back from my trip."

Britak wasn't looking forward to some parts of her journey but it was necessary as spiritual guardian of the Five Kingdoms. She would not let any nation slide into debauchery and paganism like the heathens of the Summer Isles.

It was going to be a grand spectacle which she hoped would inspire the masses to return to the glory of the Shepherd's teachings. It had been a long time since the leader of the church had made such a pilgrimage but these were desperate times.

Some rulers like Roebus could be carefully managed through surrogates but others required the direct approach. Dealing with them face to face was also the best way to guarantee there was no room for misunderstandings. It was going to be a difficult trip for her physically but hopefully the results would be worth it.

"I will see you upon my return," said Britak, making it sound like a threat.

As she marched through the palace, with her mind on the future, the aches in her body seemed far away.

She might not live to see the Five Kingdoms united as one, but she'd make sure Kell Kressia was dead and buried before her.

CHAPTER 5

Upon the ice they live, for nine parts of the year,
Frostrunners we name them for their own language is queer.
Hardy and pale, wrapped in fur, ice masters one and all,
Hunters, dreamers and deep in spirit they live like no other.

EXCERPT FROM THE SAGA OF KELL KRESSIA
BY THE BARD PAX MEDINA

"Does my father really want me to meet with the Reverend Mother?" asked Princess Sigrid.

She and Lukas were sat beside each other on a bench in what she had called the Walled Garden since she was seven years old. It was small and slightly out of the way compared to the main garden at the rear of the palace and far less ostentatious. As a child she'd always liked the peace and quiet of the Walled Garden. She could sit and read or play for hours without seeing another person.

The first time she'd been discovered here it had caused quite a stir in the palace. As it turned out, the Walled Garden was in fact, the Poison Garden, and its out of the way location had been done on purpose to minimise the risk of accidental death.

Rather than full of garish flowers that were only designed to look pretty, the plants here were functional. Some of them had colourful flowers, but others were incredibly ordinary, and most were deadly if ingested.

"Well it wasn't in those exact words," said Lukas. "But your father did say he wants you to take on more responsibility. He gets tired a lot more easily these days. I thought, where possible, it would be a good idea to delegate tasks to other people."

Sigrid turned her face away and took a deep breath until she was in control of her emotions. Her father was getting old. She didn't want to admit it but in the last few years everything about his physical appearance had changed. His skin was thinner, his hair almost completely gone and his appetite had mostly disappeared. She understood it was a natural part of getting older but that didn't make it any easier to watch, especially when it was happening to someone she loved.

"Just let me know, whatever I can do to help."

"I need you to organise all of it. A full diplomatic visit. Greet her upon arrival and then discuss the faith, in private, without making any solid promises. You'll need to be careful, though. She might look like a sweet old woman but–"

"She's as deadly as a viper. Yes, I've read the reports," said Sigrid. "Father has never been devout or particularly welcoming to the clergy, but she doesn't know me. The last time we met I was a teenager."

Lukas gave her a speculative look. "What are you thinking?"

"That it's far easier to let her assume I'm an ally than another obstacle to her grand plans," said Sigrid with a grin. "She'll never see it coming."

Kell felt as if he was choking to death. The collar of his shirt was too tight. He couldn't get a full breath and it itched as if it was crawling with ants. Unfortunately he'd managed to fit his arse into the grey trousers and they'd not split across the seam. Part of him had been hoping to get away with wearing his own clothes, but Lukas and his people knew their jobs too well.

Staring at himself in the mirror Kell barely recognised the fop staring back. Only the eyes were the same. His stomach rumbled again, reminding him that it had been a long time since his last meal. He couldn't understand why the King ate his evening meal so late.

As an honoured guest Kell was waiting to be announced. The only problem was the King hadn't turned up yet so he could take his seat. That left Kell pacing up and down the corridor while tantalising smells wafted in from another room. It smelled like chicken. Definitely chicken and there was some kind of fish as well. Probably the overpriced blue crab from the coast. To him it tasted like every other kind of crab. Some claimed it had subtle flavours that evaded all but the most refined palate. Kell snorted. It was just another con from the Seith to separate the rich from their money.

This was starting to feel a lot like the bad old days. A Frostrunner herald. A menace rising in the far north. Only this time he was older and wiser. He wasn't a naïve boy with dreams that were bigger than his balls. Last time he'd volunteered to make the journey and wasn't even paid for his efforts. No doubt the heroes had only agreed to go on the quest once they'd agreed on a large reward. As the only survivor he should have received the full amount. Of course, he'd not seen a single dinar. He'd been too young and stupid to ask.

The door rattled and he stepped back to avoid being hit in the face. Lukas appeared, this time dressed in a pale blue tunic emblazoned with a white lantern. He was the only person serving the crown who didn't wear the eagle. He worked for the King and yet was an independent voice able to offer his opinion without fear of reprisal which made him a dangerous and powerful man. Kell remembered merchants and even foreign Kings would take the time to greet him. The city might have changed but it was clear Lukas still commanded everyone's respect.

"The King is ready for you now," said Lukas, ushering him inside.

A modest dining table, with room for twenty people on either side, sat in the middle of a lavish room decorated with paintings of the King's ancestors. Ugly, fat, balding men, going back generations, stretched up one wall and down the other. Kell thought he could feel the weight of those ancient eyes judging him. Ignoring their glares he walked to the far end of the room where the King sat at the head of the table.

Time had not been kind to the King. Ten years ago Bledsoe had been a vigorous man with a razor sharp tongue and acid wit. His dirty sense of humour was one that Kell appreciated, especially the embarrassment it caused his daughter, Sigrid, when Bledsoe told bad jokes.

Now he resembled a shrivelled walnut. His skin was so lined his eyes had become two narrow caves. Short of pulling back the flaps Kell had no way of knowing if the King was awake or not. Nothing remained of Bledsoe's hair except for a dusting of snowy white making a desperate attempt to cling onto his wizened skull. The skin on his hands was so paper-thin Kell could see the bones and tendons beneath.

"Your Majesty," said Lukas in a voice so loud it startled Kell and echoed off the walls. King Bledsoe barely seemed to hear but he slowly cupped a trembling hand to one of his huge ears. "May I present Kell Kressia."

"What?" murmured the King.

"Kell Kressia is here."

The King's head, small as it was, seemed too large for his frail body which had also shrunk. It looked as if he'd stolen his clothes from a larger man as they hung off his bony frame. Slowly the King turned his head to look at Kell. Lukas gestured for him to sit down so the King didn't have to crane his neck.

Bledsoe leaned forward in his chair and peered at Kell. "Ahhh. There you are, my boy." His voice had become a silken whisper. Kell saw little that was familiar and despite everything he felt sorry for the old man.

"I'm here, Majesty," said Kell, forcing a smile.

"Trouble again. There's always something," said the King, before his head dipped towards his chest. With a sudden jerk the King came awake, peering around the room in alarm. When his eyes settled on Kell he smiled, showing a few lonely yellow teeth. "Terrible danger, boy. You're needed again. Lukas will give you all the details," he said, waving a hand at the Steward. "Now, where's my crab?"

As soon as the King finished speaking he began to doze again. Lukas jerked his head and Kell followed him through a different door, down a short corridor and into a plain room adjoining the dining hall. Half a dozen servants were poised with plates, three trays of steaming food and a decanter of wine. Standing at the back of the room Kell spotted a bard dressed in a yellow and white striped coat. An instrument case hung over one shoulder and he was muttering to himself, probably rehearsing lines.

"The King is feeling quite tired this evening," said Lukas, making an announcement to the room. "He's asked for some privacy. Your services will not be needed this evening, Master Tatt."

The bard gave a florid bow and left the room. This must have been a familiar occurrence as the servants didn't wait for further instructions. Two of them put together a modest plate of blue crab, boiled potatoes swimming in butter, purple carrots and string beans. Another servant half-filled a glass with wine and then topped it up with water. Two servants headed towards the dining room with the King's meal while the rest went elsewhere to attend their duties.

"Shall we eat?" asked Lukas, gesturing at the plain wooden table and chairs.

The smells that had been taunting Kell from afar now made his mouth water. In one covered dish he found a whole chicken stuffed with ginger, onions and roasted squash. A pot of warm lemon sauce sat ready to be drizzled over the top. The others held a variety of fresh vegetables and the infamous blue crab. Times were difficult and food was expensive, but it was different here in the palace.

Lukas passed Kell a plate and then helped himself to some

crab and vegetables while Kell cut the chicken into quarters.

"Don't be polite," said Lukas. "There's no one watching."

Kell loosened the top button of his shirt and sighed with relief. Taking Lukas's advice he picked up another chunk of chicken before loading his plate with vegetables. All of this was preamble but he was hungry and tended to think better on a full stomach.

"How is Princess Sigrid these days?" asked Kell, sucking on a chicken bone.

Lukas sighed. "She's matured, but is still constantly challenging tradition."

Kell grunted, knowing that the Steward was just being polite. That meant she was still bitter about her lot. Five Kings had ruled since time immemorial. Despite being the King's only child she couldn't inherit the throne from her father.

Superstition said if a woman ever sat on the throne the Shepherd would curse the land for a thousand years with famine and pestilence. It was a ridiculous idea, but then again, no one would ever think to kill a crow as they were favoured by the Manx. For whatever reason, familiarity or fear of the unknown, some traditions held fast over the years. Instead of ruling, Princess Sigrid would be forced to marry some dandy and then bear him children. It was another reminder that despite her father being frail, he wasn't a kind old man. He was a ruthless negotiator who used people to serve his purpose, as Kell had learned first-hand.

"So, are you ready to make the journey north?" said Lukas, as Kell was scraping his plate.

Finally they came down to it.

"Do you know the nature of the threat?" asked Kell.

"No. The Frostrunner envoy didn't know either, but it's dangerous. We're certain of that."

A dozen heads sent a very clear message. Whatever was up there in the Frozen North did not want to be disturbed.

"I'm confused about something," said Kell. "You said the envoy came to you last year. Why did you wait so long to send someone to investigate?"

Lukas sighed and looked away into the distance for a moment. "I want your word that what I'm about to tell you will not be shared with anyone."

"I can keep my mouth shut," said Kell, and Lukas gave him a knowing look. The King's Steward was one of the few people who knew the truth about what had happened.

"Yes, you can. The truth is we didn't wait. Last year King Bledsoe called for another conclave with the other Kings. Despite the nature of the threat, most of them refused to attend." Lukas's tone of voice clearly indicated what he thought of that decision. "In the interim years, since your last journey, much had changed. I won't go into detail, but alliances have shifted and those who were once stalwart friends have become estranged. Also some of them believe there are other issues that are more important."

Politics. Kell hated it and did his best to avoid it at all costs. The closest he got to it at home was listening to gossip in the local tavern. Many stories spoke about the King of Hundar, who had always been devout, becoming militant in his faith. Instead of ruling he seemed intent on converting heathens to the glory of the Shepherd. Pilgrims were being sent to all countries, armed only with their faith and a copy of the Book for protection.

With more ships crossing the Narrow Sea the lands beyond Corvan were starting to open up for trade. Seithland was a nation of merchants and if the Five Kingdoms were struggling he could see them looking elsewhere to make their fortune. It was a common held belief that the Seith loved money above all else and so far Kell had yet to meet a westerner to disprove it. He could believe the King of Seithland refusing to get involved in a journey to the north, after all, where was the profit in such a venture?

"With only the ruler of Kinnan willing to commit, he and King Bledsoe sent warriors to the north. These were names you will have heard of. None returned. Other groups were sent after them to investigate and they too disappeared on the ice."

"Is the King ordering me to go?" asked Kell, knowing it was possible although that seemed unlikely.

"I was hoping we could come to an arrangement," said Lukas, delicately sipping his wine. "Of course, whatever we discuss, I'll have to confirm it with the King."

"Of course," said Kell, wiping his mouth to hide a wry smile. He wondered how much rope the old King had given his Steward. No doubt more than enough to hang Kell with if he caused too many problems.

"I hear that it's difficult running a farm in the south," said Lukas, trying to sound sympathetic. Kell said nothing, waiting to see where this was going. "Especially when you're on your own. I was surprised to hear that you'd not married."

"There was someone but it didn't work out," said Kell, swallowing the lump in his throat. He didn't know if the Steward was poking at an old wound on purpose or not. Given the man's nature Kell suspected it was on purpose to keep him off balance.

"I'm sorry to hear that," said Lukas, but Kell didn't know if he was being genuine. "You may not be aware, but the number of warriors joining the army has declined in recent years."

Kell didn't know or care, but because Lukas had said it he knew it wasn't idle chatter. "That's a shame," he said.

"Indeed. So the King has asked me to select someone to act as a spokesperson, a symbol if you will, to inspire young people. This person would have to travel around Algany, at the King's expense of course, telling people stories of bravery and heroism. They'd receive a generous salary and comfortable rooms would be provided in the palace when not on the road during winter. I can think of no one better suited for the role than you."

Who better to inspire young people than the living legend who'd slain the Ice Lich? Historically Algany didn't have many heroes compared to other nations. Those he could recall were from a long time ago. Even now King Bledsoe was trying to find ways to profit from Kell's past deeds.

It sounded easier than running a farm but it would also mean him being around a lot of people every day. The money would be good but the thought of having people stare at him all the time, for inspiration no less, filled him with a sense of dread.

However, before he could enjoy that life he had to travel north and kill whatever was lurking beyond the Frozen Circle. "It's a generous offer, and a lot to think about," said Kell. "Would the King provide me with any funds for the journey?"

It was clear from Lukas's smile he thought the matter was already closed. "I'm confident he would make sure you had enough money for suitable provisions for such a gruelling trip."

Kell rubbed his chin in thought. "Can I sleep on it?"

"Of course," said Lukas.

Kell was escorted to his room by a different servant and this time they didn't lock the door. It was nice not to feel like a prisoner. He loosened his shirt and took off the tight pair of boots that had been pinching his big toes. Someone had thoughtfully laid out an old fashioned nightshirt on the bed that looked like something his mother used to wear. Kell considered if he should wear it or just sleep naked as he did at home.

It had been a long day and with a full stomach Kell began to doze in the chair. He dreamed about riding home after a second journey to the north. The entire town of Honaje threw him a parade. People lined the streets cheering his name. A local woman agreed to marry him and together they raised a family on the farm.

It was a nice dream up to that point, but then it took a bad turn. One day he came home to find one of his children had gone missing. The following day his wife hanged herself and the day after that his other child choked to death on a chicken bone.

Kell came awake with a start, his body covered in a cold sweat. He was reaching for the nightshirt when there was a knock at the door.

Standing in the doorway was an elegant local woman with shimmering black hair down to her waist and a shapely figure. When their eyes met she smiled in a way that made him think they were old friends.

"Can I help you? Are you lost?"

"Not at all, Kell," she murmured. Even her voice was soft and silky. It hinted at far away places and mysteries to be uncovered. She let herself into the room, trailing a hand across his chest which sent a jolt of energy down his spine. "Lukas thought you might be lonely."

From a little way down the corridor Lukas watched as Anastasia closed the door of Kell's room behind her. Kell would have a night he'd never forget and in the morning it would make him that much easier to manoeuvre. Lukas took a direct route through the palace to the King's private quarters. Bledsoe was sitting beside the fire with a book resting on his chest. The changes in the last few years were noticeable even when he was asleep. The cragginess of his face was more pronounced and he'd definitely shrunk in height.

The King came awake with a start, eyes roaming around the room before they settled on Lukas. "I actually fell asleep for real this time," he said in a strong voice that was at odds with his ageing body.

Of late they had decided to use his age and apparently frailty to their advantage. Sympathy and compassion were powerful tools that the wily King was not above using. Most people became more accommodating in their negotiations because of it, but those who failed to be moved were met with the steely gaze of Lukas. In a wheezy voice the old King would make an offer that had been carefully agreed earlier, and Lukas would enforce it or better the deal. So far it had been working extremely well. People had always said Bledsoe was cunning but they had no idea.

The King did nap in the afternoons and slept for ten hours a night, but despite his failing eyesight there was nothing wrong with his mind.

"Did the boy agree to head north?"

The King always called him that. It made sense as Kell had only been seventeen when he'd first made the journey. "Not yet, but one of Madam Sharsh's girls is keeping him company tonight."

"That's good. Just don't tell my daughter," said Bledsoe, glancing around for the Princess. Lukas knew she didn't approve of such things, especially when it meant sneaking someone into the palace. "Tell me the truth. Do you think the boy can do it this time? Stop whatever has taken up residence in the Frozen North?"

Lukas had not seen Kell in ten years so he had little first-hand experience to judge him by except the last few hours. Back then he'd been a naïve boy with dreams of being a hero. Lukas would never forget the look on his face when he'd returned to the palace from the north. The numbness. The horror that was stamped into his features.

The quest had broken Kell. He'd become fragile in a way that Lukas recognised. Warriors who'd spent too long fighting on the front lines had the same look. On the surface, at least, he seemed less haunted. Quiet years working on the farm must have healed his spirit.

"He's a lot more shrewd than before," said Lukas, voicing his thoughts. "There a certain level of cunning in his eyes."

"Good. He'll need all his wits. But, I suppose it doesn't really matter if he succeeds or not."

"In a way, it would better if he failed," said Lukas, and the King nodded in agreement. It was also more likely as last time Kell had been in the company of eleven heroes.

The offer of a job had been made in good faith. If Kell returned he would become a travelling storyteller that would inevitably inspire many young men and women to join the army. However, if he died on the ice then martyrs were powerful symbols. After all, the Shepherd's book was full of them. People making the ultimate sacrifice for their beliefs.

Lukas would have to find a good bard to craft the story of Kell's heroic death. Someone with real talent who could manipulate the crowd and evoke the emotions he needed. After that new recruits would come flooding through their doors. Then the King could send an army north to deal with the new menace. The less likely outcome was that Kell would succeed. Either way, he would serve his country.

"We should at least give the boy a chance," said the King. "After all that he sacrificed, it's the least we can do."

"I could send someone to keep an eye on him. To nudge him in the right direction," suggested Lukas.

"They'd need to be discreet."

"Yes, Majesty."

"For everyone's sakes, I pray that the emissary was wrong. Let's hope the threat is nothing serious," said the King.

Lukas murmured a brief prayer to the Shepherd. He shared the King's fear because leaving his fate in the hands of a man he barely knew, to face a danger they didn't understand, terrified him.

CHAPTER 6

Upon the gates he knocked, three times three,
With a face as pale as the moon, Kell had finally returned home.
With shaking hands and a broken spirit he confessed to the King,
That the deed was done but the others were all dead.

EXCERPT FROM THE SAGA OF KELL KRESSIA
BY THE BARD PAX MEDINA

When Kell woke up the next morning he was initially disorientated. Eventually he recognised his room in the palace but it did little to help him relax. Everything was intended to satisfy his desires and make him more agreeable. From the plush surroundings, to the lavish food, to the pleasant and willing company.

Lukas, and the King, were intent on manipulating him. The Steward had mentioned spending time alone on purpose. Why else would Lukas send Anastasia to his room? After such an encounter they would expect him to be compliant. If everything had gone according to plan it might have worked.

It had been nice to talk to someone even if she was being paid to keep him company. They thought he was as naïve as he'd been at seventeen when all he'd wanted was fame and fortune. As Kell was wondering if he would have to dress up again he received an invite to a private breakfast with Lukas. Wearing his own clothes, which had been washed and repaired, he felt more at ease.

A servant guided him through the corridors to a room with plain wooden furniture. It was much at odds with the rest of the palace. The wooden table was stained, worn and marked with dozens of rings from wet mugs and glasses. There were cuts on the surface from knives and one of the legs was slightly shorter than the others. A wedge had been shoved under it to make it level but as he rested his arms on top he felt it tilt slightly to the left.

On a side table he spotted an array of modest fare consisting boiled eggs, a chunky malt loaf, a bowl of fruit, sausages and a jug of milk. A servant carried in a large plate of steaming smoked fish and rice which she added to the rest. Lukas bustled into the room carrying some plates and a pot of tea.

"Hungry?" he asked, passing Kell a plate before helping himself to some sausages and eggs. Kell heaped a plate with food before tucking in with vigour. The smoked fish fell apart in his mouth and the rice was seasoned with fragrant spices that made his tongue tingle. Just as Kell was finishing a second plate of fish and rice Lukas brought up their conversation from the previous night.

"So, have you come to a decision?" he asked. At least he'd waited until Kell had nearly finished eating.

"Almost, but first I want to ask you something." There were still a few boiled eggs left so Kell helped himself to a couple and another chunk of fish.

He'd caught Lukas by surprise. No doubt he'd expected Kell to immediately agree to everything. "What do you want to know?"

"Why all the secrecy? Why sneak me into the city like a thief?"

The Steward visibly relaxed. He'd been expecting Kell to ask him something else. "Two reasons. First, because the truth will terrify people and start a panic. The Frostrunner clans understand the weather better than anyone. They have over forty words for snow, so they know the difference between a bad season and a real threat. At the moment the changes are minor, but you've already seen the impact." Lukas shook his head. "If nothing is done it's going to get much worse. Everyone will slowly starve and freeze to death. The truth would be too much for most people."

"And the second reason?"

Lukas offered a wry smile. "I didn't want people to know until I had your answer."

"Do you want me to hide my identity?" asked Kell.

Lukas shook his head. "Quite the opposite. If people want to know why you're passing through then tell them. Just don't tell them the whole story. Your name still carries a lot of weight, so it will give people hope. That is, of course, assuming you accept."

"Since we're being honest, the truth is I don't want to go," said Kell, chewing his bottom lip. "I'm a farmer now. I haven't even held a sword in years, but, I am familiar with the dangers in the Frozen North."

"Is that a yes?" asked Lukas, pressing for an answer.

"This isn't a threat I can ignore. I could pretend it won't affect me in Honaje, but eventually the frost would reach my farm. Then I'd starve along with everyone else." Kell took a deep breath and nodded grimly. "I will make the journey."

"I hoped you would say that," said Lukas with a big smile. "Don't worry. I'll make sure you have all the appropriate clothing and plenty of money. No more sleeping in ditches beside the road."

"Ah, the King told you about that," said Kell. He'd never shared that part of the story with his admirers. Those nights of hardship, along with the truth about the herocs, had not made it into the bard's saga. That version spoke of glorious feasts every night beside a roaring fire, not huddling under a blanket for warmth with an empty belly.

"The King told me everything," said Lukas. "When do you want to head north?"

"The sooner I leave the sooner I can return. If you don't mind, I'd like to choose my own horse. I'm not a confident rider, so I'm going to need a patient horse with stamina."

"That's fair. Let's get started," said Lukas, getting up from the table.

Kell spent the rest of the morning working with one of Lucas's assistants choosing clothing for his trip through the northern kingdoms and then beyond onto the ice. The air was so cold in some parts it could freeze exposed skin in a few heartbeats. The southern wind cut through all but the most robust clothing and he knew it had to be carefully padded and then waxed to repel water and ice.

Lukas's assistant listened carefully to his requirements and had the tailors make suitable adjustments. It would take them a couple of hours which gave him enough time to choose a horse and gather other provisions.

By mid-afternoon Kell was ready. Lukas was waiting for him outside the stables beside the horse that Kell had selected. It was a sturdy roan mare that had been loaded up with supplies. Just as Kell was checking that nothing was missing a servant came racing out of a side door carrying rope and a pair of ice axes.

Kell added them to his saddlebags which were already straining at the seams. Some of it was food but the rest was equipment he couldn't survive without in the harsh northern climate.

Wearing padded armour over his clothing and a sword on his back again felt strange. The sword was part of someone else's life. A stranger he barely recognised any more. Kell didn't want to become that person again. Not under any circumstances.

Lukas dismissed the servants and even held the horse's bridle while Kell settled himself in the saddle. The mare barely stirred, confirming that he'd made the right choice.

"Here," said Lukas, holding up a money pouch which Kell gladly accepted. It was heavier than he'd been expecting which spoke of the King's generosity or perhaps his desperation. "May the Shepherd give you strength, courage and wisdom for the journey ahead."

Kell chuckled at the old blessing. "The last time someone said that was ten years ago."

"A good omen. Let us hope the ending this time is also the same."

"I hope so."

"How long will it take you to get there?" asked Lukas.

Kell thought back over his previous journey. "At least twelve days to reach the Frozen Circle, if there are no problems. Less than half that again on the ice. There are ravens in the town of Meer. I'll send word back as soon as I can."

Meer was the most northern settlement in Kinnan. Despite its northern position Meer was still over a day's travel from the Frozen Circle. The only people who lived there were trappers, hunters and fisherman. It was a tough place at the end of the world and not somewhere he'd wished to see again.

"After thirty days, if you don't hear any word, I would assume the worst."

Kell knew that the Steward would be realistic. Lukas nodded grimly but didn't tell him what they would do if he didn't return.

"Are you ready?" asked Lukas.

Kell swallowed hard and laughed. "No, but I'd best go before I lose my nerve."

"Good luck," said Lukas, shaking his hand.

Taking his time to get used to his horse Kell set off at a walk through the palace grounds. Retracing his steps across the city, so he didn't have to contend with the hills, he carefully navigated down narrow streets until he reached the east gate. This time he paid no attention to the sprawling market. Turning his horse towards the north Kell breathed deeply while staring up at the sky. It was a relief to be out of the city. Being around so many people made him uncomfortable. Being crammed into a huge stinking city that was awash with people sounded like a nightmare.

As he became familiar with the rhythms of his horse Kell thought about what lay ahead. The money Lukas had given him was enough to start a new life. He would ride north for a couple of days, cross over the border into Hundar, and then head east for the coast. From there he could find a ship sailing to Corvan across the Narrow Sea. After that would shave his head and beard, change his name and start over.

Once Lukas and the King realised he wasn't coming back they'd assume he was dead and send another group to get the job done. Kell felt a little guilty but he countered it with a dose of reality. Last time he'd been lucky and surrounded by heroes. This time he was travelling alone.

The lands beyond Corvan were supposed to be lush with rich, fertile soil. If he found a nice plot maybe he would buy some cattle or establish an orchard. Cider at the Dancing Cricket always tasted like tart piss. Kell knew he could do a lot better.

Yes, indeed. A new life awaited him and today was the first day.

CHAPTER 7

The first pillar is compassion.
We must care for all people upon the land,
As all men and women are created equal,
And all of them are deserving of care.

EXCERPT FROM THE SACRED BOOK OF THE SHEPHERD

Reverend Mother Britak stared at the letter clutched in her hand with such hate she considered spitting on the floor. Sallie wouldn't say anything and by tomorrow would probably have forgotten it had happened, but the messenger was a different matter.

Britak dismissed him with a wave, waiting until the sound of his footsteps had receded before releasing a torrent of swear words. Sallie's eyes widened at the litany and she blanched slightly but, showing a grain of common sense, she wisely kept her mouth shut. When Britak was done she wiped the spit from her chin and accepted the proffered glass of water Sallie held out to her.

"Thank you, child." Britak noticed that she had scrunched up the letter in one hand. She attempted to smooth out the page but the damage was done and could not be erased. Forgiveness was one of the pillars of her faith and that which she struggled with the most.

The letter had come from the King in the North, Lars of Kinnan.

For years Britak had attempted to persuade him to see the light and embrace the one true faith, but all of her attempts had been rebuffed. In Kinnan, people were allowed to believe whatever they wanted and pray to whomever they chose. It was cruel and malicious. Deceiving people into thinking that trees and rocks had spirits inside who listened to their prayers and could grant them wishes. Even worse, he allowed children to be instructed in the heathen ways of their parents, spreading the deception even further. Britak was merely thinking of protecting the innocent. Such destructive behaviour had to be stamped out.

Her latest effort of distributing free copies of the holy Book, at great personal expense to the church, had come to an abrupt end. Over a hundred loyal priests, dressed as commoners, had been handing out the sacred text in Okeer, the capital city of Kinnan.

It was not illegal but apparently they had become a public nuisance, shouting and harassing people in the street. Britak knew her followers would be enthusiastic about the one true faith, but she didn't believe such over the top stories. The sacred books had been seized by King Lars and her priests locked up for disturbing the peace. In the next few days they were going to be escorted south to the border of Kinnan and told not to return. The King's letter reassured her that in the meantime her people were being well cared for and that she shouldn't worry about their health.

"Arrogant little prick," she said, grinding her teeth. "Sallie, go and fetch Heitor."

A short time later the girl returned with Brother Heitor. The nondescript man was easy to forget, being of average height and appearance. He had no official church duties but from time to time Britak sent him out of the Holy City to deal with difficult situations. She had a number of fixers like Heitor, but his particular set of skills made him the best for the task at hand.

"Reverend Mother," said Heitor, giving her a deep bow. "How I can be of service?"

"King Lars of Kinnan is being particularly obstinate," she said, moving to the window to stare out at the city. "He has refused to accept the glory of the Shepherd into his heart. Therefore, we must focus on the future of his wayward nation and look at alternative means of bringing his people into the fold."

"His son," said Heitor.

"Yes, young Prince Meinhart," she said, turning to face her herald. Some people called her special priests harbingers. Privately, she liked the nickname and the fear it created, but publicly she spoke out against it. After all, hers was a faith of love not terror.

"One day the prince will inherit the throne from his heathen father. I think it wise that when that time comes, he knows the truth."

Heitor pursed his lips. "May I ask, do you know where he is at the present time?"

This was the only tricky part of her plan. "Yes. In the palace in Okeer."

"Difficult, but not impossible," mused Heitor. Snatching the prince away from right under the King's nose would also send a very clear message to Lars. That no one was safe. Of course, she wouldn't ever be able to admit that she was responsible but it didn't matter, Lars would still know.

"Good. Send me updates."

"Yes, Reverend Mother," said Heitor, giving another deep bow before he backed out of the room.

Saving people from themselves was never easy. Progress was always an uphill struggle but she was strong enough to shoulder the burden, alone, if necessary.

As she looked out at the Holy City, Britak wondered how many years it had been since she'd visited one of the markets. Years ago she would dress in plain clothes and sneak out to browse the stalls. She loved the smell of fresh bread, the heady mix of spices and the crunch of sweet fruit.

"Reverend Mother," said Sallie, tugging on her sleeve.

Looking around at the girl Britak realised she had been staring out the window for some time, lost in thought. It was happening more and more often. While lost in a daydream her hips had stiffened and one of her feet had gone numb.

"What's next on the schedule?" she asked.

Sallie squinted down at the book on her desk and slowly read off the page. "A friendly conversation," said the girl, struggling with the long words.

Britak grimaced as she stamped her feet, doing her best to ignore the pain as blood rushed back into her legs. "Excellent. I've been looking forward to this."

One of her most important jobs as Reverend Mother was protecting the faith. Her righteous servants who served in this capacity were the Holy Inquisitors. The seventeen men and eleven women were some of the most feared people in the Five Kingdoms. One or two of them even gave Britak pause when they were face to face, but thankfully all of them were loyal to the church. Their faith was beyond reproach and they regularly had friendly chats with those who sought to pollute the truth.

Britak left the girl behind to get on with her other duties. Sallie was incredibly simple but also a gentle soul who needed protection. That included keeping her away from the more difficult aspects of Britak's job.

The stairs to the subterranean level were dangerously worn in the middle forcing her to move slowly and with caution. She hated feeling frail but Britak was also a realist. She'd hate it a lot more if she slipped down the stairs and broke a hip or snapped her neck because of pride.

When she had reached the bottom level, without incident, she took a moment to catch her breath and compose herself. Thankfully there were no witnesses. People did not aimlessly wander around these corridors.

The air was naturally cooler this far underground and perfectly still. Sounds carried a long way and as she walked past the line of heavy doors, Britak clearly heard whimpering coming from within each cell.

Under the careful ministrations of the Inquisition the proud learned to be humble, the guilty confessed, and the sins of all were cleansed with the great leveller. Pain.

At the end of a hall was a wide rotunda where the Inquisitors gathered to rest and pray, asking the Shepherd to grant them strength for the difficult work. Their breath frosted in the air and each Inquisitor was dressed in a simple grey hooded robe. A knot of them were chatting on one side of the room but they all fell silent and bowed as Britak approached.

"Reverend Mother. What a pleasure to see you," said Inquisitor Peeke, a lean-faced woman with grey eyes. From the sound of her voice Peeke found absolutely nothing pleasurable about the experience. The woman had all the emotional capacity of a rock, which made her perfect for the work. Tears and tantrums had no effect on her and she always got to the truth, no matter how long it took.

"I'm here to see Inquisitor Krebb."

Peeke swallowed hard and quickly pointed down the hallway to her left. In all things there was a hierarchy and even among the Inquisitors, who terrified almost everyone, Krebb was one they feared.

"Thank you, child," said Britak, leaving the others behind.

"Confess and be free," said someone as she walked past a chamber of truth. It was a refrain commonly heard in these corridors of suffering but rather deceptive in its wording. The accused would be freed of the lies, some blood and perhaps a few internal organs, but very few actually walked free and ever saw daylight again.

Britak made sure she knocked loudly on the door three times before pushing it open. Hanging on the far wall was a man, dressed only in a loincloth. He'd been carefully secured in a spreadeagle position to a wooden cross so that his feet didn't touch the floor. The skin of the accused was spotted with blood but there were only half a dozen small cuts on his chest. Krebb had only just begun his patient work.

"Reverend Mother. What an honour," hissed Krebb. His words were slightly sibilant because of his severe disfigurement. The Inquisitor bowed deeply, making sure that he held on to the hood of his robe. When he straightened he readjusted the material to cover the worst of his scars but it made no difference. Britak had seen the burns in full. Half of his face was a mangled mass of flesh. It was as if his skin had turned to wax, dripped down his face and then reset. Mercifully his missing eye was covered with a patch but the skin was still bright red and lumpy, like Sallie's attempt at porridge.

"We were just getting warmed up," said Krebb, turning to face the accused. He was a handsome man, somewhere in his thirties, with a good physique, a strong jaw and beautiful blue eyes. Britak knew it wouldn't be long before they were bloodshot.

"Reverend Mother, thank goodness you're here," said the man. "My name is Pastor Finch. I am a minister of the one true faith."

"You are a liar and a deceiver," said Krebb, shuffling towards his tray of implements. The wheels on the cart squeaked as he dragged it nearer. Finch did his best to ignore both it and the grisly man, instead speaking directly to her.

"Reverend Mother, there has been a terrible mistake. I believe in the Shepherd. You and I are the same."

Krebb looked up from his tray of steel implements. "What did you say?"

"That must be a record for you, Krebb," said Britak. "A confession of guilt already."

Finch looked confused. "I don't understand."

Despite the smell, Britak moved closer to Finch until they were almost nose to nose. "For years I've been hearing rumours about the subversive filth that you peddle. Secret meetings in basements. Coded messages sent by carrier pigeon. It took a long time to get someone inside your inner circle. And finally, here you are."

"All I do is spread the holy word," said Finch. "Does the Book not say '*When mankind trembled in the night, the Shepherd brought fire and with it light. But the twelve pillars were what the tribes cherished, as without them, they would all have perished.*'"

"That rhymed!" she said, aghast at his blasphemy. "The Book is not a bawdy limerick to be sung by drunks in ale houses. It is holy scripture!"

"If it helps people live a better life, what's the difference?"

"Did you think I wouldn't find you?" said Britak, ignoring his nonsense.

Finch showed no remorse about teaching others his deviant text. It was a mangled version of the Book, one that spoke about the Shepherd in disturbing ways. It even insinuated that he was an earthly being and not celestial in nature.

"The Shepherd will forgive you," said Finch, doing his best to sound benevolent, while being practically naked and hanging from the wall in chains.

Britak turned to Krebb who was testing the keen edge of one of his bonesaws. Not finding it sharp enough to his liking, Krebb began to sharpen it against a whetstone.

"I want everything. The names of all his followers. Information on who distributed the books. Places they met. Who wrote the coded messages. All of it."

"It will be as you say, Reverend Mother," said Krebb. "I will leave no stone unturned."

All copies of the deviant text had been burned and all of the miscreants, after being thoroughly questioned, were at peace. Death was sometimes a mercy, especially when the mind of the individual had been poisoned. This way the darkness would not spread any further and more people could embrace the light.

As Krebb pulled back his hood and approached the bound man Britak saw Finch's confidence, together with most of the blood from his face, drain away. It was going to be a long and interesting conversation.

CHAPTER 8

Against the maglau and the garrow they fought,
Who sought to drown and eat the heroes in the day.
But at night there was no rest upon the ice,
For the Qalamieren whispered in the dark.

Excerpt from the Saga of Kell Kressia
by the Bard Pax Medina

After riding north of the capital, Thune, for two days, Kell arrived at the small town of Mizzei as the sky was streaked through with purple and black. Thick clouds had been threatening a storm which made him glad he'd kept a steady pace all afternoon. There was nothing romantic about sleeping outdoors when it was raining. It was just cold, damp and depressing.

Kell wasted no time, paying for a room at a tavern called the Thirsty Ferret, and getting his horse stabled for the night. She'd done well today, so he tipped the groom to give her some treats.

To maintain appearances Kell decided to play the role Lukas had given him by strolling around, chatting to locals while gathering news. Predictably most of their talk was about the weather, although that was fairly typical for Alganians.

A few people asked for his name, which he shared, and each time it caught them by surprise. They would take a hard look at his face as if searching for something familiar. Admittedly he'd changed quite a bit in ten years. Long hours working on the farm had kept him fit and his face was leaner, stripped of all its soft edges. It bode well for his plan to make a new life elsewhere.

By the time he sat down for his evening meal quite a crowd had gathered. The owner was puzzled at her good fortune but didn't complain. The number of people in the common room made Kell feel a little uneasy, which was an improvement. A few years ago a large group of people would have terrified him to the point of feeling sick. Over the years he'd built up a callus, but he still didn't like being the centre of attention.

For the first hour he received curious glances but eventually a person at the bar summoned enough courage to approach his table.

"Buy you a drink?" asked a handsome local man. His black hair was shorn to the scalp and a thick pair of gloves were tucked into his belt. He had a smudge of ash on his cheek and he smelled of smoke.

"That's very kind," said Kell, holding out his hand. "Kell Kressia."

"I know. Russlan," said the smith, shaking his hand. He went to the bar and shortly returned with two foaming glasses of beer.

The rest of the room listened at a distance while feigning disinterest.

"So, is it true? The Medina saga?"

"Which bit?" asked Kell, sipping his beer.

"All that stuff about monsters on the ice."

"It's been a while since I heard it," admitted Kell. "But from what I remember, it's all true."

Russlan mulled that over for a while. "And now? Where are you headed?"

"North."

"Just travelling or something else?"

Kell saw many in the crowd lean forward to catch his answer. "I'm headed back to the Frozen North."

A roar of flurried conversation surged around the room as

groups of people frantically discussed what it meant. Everyone was waving their hands and talking in loud voices. Several began firing questions at him but in the din it was impossible to hear what was being said. The owner of the Thirsty Ferret rapped an empty glass on the bar until the noise drained away.

"Keep it down," she warned the room.

"Has the Ice Lich returned?"

"Did the King send you?"

"Is that Slayer? Can I touch it?"

People were talking over each other in a rush before he had a chance to answer. The noise began to rise until the landlady rapped the bar again.

"Last warning," she said, eyeing the crowd.

"What can you tell us?" asked Russlan, before anyone else jumped in. This time the silence held, but Kell knew it was a fragile thing.

Sweat was starting to trickle down his back from being the focus of so many people. The sooner this was over the better.

"I'm a farmer now, so you've all seen the same as me. The weather's not right. Crops are at least a couple of months behind where they should be. King Bledsoe has asked me to travel north and cross the ice again. It might be nothing!" he said in a loud voice, cutting off whispers that had started up.

"But it could be something," said Russlan.

Kell reluctantly nodded. "Aye, it could be. So, it's better to be safe than sorry," he said, tapping the hilt of Slayer sat across his back.

He had hoped to avoid notice but now that he'd been spotted he might be able to use it in his favour. If he'd travelled across country too soon the King might have become suspicious. However, if people remembered seeing him pass through, on his way to the north, it would be easier for them to believe that he'd died somewhere on the ice.

"Is it a secret? You going on this quest?" asked the smith, leaning forward on his chair.

"No. The King said I could talk about it. He just didn't want people worrying in case it turned out to be nothing."

Russlan grunted. "Makes sense. Well, you did it once, so I'll sleep better at night knowing you're heading up there again."

A chorus of support followed the smith's declaration and the building tension drained away. A normal hum of conversation filled the room and he was no longer the centre of attention. The smith shook his hand again and left. Kell heaved a sigh of relief and started to relax again.

In pairs and small groups people came up to Kell's table to shake his hand, thank him for what he'd done and wish him well for the journey ahead. No one asked any more questions about what he would be facing. It was clear they preferred not to know. Several offered to buy him a drink and before long he had ten on a tab at the bar. A skinny Hundarian merchant with jade earrings and three rings through his nose offered to buy Kell several drinks. When the Hundarian realised how many drinks were already on the tab he insisted on paying for Kell's room instead.

Although his name was widely known, Kell had never traded on it before or experienced such adoration. It took him by surprise and he felt a rush of warmth from the attention. Was this what the heroes had experienced every day? It was easy to see how intoxicating it could be.

Eventually it happened as he knew it would. A chubby Seith merchant wobbled over to his table, sloshing beer all over his clothes. Like all westerners he had a wide nose and the trademark red shirt. Looking closer, Kell could see it was actually a mix of white, green and red.

Every Seith family had their own unique pattern which told the history of their business. Although he couldn't translate all of the loops and kinks Kell recognised enough to pick up the general story. The domination of white threads on the shirt meant most of the family's money had been made from textiles, probably silk and cotton judging by the merchant's fine clothing and gold teeth. The secondary green threads indicated a smaller portion of their money came from timber.

Before the Seith tried to shake hands Kell held up his left, tucked in his thumb and showed the Seith the back of his hand.

"Luck for the journey," said Kell.

The Seith laughed and mirrored the traditional gesture. "Peace upon the road."

The old greeting had been used in Seithland for centuries but these days most had adopted the handshake.

"Tell me the story," said the merchant, sitting down without an invitation. "Not the honeyed version from the bard. The real story. The grit. The blood. The struggle."

"I'm sure you've heard it before," said Kell, trying to play it down.

"No, you tell it," said the merchant, slamming his glass on the table. Beer spilled into his lap but he didn't notice. Looking at his eyes Kell could see the merchant was already drunk. If he'd been the only person to make the request it would have gone unnoticed but others took up the cheer. Soon half the people in the room were yelling at him for the story.

The voices were overwhelming. Kell raised his hands for silence and a hush quickly fell across the room. Only the drunk Seith was left cheering.

"Be quiet, Yan," said a woman, and the merchant fell silent.

Kell realised everyone was staring at him. There was a flutter in his stomach and a lump in his throat. There was a reason the King had hired Pax Medina to pen his saga. Kell wasn't confident speaking in front of others and didn't have the skill to keep a crowd on the edge of their seats.

"Perhaps I can assist?" said someone, moving through the crowd from the back. It took Kell a moment to realise the speaker was not a woman as he'd first assumed. With delicate features and a slim build, a high-pitched voice and eyelids painted blue to match his shirt, the foppish curly-haired man was drawing a lot of stares. In addition to being short, for a Hundarian, the man's garish clothing wasn't the only reason people had taken notice. It was the thirteen-stringed oud he was carrying on his back. It was rare to see a Hundarian adult without a shaven head and multiple piercings. The bard was definitely an outsider.

"My name is Vahli and I am a bard of some renown," he said, giving Kell a bow. "May I make a suggestion?"

"Go ahead," said Kell, happy for the gaudy bard to be the centre of attention.

"Perhaps I could recount the story of your adventure, and you could jump in with any new details?"

There were a few grumbles from the crowd at that idea but Kell knew it was the best offer he was going to get. He also knew that even when the saga veered away from the truth about the heroes, he would remain silent. The only people who knew the real story were King Bledsoe and Lukas, his Steward. Not even the bard, Pax Medina, had been given the full version of events.

Before Kell had met the heroes, each had performed good deeds which had earned them a reputation. At this stage a dose of the truth wouldn't help anyone. Besides, he'd sworn an oath to take some secrets to his grave. Parents still used their names as paradigms for their children. Work hard and you'll be as brave as Cardeas. Eat all your vegetables and you'll be as strong as Bron. Did anyone ever use his name in the same way?

"That sounds like a wonderful idea," said Kell.

With a florid gesture Vahli struck a heroic pose as he strummed his instrument.

"Kell Kressia was but a young lad of seventeen years," said the bard, his voice becoming deeper and more sonorous. "He dreamed of becoming a great hero like the stories he'd grown up with. Tales of Cardeas and Bron. He wanted to be just like them, a mighty warrior of legend and slayer of savage beasts, but then the weather began to change."

As Vahli spoke, people's eyes were drawn to the windows and the sky beyond as they contemplated the weather. The familiar words and rhythm carried Kell back in time until he was travelling north, surrounded by the heroes.

If only the audience knew the whole truth. There were moments, usually when he'd drunk too much, that Kell was tempted to tell people what had really happened. Every curse and threat. Every kick up the arse. Every lie they'd told. But even when he was drunk and miserable his oath to the King held him back. His word created an invisible barrier that protected the heroes even in death.

To sully their names would bring him no comfort. Nor did he want pity about what had happened. In a way, by protecting their legacy, he was also protecting himself. Now their names and deeds were inextricably linked and Kell would rise or fall alongside them.

"Is that what really happened when the dogs died?" asked someone.

Kell realised he'd drifted off at a critical moment. In the bard's version of the story Bron the Mighty, the strongest man who had ever lived, had pulled the remaining sleds across the ice to the castle. It was nonsense, of course.

"It's true. Bron saved us all," he said, forcing a smile.

Pragor had cried, not for the dogs, but for himself. It was Kell who came up with the idea of skinning the dogs for their fur. Without their pelts everyone would have frozen to death before they reached the Lich's castle. It had been hard to believe that despite all of Pragor's past adventures he was so fragile. It was at that point, after all that he'd endured to reach the ice fields, Kell realised he wasn't the weakest in the group.

Having lost his passion for the retelling almost the moment it had begun, Kell waited for Vahli to finish.

"And with one final swing of Slayer, he severed the creature's head from her shoulders. And with that the Lich was dead," concluded the bard. "And so, Kell Kressia, a boy no longer, made the long journey home to Thule to meet with King Bledsoe."

At times he thought the worst part of his journey had not been travelling to the north but returning alone. The silence on the road had eaten away at him. It had left him with only his thoughts for days on end. At the beginning he'd spoken to the heroes as if they were still alive. When the Frostrunners found him on the ice he'd been rambling and close to death. He would have died if they hadn't taken him south to Meer.

A stunned silence had fallen over the room. Many of the listeners were agog with open mouths. Even the table of teenage boys, who had been pretending they weren't impressed, were now staring at him with awe. Most of the crowd were smiling which made it easier to spot the few that weren't happy. He wasn't sure what they'd been expecting but it didn't matter. Kell thought a few were staring at him with sympathy. At least he hoped it was sympathy and not pity. Why would they pity him?

"What happened when you returned home?" someone asked. Kell picked out the speaker, a pink-skinned Corvanese with yellow hair which made her stand out in the crowd. "Was there anyone waiting for you?"

"There was someone special when I left," said Kell, trying to recall her face. It had only been ten years ago but for some reason details about Ines were sketchy. They'd both been little more than children. At the time their passion had seemed like the most important thing in the world.

"When I returned to Honaje almost half a year had passed. Everyone thought I was already dead. By then she'd already married someone else." He'd seen her around town but she'd changed, or perhaps he'd grown up. There had been someone more recently but he never spoke about her because it was still too painful.

"Any more drinks?" shouted the landlady, breaking the silence. The spell was broken and people drifted away. When a group gathered to thank Vahli and request a few tunes Kell snuck away to his room. His legs ached from the saddle and his head was a little fuzzy from the beer.

In the end it had turned out to be a good night. Far better than at home. He didn't have to pay for his room and he'd been given free drinks. This must have been what it was like for the heroes. That thought immediately soured the evening.

On the long journey home Kell had made several promises. Never to return to the Frozen North. To live out the rest of his life in peace. The last was to remind himself that for all of their faults the heroes had given him a second chance at life which he wasn't about to squander.

Kell felt a little guilty about taking the money from King Bledsoe to start a new life, but he viewed it as his reward for services past. Feeling no regret about his decision, Kell fell into a deep sleep.

The next morning Kell walked out of the Thirsty Ferret to find that his horse had already been saddled. Holding the reins, and that of a nervous black stallion, was a teenage boy. He was tall and skinny with fuzz on his top lip in an approximation of a moustache. His trousers were slightly too short, indicating a recent growth spurt, and the leather brigandine was too big suggesting he'd borrowed it. The boy was full of nervous energy and unable to stand still.

"Thanks for saddling her," said Kell, reaching for a coin. "I appreciate it."

"I don't work in the stables," said the boy. "I'm Gerren. I heard your story last night."

"Then thanks for the favour," he said, but the boy shook his head. "What? What is it?"

Gerren took a deep breath, puffing out his skinny chest. "I'm coming with you."

Kell stared. A hundred different thoughts whirled through his head. His first instinct was to ride away. His second was to belittle the boy. Gerren wasn't old enough and going on this trip would be a death sentence. Kell wanted to conjure the worst things from his imagination and scare Gerren into staying at home. The irony wasn't lost on Kell, particularly with him now filling the role of the hero. In the end, Kell couldn't help himself because of the absurdity of it all. He laughed.

It was cruel and mocking laughter, at the boy, at himself, and the Shepherd for putting him in this ridiculous situation. Gerren took it badly just as Kell had done ten years ago, which only made it even funnier. The heroes had laughed at Kell for a long time as well.

Finally, when he was done and his sides were aching, Kell wiped tears from his eyes and snatched his reins from the boy.

"Go home, boy."

"I'm seventeen. Exactly the same age as you were. I know how to ride and hunt, and I've packed for a long journey. I'm ready," insisted Gerren, gesturing at his horse. The stallion had been weighed down with provisions. He'd also found a sword from somewhere which was strapped to his back. From his posture and the way it kept shifting about, Kell could see the boy wasn't used to its weight. He'd probably never even held a blade before.

"Who did you steal the horse from?"

"No one. It's my father's."

"And the sword?" asked Kell. This time the boy had no answer. "Go home, fall on your knees and beg for your father's forgiveness. Then go back to chasing girls, or whatever you were doing before." Kell dismissed him with a gesture but the boy didn't move. Pretending he wasn't there Kell checked his horse, making sure the saddle was secure and not too tight. His horse seemed well rested so at least the groom had done his job.

"Ready for another long day, girl?" he asked, and the horse whickered. Kell gently stroked her head and wondered if he should call her Misty.

"I'm going, and you can't stop me!" said the boy. Kell continued to ignore him, tying on his bag behind the saddle. "I'll just follow you all the way to the Frozen North!"

That caught Kell's attention. After all, he'd done the same for the first three days. Setting up his own camp at night within sight of their fire. On the second day the heroes had risen early, with the hope of catching him asleep, but Kell had already been waiting for them in the saddle.

An idea formed in the back of his head and with a resigned sigh he turned to face the boy. "Did you hear the story last night?"

"Every word."

"There's a lot I left out. There are gaps in the Medina saga as well. The kind of thing that will give you nightmares."

"I can handle it," insisted Gerren. "You managed at my age."

Kell shook his head. "No, I didn't. It was a horrible mistake. The worst of my life. It took me a long time to get over what happened. I had nightmares for years and seizures during the day. I wasn't right in the head. Everything hurt. Everything was broken inside. Do you understand?"

Gerren just stared. He had no idea of the horrors Kell had seen and the way those memories had lingered, weighing him down, eating away at his soul. It was like the tide. A relentless force intent on destroying him bit by bit, eroding his sanity and sense of self. Eventually it had felt as if there was nothing left inside.

Kell became a hollow thing shaped like a man. He'd barely been able to function. Sleep was just an idea because all he had was nightmares, but they weren't fiction. They were memories from the journey that he was forced to relive over and over. He ate sporadically, lost a lot of weight and most days had hallucinations. No one understood. The only people who might have understood were dead.

In those early days he'd lived in a small house in the centre of town. People thought he was cracked in the head. Kell had heard voices and was often seen talking to people that weren't there. He was violent and unpredictable around others but staying alone indoors only seemed to make it worse. It didn't take long for him to go from being a celebrated hero to a shunned mad man.

The local Manx, and even Sister Gail, had done their best for him, but they had other people to look after, including his sick mother. A few months after he returned from the Frozen North his mother died and he inherited a small holding. It was quiet, away from other people, and he was surrounded by nature. Plants, trees, animals, fertile soil and the changing seasons. But there was also a long list of jobs that needed to be done every day. The farm wouldn't run itself. The neighbours had done their best but it wasn't their responsibility.

That meant every day he had to get out of bed to feed the animals and tend the crops. He couldn't lie around feeling sorry for himself. He had no choice. If he wanted to eat he had to work. Running the farm gave him structure and discipline. He woke early and went to bed late. Most nights he was so exhausted he'd fall into bed and didn't dream.

It was the peace of being on the farm and its routine that slowly brought him back to life. If not for that, Kell knew he would be dead, either from starvation or he'd have taken his own life. He'd often thought about it. Even rested a blade against his throat once, pressing it hard enough to draw blood. The scar served as a reminder every time he looked in the mirror.

"Do you think you could handle cutting off a man's arm?" asked Kell. "We had to do that when Bron's wound became infected. The noise of a blade cutting through bone will never leave me but slicing the nerves was worse. Bron begged and screamed like a child. Then he wept for his mother." Kell could still see him, a mountain of a man famed for his strength crying like a little boy, huddled in a blanket as they poured whisky down his throat to try and numb the pain. He'd never been the same after that. Perhaps it was a mercy that he'd died on the ice.

Gerren swallowed hard but stubbornly shook his head. "I'm going."

Kell wondered if he'd possessed the same level of arrogance at seventeen. Of course he had. At Gerren's age he'd also thought that he was immortal and that he knew everything about the world.

"Do you have any provisions?" he asked, gesturing at the boy's saddlebags.

"Yes and money to buy more."

Kell didn't ask where he'd found the money. "How about warm clothing? Wool-lined boots and the like. You'll need them on the ice, otherwise you'll freeze to death."

Gerren's mouth fell open. "Are you saying I can go with you?"

"There's not much I can do to stop you, is there?" said Kell. "Do you have any clothes like that?"

"No, but Cade down the road might have some."

"Well, you'd best go and get some. I'm not going to hang around here all day," said Kell, looping his horse's reins around a post. "I'll be inside having a drink. Come and find me when you're done."

Gerren tied up his horse and then ran off down the road.

"Don't take all day!" he yelled after the boy.

Kell went inside the Ferret, counted to ten and then walked back out. Using a knife he split the girth on Gerren's saddle and laid it down on the road. The stallion watched him curiously, but it made no attempt to bite or kick him which he appreciated.

Kell rode out of town at a canter putting some distance between him and the boy. It was better this way. Gerren would feel foolish and then angry at being cheated of a great adventure. He hoped that, in time, Gerren would realise that being left behind was a gift and it had saved his life. There were countless times over the past ten years when Kell wished someone had done the same for him.

After a pleasant ride in the morning Kell walked his horse for a while to stretch his legs. He had lunch in the shade of some trees beside a brook where Misty drank her fill. Part of him expected to see Gerren coming up the road from behind, riding hard in a desperate attempt to catch up. He was relieved when the only travellers he saw heading north were merchants and a farmer driving cattle.

By mid-afternoon Kell had put the boy from his mind. He planned out the next few days and thought again of his new life. In a week's time he would be across the Narrow Sea in lands he'd only heard about from merchants.

He was still leaning towards an orchard. If the weather was good he could brew cider. If it was poor he could sell the apples to farmers as cattle feed. All he had to do was sit back and watch the trees grow. It would be a good life. Peaceful and quiet like the farm.

When the first hint of grey began to colour the sky, and darkness was still a few hours away, he arrived at the next village on the road. There were several unhitched wagons in a row lined up on one side of the street. The horses had been stabled in a paddock and music was already drifting through the air from the largest tavern. There were even a few tables outside where a small group were smoking hookah pipes or enjoying a drink.

Just as Kell was about to get down from his horse something caught his eye. From a narrow side street a figure slowly rode towards him with purpose. Shielding his eyes against the falling sun it took a little while for the rider came into focus.

It was Gerren.

CHAPTER 9

One by one the heroes of legend fell,
Where their blood froze upon on the ice.
Until only the boy remained and all hope seemed lost,
But with a fierce cry he charged his hateful enemy.

EXCERPT FROM THE SAGA OF KELL KRESSIA
BY THE BARD PAX MEDINA

Kell ignored Gerren as best as he could. He refused to answer any of his questions and just pretended he wasn't there.

The village was much like the others he'd passed through. Famous for nothing, busy with travellers and merchants. The only unusual thing he noticed was a lot of people were covered in grey dust which meant there was a mine.

Not far away a line of men and women from across the Five Kingdoms were waiting to collect their wages. Hard times had driven people to this but at least they would be paid for an honest day's work. It was better than going hungry.

As a young man Kell had often dreamed of wealth. The only thing of real value he owned was the farm which he'd inherited when his mother died. His father had died when Kell had been very young. All memories of his father came from the few stories his mother had told him over the years.

"You can't keep ignoring me forever," said Gerren, as Kell climbed off his horse and passed Misty's reins to a lurking stable girl.

"Are the rooms clean?" he asked, jerking a thumb at the tavern.

"Cleanest around," she promised, although her grimy appearance didn't fill him with much confidence. Nevertheless he went inside the Blind Fox. A warm meal, a soft bed and a good night's sleep. That's all he wanted.

Gerren constantly badgered him at the bar and then refused to leave Kell alone when he sat down to eat. Closing his eyes Kell savoured every bite of his venison. The food was expensive but for once he had enough money not to worry about the price. It was only going to get more expensive in the coming months.

When he'd finished eating Kell ordered some of the spiced apple pie he'd seen others enjoying. The boy briefly stopped talking to eat but now that he was almost done Kell could see he was getting ready to resume his pestering.

"Before you start," said Kell, finally addressing the boy after two hours of silence. "You need to hear a few truths. Will you listen without interrupting?"

Gerren started to answer but instead clamped his mouth shut and just nodded.

"The story you know, the one everyone is told by the bards, it's not the whole story. A lot more happened and much of it wasn't pretty. No one wants to hear about those parts but they still happened."

"But even those parts make you a hero," said the boy, bursting with enthusiasm. "Besides, I know why you tried to leave me behind."

"Really?" said Kell, raising an eyebrow.

"It was noble, but I don't need you to protect me."

"That's not the reason. I don't want your death on my conscience."

Gerren's face turned pale. "You're just trying to scare me."

"Boy, you should be scared. The things waiting in the Frozen

North are worthy of nightmares. There are places where even the Frostrunners won't tread. But I did. Twelve of us went north and only I returned. Gerren, if you listen to only one thing then let it be this. The heroes you worship, they all died screaming in pain. At the end they all begged for their mothers like frightened children. Doesn't that tell you something?"

The boy swallowed hard and stubbornly bit his lip. It was at that moment Kell knew that no matter what he said, the boy wouldn't listen. The truth wouldn't dissuade him. Even lies wouldn't work.

As Kell stewed on what to do he noticed a few people looking in his direction. He was starting to be recognised. Travellers on the road must have mentioned his name and word had spread. If he stayed in the tavern Kell knew what would happen. He'd be asked to repeat the story to another audience who were desperate for some excitement. For a short time, through his tale of misery and suffering, they would live as heroes.

With his mood soured Kell left the Fox, refusing to stop when people tried to engage him. The muscles in Kell's left leg twitched as he waited for the girl to retrieve his horse. He wouldn't stay the night. He couldn't any more.

"Where are you going?" asked Gerren, coming up behind him.

Kell didn't answer because he didn't know. He had a sudden urge to be far away from other people. To be outside without a roof over his head or walls boxing him in. He needed to see the night sky. To feel earth between his fingers. Kell told himself that the icy trickle running down his spine was sweat. It wasn't the cold hand of fear. He wasn't back in the north waiting to die. All of that was over. There were no whispering voices. It was just the wind and his imagination. He needed to get away. To fly.

Kell pulled himself into the saddle and rode out of the village as if pursued by an angry mob. Part of him was on the horse but the rest was elsewhere, trapped in the past. The nightmares that he thought long-buried resurfaced bringing fresh horrors with them. The calluses he'd built up over ten years offered little in the way of protection.

He desperately wanted to forget the past, but he couldn't. Not with time or drink. The memories were immovable and unyielding, like a perfectly formed diamond.

He was back on the ice. Desperately trying to put up a tent and help the heroes. Something was soaking into his trousers, pooling around his legs. He told himself it was just water, except it was warm and red. One of the heroes shoved him aside, his arms full of bandages. All of their faces were pale, eyes wide with terror. They knew it was already over, the wounds were too severe but desperation made them try. A final breath came and then the flesh began to cool, eyes staring at nothing. Forever.

One by one the heroes died and he witnessed it all. Every cry. Every last breath. Every prayer for their departed soul.

Time lost all meaning. Kell rode until there were only trees and the sky above full of stars. When Misty stumbled he let his horse slow to a walk. Gradually he came back to the present and found he was panting as much as his horse. They stopped at a stream to drink and he let Misty rest before checking her for injuries. Thankfully she'd carried him through it safely.

He still had nightmares from time to time but it had been many years since his last waking episode. Even pretending to make this journey for a second time was bringing up a lot of old memories.

Some time later Kell heard another horse approaching. He was sitting against a tree staring into the darkness. His clothing was soaked with sweat and he was shivering. Gerren said nothing. He gathered wood and carefully built up a fire before covering Kell with a blanket. Slowly the heat began to seep into his body and the numbness faded.

"There's a flask," said Kell, vaguely gesturing towards his horse. Gerren rummaged around in his saddlebags and eventually returned with it. The small silver flask had been a gift from King Bledsoe. "Drink," said Kell, urging the boy to have a taste.

Gerren took a sip and had a coughing fit. Kell took a long pull, enjoying the burning sensation as it passed through his body.

"Did you ever hear any stories about Kursen the Hunter?" asked Kell.

"Everyone has," asked Gerren. "My favourite is the one where he wrestled a bison bull to the ground."

Kursen had been tall, even for a Hundarian, with arms that seemed longer than his legs. Kell had expected him to be boastful and loud like many of the other heroes, but he'd been quiet and thoughtful. He smiled and laughed at their jokes but not if they were cruel. He liked to drink and had an easy-going nature, but sometimes Kursen would go for hours without speaking. During those times the others knew to leave him alone and when Kell asked they said that it was just his way. Kursen would fall under a black cloud. Eventually it would fade and his smile would return but Kell stayed clear during his bleak times. Out of them all he was the only one that Kell would call a genuine hero.

"Was the story true? Did he really do it?" asked the boy, intruding on his thoughts.

"He did. His arms were so long he wrapped them around the beast and choked it to the ground. After that it followed him around like a puppy."

Kell smiled at the memory. They had been sat around a fire, much like the current one, only back then he'd been the boy. Kursen's booming laughter had rolled out into the night as he'd told Kell about the bison.

Kell's humour faded as another memory rose to the surface. "One day, when we were crossing the ice, a sabre of maglau attacked. Kursen was injured in the fight. He pretended it wasn't serious and told no one when the wound became infected. Three days later he was delirious from blood poisoning. There was nothing we could do. We were too far north to turn back and we had to press on. But the dogs wouldn't carry him because of the smell, so we left him there to die, alone on the ice."

It wasn't the most difficult thing Kell had ever done but it was definitely one of the worst. He'd argued with the others, desperate to find an alternative. Some had wanted to wrap

Kursen in a blanket to muffle the smell and take him with them. The rest wanted to leave him there to die. By that point half of the heroes were already dead and the thought of losing someone else was too much to bear. The vote was tied until Kursen himself ended the argument by voting to be left. When Kell asked him why, Kursen said he would rather spend his final moments in peace, wrapped in silence, than be surrounded by angry voices and furious hearts.

He must have frozen to death in a few hours. By chance, Kell came across his body on the way south but with no tools there was no way to dig a shallow grave or free him from the ice. Leaving him behind a second time had been as difficult as the first.

This time the boy didn't smile or make light of Kell's story. He was starting to understand but Kell knew it was too little too late.

"You can't trust anyone. And you can only rely on yourself."

Kell knew the boy wanted to argue that he was just old and bitter, which was true, but it didn't change the facts. Showing wisdom for his age, Gerren remained silent, his face thoughtful in the firelight.

The warmth of the drink and the fire eased Kell's troubled mind. Sleep pulled at him and he willingly went towards it, keen to be away from the world and its problems.

The next morning Kell woke early to find the fire had burned down to ashes. He checked on his horse, gathered up his belongings and gently eased the boy into a sitting position against the tree. Gerren stirred, muttering in his sleep, but didn't wake. With a bit of persuasion he encouraged the boy's horse to go for a run.

As Kell was climbing into the saddle the boy's eyes fluttered open but it was too late. He tried to stand and then began thrashing about, but Kell had made sure the rope was secure about his wrists. With a bit of sweating and some fierce wriggling, plus losing a bit of skin, Gerren would be able to get out of his restraints in an hour or two. It would take him at least as long to retrieve his horse, by which time Kell would be far away.

If Gerren continued to pursue him then by the time he arrived at the next town Kell would already have left and be on the way towards his new life.

"Why?" asked Gerren, when he realised he couldn't escape.

"I told you, boy. You can't trust anyone."

"You're afraid."

Kell laughed. "Of course I am, and you should be too. The problem is you're too young and stupid to listen. Do you think Kursen and the others were never afraid? Most of them pissed themselves when we heard the Qalamieren." The colour drained from Gerren's face at mention of the ancient creatures. "Oh, that's right, boy. They're real. I've heard them and they're far worse than anything you've been told."

"You're supposed to be a hero." There was accusation in Gerren's voice but it didn't affect him.

Kell leaned forward on his saddle, fixing the boy in place with a stare. "Listen closely, because it's the last thing I'll ever say to you. If you ignore me and go north into the frozen wastes, you will die. There's no maybe about it. You have no hope and no chance. So do yourself a favour and go home."

Realisation dawned on Gerren's face and the optimism leaked from his features. "You're a coward." Kell leaned back in his saddle but didn't deny it. "You're not going north, are you?"

Kell shook his head. "I've done my part. It's someone else's turn. In a few years' time, no one will even remember me."

Gerren's struggles became more frantic. Blood began to trickle from his wrists where the rope was cutting into his skin. "I'll tell everyone about you."

The weak threat made Kell laugh. "Really? And who are you, boy? What have you done with your life? You've barely got hair on your balls. You've never been anywhere or done anything. You've never risked anything. I killed the Ice Lich and saved the world. Who do you think they're going to believe?"

For once Gerren didn't have an answer and his shoulders slumped in defeat.

"Go home," Kell urged him. "Someone else will take care of this."

A heavy silence settled over them. A few hours alone would give the boy some time to think it over.

Gerren took a deep breath and raised his chin. "Leave it," he said.

"What?"

"The sword."

"Why?"

"Because you're right. Someone else is going to take care of it. At least with your sword I stand a chance."

"You've got balls, I'll give you that," said Kell. "But do you want to know a secret? There's nothing special about my sword."

"But it's Slayer! You slew the Ice Lich with it!" insisted Gerren.

"It's not a magic sword."

"That doesn't matter. Besides, I need Slayer more than you."

"Then you'd best head for Seithland. I sold the original blade to a merchant seven years ago. This is the third Slayer," said Kell, gesturing at the sword on his back.

"Is anything about you real? Was it all lies?"

Kell didn't answer. Turning Misty around he rode out of camp.

He hoped the boy would listen but Kell recognised that stubborn look. It was possible Gerren would tell stories about him but it didn't matter any more.

Soon he would be free. Free of the past and everything that came with it. His new life was about to begin and nothing would stop him.

CHAPTER 10

The seventh pillar is charity.
When the larder is full, giving a portion is easy,
But when stomachs are tight,
The faithful share and do not hoard.

EXCERPT FROM THE SACRED BOOK OF THE SHEPHERD

Reverend Mother Britak had found the journey to Thune from the Holy City to be surprisingly productive. Normally her duties kept her incredibly busy, leaving her with insufficient time to meditate on the larger problems that needed addressing.

She'd insisted the carriage ride be conducted in silence to promote purity of spirit and encourage prayer. It would have been even more comfortable if she wasn't being accompanied by Sallie, her slow-witted maid, but appearances needed to be maintained for someone of her station.

To her credit the girl said little and seemed content with staring out the window at Algany so Britak didn't chide her on the few occasions she spoke. Sallie had a tendency to fall asleep and snore if left to meditate for too long.

As the girl gawped at the sheep, Britak focused on how best to approach her meetings in the coming days. Some of them would be pleasant, others more challenging, but all of them required that she be completely focused. She couldn't give any sign that she was no longer in full control of her mental faculties.

Only a fool would attempt to rob her but these were difficult times and people were desperate. The carriage itself wasn't richly decorated but the six pure white horses pulling it would fetch a good price. The twenty priests escorting her were a reassuring presence when they camped outside each night.

She could have stayed at any roadside tavern but, despite the honour of having her as a guest, she would not expect the owner to do so for free. To feed and house so many in one night would fill the place and cost a small fortune. Times were hard and she loathed to waste money on comfort for herself when others were in dire need. Once she reached Thune a cell in a convent would be more than enough. It was rare that she made such journeys but these days people needed hope. If her presence meant that more of them embraced the twelve pillars of the Shepherd then it was worth the effort.

As the carriage approached the gates of Thune she was surprised to see a market had sprung up since her last visit. The whole area was bustling with people but the produce she could see looked to be poor quality and the meat was expensive. There were a lot more bakers than she would have expected, all of whom were busy with long queues. Armed city guards drifted through the market, their spears poking up above the crowd, keen eyes scanning for pickpockets.

"Don't gawp, dear," said Britak, gesturing for Sallie to close her mouth. The girl had never been outside the Holy City so this was a grand adventure for her.

At the gates she saw there was a small queue of travellers. Patience. It was the one principle from the Book that she struggled with the most. Sobriety wasn't a problem. Thrift had never been an issue either as before becoming a nun her parents never had any money. It took a little time, during which time Britak tried her best to meditate, but eventually they moved forward and passed through the gate.

As she rode through the capital, Britak was pleased to see many local priests at work. There were more beggars on the streets than in the Holy City but several were in the company of priests who were handing out bread and blankets. Each time her carriage came abreast of a priest they would pause and raise a hand in salute. Britak took the time to bless each one which made all of them smile and stand up straighter than before. Theirs was a hard road that was often thankless. If a blessing from her made them feel proud she was confident the Shepherd would forgive them for such a minor transgression.

Finally her journey came to an end as they reached the palace gates. Here she alighted from the carriage while her priests spoke to the guards. While they were making arrangements she took a little time to stretch and work the kinks out of her back from sitting down for so long. Sallie watched her with such fascination it was as if she'd not seen her do it before.

"One day it will happen to you," said Britak, but the girl just stared without comprehension.

A short time later, surrounded by six priests she'd chosen with care as they were the least likely to cause problems, Britak walked through the palace grounds. Two palace guards led the way, opening doors ahead of her so that her progress was not impeded. The guards' pace was faster than Britak would have preferred, but she gritted her teeth against the pain and kept going. Besides, it was only a short walk and she needed to stretch her legs after being in the carriage for so long.

A final set of heavy double doors was pushed open to reveal her welcoming committee waiting inside. Although she'd seen various signs of wealth in the corridors the room was surprisingly sparse of furniture. Sunlight filtered into the room via narrow windows which was reflected off large mirrors on the walls. The result was a bright, welcoming room.

There were a few bunches of freshly cut flowers on simple wooden tables but no great works of art or paintings of the King and his ancestors. A shrewd mind had carefully arranged the room so that it caused her the least offence and generated little criticism.

As she'd expected, the King was not there to greet her. No doubt there would be a formal apology later, something to do with ill-health, but she knew there weren't that many years between them in age. Instead of King Bledsoe, his daughter, Princess Sigrid, stood waiting for her arrival. In fact, all of those waiting had been forced to stand as there were no chairs.

Dressed demurely in a simple grey dress with a high neck and long sleeves, Sigrid was the epitome of nobility and etiquette. Tall and elegant, her chestnut skin shone with health and her long black hair was gathered in a simple clip. She wore neither a crown nor any jewellery and still managed to outshine everyone else.

Sigrid was flanked on either side by two of the Raven, the King's elite. As ever they were dressed in their morbid black uniforms. Beside them were various palace officials, an ambassador from each of the other four Kingdoms and right at the edge of the room, the King's Steward. Lukas was a man that she despised and yet also admired for his intelligence. He was undoubtedly the one who had carefully planned the room. Lukas had faithfully served the King for decades and Britak always paid extreme care to every word she said in the man's presence. He had a mind like a bookkeeper where everything was carefully recorded for future use.

Although Britak understood the necessity of pomp and ceremony, particularly for a formal visit, after decades of similar rituals they had become tiresome. She would rather get to the real reason she'd come all this way.

The Princess welcomed her with genuine warmth, thanked her for making the difficult journey and made a few polite enquiries. Next came the relayed greetings from the other Kings, via the ambassadors, all of whom asked if she would bless their lieges with a visit in the future. She couldn't tell which of them were genuine as all of the ambassadors gave little away.

Normally at this point there was an exchange of gifts but given the circumstances Britak had not brought anything with her. She was pleased to see no servants were lurking with anything to present to her.

"I hope you will forgive me for not offering you any gifts," said Princess Sigrid. "Instead the money will be used to house and feed those in need during these difficult times."

From the irate expressions of the ambassadors it was not a popular decision. No doubt they had been hoping to flatter her with gifts to curry favour for their respective king. She was really starting to like this girl.

"A wise decision, Princess."

"I look forward to our discussions, Reverend Mother, but perhaps you would like some time to freshen up from your journey. I believe the local Bishop has arranged rooms at a nearby convent."

The Princess gave a low curtsey, much deeper than was necessary, which pleased Britak. She didn't know if it was all for show, or Sigrid's respect was genuine, but either way Britak appreciated the effort. It was going to be interesting in the next few days getting to know the Princess while assessing her devotion to the Shepherd.

In the past her father had always been courteous but had strongly opposed compulsory religious lessons in schools. But time marched on, and no matter who actually sat on the throne, Sigrid was the future of Algany.

Everyone wanted something and she was determined to find out what Sigrid desired. Once she knew that, Britak would find a way to encourage the Princess to share her vision of the future. Failing that, there were other ways of motivating her but one way or another Sigrid would fall in line. The Five Kingdoms may never been united under one King but they would be under the one true God.

After days of sleeping in the carriage Britak was relieved to spend a night in the convent. However, the thin mattress was too soft so instead she slept on the stone shelf wrapped in a blanket to keep away the chill. Once she'd performed her daily stretches, working out the kinks in her back, she felt refreshed.

The morning was cool and the light drizzle threatened to sour her mood. The cold air would make her knees ache. The Shepherd was continuing to test her and everyone else with such poor weather. The faithful would flourish and those who clung to superstition would be punished. Faith had to be tested. Those who never questioned anything were nothing more than sheep and, although she often referred to a congregation as a flock, it was made up of individuals, not slow-witted animals.

After morning prayers and a quick breakfast she set off for her first appointment. Several times as she walked through the city Britak was approached by those who recognised her. Initially they were apprehensive about her armed priests but once she was certain they weren't dangerous she made time to speak and bless them individually. Britak was genuinely surprised at the warm welcome she received from strangers. It restored her belief that good people existed everywhere.

By the time she arrived at a nondescript building for her first meeting, the aches in her knees were forgotten. Two priests circled around to the back while two more went inside to search for potential threats. The remaining two stayed nearby and were alert for danger. There had been attempts on her life in the past, but the last was a dozen years ago. Even so her priests were unwilling to take any chances. She was only allowed to enter the building when they were certain it was safe.

In the front room Fayez, the Hundarian ambassador, looked flustered, no doubt from being thoroughly searched for weapons. He quickly recovered and bowed deeply, his shaven head almost touching the grubby floor. It looked as if a stiff breeze would blow the man over but like all of his people Fayez had a wiry strength.

Although their meeting was not clandestine the unusual location provided a suitable excuse for her presence. The building was currently in the process of being transformed into the new Hundarian embassy and she was supposed to be there to offer a blessing. The walls were freshly painted, the wooden floors scrubbed and most of the furniture covered with old sheets apart from two chairs in front of the cold fireplace.

"An honour, Reverend Mother," said Fayez. He waited until she was comfortable before taking his seat opposite.

She'd previously met him on two occasions and knew him to be a humble and careful man. He never made promises he couldn't keep and if he didn't know something he would admit it rather than lie on behalf of his King. "I bring you warm greetings from my King. He apologises for not being here in person, but there are many problems back home that require his attention."

Britak didn't need him to explain. Every ruler in the Five Kingdoms was facing the real possibility that there would be famine this year or next. Hard choices would have to be made and she didn't envy their position in the months ahead.

"I will pray for him, and ask the Shepherd to give him wisdom," she promised, which made the ambassador smile. Fayez, like his King and Queen, was devout in his belief. Hundar was her strongest ally against the faithless and every year they sent missionaries beyond the Five Kingdoms to spread the word.

"Your message said it was a matter of grave importance," said Fayez, getting down to business.

Britak's smile slipped for the first time since waking up that morning. "Kell Kressia."

"That is a name I have been hearing often in the last week," admitted Fayez. "I am told he's on his way north again. To face a new evil."

"Superstitious nonsense," she said. "It's nothing more than a story concocted by King Bledsoe."

"Are you certain?"

Britak raised an eyebrow. "Let me give you some advice."

"Please, Reverend Mother," said Fayez, giving her a seated bow.

"No, not as the Reverend Mother, but at someone who has lived for seventy years. There is nothing new in this world that I have not already seen." Her recent memory wasn't perfect but events from her youth were absolutely clear. "I've seen it all before. The rise of sex cults, popular for their promiscuity, before they suddenly end in disease, violence and death. Heroes, worshipped as false idols for their bravery, who turn out to be nothing but flawed individuals. I've seen famine, flood and a five year drought where the sun was so warm the land cracked open and riverbeds were dry. Two years of bad weather is nothing. The cause is not supernatural. Ten years ago you saw it yourself. A few bad seasons that suddenly ended."

Fayez wasn't stupid but he and many others had been duped by Kell's story. The whole affair was made worse when the cursed song was spread by the bards. She had tried to have it banned in all the taverns in the Holy City but the King had ignored her request.

"Kell is an assassin, trained by King Bledsoe. He was never an innocent youth. How else do you explain that only he survived the journey?"

She waited until Fayez shrugged, unable or unwilling to answer.

"If he reaches the Frozen North again you know what will happen. He cannot be allowed to pass through Hundar." Britak knew that King Roebus was sending someone after Kell but she didn't believe in taking unnecessary risks.

People wanted a simple answer to their problems. A supernatural evil was a story for children and adults unwilling to face the truth. The world and its problems were far more complex, as were the solutions. It required hard work, dedication and time. Unfortunately the truth was a bitter pill to swallow and some preferred fantasy over reality.

"He's attracting a lot of attention on the road. People are being drawn to him," said Fayez. "I'm sure I could find a willing admirer who could get close to him."

Britak shook her head. "That's already being covered."

"Then what did you have in mind?"

"Once I could have walked the entire length of the Five Kingdoms without protection. Now I must travel with an escort of armed priests."

"Bandits then," said Fayez. "How many?"

"A dozen, maybe more."

"For one man?" asked Fayez, raising an eyebrow.

"As you said, he's attracting a lot of attention. People worship him as a hero. Some may even want to tag along on his new adventure. There can be no witnesses."

"Very well. I will send a message home. It will be done."

"Thank you."

"May I ask you a question, Reverend Mother?"

In such a meeting where they were having a frank discussion people only asked such a question before saying something uncomfortable.

"What do you want to know?" she said, thinking it was going to be a question about faith, or what happened after death.

"Have you ever considered that you might be wrong about Kell Kressia?" said Fayez, catching her by surprise.

"What do you mean?"

"What if, ten years ago, he wasn't an assassin and was nothing more than a stupid, headstrong boy? What if it was pure luck that he survived? Or what if he simply went up to the ice, let the others go ahead, and came home when they didn't return?"

"You think he's a hero," said Britak, reassessing her impression of Fayez.

"No, not a hero. Maybe just a lucky fool."

"It no longer matters. He must die," said Britak. When she came face to face with the Shepherd, there would be an accounting of her sins, but she was willing to pay the price.

Truthfully, Kell's innocence was something that she'd considered shortly after his return. The idea had given her many sleepless nights but as his fame began to grow, and more people spread the Medina saga, it became irrelevant. He was dangerous and needed to be stopped.

Besides, if he was innocent, then who had stopped the assassins she'd sent to kill him over the years?

CHAPTER 11

With familiar voices the Qalamieren called,
Crying out in grief and pain.
Tempting the heroes onto the ice,
Where they could devour their souls.

EXCERPT FROM THE SAGA OF KELL KRESSIA
BY THE BARD PAX MEDINA

After riding at a steady pace all morning Kell arrived at a town called Burston a little after midday. It was on the border between Algany and Hundar making it an ideal stopping point for travellers. Far in the distance to the north-west he could see the edge of the Breach mountains. The range was immense and the highest peak was hidden among the clouds.

All morning he'd expected to hear Gerren come riding up behind him but so far there was no sign. He knew the boy wouldn't give up, so Kell bought fresh bread and cheese from a bakery and ate it in the saddle.

This far north the air was noticeably cooler and the land more uneven. On his left were the Breach mountains. For centuries people had thought there was no way through them to whatever lay on the other side. When the first tattooed warrior appeared, someone had shot him in a panic.

Negotiating peace with the Choate had been a long and difficult process. The war had ended two hundred years ago but people were still nervous around the tribes. Kell had heard stories that Choate territory was nothing but an endless sea of pitted rocks and stinking swamps. He suspected the Choate liked the story as it kept away outsiders.

Across the border into Hundar the road split in two. The western fork led to the capital city, Pynar, and beyond that numerous mining towns and settlements. To stay away from large crowds Kell took the east road that drifted through farming settlements, forests and pastureland. It reminded him a little of home but it was too hilly and often littered with barrows where the ancient Hundarians had buried their dead. Despite not being much of a believer, Kell rode around them. It didn't pay to disturb the dead.

Just before nightfall he reached the town of Nasse. Every settlement in Hundar was always surrounded by a barrier. In villages it was often a small fence or a muddy slope bristling with wooden stakes. Nasse had a six foot wall that was old and pitted in places but it was not designed for war. Hundar had been a land where wolves and their larger cousins, the vorans, had thrived, not to mention bears, cougars and snapjaws.

Over time the wilderness had been pushed back, but every now and then a few sheep or a child would go missing. Then the hunters would don their old gear and bring down the rogue beast that didn't understand the new order.

At the exact centre of town, like all Hundarian settlements, was the Shepherd's church. It was a modest structure made of limestone with two small blue domes. The outside was fairly bland but inside it would be awash with coloured tiles, incense, glowing candles and soothing music. Going to church in Algany was sedate and tedious, but to Hundar it was a celebration of life.

Spanning out from the church, like the spokes on a wheel, were twelve streets lined with shops, taverns and businesses. After passing through the gates of Nasse he found the town stables. Placed at regular intervals around the courtyard Kell noticed blue glass lanterns. Hundarians believed they provided a soothing atmosphere for the horses.

There was an old joke about a Hundarian man whose house was on fire. The first time he ran into the burning building he came out with his horse, then his hound and finally his wife. It was an exaggeration but there was a seed of truth to the story.

At first glance everything seemed quiet. The moment he saw the grooms whispering together Kell knew something was wrong. He should have just ridden away but he was tired, hungry and Misty needed to rest.

As soon as the grooms saw him their huddle broke apart. A young girl in her teens raced up to him with a big smile. She wore a baggy black skirt that reached her ankles and a shirt embroidered with one gold crown, denoting she worked for the town and their King. The male grooms appeared to be dressed in an identical fashion except when they moved he saw they wore flowing trousers.

"A pleasure, sir," said the girl as he dismounted and handed over the reins.

Nervous sweat gathered in his hairline but he forced a smile, paid her and quickly walked away. Kell was sure that they'd recognised him. Perhaps he could grab a quick meal and then go straight up to his room. If he left first thing in the morning only a few people would know he was in town.

Music and laughter coming from one of the central streets drew his attention. It was busy with people drifting from one tavern to the next in search of the cheapest beer and best entertainment. Some were gangly locals on their way home but the majority were travellers from across the Five Kingdoms.

Several individuals waved or smiled at him in a familiar fashion which was alarming. A few people in any settlement might recognise him, but it had been ten years. Most had no idea what he looked like and had never seen him in the flesh. Even if stories about his new quest had raced ahead of him from other travellers it shouldn't be this widespread.

He'd missed something. Kell felt as if he was walking into a trap but there seemed no way to avoid it. He bypassed the first tavern, where a plump bard was recounting the Medina saga, and ignored the second that was busy with people. At the far end of the street, away from the noise, he found a more rustic tavern called the King's Blessing. As long as the bed was free of lice and the food was edible he didn't care.

Peering through a window he saw the main room was half empty which he thought was a good sign. After taking a few deep breaths to calm down, Kell pushed open the front door. Every person in the room turned towards him and their faces lit up with recognition.

The owner rushed forward babbling about being honoured that Kell would enter his humble establishment. People started cheering, applauding and then chanting his name. Sweat erupted from his pores and Kell started to panic. He tried to back away but the owner had a firm grip on his arm. The noise would draw more attention from elsewhere in town. He tried to address the room hoping that the crowd would fall silent but they were too excited. Almost immediately more people came pouring in from the street. Everyone wanted to shake his hand or pat him on the shoulder and soon the room was full of warm bodies.

Kell was shoved and guided to a chair towards the back of the room making it impossible to escape. Even more people squeezed into the room or leaned in through the open windows.

The noise level rose significantly as a dozen people tried to talk to him at once, peppering him with questions. The owner had disappeared behind the bar to serve drinks and now five serving girls were dashing around the room with trays. One of them passed by his table, dumped a glass of beer, and whirled away before he could ask her anything.

A chubby merchant from Algany, wearing a tricorn hat with four ribbons, sat down at his table without invitation. From the way she was swaying she'd been drinking for some time.

"Here he is," she slurred. "We've all been waiting for you!"

"How did you know I was coming?" he shouted, struggling to be heard over the noise. A constant stream of people came up to his table to touch him as if he were a sacred statue of the Shepherd.

"We were told you was coming," said the merchant, giving him a wink.

"How?" he asked.

"A bird came. From Burston," said the woman. The merchant lifted the empty glass to her lips and then stared at it with a puzzled expression.

"Everyone's going to come and see you," said the merchant, lifting her empty glass in a toast. "It's a celebration!"

"Let me talk to him," said a Seith woman, shoving the drunk in her chair. The merchant glared but gave up her seat to go in search of beer.

Wearing a white shirt, red jacket and black trousers, the newcomer cut a striking figure. Her jacket had threads of black and yellow running through it which meant her family's money came from mining coal and gold. The Seith merchant was lean and her long black hair was tied back in an elaborate braid. Instead of trying to shake his hand she gave him the traditional Seith greeting which Kell mirrored with his left hand.

"Luck on the journey," she said.

"Peace upon on the road," he replied, noting that her green eyes were clear. At least she was sober.

"How much of the Medina saga is true?" she asked.

"All of it," he said. "What did she mean? A celebration?"

She raised an eyebrow but still answered. "We know all about your new quest. Word came from Burston but, as instructed, we've sent birds ahead all the way up to the border and beyond into Kinnan. Everyone north of here is waiting to meet you."

It was worse than he'd imagined. Someone had just made it infinitely more difficult for him to escape. He'd hoped that his reputation would remain intact but it didn't really matter. So what if people knew he'd run? He would never see any of them again. He didn't owe them anything. Certainly not his life. Not again.

Someone had left him with no choice. Tomorrow morning he would ride straight for the coast. Where he was going they wouldn't know his name or care about his past.

The Seith woman wouldn't leave him alone. Eventually Kell realised she was after a token from his first trip to the north.

"Even if it was something small, it would be worth a lot of money," said the woman. When Kell didn't respond her eyes flicked towards his sword. "How much for Slayer?" she asked, licking her lips.

"Get away from me," hissed Kell.

"Think about it," said the schemer before she disappeared into the crowd.

Kell tried to attract the owner's attention but he was far too busy serving drinks. Every time there was a small gap in the crowd another group of people filled it, making the room unbearable hot. In desperation he caught one of the serving girls by the arm as she was passing.

"I need a room for the night," said Kell. She frowned at his hand and he let go.

"The owner has already put one aside for you," sniffed the girl before racing off.

For the next three hours a constant line of people sat at his table, all of them desperate for details that they'd not heard a hundred times before in the Medina saga. Kell received a brief reprieve when a plate of food was delivered. He'd been hungry when he'd arrived and after hours of drinking he was light-headed and famished. Kell tucked in with relish to his lamb stew and rice, savouring how the tangy limes contrasted with the herbs. A bowl of yoghurt and warm flat bread rounded out the meal.

Currently a gaggle of local shaven-headed women were sat at his table, smiling but saying nothing while he ate as Hundarian customs forbade talking through a meal. They believed it was an offence to the Shepherd and the person who had provided the food. Of course, that didn't mean they would leave his table. It was also considered rude to let someone eat alone, so he was trapped with his silent observers. Kell refused to be intimidated or rush his meal as he could see others waiting for an opportunity to speak with him.

After the group of local women left, a lean-faced man from Kinnan sat down. The hunter seemed intent on lecturing Kell about the dangers he would face further north as if he'd never been there before.

"The vorans are getting out of control," he stressed. "It's not like it was a few years ago. They're more daring and they keep coming after me. Year after year. I think it's because prey is in short supply."

Kell didn't point out the obvious. One of the reasons they might be targeting the hunter was his voran-skin coat. Vorans weren't like ordinary wolves. They carried memories from one generation to the next and that would include vendettas.

After the hunter was a local tailor, hoping to get Kell's blessing on a new style of cotton shirt. The final straw came when he spotted a familiar face at the bar. There was a brief gap in the crowd and watching him with a smug grin from across the room was Gerren.

The boy had orchestrated all of this in an attempt to trap him. If Gerren thought Kell's reputation was more important than his life he was in for a big surprise.

"Good evening, sir," said someone else sitting down. It took Kell a moment to realise the newcomer wasn't a stranger. It was Vahli, the garish bard he'd previously met in Mizzei. Today he was dressed in saffron-coloured trousers and a lime green jacket. The bard still carried his instrument in its leather case and was receiving a few stares.

"Let me guess," said Kell, tired of being pecked at all night. "You want to know how much of the Medina saga is true? Or you want some new details so that you can create your own version?"

It all came down to money. Not a single line of the original saga had been changed since it had been commissioned ten years ago. He suspected Vahli could make a fortune with an updated version.

"Oh no. I want nothing to do with the Medina saga," said Vahli, practically spitting out the name. "May I be honest with you about it?"

Kell gestured. "Go ahead."

"I found it to be overly long and somewhat lacking. I'm sure there's much you didn't include, but even so, I think it was rushed. There was no rhythm to the words," said Vahli, slipping his instrument off his back in what was probably a rehearsed gesture. He began to lightly strum it, his fingers dancing over the strings with casual ease. A few heads turned at the deep melodious sound. "It's badly written," added the bard.

His honesty caught Kell off guard and he laughed in spite of himself. Vahli raised an eyebrow, surprised at his response. The bard probably expected him to be offended at the criticism. After all it was the most famous story of his epic adventure. There had been others but for some reason they had disappeared. Kell suspected King Bledsoe and Lukas were responsible for that. "Since we're being honest," said Kell. "I think he was tone deaf and you're right, very little of it rhymes."

Even the bard's laugh was a high-pitched feminine sound. "Well, I didn't want to be the one to say it, but it's truly awful."

"So, if not a story, what do you want?" asked Kell.

Vahli's expression turned grim. His strumming produced a bitter sounding dirge. "Do you know how difficult it is to live in Medina's shadow? Every bard is compared to him. Every original song is held up against his, as if it's the best." The bard shook his head and forced a smile, lifting his fingers from the instrument. "When I heard you were coming here I couldn't resist. Especially after what you said about returning to the Frozen North."

"I'm just going on a quest of discovery," said Kell, careful not to give away any details. "It could be nothing."

"Ah, but King Bledsoe wouldn't send you unless he thought it was serious," said Vahli, proving he was more than just a pretty face. When Kell didn't deny it he just quirked an eyebrow and smiled. "I've made a decision, one I think you're going to like. I'm coming with you to the Frozen North!"

Kell almost choked on his tongue. "What?"

"Someone needs to chronicle your story, and who better than me? Be grateful I'm not an idiot like Medina. I'm going to make a note of every detail and in a hundred years' time, they'll be telling the Roe Vahli saga." The bard's eyes had taken on a faraway gleam so he missed the anger that passed over Kell's face.

First the boy and now a bard. "It might prove to be nothing. Just a couple of bad seasons," said Kell, but he already knew it was pointless. The bard had been given the opportunity of a lifetime and nothing would turn him aside. "I'm going to bed," said Kell, pushing up from the table.

Blood rushed to his head making the room spin while pain shot down both legs from sitting still for too long. As he squeezed through the crowd towards the bar people tried to engage him in conversation but he brushed them aside. When he finally reached the bar, sweaty and hemmed in by bodies, he gestured at the owner. He was still frantically trying to serve drinks and keep up with the tide of customers.

"My room?" he shouted. The owner unhooked a key from above the bar and passed it across.

"Up the stairs, last door on the right," he said.

Kell turned around and found himself face to face with Gerren.

"Going somewhere?" asked the boy.

He was tempted to punch the smug little shit in his face but held back. "To bed."

"I'll see you first thing in the morning. Nice and early."

Kell shook his head. "Boy, this doesn't change anything. I can still slip away."

"It won't be easy, with me and now a bard trailing after you."

"I'll manage."

"But what about your adoring fans?" said Gerren, gesturing at the crowd. Even now people were trying to intrude on their conversation and catch his eye. "They'll be so disappointed when you don't show up."

"I don't care," spat Kell. "I don't owe them anything." The noise from the crowd swallowed his words but a few people noticed his sour expression. "What do you want?" he asked the boy.

"I want you to tell them the truth. Tell them you're a liar and a coward." The hurt in Gerren's eyes was familiar. It reminded him of a dog that had been kicked by its master. The boy was just being petty. He didn't care what the truth would do to Kell or how it would affect everyone else.

"Going on this quest would be a death sentence for me," said Kell.

Gerren wasn't listening. "Is any part of the Medina saga true? Did you actually risk your life for other people?"

"I did, but mostly I was lucky," said Kell. "That's the only reason I survived."

"What does that mean?"

"Before I went to the north, I was just like anyone else. Sometimes I won at cards, sometimes I lost. But afterwards, everything changed. It was like I'd used up all the good luck in my life. Every drop of it was gone. Do you understand?" said Kell.

Gerren wasn't impressed. "You're saying you lost at cards."

"No, boy, I lost at everything in life. Every single time." Kell was trying to explain a decade of failure, heartache and sorrow to a boy who had never lived. He'd not risked anything, not his heart, his money or his life.

Since his return home Kell had never won at cards or dice. Not once. Every venture he'd invested money in had failed because of bad luck. Storms at sea and once a freak landslide that buried the merchant train. When he'd dared take a risk with his heart, reaching out to an old friend from childhood, she'd been delighted to hear from him. They had corresponded for months before Mona finally agreed to visit him in Honaje to see what happened next. She'd been murdered on the road by bandits.

People had said it was just an unfortunate accident that could have happened to anyone. No one blamed Kell for Mona's death, not even her family, but he knew the truth. His bad luck was responsible for her murder and the guilt of it still burned.

"Last time I survived because of the heroics of others. But eventually even that wasn't enough. One by one they all died in agony until only I was left."

"You're lying," insisted the boy, but Kell could see that he was scared.

"She cursed me," he said, saying aloud what he'd never told another person in his life, not even the King. "Right before I killed the Lich, she used her powers and cursed me. I thought it was nonsense. A desperate plea because she was about to die but then my luck changed. First it was in small ways, but over time it became much worse. So, that's why I know, in my heart, that if I go north this time I will die. A man can walk away from something like that once in a lifetime. Twice is impossible."

Something in his words finally reached the boy. Disbelief warred with sympathy on his face. He wasn't cynical enough to disregard all of it but Kell had hurt him. Gerren was feeling bruised and full of resentment. It was his anger that eventually won out.

"You can't run from this," insisted Gerren, which sealed Kell's fate.

"Then you have killed me," he told the boy.

PART TWO
Local Heroes

CHAPTER 12

The eleven were legends, one and all,
Great men with famous deeds celebrated in song.
But within the bravest a seed of fear took root,
And with each passing mile tendrils began to sprout.

EXCERPT FROM THE SAGA OF KELL KRESSIA
BY THE BARD PAX MEDINA

After a hearty breakfast Kell emerged from the King's Blessing to find a strange tableau awaiting him in the street.

By this time most locals would normally be at work and travellers already on the road. Instead he saw that a crowd had gathered, but they were not there to see him off. Gerren and the bard, Vahli, were standing beside their horses, but even they hadn't noticed Kell. Everyone's attention was focused on the figure squatting down on its haunches across the road.

It was an Alfár.

No one was really sure where they came from but there was one fact that everyone could agree on. They weren't human. There had been stories about them since his great-grandfather's time and yet they remained a mystery. Much like grizzly bears, no one had ever seen more than one Alfár at a time and never any children. This led people to believe they led solitary lives and only came together when it was time to mate.

Every once in a while one of them would show up at a town or village. They always stayed away from cities and years could pass between sightings. Unlike other travellers they didn't stop to chat, buy a beer and listen to the latest news. They drifted about settlements asking strange questions, purchasing recently unearthed artefacts and sometimes buying a Manx's entire stock of rare herbs. They looked strange but they never got into any trouble so were seen as harmless nomads.

The Alfár was roughly shaped like a tall human but that was where the similarities ended. With pale blue grey skin and slightly oversized hands and feet you might be forgiven for thinking she was a freak like those found in the carnivals. But once you saw her face there was no doubt that she wasn't human.

With a slightly tapering head rising to a bony point at the back of the crown, the Alfár had a long face with lean features. Instead of ears she had raised bony ridges with a slightly flared lip which curved forwards. One was slightly higher than the other and as someone in the crowd whispered to their neighbour, the Alfár's head bobbed up and down like an owl pinpointing the sound. Her yellow eyes, set in a sea of black, focused on the speaker and their voice trailed away.

With a cluck of her long tongue and a flick of her downy white hair, which was tied back in a ponytail, the Alfár settled back into stillness. Beyond her physical appearance there was something about the Alfár that instinctively unnerved people. Everyone was trying their best not to attract her attention and yet there was a current of small movements. People scratched their faces, coughed or sneezed and shifted about with nervous energy. The Alfár didn't move. She barely seemed to breathe and didn't blink. It was as if she had turned to stone.

Finally, after a long time, she blinked and then her eyes found Kell for the first time. His instincts told him to run but not because he felt threatened. The Alfár was so outlandish he had nothing to compare her with from past experience. He simply didn't know how to respond. There was no way to know if she wanted to fight him, fuck him or eat him. He didn't know if a handshake would insult or endear. Talking or even making direct eye contact might be seen as offensive.

In circumstances such as these it was far better to walk away but with so many people watching Kell didn't have the luxury of a quick escape.

The Alfár unfolded her limbs, rising to her full height until she was almost as tall as a Hundarian. With skinny limbs wrapped in corded muscle, wide shoulders and a narrow waist, the Alfár appeared to be female. Kell couldn't be sure, but he thought so. Her loose shirt and baggy trousers hinted at much, showing muscles and curved bare skin on her chest, but ultimately revealing nothing. As she walked towards him Kell thought her neck seemed slightly too long for her body and her gait oddly loping, as if walking was a slow and uncomfortable way of moving.

Kell had met many kings and heroes in his life but never before had he been so intimidated. As a boy he'd seen an Alfár at a distance but nothing had prepared him for being face to face with one.

Up close he could see the veins beneath her skin were black and she had a musky scent. He also noticed a light dusting of what looked like grey freckles across her nose and cheeks but couldn't be sure. When the corners of her mouth lifted he didn't know if it was a smile or not. Some predators opened their mouth to better inhale the scent of their prey before tearing them to pieces.

"You are Kell Kressia." Her voice had a strange resonance as if there were two people speaking in unison. The language was clearly not her native tongue and yet she spoke with clipped precision.

"I am," said Kell, nodding firmly. She maintained eye contact with him so he did the same.

"I know of your story and have heard the song about your journey to the Frozen North." She spoke with confidence but Kell sensed there was also a question in her cadence.

"Yes, that was ten years ago," said Kell, breaking the silence that had settled between them. The Alfár continued to stare at him expectantly. "Did you want to know something about the journey?"

The Alfár pursed her lips but didn't answer. Kell wanted to break eye contact, to look at someone else for help, but he had the impression she would be offended.

"I'm making the journey again. I'm going back to the ice because of the bad weather," said Kell. He was babbling but couldn't stop staring at her eyes. They were the colour of fresh lemons but he could also see a few specks of silver in the iris. "King Bledsoe thinks there is a new danger in the north."

"Ahhhh," she said, giving him another smile which he took as a good sign.

"Who are you?" he asked, but she didn't reply. Kell had the impression that the Alfár ignored questions she didn't like or didn't want to answer. "What is your name?" he tried instead.

"Yes," said the Alfár, apparently pleased with his question. "My name is We-loe-zahn-bree-kan-rosh-naz-shree." She took a deep breath and continued speaking another long string of sounds that he couldn't memorise. Eventually she reached the end and Kell tried to think of what to say. There was no way he would be able to remember her full name, let alone pronounce it.

"You said We-loe, at the beginning," he asked. "Can I call you Willow?" The Alfár's expression changed and he didn't know if she was thinking it over or was insulted. "It would save a lot of time."

"Time," she said, and he wondered if she even understood the concept. There was another pause. "You may use that name," she said and Kell heaved a sigh of relief.

"Thank you. Is there something else you want to tell me?" he asked, hoping she would explain why she had been waiting for him.

"Yes. Your new journey to the cold north. I will travel with you. I will see the world beyond the Frozen Circle. I will stand upon the snowy fields and see the castle made of ice. I will see where your heroes fell to their deaths." When she broke eye contact Kell felt as if a huge weight had been lifted from his shoulders. Her stare had been so intense he didn't realise how much he'd been focused on it. He suddenly became aware of the crowd that had been watching the exchange. They looked as confused as him by the whole conversation.

Willow retrieved a battered leather bag which she slung over one shoulder and a strange battle axe unlike anything Kell had seen before. It had a huge crescent shaped blade at one end of the metal haft and an eight-headed mace on the other. It looked as if it was made of steel and yet the Alfár handled it with ease. The haft of the peculiar weapon had been engraved with a series of swirling symbols which Kell assumed were words from her native tongue.

"Tomorrow. We will meet here, at this time, and travel north together," said Willow in her peculiar voice.

Kell didn't know what to say. They spoke the same language and she could understand him up to a point, but there was still a huge gulf between them. The Alfár was staring at him again, waiting for something.

"Tomorrow," he confirmed, and Willow bobbed her head. As the Alfár turned away the crowd moved aside so that none of them were standing in her way.

The whole encounter had left him dazed. It also didn't help that he'd barely slept and had woken up feeling groggy. He'd spent hours pondering what to do about Gerren and only came up with an idea shortly before dawn. Strangely, the Alfár's appearance coincided with his plan. The sandy feeling in his eyes was still there but new energy was now coursing through his body.

"I've never seen one in person," said Vahli, his eyes full of wonder. "Did you hear her voice?"

"It seems like you'll have an interesting start for the new saga," said Kell, which caught the bard's attention.

"I can't wait to find out more about her people. I could be the first to unravel fact from fiction." Vahli was practically bouncing on his toes.

"What do you know about them?" asked Kell.

"Very little, and I suspect most of it's nonsense."

"Such as?" asked Kell, hoping for something to help him navigate conversations in the future.

"Some people claim they lay eggs like a bird, but you only need to look at her body to know that's not true. For all of their differences she's like us." Vahli's gaze became distant and he bit one finger in thought.

"What else?" said Kell, distracting the bard from his daydream. "Anything reliable?"

"Not much. Stories have mentioned that they're incredibly strong and can run fast, but there's little about their culture. I do know they have a strange sense of honour."

"I think she ignored some of my questions when she didn't want to answer them," said Kell.

"They were too general," said Vahli. "I think she likes specific questions."

Kell mulled it over and thought the bard was right. In the future he would have to be precise.

"Where are you going now?" asked the boy, as Kell turned away. Gerren's constant badgering was starting to get on his nerves.

"If you're determined to come with me then meet back here tomorrow morning," said Kell as he walked off.

"There's nowhere to run!" yelled the boy.

"What does that mean?" asked the bard. It didn't matter what the boy said to Vahli. Kell didn't think the bard would believe him.

A short walk towards the outskirts brought Kell to a stout round tower. It had a single door but towards the roof there were at least a dozen small openings. The tower was made from the same stone as the town wall suggesting it had been there for a long time.

Beside the pigeon tower sat a squat wooden structure that was little more than a shack. It would probably blow away in a strong breeze which would be a blessing as the smell coming from inside was pungent. A hunchbacked woman with one eye sat in the doorway cuddling a bird to her bosom. Her huge hands almost engulfed the bird and yet with nimble fingers she carefully attached a small piece of paper to one of its legs. After settling the bird down she stood and carefully released it into the air. The pigeon circled the tower once and then flew away to the north.

"Good morning, Madam. I need to send a message."

The woman regarded him with one bright blue eye. This was her domain so Kell waited patiently until she beckoned him forward. After a bit of haggling over the price and how many birds to send they reached an agreement and money changed hands. Feeling happier than when he'd arrived in town the previous night Kell retraced his steps to the King's Blessing.

He spent the rest of the morning spreading the word by telling locals about his plan. Inevitably that led to people asking about his quest from ten years ago. After a few hours of questions the repetition started to get on his nerves. The questions were always about the heroes and never about him. After lunch he took a long walk outside the town to clear his head.

Talking about the past inevitably made him think of what happened when he'd returned home. Gerren probably thought he'd been lying but Kell truly had been cursed with bad luck these last ten years. Despite his best wishes his thoughts turned to the worst of it and the death of Mona. Taking a deep breath he looked at the sky, tried to shake off the bitterness and focus instead on what lay ahead.

It seemed as if he had no choice but to go north again. However, it would provide him with an opportunity to prove what he'd known for years. He was not without flaws but he would show everyone the truth. Compared to the heroes that they revered, he was the better man.

And if he should die on this journey then perhaps people would ask endless questions about his life as they did with the fallen heroes. If he was destined to return to the Frozen North then he needed to be prepared.

As he reached the gates of Nasse he found Gerren waiting for him with a surly expression. "I thought you'd decided to run away on foot!" Kell ignored him, but the boy trailed after him like a puppy. "I've heard what you're doing."

"It wasn't a secret."

"It won't make any difference," insisted Gerren. "You can surround yourself with as many heroes as you want, but it won't change what you are."

"Last time there were twelve of us. At the moment there are four. I see no harm in asking for volunteers to join our quest."

"Our quest?"

"That's right. If you still intend to make the journey."

"I do. And nothing you can do will stop me," said the boy, full of defiance. Kell knew he'd been just as cocky at seventeen.

"That's become very apparent," said Kell, heading for the tavern. "I'll see you later?"

"Oh," said Gerren. "All right then."

It was actually the boy's trap that had inspired him. Kell had sent word ahead asking for heroes to rise up and join him. The first time he'd travelled with eleven legends. If the last decade had taught Kell anything it was that the Medina saga had inspired others to greatness. There were always stories floating around the taverns about feats of bravery. Kell hoped that by casting a wide net across Hundar and Kinnan it would attract a good number of people. It might take a few days for them to find his party on the road but, thanks to Gerren, his route to the north was widely known. If anyone was really keen they would find him.

Survival was at the forefront of his mind. It was not guaranteed but the more heroes he recruited, the better the odds. At least this way he had a chance whereas before there had been none. Perhaps he could borrow some of their good luck as he had none of his own.

Had King Bledsoe and Lukas sent him north alone in the hope that he would recruit others? Or had they done it so that he'd fail?

It no longer mattered. Just like everyone else they'd underestimated him. Once again Kell would prove he was a survivor and a lot more difficult to kill than anyone realised.

CHAPTER 13

Across the frozen ice they travelled,
With sled dogs the colour of night.
Through a land fraught with beasts,
They braved the Frozen North.

Excerpt from the Saga of Kell Kressia
by the Bard Pax Medina

Gerren stared at Kell's back and plotted how best to expose him.

A day's ride north of Nasse would bring them to the town of Molline. It was already late in the afternoon and the four of them had been making good time. To his surprise the air was much cooler in Hundar than at home in Algany. Thinking on it, Gerren realised it made sense as it was further north. It didn't seem that bad to him, but everyone they'd met had been grumbling about the weather.

People were happy to see Kell but after they'd passed, Gerren noticed their smiles fade as they contemplated their skinny cattle and stunted crops. His dad had said it was just a bad couple of years but Gerren didn't believe him. There was something in the Frozen North again that had upset the balance and he was going to smite it. At least, that's what Kell had said but then, how could he believe anything he said?

After a couple of days away from home Gerren was beginning to realise that the world, and all of the people within it, were a lot more complicated than he'd thought. He wished there was someone he could trust who would give him a straight answer. The bard was well travelled. Perhaps Vahli would be honest with him.

Riding at the front of their group Kell was currently telling the colourfully dressed bard, Vahli, a story about life on the farm. It was fairly mundane but the bard wanted to know every detail in order to reflect how humble Kell's life had become. It sounded like a reasonable story, but Gerren knew there would be lies mixed in with the truth. Kell was probably exaggerating about his hardships in order to elicit sympathy. The coward couldn't help it. Whenever he opened his mouth it was always two parts lies to one part truth.

Gerren shook his head, annoyed at his own naïve stupidity. Just like everyone else he'd believed the story about the man who'd saved the world. Gerren had admired him and, if he was being honest, idolised Kell Kressia.

He'd risked everything to come on this journey, stealing a horse and a sword from his father, because the opportunity was not one he could miss. To ride with Kell Kressia. To make a name for himself and become a hero in his own right. Back at home it had all made so much sense. Gerren had never wanted anything so badly in his life. But all of that changed when Kell had revealed his true nature.

The man behind the myth was a huge disappointment. The only solace Gerren could find was that everyone else had been taken in by his lies. He must have told the story of his journey so many times that after a while he probably believed it himself. And now he was trying to recruit more fools to join them on another quest. So far Gerren didn't think much of their chances.

The bard wouldn't be much use in a fight and Gerren knew that Kell would run at the first sign of danger. That left only the Alfár.

Without turning around his saddle Gerren knew she was there, riding a short distance behind everyone else. A constant prickling ran across the back of his scalp and his skin regularly burst into goose-bumps as if cold. As if she wasn't disturbing and peculiar enough, the Alfár's horse was equally terrifying.

Gerren was certain he'd seen the stallion in the Nasse stables when it had been normal. Yesterday, while checking on his horse, Gerren had taken a quick look at the other animals. The black stallion had stood out from the rest, being the tallest in the stalls. It was high spirited and the owner had intended to sell him to a breeder.

Instead the Alfár had purchased it using a lump of gold the size of Gerren's fist. It had been a raw chunk as if it had been pulled directly from the earth. It was a hundred times what the horse was worth but Willow didn't seem to care.

For whatever reason horses didn't like Willow. Other animals didn't seem to mind, as long as she didn't get too close, but horses couldn't abide the Alfár. They didn't react as if the Alfár was a predator. It was something else. A deeper fear that made horses freeze and begin to shake uncontrollably.

Last night several of the grooms had witnessed the Alfár practically dragging the stallion away from the stables. Today it was a different animal.

The beast riding behind him had been changed into something monstrous.

It mostly looked the same but something else now inhabited its skin. Its huge, warm black eyes had changed. Before they had reflected the light. Now they were two pools of darkness that absorbed it. In addition, a narrow ring of yellow ran through the middle of each eye and when the beast stared at him Gerren was afraid.

The other horses were scared of it too and would instantly try to buck their rider and gallop away if it came too close. The beast did exactly as it was told and no more. It moved when the Alfár told it, grazed and would rest when instructed, otherwise it would stand perfectly still and wait. Gerren didn't know what had been done to the horse but it wasn't natural.

Gerren nudged his horse forward to ride with the others. "We should rest the horses for a bit," he said, gesturing at the stream. "Let them have a drink."

"How far are we from Molline?" asked Vahli.

Kell studied their surroundings and then glanced up at the sun. "Maybe two more hours. We have time for a rest."

When Kell went to attempt a conversation with the Alfár Gerren saw his chance to speak with the bard in private.

"I need to tell you something."

"There will be plenty of time for you to tell me your story," said Vahli, as they walked their horses to the stream.

"It's about Kell. He's not the hero you think he is."

Vahli raised an eyebrow. "What do you mean?"

"He told me he was going to run away."

The bard stared off into the distance with a faint smile. "Gerren, everyone experiences moments of fear. It's natural to be scared. There's no shame in that."

"You're not listening. This isn't about me. I was the one who sent the birds ahead of Kell on the road. I trapped him into going on this journey."

"Being a hero is all about overcoming fear." It was clear the bard wasn't paying attention. He seemed to be composing the new saga out loud.

"He doesn't care about you," said Gerren, starting to lose his temper. Vahli was no better than the rest. Worldly or not, he didn't listen. Gerren changed his mind about going to the bard for answers.

Downstream Kell's head turned at the sound of raised voices. "He doesn't care about anyone but himself," repeated Gerren.

Vahli regarded him in silence for a while before speaking. "I know what this is about."

"You do?"

"Yes."

Gerren sighed with relief. "Thank you, Vahli. I just needed to tell someone."

"It's all right. You don't need to worry," he said, resting a comforting hand on Gerren's shoulder. "I won't miss you out of the new saga. You were the first to join. That's an important moment."

Gerren rolled his eyes. "I don't care about being in the stupid saga." The moment the words left his mouth Gerren knew it was the wrong thing to say.

Vahli's eyes narrowed and his posture changed. "Being a hero means rising up, not tearing other people down," he hissed. "You're young and naïve, so I'll forgive you once, but don't come to me again with wild stories about Kell."

"Wait, you need to listen to me," said Gerren. He reached for the bard but Vahli quickly jerked his arm out of reach. From nowhere a dagger appeared in the bard's hand which he held up in front of Gerren's face.

"Mind me, boy," snapped Vahli. Gerren had thought he was nothing more than a spineless dandy, but there was a dangerous look in his eyes. He was also suddenly aware of how Vahli held the blade with practised ease. Feeling pressure against his stomach Gerren looked down to see a second blade touching his shirt. The blade moved forward enough to lift Gerren onto his toes.

"I'm listening," he said, swallowing the lump in his throat.

"Prove your worth and I'll include you in the story. Do not speak to me about this again. Is that understood?"

"Yes, sir."

The blades vanished and a smile spread across Vahli's face. "Good lad. Now run along and fill up your water skin."

Gerren numbly walked further up the creek. It wouldn't matter what he said. There was no way Vahli would believe him now. As he knelt down a shadow fell over Gerren. He looked up to find Kell standing beside him.

"What do you want?"

"It won't work," said Kell, looking over his shoulder. Gerren followed his gaze to where Vahli was juggling four coloured balls for the Alfár. He couldn't tell if Willow was bored or amazed. "I know what you're trying to do."

"I know what you really are."

"Really?" said Kell, staring out at the land. His smile was mocking which made Gerren's blood boil.

"We're heading into danger. You can't escape that."

"I'm not trying to anymore. I'm going to face it. I think I have to," said Kell.

Gerren knew he was lying. "A moment will come when you'll expose yourself, then everyone will know the truth."

"Maybe," said Kell with a shrug. For some reason he was incredibly calm and at peace. Perhaps Kell really believed that he was going to die. His story about bad luck had almost convinced Gerren.

The coward walked away leaving him to stew in silence. The others weren't willing to listen, not yet anyway. A change of tactics was needed. Gerren decided that he would play along and pretend that everything was normal. Sooner or late Kell's true nature would reassert itself.

Molline was a modestly sized town but unlike Nasse its defences were in a much better state. Kell was surprised to see the surrounding six foot wall had a small walkway that was being patrolled by four guards. Dressed in leather armour trimmed with fur, each carried a spear and had a bow slung over one shoulder. The weapons weren't decorative and looked well used. Everyone here knew how to hunt and fend for themselves.

Barely a hint of grey was creeping into the sky as they rode up to the main gate and yet torches burned at six points around the wall. Out here the wilderness was a lot closer than in the cities where they didn't have to worry about big cats and vorans tearing into their flock or stealing their children.

There was another guard standing at the gate but he just waved them inside. His eyes widened when he saw the Alfár and took a step back at the sight of her monstrous horse.

"I will return tomorrow morning," said Willow, glancing at the surrounding buildings with concern. "It is too stifling here."

"Where will you sleep?" asked Kell. They were barely inside the gate but already the Alfár looked distressed.

"Where the sky can touch the land." With that the Alfár rode back out of the gate past the startled guard. There were times when Kell felt the same about sleeping indoors. In the summer he preferred to sleep on his porch staring up at the night sky.

There wasn't a crowd waiting for them on the main street but with only two taverns it didn't take long for word to spread of their arrival. The first tavern had no rooms available so he hoped there was space in the King's Heart. Kell didn't want to camp outside with the Alfár. There would be enough cold and unpleasant nights later in the journey.

The moment he stepped into the second tavern the crowd began to applaud, many of them chanting his name. It seemed as if everyone in town had been waiting for their arrival. Vahli was unaffected by the noise while Gerren took a step back in surprise. Being the focus of so many people made Kell feel uncomfortable. He swallowed the bile rising in his throat and forced a smile through his teeth.

"Welcome, welcome," burbled the owner, coming out from behind the bar. The portly balding man had short legs and waddled like a duck. From the food stains on his apron Kell guessed he was also the cook which he took as a good sign. He never trusted a thin cook. "I have rooms available for everyone." Kell saw the owner glance out the open door and relax when there was no sign of Willow.

Kell and the others were ushered to an empty table that had been reserved while the crowd followed their every move. Under the scrutiny of so many strangers Gerren faded into the background whereas Vahli seemed to grow in stature. His chest puffed out and every gesture became a performance. From the way he kissed the back of the serving girl's hand making her blush to the delicate sipping of his ale. A number of people were already eyeing his instrument case which he'd casually leaned against the wall in plain view of everyone. Kell was happy when people shifted their focus away from him.

More people began to fill the tavern until it was standing room only, but a small pool of space was left in front of their table. The majority of the crowd were tall locals but Kell also noticed a mix of people from across the Five Kingdoms and even a few pink-skinned Corvanese. Despite that, one or two faces stuck out from the crowd.

He spotted a broad Seith woman with hands that looked as if they'd been dipped in red paint. She wore no red clothing, which was more peculiar than her stained hands. Most of the locals seemed to know what it meant and from Vahli's sour expression the bard understood she'd been branded as a thief. For such a crime the Seith woman had been stripped of everything. Her family, her history and her name. She was an outcast and no Seith would help her, even if she was dying. Thankfully other people were more forgiving. As long as she had money they would deal with her but it still made them uncomfortable.

The other person that caught Kell's attention was a woman from Kinnan who towered above even the tallest local. Generally known for being a hardy race, the Keen were most famous for their weapons. Iron from the deep mines in Hundar was supposed to be the best in the world, but it was the smiths of Kinnan who were the most skilled.

He looked for other prospects in the crowd but there didn't seem to be any. Hoping someone would surprise him Kell raised a hand for silence and a hush immediately fell over the room. "You all know why we're here," he said, cutting to the chase. From his eye corner he could see Vahli frowning. No doubt the bard would have made it more of a performance but Kell had no time for such nonsense. If anyone survived the journey then the bard could dress up this part of the story to make it more pleasing for listeners.

"Who among you thinks they are worthy of joining me on my

quest to the Frozen North?" There was a murmuring amongst the gathered crowd as people looked to their neighbours. "Step forward."

First to push their way to the front was a local man with dirt under his fingernails and a piece of straw in his hair. Kell struggled not to roll his eyes as the farmer explained why he thought he was suitable. Mostly it consisted of anecdotes that went nowhere about working long hours in the rain. Once he'd finished speaking the farmer just stood there with his mouth hanging open.

"This isn't a decision we'll make tonight," said Vahli, breaking the awkward tension filling the room. "There are many factors to consider. We'll tell everyone our decision in the morning."

The farmer shuffled back to his table to be replaced by a seven year-old with braids. She was cute and the crowd politely listened as the child regaled them with her imaginary list of accomplishments. Kell would have laughed when the girl's mother dragged her away if not for the fact that all of their lives could be at risk. As more useless individuals stepped forward Kell couldn't understand why he was the only one taking this seriously.

"Smile," said Vahli, hissing in Kell's ear.

"This is a joke," he whispered.

"It's early yet. Your call to arms only went out yesterday. I wouldn't expect us to find anyone suitable for a few days. Maybe even a week."

"A week?" said Kell, just as the applause had finished. His voice echoed loudly around the room.

"Don't," said the bard, trying to stop him, but Kell shook off his hand.

Silence fell as Kell pushed his table away and stood. He drew the dagger from his belt and ran it across the palm of his hand. Several people in the crowd gasped and others looked away as blood ran from his clenched fist.

"This isn't a fucking game," he shouted, staring at individual faces in the crowd. As he waved his hand about blood spattered on the floor and people recoiled in horror. If the sight of a little blood upset them, they were far more stupid than he'd realised. "This is just a taste of what awaits us in the north. Did you think the garrow were made up to scare children? They're savage, bloodthirsty beasts. I've seen them, and the vicious maglau. I watched as they tore a man to pieces with their teeth, just like that," said Kell snapping his fingers. "And I've heard the whispers of the Qalamieren."

A tremor ran through the crowd and all of the children began to cry at the mention of the creature's name. Several people turned pale and one woman looked as if she was ready to faint. So far the children were the only ones showing any signs of common sense. They were right to be terrified.

"Last time twelve of us went to the north but only I returned. Everyone else is dead. Dead!" This time when Kell stared at individuals in the crowd they quickly turned away unwilling to make eye contact. The silence in the room was deafening. He let it settle for a while to make sure they understood he was deadly serious. His voice dropped to a harsh whisper but they heard every single word. "There is a good chance that anyone who comes with me will die. So I need people with stout hearts. I need warriors with skill and courage. If anyone here is brave enough to battle the beasts of the Frozen North, then step forward."

The red-handed thief from Seithland shuffled in her chair but ultimately didn't stand up. There was a ripple of movement in the crowd as the tall woman from Kinnan shoved her way to the front.

Now that he could see her more clearly Kell was impressed. Dressed in worn leather armour she carried herself with certainty that everyone else was lacking. Her black hair was long on top and shaven on the sides showing off the angular shape of her strong jaw.

Hanging around her neck was a collection of large teeth from different beasts, many that he didn't recognise. She had a pair of thick daggers and carried a broadsword on her belt in the northern fashion. Several people seemed to recognise her and were staring with awe. Her expression was defiant as she wrenched off the necklace, raining teeth onto his table.

"I am Bronwyn of Kinnan. I choked a man-eating snow leopard to death with my bare hands when I was sixteen. I bludgeoned the wild boar of Gortak to death with a rock. I fought ten raiders attacking a village and I killed them all by myself. I battled Gouru, King of the Snapjaws, claimed a tooth and lived to tell the tale. I have hunted and killed men and beasts for ten years and I am not afraid."

Staring into her fierce blue eyes Kell knew everything she was telling him was the truth. Even in Honaje he'd heard stories of her.

Gerren was staring at the huge woman with his mouth agape and even Vahli was affected. With great care Kell gathered up the teeth, restringing them on the leather cord, before holding them out towards Bronwyn.

The bard had said they would tell people in the morning but Kell knew they would not find anyone else like her. "I would be honoured if you would join me."

Kell wasn't sure if she was going to refuse but slowly the anger faded from her eyes and she took back her necklace.

"When do we leave?" she asked quietly, unwilling to break the hush that had settled over the crowd.

"First thing in the morning."

"I'll be there," she promised.

For the first time since being trapped into making the journey, Kell felt a glimmer of hope that maybe they had a chance at surviving. Now all they had to do was find ten more like Bronwyn.

CHAPTER 14

The eleventh pillar is humility.
The holy understand all are created equal,
And regardless of what is acquired or achieved,
A person is measured by their heart.

EXCERPT FROM THE SACRED BOOK OF THE SHEPHERD

It was late or very early. The Anointed wasn't sure any more. All she knew was that everyone had been drinking and carousing for hours. Such indulgence should have been abhorrent to her because people were suffering. However, it wasn't sinful to forget your troubles for a while and raise your voice in song. Prayer was not for everyone.

For the most these were good, hard-working people. She would not condemn them for such a minor sin. After all, who was she to criticise them given her own sins.

She sat with a beer in front of her, head dipping towards the table in an imitation of falling asleep. Not all of it was an act even though she'd not drunk as much as everyone else. The wisest had gone to their beds long ago. Of those who remained several had already passed out at their tables but they were in the minority. The noise kept the rest of the room awake if not wholly alert.

At the centre of the celebration was Bronwyn, the big woman

from Kinnan. She was leading a group of men and women in song, without musical accompaniment, as the bard had already gone to bed. They were singing off-key, creating a horrific mangled chorus of sound, but no one seemed to care. As they came back to the chorus, with people stamping their feet and drumming their mugs on tables, the Anointed drained her glass and slowly pushed herself upright. She would have liked to join them in song but given the circumstances she wouldn't be made welcome.

The red hands had been her idea. Family was everything to the Seith. To betray one's blood was to be marked for life. In her case it was a mix of henna and paint, not the permanent dye if her crimes had been real. Eventually it would wear off but for now it served its purpose. This way everyone noticed her but no one wanted to talk for long. She was invisible while remaining in plain sight.

In truth she wasn't even from Seithland. With the right clothing and minor changes to her appearance her mixed heritage allowed her to pass as almost anyone from the Five Kingdoms. Much of it came down to how she walked and held herself. Seith tended to hunch over, although they were generally shorter than most. People often looked down on them as they were driven by a love of trade, although some equated that with greed. She had met many Seith and although some loved money above all, some were faithful to the Shepherd's teachings.

As she shuffled through the main room towards the outhouse it was clear that no one was paying any attention. Either they were too drunk or already asleep. Even those who might have done their best to avoid her were having too much fun. The owner of the tavern had sent his entire staff home but he was still in the room, snoring gently with his head on the bar.

Instead of heading to the back of the building the Anointed slipped up the stairs towards the bedrooms. She waited at the top, letting her eyes adjust to the gloom while listening to the creaking of the building. Below her the singing had stopped but now someone was bragging to the others in a loud voice. The words were slurred and much of the story seemed to inspire bouts of laughter which she appreciated.

The lanterns along the corridor wall had been doused hours ago creating a long space that was thick with heavy shadows. Peering down at each of the doors she noticed no light was showing under any of them. She hadn't thought anyone would be awake at this hour but it was always worth checking. Prudence was a form of wisdom, and although not one of the twelve pillars, it was something she kept in mind. It was better to be prepared than be caught unaware. Tipping her head to one side she heard faint snoring coming from several of the bedrooms.

Satisfied that she was alone the Anointed took out the heart-blade, a narrow file of steel no wider than one of her fingers with a slightly curved end. One quick jab in the chest and it was long enough to penetrate the heart. There would be a brief flash of pain and then her target would be dead. It was as merciful as she could manage.

She didn't believe in making her victims suffer and took no pleasure in it. Her hand and will were not her own. She was merely a tool bringing about the will of those who served the Shepherd. It was necessary that Kell Kressia die this night for the greater good. Once he was gone the blasphemy would come to an end, and then everyone would turn their faces towards the true path. One life, when weighed against the glory to come, was a small price to pay for a better future. Truly, hers was a holy task.

The Anointed had overheard Kell's conversation with the owner so she knew which was his room. He'd gone upstairs by himself but that didn't mean he was still alone. There had been ladies of the night wandering around the tavern searching for customers with money to spare. Putting an ear to his door she closed her eyes and listened.

At first all she could hear was the distant sound of laughter coming from below and someone snoring in the next room. After a while she tuned out all of the distractions and focused on the door in front. There wasn't any snoring there but she could hear someone breathing. It was slow and even, suggesting they were deep asleep. More importantly she couldn't hear anyone else in the room with him.

The Anointed was about to test the lock when a floorboard creaked to her left. Something silver flashed towards her face and she instinctively stepped back, bringing up her forearms. The dagger sliced through her shirt scoring a narrow gash across her arms. With a hiss of pain she dodged to the side, avoiding another strike before lashing out with her blade.

Her blade whipped through the air, missing her opponent, whose face was concealed in the shadows. There was no time to ask who or why as her attacker came on again, whipping their blade in a tight arc from left to right. With no openings the Anointed was forced to step back but was running out of space. She could almost feel the wall at her back. When her left heel struck the wood she raised her right foot and pushed off, launching herself through the air at her opponent.

Her knee knocked the dagger aside and collided with her opponent's chest forcing them back. She immediately followed up with a haymaker blow intended to end the fight. Her fist collided with empty air again and she stumbled. The Anointed was too slow to pull back and felt a hot line of pain across one side of her face. Blood trickled down her cheek but she didn't cry out. Pain was an old friend to be embraced. It purified the body and the mind. Instead she ground her teeth together and waited. The whole fight was being conducted in silence. The people below remained oblivious, wrapped up in a cloud of alcoholic stupor.

The light coming from below showed the outline of her opponent but she couldn't tell if it was a man or woman. Their identity didn't really matter. They were an obstacle and her holy purpose would not be denied.

Taking the initiative she charged forward, blocking a strike by grabbing her opponent's wrist in mid-air. Her red fingers tightened on the bones, grinding them together, earning a groan of pain. With her free hand she flipped the heart-blade around and tried to stab down. Her opponent grabbed her wrist and now they were locked together, struggling for dominance as each sought to stab the other.

Blood trickled into her mouth from the cut on her face but she ignored both it and the pain. It was fleeting and would pass. Her opponent was strong but as they slammed each other into the walls she could feel them wavering. A smile spread across her features as she knew victory was at hand.

Much to her surprise the Anointed was pushed back against the wall, bringing her face to face with her opponent.

"You," she said, recognising him from earlier.

With a grunt of effort she felt him flex his muscles making a final attempt to drive the heart-blade into her neck. She instinctively tightened her grip and pushed back. His dagger fell from his fingers and her smile widened. With his free hand he punched her in the side but she barely felt it. His fingers were numb and his blows lacked any real power.

The heart-blade crept closer to his face, their legs tangled together and she fell forwards on top of him trying to drive the dagger into his face. At the last second he moved his head to one side and it bit into the wood of the floor. As her full weight fell on top of him something sharp poked her in the stomach. They lay together for a few heartbeats, breathing heavily, neither one struggling. Then the strength began to leach from her body as she felt the wound.

With a cry she rolled away from her opponent. In the weak light coming from downstairs she could just see the hilt of a second dagger embedded in her side. In the shadows it looked as if the blood trickling from the wound was black. Every fibre told her to pull it out but she knew that it would only make it worse.

As the Anointed looked around for another weapon something punched her in the chest. She recognised the hilt. The heart blade had done its job perfectly and found its mark. There was a brief moment of pain and then blissful silence. The pain eased from her face as she stared into the face of her killer.

"Forgive me," she murmured.

"I'm not a priest," he said, but she wasn't talking to him.

"My sin was pride."

She'd thought herself greater than she was. She'd believed the fight already won because her purpose was just. It had made her arrogant and now she was paying the ultimate price.

"Forgive me," she whispered, just before her heart stopped.

CHAPTER 15

Young and naïve but his heart was true,
But no skill had he with a blade or bow.
From the heroes he learned at night,
To be as they were – legends one and all.

Excerpt from the Saga of Kell Kressia
by the Bard Pax Medina

After waking up, Kell lay in bed for a while trying to sort through his memories from last night. His head throbbed mildly but it could have been much worse.

Once Bronwyn had agreed to go with them the drinking had begun in earnest. For a little while his warning about what they would be facing in the north was forgotten. The whole town seemed intent on celebrating and the beer had been flowing. Kell remembered buying her three beers and being amazed at how much she could drink without it affecting her.

It became apparent early in the night that her capacity far outweighed his, so he'd quickly stopped trying to match her drink for drink. Vahli had turned his nose up at the beer, preferring wine, and Kell had cut Gerren off after his fifth beer. By that point the boy had already been swaying in his seat and singing along with the crowd.

Others had tried to keep up with Bronwyn, and Kell knew they would all be suffering this morning. Before he'd left, several had already fallen asleep at their tables while she'd kept going, singing, arm-wrestling and out-drinking everyone in the room. Eventually Kell had managed to slip away, dragging the boy to his room as well, but he'd heard the party continuing downstairs as he fell asleep.

The morning was uncomfortably bright but it was also wonderfully silent. After washing his face in cold water and dressing in fresh clothes Kell felt more human and ready for breakfast.

In the main room he found several people asleep on the floor which was sticky underfoot and stained with spilled drinks and food. The air stank of stale beer, sweaty bodies, farts and fresh vomit. The owner was nowhere to be seen so Kell went elsewhere in search of food.

A few people were drifting around the streets, many of them with sore heads, so no one stopped to talk. In fact they were doing their best to avoid him and refused to make eye contact. Despite the celebration his speech had cut them to the quick. It was better this way than the farce he'd been forced to endure. From this point forward everyone would be fully aware of the danger.

Running away had seemed like the only way to survive. The chance of starting afresh overseas had been taken from him by Gerren, but in truth he wasn't angry with the boy any more. Being alone for so long Kell was used to relying only on himself. It had been difficult for him to admit that other people might be able to help.

Perhaps his return to the Frozen North had been inevitable. Perhaps it explained his constant string of bad luck. Perhaps he should have died with the others and this would close the circle. Such maudlin thoughts were common after a night of drinking but Kell knew today it was more than that. The choice had been taken away from him so the reason he was going north no longer mattered, only the outcome.

For the last ten years it felt as if he'd been waiting for something. Perhaps this was it. He'd finally be able to get some answers to the questions that kept him awake at night. It had taken a long time to come to terms with all that he'd seen. Some of it had been about letting go of the past but the scars in his mind still itched. Try as he might, he couldn't completely ignore them.

Last time he'd undertaken this journey the heroes had made several horrible and avoidable mistakes. His had been due to lack of experience. Theirs happened because they were arrogant and had become complacent.

Now he had the experience and the skill. He wouldn't make the same mistakes or shirk from his responsibilities. Once again Kell would prove that he was the better man and that started from today.

He bought two fresh loaves and some cheese then filled a bucket with cold water. Gerren was exactly where Kell had left him last night, fully dressed and face down on his bed. The boy didn't stir when he pulled back the curtains and threw open the window.

The moment Kell dumped the water on Gerren's head he came awake with a scream, desperately trying to fight off the enemy. When the bucket was empty Kell sat down and began to eat his breakfast. Gerren was out of breath, soaked to the skin and his clothes were dripping wet. Eventually he recognised his surroundings and what was going on.

"Eat some breakfast," said Kell, gesturing at the bread and cheese. "Then we start your training."

"What are you talking about?" said Gerren, wringing his shirt. The bedsheets were drenched and Kell could hear water trickling through the floorboards.

"When the heroes realised I wouldn't go home they agreed to train me. I'd fought in the army but I was out of practice. So, every day we trained with a sword." To begin with there had been an endless series of chores. He thought they were meant to break his spirit but in reality they were waking up dormant muscles. Every night he went to bed with fresh aches in his back and shoulders, but after a few days he was more flexible.

Eventually Kursen, and then a couple of the others, had shown him how to use his sword. He'd learned a little from all of them and had gradually found his own style. Kell wasn't an expert but he knew a lot more than the boy which was nothing.

"Leave me alone," said Gerren.

"Have you ever held a sword before?"

Gerren refused to answer so Kell decided to wait him out. He was perfectly happy to eat his breakfast in silence while the boy sulked. Kell threw him a blanket when he began to shiver but he still wouldn't speak. The bread was delicious and the red cheese tart and nutty. When he was finished Kell left the rest on the table.

"If you want to survive, you need to know how to defend yourself. That means training."

"I can fight."

"With a sword?" asked Kell. He thought Gerren would lie but eventually the boy shook his head, showing he had a little common sense. "I can show you how."

"I'd rather learn from the Alfár," said Gerren.

"I don't care who you train with. Just make sure you do it," said Kell, heading for the door. "If you're still determined to journey to the Frozen North, we're leaving in an hour."

By the time Kell had gathered up his belongings, paid the owner for their rooms and saddled his horse, Vahli, Gerren and Bronwyn were waiting for him outside the King's Heart. There was no sign of Willow but he suspected they would find the Alfár waiting outside of town.

Bronwyn seemed unaffected by her drinking marathon and was currently working her way through a trencher stuffed with crackling pork and gravy. The juices were running down her chin but she hadn't noticed and was utterly focused on her food. Vahli had still been awake when Kell had slipped away to bed and this morning the bard's eyes were bloodshot. The smell of Bronwyn's breakfast turned the bard's stomach enough to make him dry-heave. By comparison Gerren wobbled in his saddle and was as pale as a three day corpse but at least he'd shown up.

If Gerren had been having any second thoughts about embarking on this trip, last night would have been the perfect opportunity to slip away unnoticed. Kell had to give him credit for showing up. He just hoped the boy was willing to learn how to use his sword.

Almost everyone was feeling a little delicate but it was still an auspicious start. A bard's retelling of this moment would paint them with bright colours rather than the drabness of reality. No doubt last night's drinking session would become a lavish banquet in a grand hall. In another ten years even those who'd drunk alongside them would swear Vahli's new saga was the truth.

With a spring in his step Kell mounted up and rode out in search of more heroes.

Gerren just wanted to curl up in a ball and die. His head was pounding, the sunlight burned his eyes and everything was too loud. Worst of all his stomach was twisted like a knotted rag. It kept trying to empty itself even though there was nothing left. The bread and cheese from Kell had refused to stay down. Gerren had been glad to leave his room with its wet sheets and the stink of fresh vomit.

Last night's celebration had started out so well. Finally someone of renown had joined the quest. A real hero. Bronwyn was an amazing warrior. She was tall, beautiful and her strength was unparalleled.

Only last night he'd seen her defeat one man after another as they challenged her to an arm wrestle. After a few beers she'd volunteered to take the fight into the street but Vahli had managed to keep it indoors much to everyone's relief. Eventually the number of challengers dwindled to none at which point she was declared the strongest and given a free beer by the owner.

The mere thought of beer made his stomach bunch up again.

Gerren remembered that the first beer had tasted fairly unpleasant. Sour on his tongue and fizzy enough to make him belch. Rather than chastise him for bad manners like his mother, the others had laughed and urged him to drink more. The second beer had tasted much the same but when he'd started on the third Gerren began to understand its magical power.

He'd been drunk before, sneaking some of his dad's rum with Malko. Even worse than the hangover was the beating that followed. Everything had been funny when he'd been drunk on rum. Last night had been different.

No one had treated him like a child. Gerren had been one of them. Not a hero, not yet at least, but he was a part of the group. For the first time in his life there was a sense of belonging.

It had been slightly spoiled by Kell's presence, but Gerren had done his best to ignore him. In fact, much to his surprise, Kell had barely added to the conversation. Mostly he sat in silence with a faraway look in his eyes. It wasn't what Gerren been expecting from him at all.

Despite the pounding in his head Gerren knew that approaching Vahli so soon had been a mistake. The bard barely knew him and had no reason to trust his word over that of the infamous hero. For now Gerren thought it wise to pretend that his crusade against Kell was over. Last night he'd apologised to the bard as well. Gerren had taken great care in singing the praises of the bard's profession and his integrity. Vahli had been delighted and had promised to write about him with fairness.

Vahli was a strange man. He always dressed like a peacock, talked softly and had a high-pitched laugh. And yet Gerren had seen women flirting with him in the crowd. Later he'd seen Vahli kissing a local woman in a dark corner. Not that he was jealous of the bard, of course.

Bronwyn. Now there was a body he'd like to explore. She was broad in the shoulders and tall but also soft in all the right areas. Even as he desperately held onto his saddle for dear life, Gerren realised he was drooling and quickly wiped his mouth.

It was around the fourth beer that things began to get a little fuzzy. He remembered challenging Bronwyn to an arm wrestle. There had been some laughter around the table but he thought it had been good-natured. Gerren distinctly remembered her calling him brave and touching him on the shoulder. When she'd leaned forward he'd received a glimpse of her impressive cleavage.

After that it was mostly a blank. He'd been told that Kell had put him to bed which was surprising. He expected Kell to push him out of a window or trip him down the stairs. It would have been one less problem for him to worry about. No one would blame Kell for such an unfortunate accident, after all, Gerren had been drunk.

There had to be a reason for his act of kindness. It was a ruse. Kell wanted to look as if he cared so the others wouldn't be suspicious but Gerren wasn't fooled. It was all a facade. Even now, as Kell chatted with Bronwyn, Gerren knew he was planning something.

Kell had been right about one thing though. He didn't know how to use a sword. Several times a day he nearly toppled over because of the unfamiliar weight on his back.

By now his parents would know that he'd run away. His father would be furious and probably take a belt to his mother. Gerren felt guilty but it was too late to turn back. All he could do was press on for now. When he returned home as a hero his life would change. They'd kick out his father out and everyone would see that he was nothing more than an angry little man.

That still left the problem of finding someone to train him. He considered asking Bronwyn; after all, there was no one more qualified. Gerren quickly changed his mind as he knew it would be difficult to concentrate if he was constantly distracted. She also struck him as someone who wouldn't tolerate layabouts. He expected her to be a tough taskmaster and he needed someone to nurture his talent not grind him into paste. Although, on reflection, part of him wouldn't mind being thrown around by her.

Gerren tried to dislodge the erotic thoughts by shaking his head but immediately regretted it. The headache had been fading but now it came back twice as strong.

"Drink lots of water," said Vahli, gesturing at Gerren's waterskin. "It will help." The bard's eyes were red and he hung over his pommel like a dead animal. In a perverse way it was nice to see that someone else was suffering. Vahli drank deeply from his own waterskin and tipped some of it over his head, wetting his hair and shirt. Gerren took his advice, drinking water until his belly sloshed.

The bard was another possibility to be his teacher. He'd shown remarkable speed and dexterity with his daggers. Then again, maybe he would be better off learning from Willow.

She was riding at the back with her head cocked to one side, staring up at something. Moving his head slowly, and shading his eyes with one hand, Gerren followed the Alfár's gaze. A crow was winging its way through the sky flying in parallel to their position. It effortlessly drifted on the thermals occasionally flapping its wings to stay aloft but was otherwise its body was perfectly still.

Gerren slowed and then had to work hard to control his horse as Willow's beast came abreast. Swallowing hard he tried to find something to say. The Alfár continued to watch the bird although Gerren sensed she was aware of his presence. She had tilted one of her shoulders towards him as if expecting a conversation.

Not wanting to plough straight in, Gerren fumbled around, trying to find something else to talk about first.

"Do you like crows?" he asked. Willow glanced at him with an unreadable expression and then back at the bird. Maybe she didn't know what it was called. Maybe she didn't have birds where she came from. Or maybe she just thought he was an idiot. "It's called a crow."

"It flies with us. Keeping track. Watching."

Gerren knew some Manx kept crows as pets and claimed they were important, but he'd never seen the birds do anything unusual. As far as he knew they just made a lot of noise and pecked at farmers' crops.

"Do you have crows where you come from?"

The Alfár lowered her chin and turned her face towards Gerren. His stomach clenched up but this had nothing to do with last night. Her unsettling gaze made fresh, beer-smelling sweat, erupt from his pores. He'd been treating Willow like she was a peculiarity, or just another person, but she wasn't. Only now, as he stared into her black and yellow eyes, did he realise that she was nothing like him at all.

On a simplistic level she looked human but fundamentally she was something else. There was no way to know what she felt or thought. Did she have emotions? Did she believe in the Shepherd or a bizarre god of her own?

"There are no crows in my homeland," she finally said. Gerren felt his courage begin to waver. He had to do this now before he lost his nerve.

"Can I ask you something?" he said, then swore under his breath for asking such a stupid question. The Alfár just cocked her head to one side and waited. "I don't know how to use my sword," said Gerren. It was an obvious thing to say. He also knew she didn't respond to statements. "I need someone to show me what to do. Will you train me how to fight with a sword?"

"I will not," she said in her strange harmonic voice. She returned to watching the bird and he sensed their conversation was over.

Gerren was relieved but a small part was annoyed that she wouldn't teach him. He smothered the angry retort as trying bluster with the Alfár wouldn't work. She wasn't a parent or a friend to be emotionally manipulated. Gerren had no idea what she felt, if anything, for him or anyone else in the group. She had her own path and much like the crow they were merely travelling in the same direction for a while.

"I wonder if anyone will ever show me how to use this," muttered Gerren, talking to himself.

"Someone will show you," said Willow, startling him. It hadn't been a question and yet she had answered. Gerren was going ask her something else when she gave him one of her creepy smiles. The last of his courage evaporated and Gerren nudged his horse forward to ride beside the bard.

The only person left who could show him how to fight was Kell. He would rather walk into battle naked than ask him for help.

That would mean admitting that he had been wrong about Kell but, despite some kind behaviour he couldn't explain, Gerren still didn't trust him.

Gerren hoped that more people would join them soon as he was out of options.

CHAPTER 16

Every day the heroes bled for one other,
Forming bonds stronger than steel.
They became brothers one and all,
A family created from sacrifice and love.

EXCERPT FROM THE SAGA OF KELL KRESSIA
BY THE BARD PAX MEDINA

After a long day in the saddle they reached a modest-sized town called Ruibeck just as night was falling. As they approached the edge of town the Alfár peeled off and disappeared into the dark.

Three times during the day Kell had tried engaging Willow in conversation. Ultimately he'd only managed to coax half a dozen words because she seemed naturally taciturn and his horse was freaked out by the Alfár's creature. When Kell asked about the not-horse, and what Willow had done to it, the one word answer made no sense. Nhill. Kell didn't know if that was what Willow had done to the horse or if it was the creature's name. The others fared no better much to the frustration of Vahli who was determined to find out more about Willow's people. Even when the bard asked a direct question the Alfár tended to ignore him. For whatever reason she seemed more comfortable speaking with Kell than anyone else, not that she spoke at length about anything.

The town was protected by a well-built eight foot wall patrolled by armed guards in padded armour. Torches burned at several points around the wall and two guards were stationed at the gate. They waved the group inside then pushed it closed and barred the gate for the night. After stabling their horses Kell walked along the quiet streets searching for a tavern.

He noticed that everyone on the street was carrying a blade or weapon of some kind, but the knives and axes were tools first and weapons second. Clothing was designed for purpose rather than fashion and there were few bright colours apart from the occasional Seith dressed in red.

Noise from the crowd drew Kell towards the first tavern. Peering through the open window he saw a decent group of people inside. A hum of conversation filled the room and everyone seemed relaxed.

That changed the moment they set foot inside.

An uncomfortable silence filled the tavern as the four of them approached the bar. Ignoring everything except her thirst, Bronwyn ordered beers for everyone and had finished hers in no time. Eventually she noticed the quiet and turned to face the room.

Every person in the crowd watched them in stunned silence. At first Kell thought it was because of Bronwyn as they were getting close to her homeland. Her deeds would be well known in this area and they were probably in awe of her. For a brief moment Kell thought it was his reputation that had shocked them into silence. Then he recognised what was lurking behind the eyes of everyone.

Fear.

They were terrified that he was going to ask them to join him.

Somehow Kell's brief speech had done what ten years of endless repetitions of the Medina saga had never achieved. It had given everyone a glimpse at brutal reality. It had destroyed the glamorous facade about being a hero.

Kell couldn't blame the children. Ten years ago he'd believed it was all comfortable beds and riches. What baffled him the most was that so many adults had deluded themselves. The bard's saga mentioned the deaths of the heroes and yet people still seemed to believe the quest had been a fun adventure. It was if they'd chosen to forget the unpleasant parts because they weren't to their liking.

As Kell studied the people it became clear that none of them were going to volunteer. There were plenty of young faces in the crowd but even they refused to make eye contact. Whatever the people felt about Kell and his companions, awe or respect, it was overshadowed by fear.

"Drink up. We're leaving," said Kell, gesturing at the beers. Kell flicked a coin onto the bar and walked out.

In the next two taverns their reception was exactly the same. There were a few teenagers desperate to volunteer but they were being physically held back by teary-eyed parents. They understood what was likely to happen if their babies rode north with him. In the wake of such widespread fear Gerren's face turned pale. He'd finally realised the truth and was starting to feel the full weight of what lay ahead. Kell thought about offering him another chance to go home but he suspected the boy wouldn't accept it, mostly out of sheer stubbornness. It would also mean admitting that he'd been wrong, which Kell knew Gerren would never do. He'd been the same at his age, arrogant and confident in his immortality.

They all ate a meal at the bar then immediately went to bed. The next morning they rode out of Ruibeck under a black cloud, each of them lost in their thoughts. Hundar was proving to be a disappointment. He'd always thought of them as hardy people but maybe he was wrong about that as well. Kell tried to shake off his malaise and remain positive about what they would find in Kinnan but even Bronwyn looked disheartened. Perhaps she was also having doubts about her countrymen.

A short time after midday they stopped for something to eat beside the road. Overhead the sky was grey and a cool wind blew in from the north, bringing with it the smell of wild flowers. Out here, between settlements, there was a lot of empty space.

Just barren scrubland and granite-littered meadows choked with bracken. There was some farmland but this far north in Hundar the land was mostly used for grazing hardy cattle and goats. Kell had seen a few of them at a distance with thick shaggy black coats and horns long enough to impale a man with ease.

There had been a few travellers on the road but for the moment they were alone. The next town was beyond the horizon and it felt as if they were the only people in the world. The moment of peace was broken by the sound of horses approaching at speed. Willow had noticed them first as her hearing was much sharper than everyone else. Kell picked out the sound of at least a dozen horses, and they were in a hurry.

At first it was difficult to make out any details but as they drew closer Kell was surprised to see they were all local Hundarian warriors. They were dressed in leather armour, steel helmets which obscured their faces, and each rider was armed with a sword or mace. Their clothing was a mismatch of different colours and they rode an assortment of horses. A burly man at the front of the group, with a shield across his back, was the only one without a helmet.

At his signal he slowed his horse and the others followed. Beside him Kell noticed Vahli had drawn a pair of long daggers from somewhere and was now standing with his arms crossed, the blades concealed behind his back. The Alfár held her weapon loosely in one hand down at her side but he sensed tension in the lines of her body. Bronwyn was as alert as the others, resting one hand lightly on the sword on her belt. Only the boy remained unaware of the rising tension.

The riders came to a halt a short distance away and for a time no one said anything. The leader stared at Kell and the others, his eyes widening at the sight of the Alfár, but his expression remained grim.

"You are Kell Kressia." It wasn't really a question but nonetheless Kell nodded.

For a moment he wondered if they were volunteers who had

come to join him on his quest to the Frozen North. Staring into the leader's eyes Kell knew that he was wrong. There was neither bravery nor compassion in those eyes. He wasn't the sort to be inspired by tales of heroism and sacrifice. They were not here to help him.

Doing a quick headcount he realised there were fifteen warriors in total.

Gerren had also drawn the wrong conclusion and was smiling at them. As the tension began to build he eventually noticed everyone else had their weapons at the ready.

"Who sent you?" asked Kell.

"Does it matter?" asked the leader, scratching his cheek.

"No way for me to change your mind? I have money."

"Thanks for letting me know. It will be a nice bonus for the boys," said the leader. He gave a signal to the others and they all dismounted. They were soldiers not mercenaries, and from their discipline it was clear the group had fought together in the past. They drew their weapons and formed a tight line.

Vahli grabbed the boy by the shoulder and shoved him back behind everyone. Right now he was more of a hindrance than a help.

Kell took a deep breath and drew his sword. Although the sky was grey Kell found himself smiling as he knew it could be a lot worse. At least it wasn't raining.

Bronwyn and the others would fight hard and kill a few but it wouldn't be enough. It would only take one or two to get behind them and then it would be over.

"Wait, I can fight," said Gerren, but the bard ignored him.

"Stay behind me," said Vahli, finally showing his blades which danced around his hands creating circles of steel. The Alfár cocked her head to one side. Kell wondered if she understood what was about to happen or why.

"Ready," said the leader, fastening his shield to one arm before drawing his sword.

Kell expected Bronwyn to jeer at the enemy or mock them.

Instead she was deadly silent. Her eyes were watchful, studying how those opposite held themselves and how they moved. One man in front of Kell kept his right foot off the ground as if in pain. Another held his sword low with the point almost touching the ground showing a lack of experience or arrogance. One of them would be the first to die.

There was a rumble in the distance. The threat of a storm and yet the clouds briefly parted, bathing patches of the land in sunlight. Kell took a deep breath, smelled the wildflowers, and readied himself.

The boy had stopped arguing but Kell could hear his ragged breathing. It was mixed with sobs. The Alfár was so perfectly still that Kell had forgotten she was beside him. Willow made a small huffing sound but he didn't know if it was a laugh or something else.

"Advance," said the leader. He inched forward and his men followed a step behind. A signal passed between two in the line and the group split down the middle, moving to the left and right.

The thunder was louder now. The storm was drawing near with uncanny speed and yet the clouds above were barely moving. Kell felt no wind on his face but he brushed it from his mind, focusing instead on the man with the bad leg. A feint to one side and the man would be off-balance. He'd create an opening and Kell would stab him right through the chest.

The ground began to shake and now the others were glancing at the sky. The Hundarian warriors began to look worried and now Bronwyn was grinning. It wasn't a storm.

Something whistled past his ear and one of the warriors in the line dropped to his knees, a bolt through his eye. Another had turned his head slightly and a second crossbow bolt took him in the throat. He began to choke, blood erupting from the wound. Panic set in as the sound of horses drew closer. It seemed to be coming from all around.

The leader urged his men to return to order and the Hundarians formed a tight ring, standing back to back. Bronwyn didn't wait.

With a roar she charged at the enemy and began to lay into them with vicious strokes. She slashed one man across the arm, punched another in the face and stabbed a third in the groin.

As Kell stepped forward to attack, someone crashed into the Hundarians from the other side. Men began to scream and the clash of metal rang in his ears. People were shoving him on all sides, screaming curses and spitting. The stink of blood and sweat filled his nostrils. His instincts kicked in and muscle memory took over. Kell readied his guard and stepped forward to engage the enemy.

More than a dozen strangers were attacking the Hundarians but in the melee it was difficult to see their faces. It was only when he glimpsed a tattooed face that he realised they'd been rescued by the Choate. Right now it didn't matter. His only thought was survival.

The warrior with the bad leg was panicking and looked ready to run but there was no escape. Kell feinted to the right and swung left in a tight arc. The tip of his blade caught the man across his chest, splitting open his leather armour. Blood seeped from the wound and before he could retaliate Kell jabbed him in the stomach, burying two feet of steel in the man's body. He wheezed once and started to scrabble around for purchase but Kell yanked his weapon free and stepped back.

Something caught his attention and turning his head Kell saw the Hundarian leader had raised his sword. Just as suddenly his arm and the weapon were gone. Kell and the Hundarian stared at the bloody stump in shock wondering what had happened. Before the man had a chance to scream, Willow's axe came down on his skull, splitting it in two.

As he looked around for another opponent Kell realised the fight was already over.

Fifteen Hundarians were a formidable group against four but even they couldn't best two dozen Choate. The blood-soaked warriors were dressed in a mix of leather and padded armour but all of them were without helmets. Their Choate rescuers, men and women, carried a curved blade in one hand and a leather buckler in the other. Strapped to their backs were their distinctive scythe-like swords for fighting on horseback.

As Kell regained his breath he noticed two more warriors a short distance away keeping an eye on the Choate horses. Each held a crossbow but they were not pointing them at anyone right now.

The Choate must have been watching him on the road and they knew his identity. Why else would they save him?

Unfortunately none of the Hundarians had survived and a quick search of their person revealed nothing about who'd hired them. When Kell approached the Choate, a burly man with triangular tattoos across his cheeks stepped forward. He was thick across the shoulders like a wrestler and had a quick smile.

"I am Gar Darvan," he said, cleaning his bloody sword on a dead man's shirt. "A good fight. Are your people injured?"

Bronwyn's armour had a few scratches but otherwise they were all fine. The boy had avoided the fighting altogether and even the bard had come out of it unscathed. Willow had killed at least a couple of the Hundarians but had no injuries at all.

"Everyone is well. Thank you," said Kell.

"A good day," said Darvan. He glanced at the sky and his smile faded a little. "Shitty weather, though."

"We appreciate your help but–"

"You want to know who sent me, yes?" said Darvan.

"Yes."

"Sadly, I must disappoint you. What I can say is that your quest is important. We will keep watch until you reach the border. Once you cross into Kinnan we cannot follow, but I think you will be safe."

Darvan knew a lot more but he was unwilling or unable to share. Kell thought about pushing the subject but changed his mind. The Choate had a strong sense of honour and it would upset them if he questioned their intent, especially after they'd just saved his life. That left Kell with only one option. To do nothing. Perhaps the answer would come in time.

"Please thank your people for their help," said Kell, pressing both fists to his chest in the Choate fashion. Darvan smiled and copied the gesture, bowing slightly over his hands.

Darvan watched Kell and his companions ride away until they were just specks on the horizon. A dozen of his best were shadowing them on the road and another group was scouting ahead for trouble. He thought it was unlikely that there would be a second ambush but he was not taking any chances.

A short time later the War General approached. Darvan was known for being thorough but on this occasion he'd been extremely meticulous with his planning. Before today he'd never had a chance to work with any member of the Blood, making this a rare and special honour. Even if he'd not been the younger brother of the High Chieftain, the War General was respected as a warrior who'd led the clans to victory many times. However, Darvan like many others, couldn't help wondering where he'd been for the past ten years.

The War General joined him on the hill, staring into the distance at the bland Hundarian landscape.

"How many?" asked the War General.

"Fifteen. All dead," said Darvan. "None of Kell's people were harmed."

"Good. You have my thanks, Gar Darvan."

"It was my honour, Dos Mohan."

"The things we do for family," said the War General, squinting at the distant figures riding north with a wistful expression. "Do you think they'll try again?"

"It's doubtful, but I have people watching them, just in case."

"That's good. I will make sure my brother hears about this."

"Do you have any further orders, War General?" asked Darvan, hoping to further impress the old warrior.

"Actually yes," said the War General, turning to face him. "I think it's time for the Magbah."

The Magbah was an ancient Choate tradition held during times of peace when the best warriors, archers and wrestlers from different tribes would compete with one another in a series of games. The last Magbah had been almost six years ago and he knew many young warriors were keen to show off their prowess. The tribes had been united as one people for many years but Darvan knew many still proudly spoke of their distant heritage.

"Will you be competing?" he asked, knowing that the War General was a fierce wrestler and one of the best with a javelin.

Dos Mohan laughed, and rubbed one of his shoulders. "I think I'm too stiff for the javelin, but I may wrestle. First the Magbah and then a celebration!" he declared.

Sometimes the drinking and feasting afterwards could go on for almost as long as the games themselves. It would be glorious.

"Where do you want to hold it?"

"I think this looks like a good spot," said the War General, glancing around. "I'll start making the arrangements."

CHAPTER 17

Around the campfires they sat each night,
Telling their glorious stories of old.
And with eyes as big as plates the boy listened,
While his heart swelled with bravery.

EXCERPT FROM THE SAGA OF KELL KRESSIA
BY THE BARD PAX MEDINA

It was late in the afternoon when they arrived at the town of Liesh, on the border between Hundar and Kinnan.

Since the attack they hadn't really talked about what had happened. The only person genuinely interested was Vahli who was busy recording every detail in his journal. Gerren was still distressed and now stared at everyone as if they were strangers. He'd uncovered the truth about being a hero. Every single one of them had a history of killing and maiming other people.

Kell had expected Bronwyn to be blasé about the attack but she'd been unusually quiet.

"Are you all right?" he asked.

"Fine," she said, although he noticed she was studying their surroundings.

"I don't think they'll attack again."

"Doesn't hurt to be cautious," said Bronwyn.

Kell slowed down to ride beside Willow. As Misty smelled the Nhill her eyes widened in terror but he kept a firm grip on the reins. "Do you want to talk about the attack?" he asked, but the Alfár said nothing. He couldn't even be sure if she was listening.

Kell tried a different approach. "Willow, are you well?"

The Alfár had been staring into the distance but now she glanced at him. "I will still accompany you on this journey. Nothing has changed."

He waited in case she had something else to say but her attention was elsewhere. At least one good thing had come out of the attack. Willow had not been put off going with them. Given what he'd seen of her during the fight, Kell was glad to have the Alfár as an ally.

To the north the terrain in Kinnan was as unpleasant as Kell remembered with few signs of life. As he peered into the distance he saw lots of winding trails cut through steep hills, rocky scree slopes littered with slate, huge chunks of granite and the odd splash of colour from wildflowers. Flashes of white hinted at rabbits and rangy mountain goats dashing up sheer rock faces but there was little else to see besides the waving grass. He'd been told there were nice parts, particularly towards the west and the capital city, but for the most part it was a craggy windswept country that bred tough men and women.

Despite being on the Hundar side of the border, the town of Liesh was built in the Keen fashion. Cut into the face of a steep hill every slate roof had the same blue-grey tiles. All of the buildings appeared shallow but typically more than half of the rooms were inside the hill, obscuring the size of each home.

The cobbled streets were sloping, narrow and only navigable on foot which made them easy to defend. Steps and winding roads seemed to be the most popular features of Keen architecture. The town was designed for function and the plain buildings had no exterior decoration. Even the pattern on the roof tiles served a purpose, channelling rain water into pipes that trickled into barrels so that nothing was wasted. Freezing winters and baking hot summers meant the Keen weren't interested in fanciful decoration that might melt in the heat or snap in the cold. The people, much like their homes, were built to last in any environment.

The group left their horses in the town stable which was situated near the gate. Much to Kell's surprise Willow decided to come with them which initially caused a few problems with the Nhill. Eventually they managed to persuade the town stablemaster to house the animal as far away as possible from the other horses.

With no wall surrounding the town Willow seemed to breathe much easier. The Alfár attracted a lot of stares but either she didn't notice or didn't care. Instead she seemed more interested in watching the birds.

Once the horses were settled they began the arduous climb towards the lower part of town where all of the shops and businesses were situated. In Keen settlements the high town was reserved for local people. To reach it you had to pass through a narrow stone arch, affectionately known as the smiling gate.

The gate was a holdover from ancient times when Keen warriors had frequently raided their neighbouring towns. A small number of defenders could hold the smiling gate, forcing the enemy to pass through it two people at a time. Burning down an enemy's business and slaughtering each other was seen as par for the course but not torching their home. In those days, before an invader could reach high town a defender would give them a red smile with their sword.

Out of respect Bronwyn received a few greetings from locals but the rest of their group seemed invisible, apart from the Alfár who attracted stares. Perhaps it was her presence but people kept their distance which didn't bode well for more recruits.

Kell's quad muscles were beginning to ache as they climbed the endless steps but eventually they reached a busy cobbled street in low town. Hawkers were standing outside their shops bellowing at the top of their lungs, their voices overlapping into a chaotic din. Fresh meat, furs, fruit from warmer southern climates and weapons seemed to dominate. Tantalising cooking smells made his stomach growl, reminding Kell that some time had passed since his last meal. Following his nose he led them to a tavern called the King's Arms. The garish sign above the door showed a bare-chested painting of the King with bulging muscles. A scantily clad woman clung to each leg staring up at him with adoration. Kell snorted at the sign but went in anyway. He was hungry and didn't want to climb another two hundred steps in search of food.

It was still early in the evening and less than half of the tables were occupied. Glass hookahs sat in the middle of several tables around which two or three people were smoking from slender pipes with bone mouthpieces. A fug of blue smoke clung to the ceiling but a wash of fresh air from their entrance brought welcome relief to those not indulging.

Several Keen watched them with lazy expressions while a few stiffened in their seats when they caught sight of Willow and Bronwyn. As well as locals there were a few Seith merchants, two faces from home and several lanky Hundarians with gleaming shaven heads. One man was asleep snoring at his table with his face pressed into the wood. The drunk had a half-empty glass of beer clutched in one hand and a partly chewed chicken drumstick in the other.

"You honour me, daughter," said the owner, coming around from behind the bar. "My name is Zoiveer." She was a broad middle-aged woman with a dark green headscarf, denoting her position as the cook. She was clearly the proprietor, suggested by the five serving boys lined up beside her. Bronwyn and the owner clasped forearms and bowed their heads slightly, a greeting reserved for honoured guests and family.

Zoiveer's smile wavered as she caught sight of the Alfár. The Keen could be quite formal with their greetings but on this occasion Zoiveer didn't welcome everyone in turn. There was no way to know how Willow would react to being touched by a stranger.

"Please, honoured guests, sit." She led them to an empty table and personally took their drinks order before hurrying away. Zoiveer cast one furtive glance at Willow, biting her lower lip, but the Alfár didn't notice. She seemed intent on studying the trailing smoke trails that were drifting around the ceiling.

The locals were minding their own business, which was an improvement from their reception in Hundar. At least no one had got up and left the room.

"Do you think any of your people will join us?" said Kell as their drinks arrived.

"Yes, but none of these sops are worthy," said Bronwyn, grimacing at the room.

The boy had been unusually quiet and almost dazed since the attack. It was probably the first time he'd seen someone die. The stories made death sound grand and heroic.

Vahli was trying to coax a few words out of him. "Gerren, would you like a drink?" he asked, pushing a mug of beer across the table.

"I'm hungry," said Gerren, staring at their surroundings for the first time. "Can we order some food?" he asked.

"Soon," said Vahli, trying to placate the boy while sipping his wine. His apprehension turned into a surprised smile. "Delicious," he said, holding up his glass.

Kell noticed Willow was now staring at one of the other tables where two local women were blowing trails of smoke out of their mouths. At first they weren't aware but eventually the intensity of the Alfár's gaze drew their attention. Their attempt at friendly smiles wavered and soon their enthusiasm for the hookah wavered too. After settling their bill they scurried out of the tavern.

"Do you have them in your homeland?" asked Kell, making another attempt at conversation.

"No," she said, and he thought Willow sounded puzzled. She was still staring at the table.

"Do you know what it's for?"

"No." Willow gave Kell that strange half-smile, turning in her chair to face him. Then she waited.

"It's for smoking tobacco," said Kell, gesturing at the bowl. "You draw the smoke into your body." Her face gave nothing away so he had no idea if she was satisfied with his explanation or not. Assuming her silence meant she didn't understand he continued. "People do it because it feels... nice." Kell was sincerely hoping he didn't have to explain what nice meant. Thankfully Willow understood as she smiled, apparently satisfied. Her attention shifted to something out of the window and Kell sighed in relief. Every day he looked for commonalities between humans and Alfár but often came up short.

Vahli had been listening intently to their conversation and was now furtively scribbling down notes in his journal. The hidebound book never left his person and Kell suspected it would form the basis of the new saga.

"What are you writing?" asked Gerren.

"Nothing," said Vahli. "Drink your beer."

Much to Kell's surprise the boy did as he was told.

Kell enjoyed relief from not being on his horse. His arse was gradually changing shape and in another week it would have moulded itself to fit his saddle.

A short time later the owner returned with two boys holding up a large wooden display board between them. Arranged across it were several cuts of beef and pork. Kell didn't even ask about the price as he suspected it was going to be high. Honoured guests or not, meat was increasingly expensive these days and Zoiveer had to earn a living. Thankfully Lukas had given him a hefty purse for the journey.

They all made a selection except Willow who seemingly stared without comprehension, so Kell made a choice on her behalf. Zoiveer returned to the kitchen and shortly after Kell heard the tantalising sizzle of meat being cooked.

"Why did the Hundarians attack us?" asked Gerren.

"We don't know," said Kell.

"Why would anyone want to stop us?" said the boy. He sounded desperate to understand, as if to make sense of the deaths he'd seen up close. Vahli took him to one side where he spoke quietly to Gerren in a soothing voice. Whatever he said seemed to help as when they returned to the table Gerren seemed a bit less frazzled.

Gerren's question had been a good one and it had been bothering Kell. Who would benefit from killing him and the others? How would anyone benefit from starvation? The only notion that made sense was that someone didn't believe the threat was real.

"I'm more interested in the Choate," said Vahli, holding his glass of wine up to the light. "Why would they suddenly take an interest in our business? Do you know any Choate?" he asked, turning towards Kell.

"No." Strictly speaking that wasn't true but the only Choate he knew was his barber and Kell didn't think he was worth mentioning.

"Does it matter?" said Bronwyn, startling everyone with her gruff tone. "Someone in Hundar wanted to stop us and they failed. The reason will come out or it won't. All of that is for another day. Today we're alive. Let's focus on that."

"I'll drink to that," said Kell, raising his glass.

"So what do we do now?" asked Gerren.

"Wait," said Bronwyn, staring at the front door, "and hope that someone else wants to join us."

Every time it opened she sat up in her chair, expecting every newcomer to approach their table and present themselves for consideration. But each time it was just another customer, coming for a drink or a spell on the pipe. After they caught sight of his party, or perhaps it was the Alfár, many people only stayed for one quick drink and then left.

When their food arrived Kell tucked in with relish but was still annoyed that no one had come forward. He temporarily forgot about them as he enjoyed his tender, juicy steak. The spices slightly burned the edges of his tongue while the sticky rice and yoghurt helped soothe the pain in his mouth. Bronwyn ate with her usual vigour but he could see she was equally frustrated. Not even one hunter or farmer with a pitchfork showed any willing.

By the time they'd finished eating everyone's mood had soured. Willow had eaten everything on her plate except for the meat which Bronwyn and the boy split between them. When a shadow fell across their table Kell was elated but his smile quickly faded. It was the drunk who'd been asleep at his table.

Now that he could see the stranger's face Kell realised he was from the Summer Isles. With swarthy skin, curly black hair and matching beard, plus a solid build he might have been a suitable candidate, if not for the stink of beer and bloodshot eyes. On his waist he carried a curved heavy blade and a pair of daggers. Dressed in worn leathers that left his arms bare Kell noticed a lack of scars which was uncommon for any seasoned warrior.

Then again people from the Summer Isles didn't follow the Shepherd and their peculiar beliefs had something against marking the skin. Tattoos and piercings were not permitted and any warrior with a visible scar was seen as inept. Those who pierced their ears, noses or other body parts were shunned and had little choice but to live in the Five Kingdoms.

"Can we help you?" asked Vahli, far more politely than Kell would have managed in his current mood.

"I'm here to travel with you to the Frozen North," he declared. If the newcomer was intimidated by their group he didn't show it. Then again, he was probably too drunk to see their faces.

"And who are you?" asked Kell.

"I am Malomir, King of the Summer Isles, renowned hunter of beasts and men. I have fought and bested every animal that swims, flies or walks in the Five Kingdoms. I slew Kronk the one-eyed voran, terror of the east. I killed Torru-gora in the jungles beyond Corvan. I even fought Gouru, King of the Snapjaws and lived. As a prize I claimed one of his teeth."

It was his last boast that made Bronwyn laugh before she pulled out the tooth necklace from under her armour. "You're a liar. I fought Gouru and claimed one of his teeth." She held up a large curved tooth almost as long as Kell's hand.

Malomir grinned and produced an identical tooth from his pocket. "I always wondered who else had bested him. There was a gap in his mouth, here," said Malomir, gesturing at the right side of his face. Bronwyn seemed satisfied but Kell wasn't as easily fooled. Clearly the man was a liar and a scam artist. In some ways he reminded Kell of the heroes. They often exaggerated their deeds to make them sound more impressive. He'd probably found the tooth in a swamp.

"Vahli, have you ever heard of him or his deeds?"

"I have heard of Kronk," mused the bard. "Although I don't recognise his name."

"I am famous across the north," bragged the Islander.

"You're mad," said Gerren. "Even I know there's no king in the Summer Isles."

"The boy does have a point," Kell admitted. "No one has ever ruled the nine islands."

"Seventeen," said Malomir, swaying slightly before he steadied himself on their table. "There are seventeen islands. Admittedly, some of them small, with only a few huts, but I am King of them all. Everyone agreed."

"I think you are mad," said Bronwyn. "You probably stole that tooth."

"I took it from him at great cost," insisted Malomir.

"Do you have any scars to prove it?" she asked.

At this Malomir showed the first signs of discomfort but eventually he nodded. "Thankfully they are not in the open. I would be happy to show you in private. Perhaps we could compare scars?" he suggested, giving Bronwyn a salacious wink.

"Perhaps," she said, with a faint smile.

"I am also hung like a horse. I could show you my cock as well."

Gerren sprayed beer across the table while Vahli suddenly became more interested in the Islander, eyeing him up and down. Malomir winked and the bard giggled in his high-pitched voice. The Alfár appeared to be listening but she was neither embarrassed nor amused. If Kell had to guess from her lack of an expression he would have said Willow was puzzled.

Bronwyn remained unflustered. "It's probably another exaggeration," she said.

"I'll show you," said Malomir, starting to unbutton his trousers.

"Not here," said Kell, noting the horrified expressions of the other customers.

"Later then," he said. "So, when do we leave?"

Kell looked at the others hoping someone had a good reason to refuse the Islander's offer. Clearly Malomir was insane, not to mention a liar and a loudmouth, with a very high opinion of himself. Even if half of his claims were true, which Kell doubted, he didn't think they could trust the newcomer.

None of the others had come up with a legitimate reason to turn him away so Kell made one last attempt.

"It's going to be very dangerous. You might die."

"What is life without risk?" asked Malomir with a shrug.

"What about your family? Won't they miss you?"

"I have no family."

"Not even a Queen?" asked Bronwyn.

"Alas no, but perhaps one day I will find the perfect woman."

Kell slapped Vahli on the shoulder, startling the bard from his reverie. "A little help!"

"I think he would make a fine addition to the group," said the bard.

"Useless," muttered Kell.

"Are you really a King?" asked Bronwyn.

"I am," declared Malomir. "The Summer Isles are a paradise. Golden sandy beaches and crystal blue water. Lush forests bursting with fruit trees and wild animals. And the people, they are the friendliest in the world."

"Then why would you ever leave?" asked Kell, trying to catch him in a lie. "If it's so perfect, why come here to such a harsh and rugged landscape?"

"I was lonely," admitted Malomir. "And bored because it's so quiet. Nothing exciting ever happens. I came to the mainland in search of adventure, and where better than in the company of Kell Kressia, the living legend."

The attempt at flattery slid off Kell as easily as insults. Both left him feeling bitter and angry. People only offered praise when they wanted something from him.

When no one spoke up against Malomir it became clear they were going to be stuck with him. If he was half decent with his sword then he might prove useful in a fight. Besides, when they reached the ice they'd soon learn if his stories were nothing more than hot air.

Malomir's arrival also gave him an idea for something that he'd been mulling over for a while.

"You can join us on one condition," said Kell.

"Name it," declared Malomir.

Kell leaned forward and whispered it in his ear. The Islander just raised an eyebrow in response. "That sounds fair."

"Welcome," said Kell, offering Malomir his hand.

And now they were six.

CHAPTER 18

The twelfth pillar is love.
Speaking the words is easy and costs nothing.
Offering love in the face of wrath and evil,
To the enemies within and without is righteous.

EXCERPT FROM THE SACRED BOOK OF THE SHEPHERD

Reverend Mother Britak had guided King Roebus through all manner of difficulties, but never had she seen him so distraught. His hands were shaking, he couldn't stop pacing up and down and he looked on the verge of tears.

Rather than conduct this meeting in the throne room he had opted for a less formal setting. The room was still garish and too lavish for her tastes with silk curtains, expensive rugs and a roaring fire, even though there was barely a chill in the air. It was all so wasteful.

The weather was noticeably cooler than only a few days ago but she didn't let it prey on her mind. It was merely a phase and part of a cycle which she'd witnessed before. A few of her novices had begun to mutter about supernatural dangers being responsible for the chill. They were learning the error of their ways for listening to gossip and publicly spouting such blasphemy. Sadly she could not discipline the King with the same ease.

"What's happened?" she asked, cutting straight to the quick.

"There, on the table," he said, pointing to a huge brass monstrosity that had been fashioned into the shape of four lions holding up a sheet of glass. A large unadorned wicker basket sat in the middle. Britak knew whatever was inside could not be dangerous, as it would never have reached the King; nevertheless he'd been severely traumatised by its contents.

Peering inside she was surprised to see a pair of severed hands. They'd been carefully wrapped in a thick black cloth which she clinically noticed wasn't marked by even a single drop of blood. More peculiar than the bloodless hands was that they had been painted red.

"Is this a threat from someone?" she asked. The King was muttering to himself as he paced about. "What does it mean?" said Britak, working hard to supress shaking him by the shoulders.

"As we discussed I sent someone, to take care of Kell," he said, glancing around at the walls. They were alone but anyone who accidentally overheard their conversation knew how to keep their mouth shut. "That's all that's left of them. It arrived this morning from Algany."

She'd been arrogant to assume King Bledsoe hadn't put someone in place to protect Kell, and more importantly, his plan to elevate Algany. Pride. It was another sin for which she would have to pay penance.

"He's going to come for me," said Roebus. "I should double the number of guards around the palace. And hire a food taster!"

"Those are all wise precautions. However, do you think if King Bledsoe intended to kill you he would send a warning first?"

It took a while but eventually the words penetrated Roebus's thick skull as he stopped pacing and turned to face her. "A warning?"

"Yes. He's telling you not to interfere."

"Then he's not trying to kill me?"

"No." Not today at least, although she didn't say that part aloud in case it sent Roebus into another panicky spiral.

"Then what should I do?" he asked. "There's growing support for Kell to succeed. A lot of people are worried about feeding their families."

"There's no proof that the danger is real," said Britak.

"Whether you believe or not isn't important." Roebus held up a hand before she could protest. "Farmers across Algany and Seithland are complaining about their crops. And they're not the only ones. Less food means less trade and that affects everyone."

Britak took a deep calming breath before speaking. "King Bledsoe is old. He won't live forever."

"What are you saying?"

"Even if this farcical quest goes in his favour his level of popularity won't matter when he dies. In fact, it's possible that the King of Algany could die at any time."

"No," shouted Roebus. "Not him, I forbid it. You will not interfere!"

"I was not implying anything," said Britak in a soothing voice. "My point was, we should let nature take its course. Whenever it happens he will be remembered as a great king, but his successor will have to earn the favour of his people. You need to stay strong, hold tight to your faith in the Shepherd and all will be well." She could see from his guarded expression that the King remained unconvinced. "There's something else, isn't there?"

"Kell is no longer travelling alone. He's gathered together a group of unusual characters to help him. There's a bard, a woman from Kinnan, an Islander and even one of the Alfár."

Britak hissed through her teeth and sketched the crook in the air with one hand for protection. They were unclean abominations. Freaks that refused to die.

No one, not even her predecessors with their extensive journals, knew where they came from. Many had gathered clues that it was somewhere across the Narrow Sea in a land beyond Corven, but there was little solid evidence beyond that unifying fact. Nothing in nature resembled them or was related to them. At first Britak had thought of them as sideshow peculiarities, freaks of nature to be pitied, but over the decades she'd realised they were something much worse. They were the living embodiment of human sin.

Whenever they showed up, trouble followed in their wake. They were harbingers of bad times and never surfaced before a long spell of peace. Next year people would be hungry until the harvest came in and that would lead to unease and possible conflict across the Five Kingdoms. She should have seen it coming.

"Kell has damned himself by promoting his belief in the supernatural and now he's allied himself with an abomination. There really isn't anything he won't do."

"They're travelling through Kinnan and will arrive in Meer in the next few days. That could be our last opportunity to stop them," said Roebus.

"No, I think a different approach would be better," said Britak, forcing a smile. Her blood was still boiling at the thought of the Alfár but to Roebus the creature was nothing more than an oddity. He didn't understand what it meant for the future.

"The Frozen North is a dangerous place. Only heathens and the insane would volunteer to travel onto the ice. Last time there were twelve of them and only Kell returned. How many does he have this time?"

"Five followers."

"Then the chances of him returning are slim. And even if he did make it back to Meer, he would be exhausted, maybe injured and probably close to death."

King Roebus nodded sagely in agreement.

Mother Nature was not kind or caring. She was brutal and relentless. She was the sort of mother Britak admired. To survive Mother Nature you had to be willing to fight her every step of the way. The beasts on the ice would thin the herd. Britak would make sure Kell, and whoever else made it back to Meer, never returned home.

Obviously Kell and the Alfár had to die, but she had to ensure the bard did not survive. She'd already been forced to endure ten years of that Medina dross which refused to go away. She would not tolerate a new song about the so-called hero, Kell Kressia. If that happened his reputation would only grow and she'd never hear the end of it.

"Now is the time to be patient," she advised the King. "It may be that none of those who set foot on the ice will return."

"I pray to the Shepherd it happens that way," he said.

Britak was happy to leave the King's presence and return to work. Whenever she was around him for too long Britak felt her intelligence begin to drop.

She set a steady pace towards the rectory, her mind on the future. Roebus was a pathetic excuse for a King. As time passed he seemed more unwilling to make difficult decisions even when they would benefit him in the long run.

Sadly his eldest son, and heir to the throne, was another weak-chinned fool that wasn't much better than his father. She'd hoped that Roebus had at least another ten years on the throne but now she had her doubts. If he found it difficult to make small decisions then it might take him months to make up his mind about something really important. That was time she didn't have to waste on his dithering. Time relentlessly marched on and every morning it became a little more difficult to open her eyes.

Britak wondered if she should have invested more of her time in the King's son instead. A feisty young wife would fire his blood. So far the King's new wife had lifted his mood but he was only a little more pliable than before. Her spy would just have to work extra hard so the King did as he was told. Either that or Britak would see to it that he was removed.

She left her escort at the front door of the rectory and marched through the hallways towards the garden. Roebus squirmed when making a decision but once it was done he spared little thought about the outcome. Such thoughts kept her up at night. They haunted her dreams and weighed on her soul.

Using a small knife Britak cut a dozen pale roses, gathered them in a ribbon and then set off for her rooms.

She knew her relationship with the King was a peculiar

partnership that few would understand. He gave the orders but she was the one who paid the price. While he slept soundly in his bed she suffered in his stead. It didn't matter that someone else had given the order or that it was necessary. She knew committing such grave sins were a stain upon her soul. The guilt of her actions would not be easily assuaged.

After entering her private rooms Britak stripped out of her clothing and then took the time to carefully hang up everything in her wardrobe. The tiles were cold against her bare feet but she did her best to ignore the pain. With the flowers clutched in one hand she lit several candles inside her private chapel before locking the door so that she would not be disturbed. Her people knew better than to enter her rooms without invitation but she couldn't take any chances.

With a sharp twist of her hands Britak beheaded all of the roses. The colourful petals fell to the floor but she ignored them. Their softness served no purpose. It was the stems that interested her. Taking down a leather cord from the wall she wove it through and around the stems over and over until it formed a long and flexible tail.

Kneeling down wasn't easy but she endured the indignity of almost falling on her face from performing such a simple task. She was getting feeble. Her flesh was starting to fail but her will remained as solid as iron.

Gritting her teeth Britak unfurled the whip to its full length and then mercilessly brought it towards her body with all of her strength. The rose thorns dug into the flesh of her back ripping the skin open in a dozen places. With both hands she yanked the whip away, tearing it free from her body. The pain was mild and she felt no better for the sins she bore. Blood trickled down her back but she paid it no attention. The guilt remained and she needed to repent.

The whip struck her flesh over and over but she refused to cry out in pain. Crying was for children. Even though the agony was beginning to mount she would suffer in silence.

As her efforts continued, sweat ran from her pores. The cuts in her flesh began to burn. Britak was clenching her jaw so tightly her teeth were squeaking.

The whip came down again, ripping a series of tears across her ribs and shoulders. She would continue until the guilt began to ease. No matter how long it took.

Towards the end, when her strength was ebbing away, the torture of her flesh opened a window of clarity in her mind. In that moment all of the lies and conceit faded away leaving her bare and honest. The pain was gone and she knew the simplest truth of her heart.

She would do anything, remove any obstacles, commit any sin, to bring the Shepherd's word to the Five Kingdoms, because it was righteous. Britak smiled through bloody teeth and felt the remaining guilt fade away.

CHAPTER 19

Once inside the Lich's castle the end seemed near,
But the fight continued for the surviving heroes.
As the walls and even the floor did move,
Hiding a host of traps designed to kill them all.

Excerpt from the Saga of Kell Kressia
by the Bard Pax Medina

The following morning they rode out of Liesh into the heart of Kinnan.

To the east were the Dralle mountains and beyond them, Okeer, the capital city. Situated on the coast it was sheltered from the harsh northern weather. The city was a monument to the history of the Keen people who had been living there for centuries. Okeer was the template upon which all others were modelled, a sprawling city, on many levels, built into the face of a mountain.

The city had never been conquered, a fact that every proud Keen would tell you if given a chance. This was both a testament to its design and that the Keen were a hardy race. That fact gave Kell hope that they would find a few others to join their quest. Despite the presence of the Alfár he wasn't confident about their success, given that he knew what lay ahead. Kell wanted to recruit at least another four people before he could begin to relax.

As he huddled into his coat he noticed the temperature was continuing to drop. He didn't need his gloves but it wouldn't be long. Soon his fur-lined boots and hat would become permanent fixtures for survival.

Kell had suggested they follow the west road which was the most direct to their next destination. However, such a path took them away from the more populated areas. Gerren and Vahli wanted to divert east to the capital in the hope of bolstering their ranks. Bronwyn had surprised everyone by suggesting they head away from the city on the west road.

By now word of their journey had spread throughout the north. People knew how to find Kell and where he was going. If they needed any proof they only had to look at Malomir. Despite being fairly drunk the Islander had managed to track them down. The fact that no one else had been waiting spoke volumes.

People were scared. Part of him could understand. After all, he'd intended to run away and start a new life. But there were some things you couldn't leave behind, no matter the distance. Kell had too many unanswered questions about his past. A return to the north could be the only way he would ever know any peace. He'd thought the trauma was gone, or at least buried deep, but it had taken very little for the nightmares to resurface. The last ten years were already starting to feel like a dream.

They veered away from civilisation and took the west road through the more barren parts of Kinnan. Bronwyn rode in silence, disappointed at the cowardice of her own people, while Gerren brooded about the fight with the Hundarians. Even though the boy hadn't killed anyone, Kell suspected he would still have nightmares for weeks.

Malomir was still hungover and dozed in the saddle and Willow trailed behind so the Nhill didn't upset the horses. That left Kell alone with the bard. Vahli seemed intent on recording every detail about his life, even mundane facts from his childhood. For some reason the bard thought people would be interested to know he'd had a stuffed bear as a child and pretended to be a warrior with a wooden sword and shield.

"Tell me something no one else knows about your first trip to the north," said the bard, changing the subject.

Kell raised an eyebrow. "Like what?"

"You tell me. Were there any details left out of the Medina saga?"

"Lots of things. How about when most of the heroes got a bad run of the shits from poorly cooked meat?"

"I meant something inspirational about the heroes. Or maybe something small about their personalities."

"People always talk about them that way," noted Kell. "The heroes and then me, separately."

Vahli sighed. "Yes, yes. You're a hero too. I'm just trying to understand them."

"Why? They're all dead," said Kell, feeling his temper flare. It had been this way for ten years. People never tried to understand him or what the journey had cost. Maybe if he'd died along with the others they would be equally fascinated.

"Fine. You want to know something new? Reeman used to beat his wife. He spent more time on the road than he did at home. After a while he was certain that she was sleeping with someone else when he was away. He'd get drunk, go home and beat her. The next morning he'd beg for her forgiveness. Is that personal enough for you?"

"It's not true," said the bard.

"There's more," he offered, but Vahli didn't take him up on the offer. No one was without flaws and the heroes had more than most.

The heavy silence that hung over Bronwyn fell across the rest of the group. With no other distractions Kell was free to study their surroundings.

Rolling craggy hills stretched out in all directions. Covered in an endless sea of grass, the tide of waving blades was broken only by the network of dry stone walls which carved up the land into peculiar shapes. As they crested another hill Kell looked down onto a large multicoloured patchwork quilt made up of greens, yellows, oranges and purple from large patches of heather.

Standing in the middle of some fields was a huge lonely tree. Too big to be dug up, its windswept branches provided limited shelter from the sun and rain. Thorny green hedgerows had sprung up within the shadow of many walls and flourishing within were bright wildflowers that attracted insects and birds. Clusters of gaping fist-sized holes in the earth suggested the presence of rabbits but he couldn't see any at present.

Apart from the walls and the occasional farmhouse there were few signs of habitation. The land had a rugged, timeless quality. Out here hardy sheep and goats outnumbered people twenty to one. In the distance Kell saw a huge grey flock moving across a field being herded by a single figure with a crook.

The nearest settlement from Liesh was two days' ride, forcing them to camp out for the first time. Before the light faded Kell kept his eyes open for a good spot. He didn't want to end up stumbling around in the dark or hunkering down beside the road because they'd waited too long. When the path dipped towards a valley with a shallow brook and a copse of trees he called them to a halt. Out of the wind, with fresh water and wood for a fire, they would be hard pressed to find a better site.

As they tied up their horses he noticed others had used it in the past. Someone had dug a fire pit and ringed it with large stones. There was even a collection of wooden stumps to sit on.

As soon as her beast was tethered and had been fed, Willow walked back up the road and disappeared into the gloom. The others looked at Kell expectantly but he just shrugged. He wasn't the Alfár's keeper and they knew as much about her as he did, which was next to nothing. He still didn't know why she had decided to make this journey. He could guess at the motives of the others, but Willow's remained a complete mystery. One day he would hopefully find out but Kell wasn't certain of anything when it came to the Alfár.

Kell collected some fallen branches and started building a fire in the hope that someone else would volunteer to cook. One of the many reasons he'd frequented the Dancing Cricket was that even after all these years he still had no talent for cooking.

"Get up boy," said Malomir, nudging Gerren who'd settled beside Bronwyn. She was busy sharpening her weapons while he'd been dozing off. Vahli was focused on his oud, ear bent to the strings as he carefully tuned the instrument.

"What for?" asked Gerren.

"It's time for your training," said the Islander, walking over to the copse of trees. Kell pretended not to know what was going on but his one condition for letting Malomir travel with them was that he trained the boy how to fight.

It was likely that Gerren had never even held a sword before and Kell was certain he wouldn't survive without training. A few days wouldn't make him a swordsman but they wouldn't be sparring against skilled warriors. It would be a battle for their lives against savage beasts that lived in the most inhospitable part of the world.

Malomir studied the trees around them before selecting a white ash. With a hatchet he cut two sturdy branches as long as his arm then clipped off any twigs and leaves. Malomir threw one of them to Gerren who fumbled the catch.

"Lesson one. We'll work on your hand-eye coordination," he said with a smile. Bronwyn snorted and went back to sharpening her sword.

As Malomir began the boy's first lesson it didn't take Kell long to see how inept Gerren was with a stick. It was a good thing Malomir hadn't started him out with a real sword.

The heroes had been impatient and had often shouted or kicked Kell when he got something wrong. Malomir was the opposite. He remained calm and seemed to have infinite patience, even when Gerren failed to follow the simplest of instructions. Instead he changed tack and made the boy run through a series of stretching exercises to wake up dormant muscles.

While they exercised, Kell gathered more wood for the fire.

Eventually he coaxed a spark from the leaves and slowly added twigs and then larger pieces of wood. About an hour later Willow returned to camp and with a flourish dumped three fat rabbits on the ground beside Kell.

"I'll skin them," offered Bronwyn.

"I can make a stew," said Vahli, finally pitching in now that everyone else was doing something. "I can't promise a king's feast."

"As long as it's well cooked. Diarrhoea can kill the same as a sword," said Kell.

Everyone settled into a routine around the camp with the exception of the Alfár. She seemed fascinated with the actions of others. Her dark eyes flicked between him working on the fire and Malomir practising with the boy. Kell wondered if the rumours about Alfár always being alone were true. Did she ever feel lonely? Did she dislike cities because she saw such large gatherings as unnatural? Or was it something else? Kell was about to ask when he saw a terrible longing in her eyes which made him turn away. His questions could wait for another day.

Vahli turned out to be a much better cook than Kell expected. With some wild onions and herbs, padded out with potatoes and carrots bought in Liesh, the stew was quite tasty. Everyone munched away in a happy silence, dipping chunks of bread, until the pot was empty. This time Willow ate everything, including the meat, which Kell knew she had avoided in the past. It was a mystery for another time. Right now he had a full stomach and was feeling sleepy. They all dozed by the fire as Vahli strummed away on his instrument.

"Tell me about when you slew Kronk," said Vahli to Malomir, taking out his journal. "I've heard stories of him but only in passing."

"Ah, he was a fearsome beast," said the madman, wiping the corners of his mouth with a sleeve. "Grey and silver fur all over, denoting his great age. He had huge shoulders, and his eyes, they were as green as virgin grass."

Kell cracked one eye open and watched the others listening to Malomir's tale. There was probably some truth to the story but he'd heard enough lies in his time to know the Islander was exaggerating. Some of the details were vaguely familiar, probably overheard one night in the Dancing Cricket, but Kell didn't recall anyone mentioning Malomir by name. Surely everyone would remember who had slain the fearsome beast?

Bronwyn was leaning forwards, listening so intently that she didn't notice Gerren staring. Kell knew the boy would have better luck with one of the horses. Willow sat a short distance away from the fire so that she was partly in shadow but he could see her yellow eyes were focused on Malomir. Occasionally Kell recognised the emotions on her face and could guess what the Alfár was thinking. More often her expression gave nothing away and she was like a closed book. He had no way to know how the Alfár viewed the world. As Willow listened to the story, Kell couldn't tell if she was impressed or amused.

"He was a vicious creature, and even at the end, when he'd been abandoned by his pack, Kronk showed no fear. He would have torn out my throat if he had the strength." Malomir bowed his head for a moment in respect. "I made it swift, to prevent his suffering. With one clean stroke I took off his head. I claimed one of his teeth and burned the rest of his body."

He carefully unfolded an item from his pack holding up Kronk's tooth. The voran tooth looked no different but Malomir handled it with reverence. As Bronwyn launched into one of her own stories Kell shuffled back from the fire to sit closer to Willow. The Alfár showed no signs of discomfort at his proximity. Kell wasn't even sure she knew he was there until she gave him one of those peculiar half smiles.

"Everyone has come on this quest for their own reasons," said Kell. "They all want something but I've no idea why you would put yourself through this. By coming with us your life is at risk. We were lucky with the Hundarians. If not for the Choate turning up we'd already be dead."

Willow cocked her head slightly as he spoke but didn't reply. Nevertheless Kell could see that she was listening.

Kell still had no idea who wanted him dead or why the Choate had come to their rescue. Maybe Lukas and King Bledsoe would know. It might be worth sending them a message from Meer.

"In a few days' time we'll reach the town of Meer. Then we'll be travelling across the ice. The Frozen North is a harsh and dangerous landscape. If you've heard the saga then you know about the creatures living there." Kell took a deep breath to try and calm his nerves about what lay ahead. "Why are you making this journey?"

The Alfár glanced up at the sky and then did something Kell had never seen before. She laughed. It was there and gone. A brief chuff through her nostrils and mouth but he thought it was a chortle, as if she were also wondering why she was here.

"My people and your people are very different," said Willow in a quiet voice that forced Kell to lean forward. For whatever reason she didn't want the others to overhear their conversation. "Some things are the same. Two eyes. One mouth. Most things inside, different," she said, tapping her chest and then her head. "I would know more of what makes you choose. Talking is difficult. Talking is like dancing. There is air and movement. Room for deception. Only in action, in difficult times, is there truth, is there understanding."

"You're putting yourself through all of this, just so that you can better understand humans?"

"It is not the only reason," admitted Willow.

"Then why else are you here?" he asked.

The Alfár fidgeted and seemed uncomfortable with the question hanging between them. Kell waited, despite her reluctance, because he needed to know.

"I wish to understand the beasts that live in the north," she finally said. "Sometimes humans are afraid of an animal because they do not know what it wants. Other times, when the animal lives too close to your settlements, like the mountain lion or the wolf, you kill it."

"Wolves and lions kill cattle and sometimes children."

"They are predators. They are not malicious and take no pleasure in it. Hunting is only for food. For survival."

"I suppose that's true," Kell conceded.

"On the ice, are the beasts the same?"

It was the first time Willow had asked him a question. On the periphery he was aware the others were still talking, except Vahli who was intently watching them from across the fire. Shadows moved across the Alfár's face creating peculiar shapes, reminding him that she wasn't human.

When Kell looked into the eyes of a stranger there was always a connection. With the Alfár that spark was missing. She made him feel uneasy, as if she didn't belong.

"Some of the animals in the Frozen North are different," said Kell, thinking back. There were few details from his ordeal that had faded as they continued to haunt him. "The garrow are cruel. I think they delight in the chase and they kill more than they can eat. Vorans are fierce but maglau are worse. Vicious."

The corners of Willow's mouth lifted. "Something in them is broken," she volunteered.

"Maybe," said Kell. "Or maybe their prey was too abundant and over time they began to enjoy killing."

Somewhere in the distance Kell heard a faint howling. Conversation around the fire dried up as everyone waited. Another wolf answered but its howl sounded even further away than the first.

"They sound close," said Gerren, his eyes wide with terror.

"Having someone keep watch would be a good idea," said Malomir, clapping the boy on the shoulder. "Well done for volunteering to go first."

"What? I never–"

"Four hours, and then I will relieve you," said Malomir, gesturing for Gerren to sit beyond the glow of the fire. The boy was about to protest when he noticed everyone watching. "Don't forget this," said Malomir, offering the boy his sword. Gerren picked up one of the stumps and carried it a short distance away before grumpily sitting down with his back to the fire.

Kell turned to ask Willow another question when he saw that she had lain down with one arm across her face.

"Did I ever tell you about Torru-gora?" said Malomir, directing his question at Bronwyn whom he seemed intent on impressing.

"I'm bored of stories," she said. "I need entertaining."

"I could play you a song?" offered the bard.

"No," said Bronwyn getting to her feet. "You, come with me," she said, gesturing at Kell.

"Where are we going?"

"Somewhere private."

"Why?" asked Kell, although he had a good idea.

"You're famous. You've slept with lots of women, yes?"

"Some," he said. It had actually been very few, and before his night with Anastasia, it had been years since the last time.

"Show me what you've learned," she said, grabbing him by the arm.

"That's very generous," said Kell, struggling to find the right words. "But I'd rather not leave the safety of the fire."

"Don't worry, I'll protect you. Or we can do it here and you can show the others your hairy arse."

"You should try dancing with me," said Malomir. "You won't be disappointed."

"In my experience, men who talk big are small where it counts," said Bronwyn leading Kell away from the fire. She pulled him by the hand through the copse of trees until the glow of the fire was barely visible. There was just enough light to see the outline of her body.

"Come on," she said. He heard what sounded like her sword dropping to the ground and then her armour. "Take off your clothes."

It was the first time in his life that a woman had taken charge and Kell didn't know what to do. He heard the whisper of material and the thump of her boots coming off. When she grabbed him by the waist he nearly screamed in surprise.

"Let's see what you've got," she said, moving a hand over his crotch. As her hand began to rub him Kell was so startled he froze. She tried for a while before they both realised nothing was happening.

"That's disappointing." Bronwyn returned to her pile of clothes and began to get dressed.

"Why did you come on this journey?" asked Kell. In the gloom he couldn't see her face but Kell guessed she was surprised as she paused with one foot off the ground.

"That's what you want to ask me?" she said, gesturing at herself. "You've barely even looked at me."

"I've seen women before."

"There are no women like me," she said. He agreed but held his tongue as she was clearly angry about something else.

"So, why are you here?"

"You're not what I was expecting," muttered Bronwyn under her breath, but with no ambient noise he heard every word. "I came because I was bored."

Kell raised an eyebrow. "That's it? Boredom?"

"Do you have any idea what the last ten years have been like for me?"

"I've been living on a farm in the south," said Kell.

"That sounds boring."

"You'd be surprised," he said with a wry smile. "So what have you been doing?"

Bronwyn snorted. "Everything. I've been travelling across the Five Kingdoms in search of a challenge. Something that would test my limits. Every time there was a story about some monstrous beast causing trouble I tracked it down and we fought. The end was always the same. I won. After that I tried to find someone as strong as me, but there's no one out there. Then I hunted the most dangerous criminals to collect bounties, but even when given the chance, not one of them could defeat me. Do you have any idea what that's like?"

"No, I don't. I'm sorry." Until now Kell had thought Bronwyn fairly shallow but she was deeply troubled. There was a lot of bitterness behind her eyes which he hadn't noticed before.

Life was a constant struggle. Overcoming obstacles made any accomplishment that much sweeter. He'd never been the best at anything but he could imagine how frustrating it must be if everything was always easy.

"So now I just enjoy myself and take what I want, because who is going to stop me? You?" she said, looming over him. Bronwyn raised a fist as if to punch him but when he didn't react she dropped her hand. "Then I heard about your call to arms. It will give me a chance to fight the beasts in the north. Perhaps one of them will prove to be interesting."

"You'll get your wish," said Kell, remembering the dying screams of the heroes. "They're vicious and bloodthirsty."

"Good. I'm looking forward to it," she said with enthusiasm.

"What happens afterwards?"

"After?" said Bronwyn.

"If we go to the north, and somehow survive, what will you do then?" asked Kell.

Bronwyn opened her mouth but quickly closed it again, unable to answer. "I don't know. Look for something else I guess," she said after a long pause.

"What about next year? Or in five years' time? Where do you want to be?"

Once again he could see that she hadn't thought that far ahead. Bronwyn lived only for today. They were of a similar age but it seemed as if she'd never thought about the rest of her life. He had hopes for the future, involving children and a wife, but all of her dreams were limited.

He knew from experience that such big questions were like weights. The more time that passed without addressing them the more difficult they became to ignore. Eventually she'd have to deal with them and think about her future. Kell left her alone to think it over.

Gerren's arse was growing numb from sitting on the tree stump. As if that wasn't bad enough he was too far away from the fire to benefit from the heat. Even worse, Bronwyn had dragged Kell off into the trees. Out of everyone, why did it have to be him? Life just wasn't fair.

Behind him the Alfár was asleep while the bard and Malomir were having a whispered conversation about her.

"The Alfár aren't from the Five Kingdoms," insisted Vahli. "I've studied history."

"My friend, you are mistaken. They were here before us."

"I think she's from across the Narrow Sea," said Gerren, turning around to join their conversation.

"You're supposed to be keeping watch," said Vahli.

"Three more hours, then you can talk with us," said Malomir.

With a sigh Gerren turned back to staring into the dark. His eyes had been dazzled by the fire so it took a while for them to readjust to the gloom.

The two continued to argue about Willow but Gerren wasn't really listening anymore. Instead he looked up at the night sky trying to find something of interest. Clusters of stars glittered above his head whose names he vaguely remembered. As a young boy his mother had told him stories of glorious heroes that had died while saving the world. Because of their bravery the Shepherd cast their bodies into the night sky, immortalising their names with stars. Gerren couldn't understand how he'd ever believed such nonsense.

The truth about heroes, and people in general, was proving to be a lot more complex than he'd realised. He now viewed everything he'd been taught by his parents and school teachers with suspicion. Gerren only had to look at Vahli to realise that not everything was simple. He'd mocked the bard and didn't think very much of him or his profession. But when the Hundarians had attacked them it was the bard who had placed himself between Gerren and the enemy.

Thankfully none of the Hundarians had reached him, but that

hadn't stopped Gerren from being afraid. In contrast Vahli had been utterly calm and poised for a fight that never came. As soon as it was over the bard's first question was to ask if Gerren was injured.

Several times a day Gerren was made aware of how little he knew about the real world and that, up to now, his life had been sheltered. He was beginning to trust his instincts over what he'd been told and what he'd seen with his own eyes. He knew that Vahli was a good man who cared about others. The bard was someone he could trust.

As Gerren's mind turned back to the attack he recalled how the others had fought. Bronwyn had killed two of them in the blink of an eye with the Alfár only a step or two behind. Her peculiar weapon proved to be deadly and she had cut down the Hundarians like she was scything wheat. Even Kell had played a role in the fight. His style was not as graceful as the others but he'd surprised Gerren with his swordsmanship. Maybe he'd been too hasty in turning down training lessons from Kell. He guessed it didn't matter much now as Malomir was teaching him.

Kell could have run but instead had stayed and fought the Hundarians. It didn't make any sense.

As he struggled with an endless series of questions Gerren shifted about the tree stump to stop his arse going numb again. As he watched the darkness he found that his eyes were starting to play tricks on him. There had been nothing to see for hours and now it was creating false images. At one point he thought there was something moving in the darkness. He was about to alert the others when he stopped. Not wanting to embarrass himself, in case it was a rabbit, Gerren walked forward a few steps to take a closer look.

Behind him the horses stirred and one or two whickered but he kept his eyes forward. He could definitely see something moving about but it seemed very slow. Bronwyn had mentioned something about lynx and wildcats that hunted at night. It was probably just a little cat stalking a rabbit.

A second flicker of movement on his right drew his attention and Gerren felt his stomach muscles contract in fear. Something much larger than a wildcat was stalking towards him on the right while something else moved in from the left. As his mouth opened to alert the others he saw several sets of green eyes glowing in the darkness.

The voran pounced.

Gerren screamed and desperately tried to draw his sword. A massive grey and brown beast knocked him backwards forcing the air from his lungs. Its weight pressed down on his chest and it tried to rip out his throat with its teeth. Gerren screamed and thrashed about but the beast held on. He managed to get a forearm under its jaw and fought to keep it back as drool landed on his face. He could feel its back feet clawing at his stomach, trying to disembowel him.

Darkness crept in around the edges of his vision from lack of air. Despite using both arms to keep it back the voran's teeth crept closer to his face. He could smell its fetid breath and see the black edges of its red gums. Pain flared in his stomach as its claws found their mark. Hot blood began to trickle down his sides. Sensing that its prey was growing weaker the beast redoubled its efforts.

Gerren was vaguely aware of other shapes flying past him on either side towards the camp. The rest of the pack would be keeping everyone else busy.

It was at that moment Gerren knew that he was going to die. No help was coming.

CHAPTER 20

The Frozen Circle came into view,
It was the point of no return.
Where the land became a distant memory,
And the ice ruled all.

EXCERPT FROM THE SAGA OF KELL KRESSIA
BY THE BARD PAX MEDINA

The darkness continued to close in on all sides as Gerren fought for his life. The voran was too strong and he couldn't breathe. For a moment he thought about just giving up and letting go. All he had to do was stop fighting. There would be a flash of pain as it ripped out his throat and then it would be over.

In that moment Gerren knew that Kell had been right. He hadn't been anywhere or done anything. He'd only kissed one girl and it had been awkward, their teeth clicking together. He hadn't even left his home town before coming on this trip. What did he know of the world? He'd been so arrogant but it was far too late. This should be the beginning, not the end of his life.

Gerren tried to scream in defiance at the slavering voran as it shook him about but he didn't have air in his lungs. Instead all he could manage was to hiss at it from between clenched teeth and glare.

Something silver flashed past Gerren's left eye and the weight of the voran was lifted off his chest. Wheezing like an old man he took a deep and painful gulp of air. The black spots cleared in time to see Willow flip her strange weapon and bring the mace down on the voran's head. The force of the blow drove the weapon deep into the beast's skull, spraying blood everywhere. The voran dropped to the ground on all fours, blood trickling from its mouth but Gerren could see that it was already dead.

The Alfár knelt down beside Gerren and quickly ran her hands over him. "You will live," she said, despite one of her hands coming away with blood. "Press," she said, guiding his hand to the wound on his right side. Gerren cried out in pain as he pressed down. Willow put a hand beneath his back and another under his knees and suddenly Gerren was flying. He was held against her chest as Willow carried him like a child. Being so close to the Alfár he could smell her. She had a strange musky aroma that he struggled to describe. He felt safe in her arms but all too soon she was setting him down on the ground out of the way. She drew Gerren's sword for him and pushed it into his free hand. Without saying another word she retrieved her weapon and ran back into the fight.

Closer to the fire Gerren could see the others battling a pack of vorans. It was his first glimpse of one from a distance and he noticed they were much larger than normal wolves. Their bodies were also a different shape with sloping backs due to their broad shoulders and long front legs. With short fat necks and wide faces they had powerful jaws that could easily crush bone. In the dancing firelight he saw they had short coats of brown and black fur, flecked with silver.

Several vorans were already on the ground but everyone was still fighting hard against the others. The air was full of growling and snarling from the vorans and shouting from his friends. Rising above it all, rolling across the hills, was Malomir's laughter.

With a graceful swirl of his blade in a downward slice he severed one voran's spine, spun on his back heel and slashed another across the muzzle. And all the while he cackled as if he'd just heard the funniest joke in the world. Kell was right. Malomir was insane.

Beside him Bronwyn fought in deathly silence laying about with her broadsword in tight sweeping arcs, driving back the beasts. When one attacked from the side, launching itself at her, she casually stepped out of the way and sliced off one of its back legs as it sailed past. Before it had a chance to recover she pinned it to the ground, burying the blade deep before ripping it out, spraying blood in an arc. This drove the other vorans into a frenzy and she would have been overrun if not for the Alfár.

With methodical chopping motions like a woodcutter hewing trees, Willow hacked and sliced with her axe. Against her relentless onslaught and her unprecedented strength the vorans fell back but they didn't run.

Spinning her weapon Willow slammed the mace into one beast so hard that it was thrown off its feet. It collided with its neighbour and both went down. Before they could recover Bronwyn stepped forward, driving her blade down through one voran's neck, pinning it to the beast beneath which was also impaled.

On the other side of camp Vahli's whirling daggers reflected in the firelight creating silver arcs in the air. Red lines appeared along the flanks and muzzles of the beasts that yelped and pulled back out of reach. His speed kept them at bay and whenever one of them risked getting closer he stabbed them so quickly Gerren barely saw him move.

Kell was in the midst of the battle too, fighting alongside the bard. With a sword in one hand and a flaming torch in the other he lunged and sliced at the vorans. His face was twisted into a grimace and Gerren didn't know if he was angry or scared.

When Vahli cut one beast across the face it fell back a step giving Kell an opportunity to lunge forward while it was distracted. Kell shoved the torch into its face setting its fur alight. With his other hand his sword came down like an executioner's axe, biting deep into the voran's neck. The blow was badly timed but it still gouged a deep trough. Dark blood ran from the jagged wound and the beast stumbled to the ground. Kell and Vahli fought with stubborn determination, patiently waiting for the right moment, while the others were aggressive, emboldened by their prowess.

Bronwyn and Willow began to fight as a pair, butchering any vorans that were ferocious enough to attack them. Only Malomir fought alone but it quickly became apparent that his skill with the blade was far beyond what Gerren had suspected. Every movement seemed to be part of an elaborate dance as he flowed between every stance. It was as if he could anticipate where the enemy would be and every bite or snap of jaws caught nothing but thin air. Realising they were losing the battle three vorans went after Malomir as he was fighting alone and that was when he began to spin.

His whole body turned, his head whipping around faster than the rest, coming to face forward first. And with it came his heavy blade in a glorious arc of silver, slicing into the beasts. On his left he severed a foreleg, on the right another voran took a cut across the face losing an eye, but the beast in front suffered the worst fate as its head was split open down the middle.

When Gerren heard a growling coming from nearby he spotted a voran stalking towards him. With one hand pressed to his wound Gerren forced himself upright, using his sword for balance. His head swam and he was afraid of blacking out but it quickly settled.

The beast was small compared to the others but it had a network of scars across its face. Gerren frantically tried to remember what he'd seen the others doing with their swords but his mind went blank. The voran drew closer, drool dripping from its muzzle. He saw its eyes focus on his injury and its growling deepened.

At that moment Gerren realised he was the easiest prey in their group.

The scarred beast continued to creep closer but for some reason it didn't attack. The hair on Gerren's neck lifted and he quickly turned his head, alert for danger. Behind him on his left he saw another voran edging closer. When their eyes met it huffed, rose to its feet and charged. Gerren screamed and managed to lift his sword and point it at the wolf hoping to impale it, but its body knocked the blade aside.

This time when its weight landed on him Gerren was prepared. The fall rattled his teeth and the back of his head hit on the ground, but he stubbornly held on to his sword. With his free hand he kept the voran's jaws at bay while trying to stab it with the other. From his eye corner Gerren saw the scarred beast coming towards him and knew that he couldn't fight both of them.

The point of his sword nicked the voran's stomach a few times, drawing blood but none of the wounds were severe. In desperation Gerren brought up both knees towards his chest, momentarily lifting the beast off him. Angling the sword he dropped his legs and his arm was driven towards the ground as the voran's full weight landed on him again. Its growl turned into a howl of pain that deafened him in one ear as his blade was driven into its body. With blood-slicked hands he tried to drive the sword deeper but only managed to saw it back and forth, opening up the wound.

Something hot and sticky flowed over his body and steaming innards flopped out of the beast. With its remaining strength it yanked the weapon from his hand and tried to escape. It managed a few steps, leaving a trail of intestines and blood, before flopping down on its side. Gerren's sword was still buried in its body up to the hilt leaving him defenceless.

The scarred voran showed far more teeth than he'd seen before. Gerren thought it was smiling at him. A moment later its head was smashed to a pulp as Willow's mace came down with lethal force. The Alfár nudged the voran with her boot but it was already dead. Stumbling to his feet Gerren approached the beast he'd wounded and saw although it was still alive it was close to death.

He was about to retrieve his sword when Willow knelt down beside the voran. Instead of killing the beast she held up one hand just above the voran's head as if bestowing a benediction. Gerren didn't know how the Alfár dealt with death. He didn't know if she was praying or doing something else. Willow's eyes were closed so she didn't see Gerren moving nearer to get a better view. But there was nothing to see. The beast had died but the Alfár was still focused on it, as if searching for something.

Glancing around the camp he saw the fight was over. All of the vorans were dead and everyone else was alive.

When Gerren turned back Willow was yanking his sword from the voran's corpse. The Alfár held the blade out to him still dripping with blood and viscera. For the first time since he'd stolen the sword from his dad Gerren didn't want it. Willow sensed his reluctance but insisted.

"There's always a cost," she said.

When Gerren took the sword he thought its weight had doubled. It took three attempts before he was able to sheathe it over his shoulder. A wave of tiredness swept through his entire body and he stumbled.

"Are you injured, lad?" asked Malomir, resting a steading hand on his shoulder.

"My side," he said, remembering where the voran had cut him.

"Sit down, let's take a look," said Malomir, directing him towards a spot by the fire. Vahli was adding more fuel to the blaze while Bronwyn checked to make sure all of the beasts were actually dead.

Kell was sitting on the far side of the fire staring at his blood covered hands. His sword lay forgotten on the ground and his eyes were haunted. Gerren could see his lips were moving but he couldn't hear the words.

Malomir probed the wound in his side and Gerren yelped in pain. "You're lucky, it's not too deep. Your brigandine held up for the most part. A few stitches and you'll be fine."

"I couldn't breathe," said Gerren, remembering the weight of the voran on his chest, its claws and the stench of its breath. His stomach muscles began to clench and his hands shook uncontrollably. A fresh wave of sweat erupted from his pores and the trembling became worse. "I couldn't breathe," he said again and suddenly it was true. He couldn't get a full breath. He was suffocating and there was something constricting his chest. Gerren pulled at the collar of his shirt which was too tight. He scrabbled at the straps of his armour but his fingers wouldn't work.

"Easy lad, easy," said Malomir, helping him out of his jacket. "You're safe now. You're safe, Gerren." He kept murmuring platitudes but the frantic pounding of Gerren's heart told him it wasn't true. He was in danger. "Hold on, it will pass."

"Need to get away," said Gerren. He didn't know where he was going. It just had to be away. He tried to stand up but Malomir kept him in place with a firm grip on his shoulder.

"Drink this," he said, pressing something cold and metallic into Gerren's hands. He took a deep pull thinking it was water and immediately felt the burn of something down the back of his throat. The fiery alcohol had a spicy aftertaste and it quickly kindled a blaze in his stomach. "Take another drink. Slowly now," said Malomir. Gerren took a smaller sip and the heat spread to his extremities. His fingers and toes tingled and the danger felt a little further away.

He didn't know how much time passed but at some point his heart began to slow. The shaking eased and the tight band of pain around his chest faded.

Gerren came back to himself, bent forward over his knees staring down at the ground as he took deep breaths. He stayed like that for a while listening to the rest of the camp. When he straightened he expected laughter at his expense but no one was paying him any attention.

Bronwyn and Malomir were clearing away the dead bodies, dragging the wolves into the darkness. Kell was sipping from Malomir's flask and although his hands weren't shaking there was definitely something wrong with him. Kell's eyes were too wide and although he was staring at the fire Gerren could see that his mind was elsewhere.

"Feeling better?" asked Vahli, sitting down beside him. In one hand he was carrying a small leather case.

"Is he all right?" whispered Gerren gesturing towards Kell.

The bard opened the case to reveal a sewing kit replete with an assortment of needles and colourful thread. "He'll be fine. Lift up your shirt."

"Do you know what you're doing?"

"I thought I'd be using this to repair my clothing, not stitch you up, but I'm more than capable." The bard threaded the needle with ease and held up the shiny pin to the light. "Unless you'd rather do it yourself?"

Gerren swallowed hard and turned away. He didn't want to watch the needle being stuck into his flesh. Clenching his jaw Gerren gestured for the bard to get on with it. By the time it was done Gerren was hissing through his teeth. Risking a glance at the wound he saw a neat row of small stitches holding the puckered flesh together.

"Use some of the citrus root," said Malomir, handing a bulging pouch to the bard. Inside were several packets of herbs, bandages and peculiar dried plants Gerren had never seen before.

"What does it do?" asked Gerren as Malomir added water to a small amount of yellow root. He mashed it together until it formed a paste which he lightly applied to the wound.

"It speeds up the healing and prevents scars," he said.

In addition to the salve they wrapped him in a bandage which prevented Gerren from having to look at the injury.

Moving around the camp the bard used his nimble fingers and Malomir's herbs to treat wounds for Bronwyn and then Kell. He was still in a fugue, staring at nothing. He didn't even flinch when Vahli jabbed him with the needle. Malomir had avoided any injuries and Willow declined when the bard pointed at his sewing kit and herbs. Gerren had seen the Alfár fighting up close. She had thrown the voran off him with ease and smashed the skull of another to a pulp. She was far stronger than any of them realised. She had also saved his life twice in one fight.

Gerren's limbs felt unsteady but he forced himself upright, wincing as the stitches in his side were pulled tight. With shuffling feet he approached where the Alfár was crouched. She sat in the shadows a short distance from the fire but her eyes were focused on the flames.

"I just wanted to say thank you," said Gerren. Willow didn't look up at him but he saw her body shift in his direction. "You saved my life. So I just wanted to say that. To give thanks." Even after travelling with the Alfár for a few days there were times when he wasn't sure if she really understood their language. She had peculiar gaps that he thought she bridged with silence, letting people ramble on until they said something she recognised.

Willow briefly made eye contact and she gave him what he hoped was a smile before returning her gaze to the fire. The others hadn't noticed her ritual with the voran. Gerren that knew he should leave it alone but curiosity made him ask.

"What were you doing with the dying wolf?" Her unsettling yellow eyes shifted and he felt the full weight of her stare. Gerren's bowels threatened to loosen and he swallowed the lump in his throat but didn't turn away. "Were you searching for something? Or praying?"

"Not praying," said Willow. Gerren noticed she was no longer smiling at him. Perhaps she already regretted saving his life. "Looking for the malice."

"What does that mean?"

"Its heart was pure." Willow sounded pleased but Gerren had no idea why. Sensing their conversation was over he shuffled closer to the fire and flopped down on his blanket. He shouldn't have bothered asking. Speaking to the Alfár never made any sense.

After such a fight he'd expected drinking and laughter with each of the heroes telling the others about their best kills. Instead a peculiar hush had fallen over everyone. Bronwyn was busy cleaning her weapons but he could see her mind was far away. Kell had apparently gone to sleep and even the normally boastful Malomir was lost in thought.

Vahli had taken the next watch but he was furiously scribbling away in his journal, head bent towards the page. An army could march through their camp and the bard wouldn't notice. Gerren wondered what Vahli would write about him. How would he be portrayed during the fight? As a cowering child who had to be rescued? Is that how he would be remembered in years to come?

Perhaps Vahli would ask him what he'd been thinking about during the fight. That meant he would have to lie. He couldn't tell anyone he'd thought about giving up, otherwise they'd call him a coward. Then he'd be no better than Kell.

Looking at Kell's back, Gerren remembered how he'd stood shoulder to shoulder with the bard. He hadn't run. It him wonder again how much of the Medina saga was true.

Gerren felt off balance but this time it wasn't a hangover from the fight. Every truth he'd held dear, foundations upon which he'd built his beliefs, were turning out to be lies. He didn't know who he could trust which left him only with his instincts.

Right now he was certain of only one thing. He'd come very close to dying. If not for the others he would be a slab of cold meat. The thought of being moments away from death again terrified him more than anything. He realised his gut was sure about something else as well. Leaving home to chase after Kell had been the biggest mistake of his life.

For the first time since he'd come on the journey, Gerren thought about running away.

CHAPTER 21

Every night they slept in the cold,
With death all around them, above and below.
For if the ice should break,
No one would find their watery graves.

EXCERPT FROM THE SAGA OF KELL KRESSIA
BY THE BARD PAX MEDINA

The morning after the fight brought little in the way of relief. Kell had slept fitfully and woke with a stiff back and sore neck from lying awkwardly on the ground. The muscles in his shoulders ached from swinging his sword and it was only now that he noticed the bandages across his left arm and ribs. He didn't remember anyone sewing him up but then again he didn't remember much that had happened after the fight. He had a vague memory of watching the fire but little else.

Rain had fallen in the night leaving the ground soggy underfoot. As he relieved himself against a tree his yellow stream merged with other rivulets running downhill. Faint patches of mist clung to the ground but they did little to conceal the bodies of the vorans. They had already attracted a swarm of flies and once they'd moved on, a horde of scavengers and insects would come to feast until all that was left was a heap of bones and scraps of fur.

Kell stared down at the corpse of a black and grey voran. Even in murky daylight it was no less intimidating. They didn't look like any other animal he'd ever seen. Neither dog nor bear nor wolf, but a horrible jumbled mix of all three. If the priests were right and the Shepherd had created all of the beasts and birds then the Almighty had a twisted sense of humour. Why would He create such a vicious killing machine? What purpose did it serve? Did it exist to inspire fear? Was that its purpose, to remind everyone of their mortality?

A huge purple tongue lolled from its open mouth which was full of sharp yellow teeth. One blue eye seemed to be watching him as he bent down to get a closer look. Its fur was cold and damp to the touch and beneath that its flesh felt like stone. It wasn't particularly ripe but there was a faint whiff of rot that would only get worse.

Fighting against the Hundarians had been unexpected but it hadn't crippled him. Last night had been too familiar. It had brought back a host of old memories where he'd watched the heroes being torn apart. First by the vorans and later by the vicious maglau. More than seeing the wolves it was their musky aroma that had triggered the memory.

Somehow the past and the present had merged in his head. He'd been fighting with Vahli against the vorans, but at the same time he'd been a scared boy standing beside Bron and Kursen battling for their lives.

When the last beast was cut down by Willow he should have felt elated but instead he'd been numb. All he could focus on was the blood. It was everywhere. Splashed across the ground. On his clothing and in his hair. He even had some on his face and had tasted it by accident. Some of the blood was his and some belonged to the wolves, but there was just so much. Only now as he stared down at the dead vorans did it realise how much of it had been in his mind.

"Claiming a souvenir?" asked Malomir. The mad Islander held up another tooth, bloody at one end. "I took this one off the grey beast that tried to gut me last night." He laughed at that, as if the idea of dying was funny, or perhaps he was simply glad to be alive. Or he was just cracked in the head, which was the most likely explanation. Kell had seen him during the fight and didn't think he'd been in any real danger. There wasn't a scratch on him compared to everyone else. Gerren had been lucky. If not for the others, and his armour, he would have been ripped apart.

"We should get moving," said Kell, leaving the voran's teeth alone. "It's going to take us at least another two days to reach Meer."

They rode out under a murky grey sky that stretched unbroken to the horizon. The overnight rain had vitalised the grass and heather, making the colours more vivid, but it did little to lift his spirits. The others were equally subdued and for a time they all rode in silence. A fine rain began to fall and then it refused to let up for hours. By the time they stopped to eat lunch Kell's skin was clammy and his clothing soaked through. Water continually trickled down the back of his neck and after a while he began to shiver in the saddle.

Despite the awful weather everyone remained alert for danger. It didn't matter that they didn't see another living soul or any large animals. Their heightened watchfulness never wavered. Kell's head dipped towards his saddle a couple of times but he saw the others were just as tired.

The afternoon was equally miserable and long before nightfall Kell made a beeline for a small forest. No one complained about stopping early as they all needed to rest. The thick canopy was a blessing as it allowed him to find dry wood for a fire. Only the Alfár was unaffected by the weather despite the fact that her clothing was also wet. It made him wonder how she would fare with extreme cold in the Frozen North.

Once everyone had changed into a dry set of clothing and the fire was built up, absent smiles began to return. They hung up their soggy clothes to dry and settled into the same routine from the previous night. Malomir immediately took up the two staves and began running Gerren through a series of drills. Kell expected the boy to complain but tonight he practised in silence. Perhaps his close encounter with the vorans had made him realise the danger. Once warmed up they began to spar but each round came to the same inevitable conclusion with Malomir delivering a killing blow. After each death he would instruct the boy on his mistake. Gerren listened intently and never said a single word.

While Kell tended to the fire Vahli prepared the food. Willow picked up her weapon and walked out of camp. Less than an hour later she returned with four fat grouse which Bronwyn butchered for the pot. They ate well and stayed close to the fire as beyond the trees the rain continued to fall. The patter of rain dripping off the leaves was so soothing that Kell began to doze by the fire.

This time when Malomir called for someone to take first watch there were no complaints. Willow surprised everyone by standing up and moving to stand beyond the glow of the fire, facing outwards towards the dark.

"I guess that means she's taking first watch," said Vahli.

"She comes from somewhere hot, in the east," said Malomir.

Their discussion from the previous night resumed but no answers were forthcoming. Willow must have been able to overhear their conversation but she didn't offer an answer. To change the subject Kell asked Bronwyn to tell them about one of her adventures. Unlike Malomir she wasn't as verbose. The bard had to extract the full story with a series of questions as he made notes in his journal. As she spoke Kell looked into the darkness. At first he couldn't see the Alfár. She was so perfectly still, Willow was more like one of the trees than a person.

The warmth of the fire, the patter of the rain and the murmur of voices lulled him asleep. He came awake a few hours later as Vahli gently shook him by the shoulder.

"Your turn on watch," he said before lying down. The rest of the night passed without incident with Kell keeping watch until the sun rose.

The morning was frosty and for the first time Kell felt it was cold enough to wear gloves. As they continued on the road north the temperature continued to fall until everyone was wrapped up in multiple layers of clothing.

This far north in Kinnan the land became even more rugged. The sea of grass continued but now it was an unpleasant yellow marred with patches of dead brown earth. The terrain was like a rumpled piece of cloth making it difficult to see very far in any direction. In addition dozens of bulbous protrusions of granite, twice as tall as a man, blocked their view. Scrubby bushes which had forced their way up through cracks in the stones were the closest thing they'd find to firewood. Deceptively appealing bright orange mushrooms and beige moss flourished in shadowy nooks breaking up the monotonous colour of the land. Kell had always hated this place and thought it was a miserable part of the world. He couldn't think of a worse place to live and yet some people had chosen it as their home.

At midday they passed through a knot of houses, not large enough to even be called a village, as there wasn't a tavern or anything designed for travellers. Fashioned from quarried stone the six houses stood protectively around a central well. One of the locals sold them some bread but they had little else to spare and every face was lean and weather-beaten. They refilled their waterskins from the well and moved on.

Flurries of snow drifted down and the horses' breath began to steam, apart from the Nhill. Whatever Willow had done to the creature it didn't seem affected by the weather, but then again, neither was the Alfár. Everyone else wore gloves, scarves and hats, but she was still dressed in only a shirt, a light coat and thin trousers.

Kell knew they couldn't reach Meer by nightfall but none of them were particularly keen on the idea of sleeping outside in the cold. They kept the horses to a brisk pace, slowing to rest them often but always moving forward.

When the murky sky began to darken they moved off the road which had frozen solid into a mosaic of rock-hard grass and mud. The only shelter they could find was in the shadow of a large cluster of rocks in the lee of a hill. It kept them out of the wind but with no wood to burn Kell knew they were in for an uncomfortable night.

Kell wrapped himself in a blanket and ate a cold meal of bread, cheese and fruit. Malomir and Gerren didn't spar and for once Willow remained within the camp. The air was so clear Kell found he was staring up at the sky and the few bright stars visible overhead. A short time later another dusting of snow began to fall, slowly coating everything in white.

"Was it this cold last time?" asked Vahli, whose teeth were chattering despite his gloves, hat and blanket.

"No, it was worse," said Kell. "When we stopped off at those houses, their well was frozen solid. We had to wait until we reached Meer for fresh water."

"Then it's not as bad this time."

"Maybe."

"What's does that mean?" asked the bard. Kell noticed the others were listening as well and he thought they deserved to know the truth.

"Last time no one knew what it meant. When the weather changed they were unprepared and a lot of people starved. This time, people should've realised sooner and made plans. Instead they just stood around, doing nothing, waiting to be saved. Even if we stop this, whatever it is, the harvest is going to be lean this year. It's going to get a lot worse before it gets better."

"Well, that's an uplifting thought," said Vahli. "Malomir. Perhaps you could tell us another story."

The Islander was trimming his beard but the opportunity to be the centre of attention was too much for him. He loved an audience as much as the bard and happily put down the mirror and knife.

"Did I ever tell you about the time I fought a chimera on the Summer Isles?" said Malomir.

"A what?" asked Gerren.

"Do you not have them here?"

The boy's expression was incredulous but for once he wasn't alone in his scepticism. "There's no such thing."

"Of course there is," said Malomir with another stupid laugh. He was always laughing. Kell's first impression had been right. The Islander was mad. Everything seemed to amuse him. Even the prospect of his own death during a fight. "They're about the size of a striped jungle cat, but they have two heads instead of one."

"That's not a chimera," said Vahli. "They're supposed to have a ram's head and a snake for a tail."

"I think you're confused, my friend," said Malomir. "What you're describing is a myth."

"And what you're talking about belongs in a carnival tent," said Kell. "I once saw a cow with two heads. That doesn't make it a chimera!"

"This was no cow. It was a fearsome and vicious beast," said Malomir, who was still smiling, but now it was through his teeth. Kell shook his head and Gerren laughed.

"Did you ever see another chimera like it?" asked the bard.

"No, it was the only one."

"There you are then!" said Vahli.

"It was a chimera," insisted Malomir.

"Just shut your mouth," said Bronwyn. Her voice was low and Kell could see the tension in her shoulders. Malomir ignored her but the others fell silent and moved away from Bronwyn. Only Willow seemed immune to the sudden change in atmosphere. "All you do is lie, all day long. All of your stories are lies."

"I never lie."

"Shut up!" roared Bronwyn, storming to her feet. Malomir didn't seem intimidated as he slowly rose to face her. Gerren scuttled out of the way so that there was no one standing between them.

"Or what?" asked the Islander, raising an eyebrow. "Is your blood boiling? Are you angry?" he said, but Bronwyn didn't need to answer. "What will you do? Fight me? Or maybe you'll drag someone else off into the dark to scratch the itch. Maybe Willow or what about the boy? You could give Gerren a real lesson."

At the mention of his name the boy started to stand up, a hopeful expression on his face, but Vahli pulled him back down. "Idiot boy," muttered the bard, clipping him around the ear.

"I'm sick of your bragging. Sick of your stories," said Bronwyn. She was breathing heavily and Kell noticed her hands had tightened into fists.

Malomir remained calm and utterly still. "That's not the reason. I think you're afraid."

Bronwyn laughed. "You think I'm afraid of you? I've never lost a fight against any man or beast. I always win."

"Exactly. You're afraid that you'll always be alone. That you'll never meet your match. You're lonely."

With a roar Bronwyn launched herself at the Islander as if she were going to throttle him to death. With uncanny grace he danced to one side and tripped her as she went past. The warrior's legs tangled together and she stumbled to one knee. She was back on her feet in a flash, trying to make another grab for him. Malomir grabbed one of her wrists, pulled her forward off balance and tossed her over his hip. Bronwyn let out a squawk of surprise before she went flying upside down and landed heavily on her back, driving the breath from her body.

Wheezing she rolled over onto her side and made it onto all fours, taking deep gulps of air. Her breathing was returning to normal but before she'd fully recovered she pushed herself upright and attacked again. This time she came forward more cautiously and when Malomir tried to dodge to one side she grabbed him by the arm and drubbed him across the face with her right fist. His head snapped back but it didn't seem to slow him down as he retaliated with a jab of his own. The blow barely moved Bronwyn's head but the look of surprise on her face quickly faded. She touched her nose and came away with a small streak of blood.

Kell wondered about the last time she'd been punched in the face and what had happened to her opponent.

Bronwyn's expression turned into something ugly and with a feral roar she charged at Malomir. Lifting him off the ground around the waist she flung him bodily through the air. Before he'd really settled she pounced on top and tried to hammer his head through the ground. He moved his head to one side and her fist slammed into a rock instead. As she reared back in pain he scissored his legs, caught her in a head lock and flipped her to one side.

Biting and snarling, the two of them rolled away down the hill, punching and kicking each other. Kell could still hear them in the darkness but they quickly faded from view.

"Shouldn't we go after them?" asked Gerren. "Try to stop the fight?"

"You're more than welcome to try," said Vahli. "But I'd rather not get in the middle of those two."

"But they're trying to kill each other," said the boy.

"If they wanted that they would have drawn their weapons," said Kell. The boy ignored him and kept staring into the darkness. Somewhere in the distance Kell could still hear the pair of them fighting and he wondered how long it would go on.

Willow glanced into the dark and Kell thought she was about to say something. Instead the Alfár wrapped herself up in a blanket and lay down. With nothing else to do Kell did the same but sleep evaded him.

The ground was hard but it wasn't that cold, not yet any way. He'd experienced far worse in the past. On the journey south, after he'd killed the Lich, Kell had made a promise to himself that he'd never be that cold again. He'd also sworn that he would never return to the north and now he was breaking his word twice.

A noise drew his attention and he looked up in time to see Bronwyn and Malomir returning to camp. Their clothes were torn and bloody, each had bruises on their face and Malomir was limping on one side. But they were smiling and he could smell the sex on them.

Bronwyn lay down and the Islander spooned up behind her,

before covering them both with a blanket. He heard muffled laughter and the low murmur of voices before they eventually settled down.

Rolling over Kell tried to get comfortable but found no relief. As much as the pain in his back bothered him it wasn't what stopped him falling asleep. He'd fought monsters most people thought were myths. He'd changed the fate of the Five Kingdoms and yet, despite all of that, he was still afraid. He had many fears but if he was honest, the worst was that he'd die without anyone really knowing him. The real him, not the facade everyone talked about.

In the early hours of the morning, bone-tired and sandy-eyed he realised something else. As a young man he'd always chosen the easy path. Kell had never pushed himself to the limit until it became a matter of life or death. Fighting alongside the heroes he came to realise they weren't great men. Most of them were greedy, selfish and arrogant. He'd aspired to be them until he saw past the illusion they projected. Away from other people the masks came off and he saw their ugliness.

After that all he'd wanted was to be better than them. Now, they were all dead and he was alive, but people still talked about the heroes.

No one really knew what he was capable of, least of all himself, but Kell decided that now was the time to find out.

CHAPTER 22

The glistening spires rose high into the frozen air,
A beautiful nightmare surrounded by death.
And waiting within was the Lich,
The architect of an endless winter.

EXCERPT FROM THE SAGA OF KELL KRESSIA
BY THE BARD PAX MEDINA

At the end of another long and blustery day they finally arrived in Meer, the most northern settlement in Kinnan.

Throughout the morning Kell had noticed the scrubland gradually changing, becoming more level with fewer rocky growths. The hills became smaller while the temperature continued to fall. A constant flurry of snow followed them throughout the entire day, sometimes gusting straight into their faces, sometimes blowing hard against their backs. Everyone was wrapped up head to toe and yet somehow a little snow managed to get inside their clothes. Even Willow had finally covered up in a thick jacket and gloves but had decided to forgo a hat. Kell wondered if she felt the cold at all and was merely covering up to make them feel more comfortable.

Already hard underfoot the mud was replaced with a sea of frozen soil that crunched under the horses' hooves. The permafrost stunted the growth of everything except the hardiest lichen. It sadly added no colour to the dull and seemingly lifeless tundra.

Across the plain, rainwater gathered in small depressions creating stagnant pools covered with floating yellow scum and insects. There were no birds, plants or trees and no signs of life except for biting flies. The featureless landscape extended to the horizon making it difficult to judge distance.

For three hours in the afternoon they rode across the blank tundra. The only way to know they were making any progress was the movement of the hazy sun overhead. Hidden behind a solid blanket of cloud it provided no heat and little in the way of light. They all travelled in a daze, seemingly trapped in a monotonous nightmare that was without apparent end.

Finally, as the sun began to weaken, the ground started to change. Broken rocks and jagged pieces of stone disrupted the featureless surface. It was now cold enough for the drifting snow to settle and deep banks began to form creating the illusion of hills and valleys. Gradually a black dot appeared on the horizon which slowly grew in size.

An hour later as they rode down to Meer the track became a sea of mud, churned up by the constant passage of travellers. As the entirety of the settlement was revealed they all took a moment to study it.

"What a shit-hole," said Gerren. It was the first time the boy had seen it but Kell was in agreement. Ten years on and it was still the same festering pile of rotting buildings that looked as if they would blow away in a strong breeze. Crumbling slabs of basalt formed the walls of the dozen large buildings that were visible above ground. Their roofs were a jumbled network of rare and precious wood, waxed sheets, rope and hides which were constantly being repaired to make them waterproof. Icicles hung from every surface and deep banks of snow sat against the western wall of each building.

More common were bulbous stone arches set low to the ground. These led to subterranean homes and businesses that sat under a permanent layer of thick ice. Dozens of stone chimneys poked out of the ground, each one spewing a column of grey smoke. The buildings above ground were reserved for businesses that couldn't be under the ice including the farrier, the stable, the abattoir and the tannery. A cloud of noxious gas hung over the last, adding an unpleasant miasma to the already strange brew of smells.

To the west of town were the homes of the nomadic Frostrunner clans who periodically visited Meer to trade. Their hide-covered yurts sat in neat lines, beyond which were vast herds of reindeer. The huge beasts provided almost everything the clans needed and the rest came from bartering meat, fur, animal hide and horn. To the east of town, as far away as possible from all other animals, were the kennels where dozens of yapping sled-dogs were being reared and trained.

Beyond the settlement to the north, glittering like thousands of jewels scattered carelessly on the ground, was a sea of snow and ice. At first it appeared to be featureless but Kell's eyes began to pick out other colours; pale blues, deep purples and even splashes of red from buried algae. There were some colours he couldn't name and was surprised that he'd forgotten about them over the last ten years. A day's travel to the north was the Frozen Circle. An unmarked line on the sea of ice where the land ended and the only thing beneath your feet was icy cold water.

"Let's get something to drink," said Kell, steering his horse towards the stable. The others followed except Willow who held back and then dismounted from her creature.

"The Nhill cannot stay here while we travel on the ice. It would not survive," said the Alfár, gesturing at the town. "I will take care of it and follow."

Kell had a good idea what Willow meant and quickly turned away. He didn't want to see what happened. At some point in the past the Alfár's mount had been a living, breathing horse, but not any more. Perhaps it was mercy to end its suffering.

The largest building above ground, and still in the best condition, was the stable. Before they reached the huge doors Kell was met by a tall Hundarian dressed in furs. The man had arms as thick as Bronwyn's and a dent in one side of his skull. When he smiled, which was often, there were several missing teeth on one side of his mouth. Bomani's beard was a little more grey than Kell remembered but other than that he hadn't changed in ten years.

"Here you are," said the stablemaster, as if he knew they were coming. He embraced Kell in a huge bear-hug, lifting him off the ground with ease. His laugh was a low rumbling sound that came from deep in his chest. Its familiarity immediately put Kell at ease. "I was just telling someone about you. A little scrap of a lad and now look at you. All grown up with a beard."

"It's been a long time," said Kell.

"Too long," said Bomani.

"Given how much you drink, I'm amazed you still remember me," said Kell.

"Ahhh, I'm a big man, with big appetites," said Bomani, patting his slightly round belly. "Besides, how could I forget my favourite adventurer?"

Kell made the introductions and then for the sake of appearances haggled about the price of stabling their horses. He knew the stablemaster was giving him a fair price but he'd missed Bomani's warmth. Without really knowing how long they would be on the ice, and if they would even make it back, Kell paid for a few extra days. He knew his old friend wouldn't sell their horses the day the money ran out. If they all died on the ice Bomani would make sure the animals went to a good home. The stablemaster wouldn't still be working with horses if he didn't care about them, especially after one of them had knocked out half of his teeth and dented his skull.

"Will I see you for a drink later?" asked Kell.

"Of course. It's your turn to pay," said Bomani.

They left the horses with him then went to find lodgings.

"What about dogs and sleds?" asked Vahli.

"Tomorrow, please. I want to sleep in a real bed. This will be our last chance."

"My arse is frozen solid from the saddle and I can't feel my toes," said Bronwyn.

"I could do with a warm meal," added Malomir.

Since King Bledsoe had been so generous, and with contributions from the others, they had enough money to pay for their own rooms at the Lucky Fish tavern. Even though he entered his own room Kell suspected Malomir wouldn't be spending much time in his bed. Kell made sure his own room wasn't next to Bronwyn's before he went in search of a hot bath.

Two huge pools of steaming water sat in a large underground chamber. Heated from boreholes dug deep into the earth, the hot springs were the only thing Kell had missed about Meer. After stripping naked he scrubbed his skin all over with soap and a coarse brush then lathered off with warm water. Only then was he allowed to get into the glorious hot water. His body ached and he was already sick of feeling cold. Kell heard other people coming and going but he kept his eyes closed. The heat seeped into his body and gradually it warmed him through. After a while Kell began to sweat but he stayed until his muscles had eased.

Back in his room he dressed in clean clothes, brushed his hair with his fingers and felt like a new man. With his stomach growling he went in search of food and a cold beer.

Like all of the buildings underground the corridors of the tavern were narrow and the ceiling low. It made Kell slightly claustrophobic but at least he didn't have to walk hunched over like Bronwyn whose head scraped on the ceiling. The only place where she could stand upright was in the centre of the main room which descended in concentric rings. People sat on cushions on the floor on all levels or stood at the bar which resided in the bottom of the shallow bowl.

The crowd in the Lucky Fish were a mix of people from across the Five Kingdoms but all of them were cut from the same cloth. Grizzled, hardy and hairy. Every face was lean and there wasn't a man in the room without a beard or moustache to keep them warm. Regardless of origin all of them, men and women, had skin like worn leather. Chafed by the wind, rain and glare of the sun, faces often had a pale lower half from being permanently covered and a tanned upper half.

Those who came to Meer did so because it was necessary. No merchant would volunteer to travel to the coldest place in the world. Those with the means forced others to do it in their stead. The people here were the kind who needed the money and couldn't say no. Every visitor was hard-working, straightforward and without airs and graces.

Red-shirted Seith mixed with Keen, Hundarians and Alganians without any of the usual rivalry. Dotted in among the familiar faces Kell saw clusters of ice-dwellers. The Frostrunners always slept in their yurts when visiting Meer but they often stayed for a few drinks after trading with the locals. In truth the clans were the true natives and everyone else was a visitor this far north but they never complained. They relied on their southern neighbours for many things they couldn't find here.

Around the upper ring of the room there were stacks of fur-edged coats and boots, drip-drying, while everyone walked around in their socks or bare feet. Kell happily yanked off his boots and left them beside the pile. The tiled mosaic floor shone from being polished by so many feet and light came from lanterns set in alcoves around the room. Nothing hung from the ceiling, which was made from a huge slab of grey stone. Around it were a number of hidden narrow channels that allowed air to circulate, although it didn't stop the room from smelling like wet dog. Heat came from four stout metal stoves which were constantly being fed with a supply of reindeer dung.

Kell had barely started on his first beer when the others joined him at the bar. Malomir and Bronwyn had bathed as their wet hair shone in the light. Gerren was still a little pungent from the saddle but he probably wasn't used to bathing with strangers.

As it was his last chance to entertain, the bard had changed into one of his garish outfits, a mix of green and purple that jarred the eye. Vahli carried his instrument carefully in both hands and many people followed his progress through the bar. When the Alfár entered the room a few heads turned in surprise, and one or two people stared, but they quickly went back to minding their own business.

"How about something to eat?" suggested Kell, once everyone had a drink.

Sat around one of the low tables they ate generous slabs of reindeer steak, dripping in a tangy apple and redcurrant sauce, with greens and roasted potatoes. The black beer was icy cold and for once the bard didn't turn up his nose in favour of wine. Willow ate everything on her plate except the meat which the others shared between them. For a short time there was the illusion of harmony around their table, but all too soon it fell apart.

"Boy, you smell," said Vahli, nudging Gerren with an elbow. "You should bathe."

"I was going to, but there were other people in there. Naked people. Some of them were women," whispered the boy.

"No one cares. There's nothing to be afraid of," said Vahli, trying to put the boy at ease. Gerren's face turned pale and he hurried from the room. "What is wrong with him?" The bard shook his head then excused himself to entertain his audience.

"Poor lad. I doubt he's ever seen a naked woman before," said Malomir, gulping down the last of his ale.

"Well, don't look at me," said Bronwyn. "I'm not going to show him."

"I think that's a good idea. You'd ruin him. Then he'd think every woman was like you," said Malomir.

"That's true," she said and Malomir laughed.

She was unlike any other woman Kell had ever met. When she and Malomir had first argued he'd thought the Islander was wide of the mark. Wherever she went, even among her own people, Bronwyn would stand out. People viewed her with respect, but she would forever be an oddity that didn't fit anywhere.

She'd needed to find someone who was her equal. For whatever reason it seemed as if she'd found that in Malomir. Kell didn't understand why the Islander was on this journey, but the loneliness he'd sensed from the mad man had faded of late. He was glad they'd found each other.

"What are you grinning about?" asked Bronwyn.

"Nothing," he said. "I'm going to check on the horses."

As he pulled on his boots the first notes of a tune echoed around the room from Vahli's oud. His nimble fingers danced across the strings and a complex and mournful melody filled the space. Every face turned towards the bard whose presence swelled under the scrutiny of so many fans. His reason for coming to the north wasn't a mystery. Vahli couldn't bear living in the shadows of mediocre talent like Pax Medina. It was selfish and petty but no different from any of them. None of them were here, with the possible exception of Willow, for selfless reasons.

At the moment the Alfár was watching Vahli perform an old classic with what Kell thought was a puzzled expression. Malomir and Bronwyn had snuck off somewhere leaving her alone at the table but Willow didn't seem to notice. As much as she was watching the story unfold, Willow was studying the crowd with the same baffled curiosity. At a distance the Alfár looked similar to everyone else and yet they were fundamentally different. What stories would Willow tell her people about them if she made it home?

Kell bought two beers from the bar and snuck them out the front door into the freezing cold.

In Meer the hours of darkness were shorter than elsewhere and the further north they went, the fewer they became. As they travelled across the ice they would quickly reach a point where the sun didn't set at all. It would stay like that throughout the summer until the autumn equinox when blessed darkness returned.

Slush and mud squelched at Kell's boots as he slogged down the street towards the stable. Warm yellow light showed through a crack in the doors which he took as a sign that Bomani was still inside. As Kell raised his hand to knock on the wicket gate he heard raised voices. He couldn't make out the words but the low patient rumble told him the stablemaster was one of the speakers. The other voice was muffled but familiar. Kell eased open the door and slipped inside hoping he wouldn't be noticed. Standing at the far end of the stables Bomani was deep in conversation, trying to persuade Gerren not to leave Meer.

Gerren raced out of the bar and headed straight to his room. This had all been a terrible mistake. He should never have come on this journey. He should have turned back when Kell had given him the chance, especially when he'd been tied to a tree. He should have gone home, said he was sorry, and carried on with his real life. But he'd been too stubborn and proud. He'd been determined to prove that Kell was a coward. It didn't even matter anymore, he was no better because he wanted to run away.

Every night the dream was the same. His armour didn't hold and the voran tore him apart, but he didn't die straight away. Instead he watched as it feasted on his innards, gulping them down like sausages.

He'd wake up sweating, crying sometimes, muffling the sound by stuffing a blanket in his mouth until it passed. He'd wipe his face, tell himself it would be all right because he was surrounded by heroes, but it didn't make any difference. They couldn't always be there to protect him. Last time he'd been lucky. If not for the Alfár saving him, twice no less, he would have died.

The lessons with Malomir were a joke. He did everything he was told but Gerren knew it wouldn't be enough. A few days of learning how to fight with a sword wouldn't change anything. If he had years then maybe, just maybe, he'd stand a chance in a real fight. Even then it still relied on a lot of luck, especially on the ice where it was always so slippery.

Gerren wasn't sure if he believed Kell's story about being cursed but he'd been telling the truth about one thing. Luck had played a big part in his survival but this time they had half the numbers.

He had to leave right now. Get on his horse, ride south and

forget about all of this. Forget about being a hero, having a legacy and being rich. Right now he just wanted to live. To go home, back to where everything made sense. Back to a place where the fear couldn't reach him.

Gerren stuffed all of his belongings into his bag, gathered up his sword but didn't put it on his back. He wasn't a warrior and wearing it did nothing but put him off balance. After pulling on his boots and hat he went to the back door of the tavern and hurried out into the snow.

The wind was bitterly cold and it cut through his clothing. The sweat coating his skin froze and he shivered but kept moving, forcing his legs forward through knee-high snow until he reached the stable. The stablemaster saw him coming and his huge smile faded when he saw how Gerren was dressed.

"It's a little late for a ride," said Bomani.

"I need to go home. Now." Gerren looked up and down the stalls. If he didn't get on his horse soon he might start crying. "Where's my horse?"

"Resting," said Bomani, slowly approaching. He spoke calmly, hoping to soothe this problem away, but Gerren's mind was made up. Talking wouldn't change anything.

"I need to saddle him. I'll do it myself."

"Riding in the dark is dangerous. Your horse could fall and break a leg, plus you'd freeze to death out there. Wait until the morning."

"I can't," shouted Gerren. "I can't," he said again, quieter. He'd made one bad decision after another. This was the only way he'd survive.

"Let me help you," said Bomani.

"You can't," said Gerren. "It's too deep. I need to get away."

"Running won't make the fear go away," said a voice behind him.

Gerren spun around and felt his heart sink as Kell walked out of the shadows. He'd hoped the others would have been too busy to notice he was missing. By morning it would have been too late.

They would have gone on without him and been no worse off. The last person he'd wanted to see him running away was Kell.

"Have you come to gloat?"

For some reason Kell was carrying two glasses of beer. He offered one to Bomani who took the beer and hurried out the door. "No, to say that I understand."

Gerren snorted. "What does that mean?"

"You thought you were ready to face anything." Kell sat on a bale of straw and took a sip of beer. "You'd heard the stories a hundred times and knew that was what you wanted. A real life, full of adventure. Not a boring one like your parents. They never seemed happy. Always complaining about other people or not having enough money. But the heroes, they were larger than life. People loved them. They'd buy them drinks, give them free food and rooms, and the women, they loved them too."

Much of what he was saying was familiar but Gerren had the impression Kell was also talking about himself as a boy.

"It all looked so easy. You already knew about the dangers so there wouldn't be any surprises. But hearing about monsters, that's just words. Seeing them up close, it's different." Kell was staring at the wall but his eyes were far away. "It was the vorans, wasn't it?"

"Yes." There seemed little point in lying since he'd been caught trying to run away.

"For me, it was a mountain lion. We were only a day outside of Liesh and it just wandered into camp. At first I don't think it even realised I was there. But then the others saw it and drew their weapons. And I swear I saw its eyes change." Kell held up one hand towards something but then let it drop. "Its gums peeled back and then it started growling. And its claws, they were so sharp. I still have a scar," said Kell, touching his left side. "That's when it found me. The fear."

"How did you get rid of it?"

"I didn't. Instead I hid it from the others. They were heroes, so they always charged into battle. Whenever we met something dangerous they went straight in and I just stayed around the edges, killing the maimed and stabbing the dying to finish them off. I thought, in time it will get easier. I'll toughen up and then I'll be just like them. I told myself the fear would go away and I'll feel whole again. Then it was over and everyone else was dead. I returned to Algany as a hero but it was an empty victory."

"I don't understand," said Gerren.

"The fear followed me home."

Gerren was even more confused. "You want me to stay?"

Kell shook his head. "Over time the fear will fade. Ten years ago I was afraid of everything. It's taken me a long time to recover. Now, I'm just afraid of dying. I'm not ready. That's why I was going to run, but somewhere along the way I realised something. I need to be here." Kell took another drink and a wry smile touched his face. "I've been carrying around this huge weight. It's like a boulder hanging from my neck. It's never going to go away unless I make it. So I have to go north, and I might die, but there's a small chance that I'll live. Maybe the curse is real and it won't make a difference, but I'm making the choice. I won't have anyone or anything tell me what to do. Don't let the fear decide for you."

"I don't want to die. Coming here was the biggest mistake of my life!" said Gerren, finally able to say it out loud. The anguish in his chest was like a vice, squeezing his heart. It was such a relief to finally put it into words. "I'm sorry, Kell. I should have listened to you. I should have turned around and gone home days ago, but I just wanted—"

"It doesn't matter any more. The only thing you need to decide is why you're here. Why did you really come on this journey?" asked Kell. Gerren started to answer but Kell held up a hand. "Take some time and really think about it. Tomorrow morning, if you want to go home then no one will think any less of you. But if you want to travel north with us, then make sure it's for the right reasons. Your reasons, selfish as they may be. Just make sure you understand why you're doing it, Gerren. You can hide from other people, but you can't hide from yourself. I'm proof of that."

Kell held his gaze for a moment then walked out the door. Gerren sank down onto the ground and stared at nothing, his mind whirling. He wiped his face and found that it was wet. Had he cried in front of Kell? It didn't matter any more. Kell had proven, time and again, that he wasn't trying to escape or turn back. He might have been a coward in the past but not anymore. Gerren knew that he was the only one in the group.

Why was he really here? Gerren returned to his room and spent the rest of the night thinking about the answer. His body ached, his eyes were sandy but his mind wouldn't let him rest until he knew the truth.

All night the same thoughts went around and around. Every time he asked himself the question he tried to evade it with humour or by deflecting the blame onto other people, but in the theatre of his mind there was no escape. He relentlessly pursued the answer, brushing aside excuses, his pride and lingering fear. Kell had been right again. There was nowhere to hide. Gerren might be able to fool others but never himself.

Why had he come on this journey? What was he searching for? What did he really want?

For hours this went on and gradually he wore himself down until the truth began to take shape. Morning, when it finally came, found him exhausted but happy because he had an answer.

Feeling at peace Gerren made a decision.

PART THREE
The Frozen North

CHAPTER 23

Given that he was awake at a ridiculous time of morning Gerren decided to take advantage of the quiet. Before anyone else woke he went to the underground bathhouse and scrubbed himself clean then enjoyed a brief soak in one of the heated pools. Mercifully he was the only one there but, just as he was leaving, two women went past him in the other direction. He idly wondered what might have happened if he'd stayed in the water. The others were right. He'd never been with a woman and would probably just embarrass himself. Ignoring his urges he went in search of food as his stomach was rumbling.

The others weren't awake yet so Gerren ordered some breakfast, thick porridge filled with dried fruit and sweetened with honey. Huge slabs of bread, smeared with bright yellow butter, a plate of eggs with pieces of blood sausage cut up into it and a big mug of strong coffee. By the time he'd nearly finished eating Gerren felt awake. The first to arrive was Vahli but the others were not far behind with Malomir and Bronwyn arriving together. Their hair was wet and they both had flushed cheeks but Gerren suspected it had nothing to do with an early bath. Erotic images stirred in his mind but he bit the inside of his mouth to stop himself saying something stupid.

Kell entered the room next, pausing on the threshold in surprise at seeing Gerren at the table. He seemed pleased but said nothing.

The others seemed unaware and Gerren was thankful that Kell hadn't told them.

The room began to fill with other customers and the smell of cooking meat and coffee swirled through the air. The Alfár arrived last and once again ate everything except the meat which the others shared between them. He watched with fascination as she picked out every little piece of blood sausage, piling them up on one side of her plate. Gerren wasn't alone in wondering about her peculiar behaviour.

Strange eating habits aside Gerren was glad Willow was going with them. He'd seen how lethal she was with her strange weapon, smashing the vorans apart. She was so strong and had carried him like a baby after he'd been attacked. With the Alfár fighting beside them Gerren thought they stood a much better chance against anything that crossed their path.

"I'm glad you're with us," he said to Willow. Despite whispering the others overheard and Gerren felt his cheeks flush. He had no idea if the Alfár understood but she gave him a half smile briefly showing her teeth.

Once they'd all finished breakfast they wrapped up against the cold with multiple layers of clothing plus scarves, hats and stout boots. Kell then led them to one of the buildings above ground to hire some dogs. After some haggling they were assigned three dogsleds with six huge dogs pulling each. The animals were far larger than Gerren had been expecting and their long faces reminded him of wolves. While they stood around shivering, the dogs were completely unaffected by the snow, playing with each other as if it was spring.

As Gerren followed the others about from one place to the next, buying tents then bartering over waterproof reindeer boots, he kept glancing up at the sky. It was bright blue with only a thin layer of cloud but little heat reached them from the sun. After only a short time outside his breath frosted on the air so he pulled up his scarf to cover the bottom half of his face.

Apart from Kell everyone was unfamiliar with the extreme

landscape and how to safely travel across it while handling the dogsleds. Gerren did his best to listen while the kennel master explained verbal commands and how to look after the animals at night but found he was easily distracted. His attention kept being drawn away by the smallest of things, perhaps it was because he hadn't slept. At one point he noticed any time of the Frostrunners passed them in the street they stared at Willow. Each made a brief gesture with one hand, something he'd never seen before, but it didn't look friendly. If he had to guess he would have said they were warding off evil.

"Gerren," said a voice. He looked around and realised the others had already wandered away leaving him alone with Kell. "Let's take a walk."

Kell led him away from the dog pens towards one of the other buildings above ground. Despite the doors being closed the awful stink told Gerren it was the tannery.

"I lay awake all night, thinking," he said.

Kell took a wide berth around the building towards the next. "I was surprised to see you this morning."

"I've found my reason," said Gerren. "I know why I'm still here."

"Whatever it is, keep it to yourself," said Kell.

"But–"

Kell held up a hand. "Gerren, I don't need to know. It's not for me to judge. Hold on tight to it, because the days ahead are going to be the most gruelling and dangerous of your life. So I hope it's enough to see you through."

Gerren wanted to tell him why he'd chosen to stay. It had taken all night but he'd forced himself to keep digging until he found the truth. He wasn't doing this for fame, money, power or even women. He was doing it because even at home, surrounded by friends, Gerren felt alone.

When he listened to friends' conversations Gerren always felt on the outside, unable to relate. He thought he'd shared their aspirations but somewhere deep inside there was a line that separated them. But here, among this group of people, far away from everything familiar there was a sense of camaraderie. Although he was the youngest and least welltravelled, much of what they were experiencing was new to everyone.

The sense of danger was no longer appealing. It had been extinguished by the voran attack. But somewhere in that willingness to face the unknown together, Gerren felt as if he belonged for the first time in his life. He was part of something that was greater than himself. He didn't know if he believed in the Shepherd and if being here was his purpose, but in his heart he knew that it felt right.

"I'm ready," said Gerren, hoping that it was true.

On three sleds they headed north, away from Meer and the safety of the community. Some of their belongings had been left behind in storage so they only carried the essentials onto the ice. Kell had thought Vahli was going to cry when he'd left his oud in town but from this point forward it served no purpose. They wouldn't be sitting around the campfire at night telling stories or singing songs. Besides, space in the tents was very limited and the instrument was too bulky.

It had been many years since Kell had last been here and yet the stark beauty was as familiar as it was haunting. Beneath the glittering sea of ice was a final hard crust of land; a safety net against certain death composed of frozen earth, tiny clumps of brown plants, tree stumps and thousands of tumbled grey stones. The dogs moved around these obstacles without having to be told. They eagerly ran north as if they were being pulled towards a finish line that only they could see.

The bright white of the ice and snow didn't bother the dogs but Kell insisted that everyone wrap their eyes in the thin layer of cotton. It reduced visibility but also protected them from the blinding landscape. Every surface reflected the meagre light of the sun a thousand-fold creating dazzling patterns of colour.

Although the land was perilous Kell wasn't particularly worried by crevasses. It was what roamed above and below the ice that bothered him. Only the toughest beasts made the Frozen North their home and they were not known for their compassion.

As the dogs ate up mile after mile Meer receded into the distance. It wasn't much of a place, a travellers' rest full people driven there by ill-luck, but it was their last refuge. If they encountered something dangerous, crying out for help was a waste of breath as there was no one to hear their pleas. They were completely on their own.

As ice began to form on the outside of his clothing, building up layer by layer to create a new skin, Kell felt himself changing on the inside. There was a stripping away of unnecessary thoughts that served no purpose in such a place. A refocusing on vital skills that would give him a better chance of survival.

With the wind whipping past his ears he glanced around to see how the others were faring. Behind him Willow's head continually moved from left to right as she stared in wonder at their new world. The intense cold finally had an impact on the Alfár. She was wrapped up like everyone else from head to toe apart from the top half of her face. The glare had no effect on her eyes making Kell wonder how far she could see across the ice.

Gerren had surprised everyone by volunteering to travel with Vahli which made things a lot easier. Whatever his reason for staying it seemed as if the boy was finally starting to grow up.

On the last sled Bronwyn and Malomir were huddled up against the cold. He rode on the back, shielding her from the wind, while cautiously steering the dogs. It was the first time Kell had seen Malomir uncertain about anything. It was a refreshing change from his usual swagger.

As well as keeping one eye on the dogs Kell scanned the snow and ice for signs of life. This close to Meer there was still the risk of encountering a wandering snow bear or roaming sabre of maglau. It would be far worse once they crossed the Frozen Circle as there would be dangers beneath the ice as well. Occasionally Kell spotted tiny flickers of movement at the edge of his vision, but by the time he turned his head they was gone. It could have been a snow fox or snow hare but the dogs never veered off course to investigate.

The dogs flew over the snow with unbelievable endurance. After a few hours Kell called for a stop to give them a rest and everyone else a chance to stretch their cramped muscles. By the time they stopped in the evening the sky had barely changed colour. There was a slight dimming of the light, so that the reflective glare was not as severe, but little else was different.

Following Kell's lead the others immediately looked after the most important thing they'd brought with them: the dogs. Without them no one would survive the journey to the Lich's castle, and hopefully back home. The distance was too great to traverse on foot. Their wellbeing came ahead of everyone else's. A large portion of the supplies on every sled comprised huge slabs of meat and bags crammed with straw for bedding.

With short-handled wide spades they all dug shallow pits in the snow to shield the dogs from the wind. The hardy beasts had remarkable stamina and their thick coats allowed them to sleep outdoors at night but even they had their limits. Once all of the dogs had gobbled up a vast amount of meat Kell and the others lined the pits with straw. The dogs from each sled all curled up together, sharing body heat, and promptly went to sleep. Only then, already tired and sore, did the others begin to assemble their tents and think about food for themselves.

With a small oil burner sat on a metal tripod they melted snow to make tea and create a thick broth that was full of fatty stewed meat and vegetables. Although they hadn't worked as hard as the dogs, everyone needed to eat a lot of food to keep them going. In this climate a lack of water was also a problem so Kell suggested everyone drink plenty as well. Willow picked out the meat from her stew and Kell made a mental note to ask the Alfár about it when they were alone.

"Tell us, what kind of beasts are we likely to meet out here?" asked Bronwyn. She'd explored much of the Five Kingdoms but he was the only who had even been this far north.

"There are bears, which are powerful and dangerous, but they tend to keep their distance unless they're starving," said Kell, thinking back to his first trip across the ice. "They're also solitary animals, so they're unlikely to attack a large group."

"Is that it?" asked Malomir. He sounded disappointed by their deadliness.

Kell shook his head. "Bears are the least of our worries."

Vahli had been scribbling in his journal but now he looked up from the page. "You mean the Qalamieren."

Even saying their name made Kell uncomfortable. "Amongst other things. They are some kind of dark spirit. No one really knows for sure, but if we hear their song, all we can do is run and keep running. If they get too close then we die. It's that simple. There's no way to fight them and no one ever survives."

A heavy silence fell across everyone and Kell let it settle so they understood.

"There are also horned sharks, on the ice fields, but the most worrying beasts are the maglau."

"What are they?" asked Gerren. His voice wavered but Kell pretended not to have noticed.

"They're pack animals, but they're not wolves. They're something else. A savage and primal beast. Their skulls are very thick so swords will just bounce off. Weak spots are the belly, mouth, flanks and if you're lucky, behind the neck."

Kell outlined some of the beasts' tactics, sharing everything he knew about them. For once Malomir didn't brag about having faced something similar in the past and he listened in rapt silence.

"What about the Lich?" asked Vahli.

"She's dead," said Kell.

"Are you sure?"

"I cut off her head, Vahli. Nothing can come back from that."

"What was she like?" persisted the bard. "No one ever talks about that."

As he glanced at the faces of the others in camp Kell realised they were all equally intrigued. Details about the Lich in the Medina saga were vague and only he had seen her face.

"She was beautiful, majestic and terrifying, like an avalanche," said Kell, casting his mind back. "I found her, alone, in the heart of the castle. She glared down at me from her throne like I was an insect." He'd been terrified, ready to piss himself, but a stubborn part of him had refused to give up.

"What else?" asked Vahli, his hand moving across the page of his journal.

"Her eyes were mesmerising. There are times when I still see them, staring back at me from the shadows," said Kell. "Sometimes, I think all of this is a dream and that I actually died on the ice with the others. At least, this way, I'll know for certain, one way or another."

The others were staring at him now, with a mix of awe and pity. No one outside his home town really knew about his breakdown, the nightmares and the long road to recovery. Everyone thought he'd just come home from his adventure in the Frozen North and carried on living as before as if nothing had happened. They had no idea of the time he'd lost and what had been taken from him. To this day, he still wasn't whole.

"I think it's time for bed," said Kell.

The waxed tents were wider than normal and low to the ground, so that there was just enough room for two people plus their gear. On hands and knees Kell crawled inside and wrapped himself up in his sleeping pouch and a blanket. Changing clothes and bathing were luxuries they would have to do without for a while. Although he didn't smell yet it would be different in a few days. Willow crawled in once Kell was settled and to his surprise the Alfár stripped off her shirt and trousers leaving only a light vest and shorts. He caught a few glimpses of rounded flesh and didn't know if it was muscle or something else. Despite the climate Willow only covered herself with a light blanket. Kell had not been this close to the Alfár before and through his clothes and the blanket he could feel heat radiating from her body.

Despite the long day of travel the brightness outside intruded and Kell struggled to fall sleep. He heard a long exhalation of breath and turning his head was surprised to see Willow staring back. Her eyes were still unnerving and he quickly looked away in case he was drawn in. Kell pulled the blanket tight around his shoulders to try and chase away the lingering chill in his fingers and toes.

"It's too bright outside," whispered Willow.

"It will be like this for days once we cross the Frozen Circle. The next time we'll see real darkness will be back in Meer." Of course, that would only happen if any of them survived. Kell was trying not to dwell on it but that was becoming increasingly difficult given what lay ahead.

"Tell me something," said Kell, changing the subject. "Why do you only sometimes eat meat?"

The Alfár was silent for a long time before answering. "In my homeland we have difficult times. Food is sometimes hard to find. Life struggles. Here it is abundant. Clean. Safe. To kill something pure, to take it away when everything is so fragile, is not an easy choice. I will only eat what I have killed."

"But it's different here," said Kell.

"But I am not," said Willow.

Kell tried a different subject. "Can you tell me something else about your homeland?"

"In the long winter I ate many things I would not consider food, just to survive." Willow raised her eyebrows and Kell was suddenly unnerved by the way she was staring at him. She gave him one of those peculiar half smiles, showing a lot of teeth, and the hair began to stand up on the back of his neck. The moment stretched on but then it was broken as the Alfár made a strange whooping noise. Her whole body was shaking and her teeth clacked together. Eventually Kell realised she was laughing at him.

"That wasn't funny," said Kell, as sweat trickled down the back of his neck. He'd been sure Willow had been about to take a bite out of him.

"I think it was a little funny," said Willow.

"Well, it proves something else we have in common. You do have a sense of humour."

"We can laugh," said Willow. "Although, among my kind, it is not a sound often heard these days."

"Where are your people? Where is your homeland?" asked Kell. Everyone had theories but no one really knew. If he was ever going to find out, now was the time to ask.

"It is not far. You can reach it across the sea," said the Alfár, confirming what others believed. "But it is also here."

"I don't understand. What—" Kell's next question was interrupted when Willow put a finger to his lips. A tremor of a different kind ran through his body at her touch. Now that the two of them were alone, breathing the same air in a small tent, he became aware of her musky and exotic scent. Kell gently eased her fingers away from his mouth but held onto Willow's hand.

"I'm just trying to understand you," he said. "I know why the others are here, or I can guess, but I can't read you. So I have to ask questions."

Questions made her uncomfortable but Willow rarely volunteered information so it was the only way. The others had talked about Willow many times when she was in earshot and not once had she corrected their assumptions.

"I am here, where many others refused to walk," said Willow. "I am a friend. And I will help you on this journey, is that not enough?"

The Alfár was right. It didn't matter where she came from. It didn't matter that she looked different from the rest of them. It didn't even matter if she had her own reasons for coming. Willow had chosen to place herself in danger by travelling beside him. Many others had turned aside because of their fear. The Medina saga might have inspired people but only a handful had been willing to put their lives at risk.

There were more important things to focus on and in the days ahead Kell knew they couldn't afford any distractions. Out here on the ice a moment of hesitation could mean the difference between life and death.

"It's more than enough," said Kell, giving Willow's hand a squeeze.

As he settled down to sleep Kell pulled his blanket tight to try and get rid of the lingering chill. He heard movement and then felt Willow wrap her arms around him as she hugged him from behind. Almost immediately he started to feel warmer from sharing her intense body heat. They were so close to one another that Kell thought he heard Willow's heart beating except there was a double rhythm running through him.

Ignoring the questions and pushing aside his confusing feelings Kell focused on sleep and soon drifted off.

Gerren lay awake for a long time, staring at the ceiling of his tent. He tried not to fidget, as Vahli was asleep, his breathing deep and even.

Kell had told him, time and again, that the Frozen North had been terrifying but he hadn't really believed him before now. There had been something terribly sad and desperate in Kell's eyes. A savage pain that made Gerren look away. He didn't understand how anyone could carry that around inside them.

"Go to sleep, Gerren," said Vahli.

"I thought you were asleep."

Vahli rolled over. "I can hear you thinking."

"I had no idea what the first journey did to Kell. He's…" Gerren trailed off, trying to find the right word.

"Broken," said Vahli.

"Yes, broken inside."

"And now you're worried the same will happen to you."

"To all of us. Or worse," said Gerren. The others had great deeds to their names but so had the eleven heroes and all of them had died on the ice. "I don't want to die up here," said Gerren, biting his bottom lip to suppress a sob.

"Nor do I," said Vahli, briefly gripping his hand. "So, all we can do is trust one another, watch each other's backs and fight as hard as we can. Can you do that?"

"Yes."

"Good. Now get some sleep."

Bronwyn had a moment of peace, where she could forget about everything, but once it was over and they lay together in sweaty silence it all came rushing back. The endless questions with no answers. The niggling doubts and worries that plagued her mind. The yawning chasm of loneliness that sometimes made it difficult to breathe and could make her thoughts become self-destructive.

"Do you think the others heard us?" she asked, keen to banish the silence.

"They probably heard us back in Meer," said Malomir, running a finger down her bare back. The air in the small tent was still warm but she knew it wouldn't be long before the freezing cold seeped in again. Brushing his hand aside she pulled on her shirt before wriggling back into her trousers.

"What is it?"

"Nothing. I just don't want to get cold," she lied. A small line appeared between Malomir's eyebrows but he said nothing. "Tell me about your family."

One of his eyebrows rose in surprise. "What do you want to know?"

She knew why she'd asked the question but wasn't ready to share the reasons. When she looked at Malomir she could see they had much in common, especially the loneliness, but there was much she still didn't know.

"Do you have any brothers or sisters? Are your parents still alive?"

Malomir shivered and began to pull on layers of clothing as he spoke. "One sister, three years younger. She's married and has two, no, three children. She only ever wanted a big family, a good home, a peaceful life. She is content."

Bronwyn could hear the envy in his voice. "And your parents?"

"Dead. They sailed and fished all their life. One day a storm claimed them. We found pieces of their boat. A few days later their bodies washed up on the shore of a neighbouring island."

It was an old wound but there was still pain behind the words. "How old were you?"

"Thirteen. Almost a man. I started working as a fisherman the next day."

"Wait," said Bronwyn, realising something. "Your parents weren't royalty?"

Malomir's grin was infectious. "I am the first King of the Summer Isles. There are no palaces in my homeland. Each island was its own nation until I united them." Malomir's smile faltered and he turned his face away to pull on his boots.

"What about your family?"

"Dead," she said quickly, not wanting to share too much. Not yet. She smiled when their eyes met to show that it didn't hurt. "It was a long time ago."

"Is that why you push yourself so hard?" asked Malomir. Even with so little he could see right through her. He was a lot more perceptive than she realised. Or perhaps it was because he was also trying to live up to an impossible ideal.

"One of the reasons, yes," she said, hoping he wouldn't pry.

"Whenever you're ready to talk, I'm here," said Malomir, lying down and getting comfortable. She smiled at his back, grateful that he hadn't pushed. Bronwyn covered them both with a blanket and cuddled up against him.

CHAPTER 24

The following morning, after another hearty breakfast, they were back on the ice racing north again. The air was so cold it ached to breathe even through the material they all wore across their faces. Almost every bit of bare flesh was covered but it didn't seem to make a lot of difference as Kell's fingers still tingled.

The sky remained a relentless, bright blue dusted with a few wispy clouds. The sun was hidden from view and this was how it would remain for the next week as they travelled in the Frozen North. Darkness had abandoned them but that didn't stop the nights from being more severe.

Today he rode on the back and Willow was on the front, her long limbs folded up. They would take turns steering the sled but for now her keen eyesight was scanning ahead for problems.

Long before what Kell thought was midday they crossed over the Frozen Circle leaving behind the land. There was no visible marker or sudden change but he felt a shift underfoot. There was a slight imbalance in his ears which left him dizzy for a moment. The others gave no indication they'd noticed which made Kell wonder if it was all in his imagination.

Beneath the smooth runners the snow changed from a crunchy packed layer into something thick and tough. Before they had sailed across the surface, barely leaving a mark, which was soon erased by drifting snow. Now the combined weight of each sled cut deep channels as if scoring wood. Glancing behind Kell could see their tracks extending far into the distance.

Beneath the deep snow, and the dense layers of ice, was the freezing ocean. The water was so cold it could kill a person in a few heartbeats. The niggling fear that had been lurking at the back of his mind tried to push its way forward but he ruthlessly squashed it. Kell would not be beaten or controlled by fear. If the worst should happen then at least it would be quick. There were far worse ways to die out here.

Movement on his right caught his attention and in the distance, keeping pace with their sled, was one of the snow bears. Despite its jet black eyes and nose, its thick white coat made it easy for such a large beast to disappear. This particular bear was a massive beast and it seemed to have taken an unusual interest in them.

Occasionally they attacked travellers but it was uncommon. Against three fast moving targets, each with six dogs that could cause an injury, it seemed unlikely it was a big risk. After a while it dropped back and then disappeared as another flurry of snow hid it from view. Kell heaved a sigh of relief and let go of his sword.

As the wind picked up and changed direction, throwing snow in their faces, visibility became poor and they were forced to slow down to avoid obstacles. Kell was squinting and yet still almost missed the grey lump protruding from the snow. At the last moment he yanked the dogs to the left in a vain attempt to avoid a collision.

One of their runners clipped the obstacle and they teetered at an angle until Willow leaned her weight in the opposite direction, resetting them on the snow. Kell eased the dogs to a stop and then waited for his heart to slow down.

The other two sleds had seen them suddenly veer to one side and had managed to avoid any damage. A quick check of the sled showed nothing obvious but it was possible one of their runners had been cracked. A more thorough inspection would be needed but first he wanted to see what they'd hit.

Half buried in the snow they found the remains of another

traveller. The sled was more or less intact but the harness was shredded by tooth or claw. Either the dogs had chewed their way out or something else had dragged them away. There was no blood in sight but in such a constantly shifting landscape it would be quickly buried.

It was hard to know how long the half-chewed man had been lying there as his skin was frozen solid. Something had ripped off one of his arms at the elbow and one of his legs at the hip. There were bite marks on his ribs and his shirt had been torn open. Most of his organs were gone and stray bits of viscera were strewn across the snow. Unfortunately he still had both of his eyes. An endless grimace of agony was stamped onto his rigid features.

A quick search of the sled revealed anything edible had been ripped open and taken by scavengers. Three metal oil tins had been left behind. As Kell added the dead man's fuel to his sled he noticed the others were watching.

"There's nothing we can do," he said. "The ice is too thick so we can't bury him very deep, and even if we tried, they'd just dig him back up."

"Maybe a prayer?" suggested Vahli. Kell wasn't really sure he believed in the Shepherd but he gestured for the bard to get on with it. They couldn't linger for long in case whatever had been eating the man came back.

He could barely see past the end of his nose. They needed to get clear of the snowstorm and back onto the open plain. The dogs had keener noses than anyone so they would be the first to smell if anything was approaching. That didn't stop him nervously looking around as Vahli muttered a prayer for the man's spirit.

One of the dogs chuffed and Kell was instantly alert, reaching for his sword. The others dogs had noticed something was amiss as they stood up and began to pull at their harnesses. A couple began to keen, staring into the snow for whatever they could smell.

"We need to go," said Kell. "Now!"

Thankfully Vahli had finished so there wasn't an argument. The others noticed the change in the dogs and drew their weapons.

Willow had her strange weapon in one hand and her eyes were focused on one point to their left.

"Can you see something?" asked Kell, unsure if her eyes could penetrate the storm.

"There's a shape. Watching. Waiting," said the Alfár.

"Move, move!" said Kell, mushing the dogs the moment he felt Willow's weight settle on the sled. The dogs were eager to be off and quickly ploughed ahead into the whirling snow. Willow's head swivelled to the left and then behind them, fixed on something. Only when they'd put some distance between them and the dead body did Willow relax and put away her weapon.

"Was it the bear?" asked Kell.

"Maybe," said Willow. "Is that normal?"

"They usually stay away from people. If they're desperate they might attack."

Perhaps the bear had simply been guarding its meal and was upset that they'd disturbed its larder. There was no way to know if the bear had killed the traveller or stolen it from another predator. Kell tried to brush aside the image of the dead man's face but it lingered in his mind. It was a stark reminder about the dangers of being in the Frozen North.

A flicker of movement on his left side caught Kell's attention but he was too slow to react. Something massive collided with the sled sending him and Willow flying through the air. He landed on his shoulder and slid across the ground, ploughing a furrow through virgin snow. Startled by the attack the dogs kept going and were soon lost from sight. The other two sleds slowed down and came to a stop beside Willow. Everyone had drawn their weapons but there was no sign of whatever had attacked them.

Kell had barely made it to his feet when a snow bear appeared on his right. The scar-faced beast charged at him in a frenzy. Its deafening roar shook the ground and the other dogs tugged at their harnesses, desperate to escape.

All thoughts fled as Kell stumbled backwards to avoid the bear's claws. His legs tangled together but he managed to avoid tripping over. If he fell the bear would immediately tear off one of his legs, or shake him and snap his spine.

It made another clumsy swipe, as if its heart wasn't really in the attack, which made him even more worried. The beast was huge and looked well-fed with powerful shoulders and a thick coat, so it wasn't attacking because of hunger. It seemed to be teasing him. It was almost as if it were trying to shepherd him towards something.

"It's not alone!" shouted Kell, but his voice barely travelled through the whirling snow. Only Willow heard and the Alfár immediately spun around to face the opposite direction. A second beast came charging in from the right, knocking Gerren and Vahli aside with its shoulder, swiping at the others. Willow's weapon came down but she only caught the bear a glancing blow on a shoulder. Kell didn't see any more as the lazy bear in front suddenly changed its demeanour. Its playful teasing turned into full-on assault as it charged at him with tooth and claw.

Gerren spat snow from his mouth and wiped the stinging ice from his eyes. Part of him was convinced his vision would clear just in time to see the bear's claws coming towards his face. Instead he witnessed Malomir and Bronwyn battling back and forth with one beast while Kell and Willow struggled against a second. Both animals were huge with long black claws and powerful jaws full of sharp teeth. One bite and Gerren knew it would be over.

His hands began to shake but it had nothing to do with the biting cold. As Gerren helped Vahli to his feet his heart began to pound. The fear inside was telling him to run and hide. To turn away and live another day. He tried not to listen but it was so loud. He didn't want to let his friends down but at the same time he didn't want to die.

"Deep breaths," said Vahli, drawing a short sword he'd taken to wearing since leaving Meer. The short double-edged blade had a tapered point making it ideal for stabbing or slashing. Gerren didn't know how his sword would fare against the bear's thick coat but the time for worrying was over. The bard clapped him on the shoulder and together they charged at one of the bears, screaming wordless battle cries at the top of their lungs.

The bear turned its head slightly, catching sight of them, but it didn't run. Gerren wasn't sure if its behaviour was normal but both animals seemed highly intelligent. When Bronwyn tried to overpower the bear it stood up on its hind legs towering over the tall warrior. Its paws came down on her shoulders which sent her to the ground. Her sword went spinning away leaving her defenceless. Malomir cried out but didn't slow his attack. His heavy sword cut a long red line across the bear's side but it merely growled in response. As it turned to face the Islander Gerren and Vahli came within striking distance.

Using both hands Gerren brought down his sword with all of his strength on the bear's flank. The blade bit through the fur and flesh but then stopped, jarring his arms as it struck bone. The beast lashed out with a back foot ripping the sword from his grip which then disappeared into the snow. The glancing blow clipped Gerren on the shoulder and he landed face down. He could hear the bard while Malomir roared as if he'd become an animal.

From the corner of his eye, Gerren saw the Alfár's axe come down on the other bear's side and he knew it would soon be over. Willow and Kell would defeat their beast and then the six of them would fight together to kill the other. Gerren felt his heart sink as the impact of Willow's axe seemed to have little effect. The bear yowled but belying its size the beast quickly spun around striking Willow across the chest. It was the first time Gerren had seen the Alfár in pain. She hissed through her teeth and touched a hand to her chest coming away with something blue.

Before it had a chance to attack again Kell's sword hammered into the beast's head, cutting off one of its ears, shearing away fur and flesh. The bear yelped and scrambled back before it began to circle Kell and Willow. The fight was not going to be over as quickly as Gerren had hoped. The best he could do was try and help his friends.

Clenching his jaw against the pain Gerren forced himself up to his knees and then his feet. A quick search showed that his sword was dangerously close to the bear's feet. The animal was currently struggling against Bronwyn and Vahli who were alternating their attacks on either side to keep it distracted. Malomir was on the ground, a hand pressed to his side and he was breathing hard. Gerren looked around for another weapon knowing that the small dagger on his belt wouldn't be enough but there was nothing to hand. He felt useless but kept searching.

The fight had churned up the snow and beneath it he glimpsed the ice. Something sharp was poking up and Gerren carefully lifted the item from the snow. The shard of ice was as long as his forearm and it tapered to a point. The edges were so sharp they cut through his gloves into the flesh of his hands. Gerren wrapped it in his scarf as blood dripped onto the snow. While the bear's back was turned he ran forward and brought the icy shard down on its rear.

The point snapped on impact but momentum drove a small portion of the ice into the animal's flesh. As the bear turned its head Bronwyn's sword came down on its neck, gouging a huge trough that squirted blood into the air. But the beast wasn't done. One of its paws slammed into Bronwyn so hard that it sent her cartwheeling through the air. She landed some distance away and skidded out of sight across the snow.

As Malomir's sword came down on the bear's left, Vahli attacked from the right, stabbing it in the side over and over again. Roaring in pain it turned around, clipping Vahli with its head, its teeth ripping at the flesh on his arm. Gerren saw his chance and made a desperate grab for his sword. As his fingers closed around the grip a shadow fell over him. Looking up he saw the bear's jaws rushing towards his face.

Screeching in terror he dove to one side and felt something catch one of his legs before he scrambled away. There was a flash of pain but as he turned around with his sword held ready he realised why the bear hadn't attacked him.

The blood loss from its injuries was finally taking a toll. Malomir's heavy scimitar hacked huge chunks out of its side and the bear's attempts to keep him at bay were slower than before. It snarled and snapped its jaws, swiping at him with its paws but it continually missed the Islander.

A deafening roar on Gerren's left drew his attention where Kell and Willow were delivering a final blow to the scarred bear. Using her full height the Alfár raised her mace on high and then brought it down with such speed it whistled through the air. There was a sickening crunch as it impacted with the bear's skull and it dropped to the ice, leaking blood and brains. Kell's sword came down a moment later, striking it in the neck and then a second time until the light faded from the beast's eyes.

On his right Malomir was now standing with his sword pointing towards the ground. The bear had turned to face him but it made no move to attack. It barely had the strength to remain on its feet and the pool of blood around it had grown. Bronwyn appeared out of the snow charging towards the bear and with one final blow she severed the beast's head from its body.

It took over an hour for them to retrieve the dogs and by then Kell was so exhausted he almost fell asleep on his feet. Thankfully the sleds had toppled over in the dogs' frantic attempt to escape. Despite the weight and awkward burden they had managed to pull the sleds a good distance before the weight of snow stopped them. It took a while to coax the dogs back to camp and longer to calm them down. One or two nosed at the bear carcasses, tearing aside skin to nibble at the meat.

As Bronwyn and Willow butchered the bears Vahli did his best to see to their wounds with needle and thread. What was left of the bears would draw scavengers so they rode at a slow pace for about an hour before finally stopping. By that time Kell could see everyone was on the verge of collapse but they still had chores.

They fell into the same routine as the previous night, digging pits for the dogs, feeding them and this time trying to calm them down before they would settle. It was still early, perhaps mid-afternoon, but everyone was famished and they ate more of their limited supplies than was wise. They might be able to supplement their stock with fish but there was no guarantee. Kell knew it might be a decision they later came to regret but his mind was too tired to dwell on maybes. As soon as they'd put up the tents everyone crawled into their blankets to sleep.

Kell's whole body ached, from his tired arms and shoulders, right down to his burning thighs. A huge weight settled on him, threatening to pull him down into sleep. He willingly went towards it but a small worrying thought kept him awake.

One bear stalking them was unusual behaviour but not unheard of so Kell had put it from his mind. Now he wondered if it had been a scout for the others. Such an idea seemed ridiculous as he'd never heard of snow bears working together. They were solitary animals that spent most of their life alone. Even if the bears had their own language, how had they coordinated their attack? He'd not heard any sounds before the first bear charged his sled. So how had they been communicating with one another?

The bears had also seemed unusually alert, or perhaps it was simply a figment of his exhausted mind. A darker thought occurred and then wouldn't leave him alone. One Kell had dared not consider until now. What if this was the work of the Ice Lich?

Everyone thought a new power was responsible for changes to the weather but Kell began to wonder. The creeping cold felt like its work which made no sense. He had killed the Ice Lich and yet here he was, ten years later.

No one knew where the Lich came from or how it had amassed its power. As the only person to see it up close he was the most familiar and yet was none the wiser. The Frozen North was the territory of the Frostrunner clans but if they knew anything about the Ice Lich they had not shared it with anyone. Both times an emissary from the clans had travelled south to deliver a warning but nothing more.

"Has something like this happened before?" asked Willow. Her radiant body heat was not as intense as the previous night indicating her level of exhaustion. "Have you heard any stories?"

"No. Bears only attack when they're desperate for food." He'd been told they fought for territory and during their mating season but lethal attacks on people were rare. Such stories were the gossip of Meer but no one had ever whispered about snow bears working together.

"Both bears were well-fed," said Willow, echoing his own thoughts. Their behaviour was an aberration which meant something had compelled them, against their nature. Kell waited for the Alfár to say something more but Willow had fallen sleep.

A prickly feeling ran down the length of Kell's spine. Something didn't want them here. Even worse, it was already aware of their presence and it had the power to influence animals.

They'd barely crossed the Frozen Circle and were at least three days' travel from the castle. Until they arrived there would be no way to know if it was the Ice Lich or something else.

CHAPTER 25

The following morning Gerren could barely get out of his tent. His body felt like one giant bruise. His hand was throbbing from where the ice had cut him and he had difficulty straightening his fingers. Vahli had done his best to bind them but the cuts weren't deep enough for stitches. That didn't stop them from hurting badly enough to wake him several times during the night. Groaning quietly Gerren tried not to disturb Vahli but in such a confined space it was almost impossible.

Last night, before they'd fallen asleep, Gerren had admitted his many failings to the bard. For being swayed by the opinion of others he'd thought were wiser. For trying to tear down Kell when he was no better himself. Mostly Gerren admitted to being afraid. Afraid of dying. Afraid of never fitting in. Afraid of freezing to death in the Frozen North. Afraid of being torn apart by the wild creatures. Afraid of being alone for the rest of his life.

Vahli had listened to his tirade in silence. Eventually, when Gerren had run out of words, the bard gave him a sage piece of advice. Before he could begin to move forward Gerren had to forgive himself. Everyone started off young and ignorant. The key was to learn from the past.

Gerren was struggling with a lot of things, such as being naked around other people, but he was trying not to speak his mind without first thinking it through. Thankfully since crossing onto the ice he didn't have to get naked anymore. Of course that was both a blessing and a curse. After a couple of days the smell was considerably worse in a confined space.

The compact tents meant they had few secrets and Gerren soon learned much about Vahli that he suspected no one else knew. The bard often muttered in his sleep and had dreams where he was fending off someone. He didn't know if it had something to do with Vahli's family and didn't feel comfortable asking about it.

As he'd suspected, the bard wore makeup which he carefully applied every morning despite then covering his face with a scarf and woolly hat. It concealed minor blemishes but also a faint scar across his jaw which Gerren hadn't noticed before. As well as carrying a short sword Vahli had four daggers on him at all times, including one up a sleeve. The speed and familiarity with which he strapped them to his body suggested it was a routine he'd done for years, which was both surprising and a little scary.

Every day Gerren was learning there was much more to all of his companions than he'd assumed upon first meeting them. He would even include Kell in that category now that he understood him a little better.

Gerren tried to ease into his overcoat without waking Vahli but the sound of material rasping together was extremely loud in the tent.

"I'm awake," muttered the bard. "You don't need to creep about."

"I'm sorry."

Vahli flapped one hand. "Just let my head settle."

That was something else Gerren doubted the others knew. Every morning when he first woke up Vahli experienced a period of dizziness. At first Gerren had assumed the bard had been sipping from a flask but there was no alcohol on any of the sleds. Much like the makeup that Vahli applied every morning his smile concealed many secrets.

"You were very brave yesterday," said Vahli.

Gerren laughed until he saw the bard's expression. "I was terrified the entire time."

"And yet you still attacked the bear, with a shard of ice, no less. That took courage."

"It didn't feel brave. It was stupid, but I didn't think my dagger was going to hurt it."

"You'd be surprised," said Vahli, drawing one of his blades. "A keen edge can do a lot of damage, but sometimes the shock of a shallow wound is enough to win a fight. Surprise will make an enemy hesitate and that gives you an opportunity."

"To do what?" asked Gerren.

"Fight or run," said Vahli with a grin. "Here," he said, passing over one of his longer daggers. It was an elegant narrow blade with a tapered point as long as Gerren's hand. The edge was finely honed but the handle was worn from use.

"I can't take this."

"Keep it. I have others," said Vahli, producing a fifth dagger from somewhere.

"How many blades do you have?"

The bard grunted. "A few."

Gerren had thought he was nothing more than a dandy but there was a lot more to Vahli than his profession and bright clothing. They had all seen him scribbling notes in his journal for the new saga, but only Gerren had seen him writing in a second notebook. Sneaking a quick glimpse had revealed a language he didn't recognise, leaving him with more questions.

Once they were both dressed and wrapped up against the cold they finally opened their tent and went out into the snow. The initial shock always took his breath away and the first lungful of air hurt deep inside his chest. It soon passed and then came Gerren's favourite part of the day: feeding the dogs. The animals were all well trained, friendly and affectionate, even more so than usual when he fed them huge pieces of meat. All of the dogs gobbled up the fresh chunks of snow bear with relish while he cleared away the straw then got them into their harnesses.

An hour later, after a quick breakfast and a hot cup of tea that warmed him up for a while, they were racing north again. As the dogs ran across the icy landscape it sometimes felt as if they were flying behind them on the sled. The runners seemed to barely touch the snow and Gerren imagined they could drift up into the air.

Today the sky was a uniform bright blue and utterly featureless without a single cloud. He'd never spent much time considering the colour of the sky but now that it never changed Gerren realised he was already bored and missed the variety.

A gentle nudge from Vahli served as a reminder that he was supposed to be watching for trouble instead of daydreaming. After yesterday's attack by the bears everyone was more alert and any time they saw another animal they tensed up.

In the distance on Gerren's right he spotted something moving. Before he might have dismissed it but the tension pouring off the others made him tug on Vahli's arm and point. The bard stared where Gerren was indicating but shook his head. He hadn't seen it but nevertheless Vahli warned the others.

Their field of vision was restricted by sweeping snow showers that criss-crossed their path or sometimes blew straight in their faces when the wind changed direction. At the moment a cross-wind sweeping in from the west made it difficult to see anything beyond a dozen paces on their right side. If an attack was going to come from anywhere Gerren reasoned it would be from the east. He kept his attention focused in that direction as Vahli steered the sled.

Something was moving out there. This time the bard saw it and so had the others. It was smaller than a bear and seemed to have a loping grace Gerren associated with their dogs. The wind was blowing in the wrong direction so thankfully their dogs couldn't detect its scent.

"What is it?" said Gerren, but Vahli shook his head.

"Maybe a snow fox…" Either he trailed off or his words were snatched away by the wind. Gerren saw the lines between his eyebrows deepen and the bard's short sword appear in one hand. It didn't make sense. Why were they being targeted? What was it about them that attracted the wild animals? He guessed it could be the meat they were carrying for the dogs. Perhaps if they left some behind it would draw them away. He suggested the idea to Vahli who considered it but then shook his head.

"We can't afford to slow down or stop. It might be another ambush. Best we try to outrun whatever is lurking out there."

Gerren hadn't considered that. He could only just make out the rough shape of one beast, roughly the size of a large dog, but there could be a dozen more just out of sight. Last time they'd seen one bear and the other had surprised them from the opposite direction.

They stuck to the same bearing and pressed on but their shadow never left them. When the terrain became more uneven and they had to slow down to clamber up snowy ridges Gerren braced himself for an attack but it didn't come. They sailed down the other side, gaining speed, and he thought they'd lost it only for it to reappear shortly after. It always stayed at the same distance and continued to keep pace. The dogs could keep this up for hours but eventually they would need to stop for rest.

Gerren's muscles were beginning to ache from being in the same position for so long that his arms and legs began to cramp. He tried to ease the tingling pain but it was difficult within the confines of the sled. Vahli rode behind him and he was tucked in amidst the supplies creating an uneven but sheltered seat. It was a lot more comfortable and warmer than being on the back but, like the dogs, he needed a break. Perhaps whatever was stalking them hoped they would keep running until they had tired themselves out and then attack.

When Gerren's stomach began to grumble he realised it was well past the time they normally stopped for lunch. The dogs showed no signs of slowing yet but he could see everyone else shifting about in discomfort from being on the sleds for so long without a break.

"We need to stop soon," shouted Kell, slowing his sled so that they could hear him.

"I think it's counting on that," said Malomir.

"If we keep going, the dogs will be exhausted. We may need a fast escape and they won't have the energy. Neither will any of us." Kell's reasoning was sound. They might be able to fight off whatever was out there before it called in anything else, but not if they were tired.

"We'll stop at the bottom of that ridge," he said, pointing to a thick line of snow to the west. "Feed the dogs as normal but keep your weapons ready in case of an attack. Bronwyn, Willow, stand guard."

Gerren's heart began to pound fast and hard. His hands tightened into fists and he tried to slow down his breathing. Looking to the others for strength he saw they were calm and steady, at least on the outside. Kell had a steely glint in his eyes that Gerren had not seen before. Unfortunate circumstances had brought him to this place, against his wishes, and yet now he refused to surrender. The others had chosen to be here, like him, which made Gerren's chest swell with pride.

As the sleds came to a stop the fear made his stomach churn, but he refused to let it be his master. Gerren tried his best to ignore it as he drew his sword.

As Gerren and Vahli fed the dogs, Kell mashed up ice for their water while keeping an eye on the murky shape in the distance. It had settled down onto its haunches, suggesting it was a wolf but he'd never heard of one so far north, nor one so attentive. But these were abnormal times and perhaps all beasts were now under the sway of some outside power. Even more worrying than that idea was that its reach extended this far.

Perhaps he was wrong. Perhaps this wasn't the Ice Lich. Kell wasn't sure if that was a comforting thought or not. Either the Ice Lich was still alive and its power had changed over the years or they were facing something new.

The others were relying on his knowledge to guide them, but all of his experience would count for nothing if their enemy was an unknown.

The dogs had finished their meal and the others now gathered beside him in a semi-circle. The ridge behind provided them with cover from the wind but the drifting snow blowing over the top trickled down the back of his neck.

All of the heroes had died in the Frozen North. Was it luck that had saved him ten years ago? Or should he have died alongside the others? If that was his fate then he would not lie down and just let it happen. Whether it was the Ice Lich or something else, he would fight until the end.

"Come on then," said Kell as he rolled his shoulders. He was still sore and aching from yesterday's fight but he pushed the pain to the back of his mind.

As if it had heard him the solitary beast approached. As its shape coalesced into one he recognised, Kell's stomach clenched with fear. It was a maglau. Although it was only slightly larger than one of their sled dogs the canine beast was something primordial. A beast that should have died centuries ago but had stubbornly held on in this last frozen bastion.

With thick grey fur and a broad stocky frame that was packed with muscle the maglau was a powerful animal that had thrived despite the harsh climate. Its razor sharp teeth and claws were effective weapons but they were not what made it such a dangerous killing machine. A short bony frill, which encircled the top portion of its head, was studded with blunt protrusions. The longest two were above its forehead which it used to ram its enemies, stunning them or punching through their defences. Kell had seen how much damage their horns could inflict on armour and the flesh beneath. Several of the heroes had come away with broken ribs and Kursen had eventually died because of his injuries.

"Just one?" said Malomir.

Kell was already shaking his head. "There are always seven maglau in a sabre."

The beast at the front was the scout. Small, compared to the rest, it was designed for speed and endurance. Walking in a line directly behind the scout to conceal their numbers came the beta, a beast twice as big as the scout. One of its horns was snapped off and Kell could hear a deep rumbling coming from its chest. Four more maglau came after it until he saw the alpha at the rear, a huge black and grey monster with blue eyes.

"Remember, don't bother with blows to the head," said Kell, watching as the pack began to spread out. The sled dogs had noticed the maglau and were now whining and cowering behind the sleds. The maglau were trying to flank them, gradually spreading out in a semi-circle of their own.

On his far left stood Willow. The Alfár held her peculiar weapon ready in both hands, her head cocked to one side as she assessed the creatures. On the far right was Bronwyn, gritting her teeth and snarling back at the beta which was staring directly at her. Kell knew the maglau would have great difficulty getting past either one of them if they wanted to attack from behind.

There was no signal. No change in their posture. Between one heartbeat and the next the maglau charged. Kell saw Willow spin her weapon around as a maglau ran forward, sweeping it in an upward arc which caught the beast under the jaw, punching a hole in its head. Bronwyn bellowed on his right, slamming her shoulder into the beast's head which sent it reeling. Then Kell only had eyes for the maglau in front which put its head down and tried to break his legs with its bony head.

Moving on instinct his sword came down, bounced off its thick skull, barely broke the skin and drew only a small trickle of blood. Its snapping jaws tried to grab a leg and he retaliated by kicking it in the snout. The maglau yipped in pain and danced back a few steps but he didn't pursue it. Kell knew it was trying to draw him forward and isolate him from the protection of his friends on either side. They had a sly intelligence, far beyond the normal cunning of other beasts. When the maglau saw that its ruse hadn't worked it changed tactics.

Pairing up with one of its pack the two attacked him together. Kell kicked out at one and jabbed his sword at the other's face, catching it across the mouth. The beast squeaked in pain but didn't fall back. As blood spattered on the snow it snarled and made a feint at Gerren beside him. Despite his warning the boy tried to hammer the maglau with his sword. The beast didn't even try to dodge and simply lowered its head, letting the blade ricochet off its skull. Kell was forced to dodge to one side to avoid Gerren's blade and that was when the other beast attacked. Its skull connected with Kell's hip and one of its horns punched him in the stomach, driving the air from his body. As he gasped for breath and fell to one knee it came forward, trying to grab his wrist and wrench his sword away.

Screaming as if in pain Gerren swung his sword with both hands at the maglau. The blade caught it on the shoulder, bit deep and knocked it to one side, saving Kell from being savaged. The other slammed into Gerren's leg, bowling him over and then Kell was fighting for his life as the injured maglau tried to rip out his throat.

He managed to get his sword up in time but the beast grabbed the blade with its teeth and refused to let go. As they struggled for control of the sword he tried to push the beast away but it was stronger than him and too heavy. Its whole body was pressed against his making it impossible for him to reach the dagger on his belt. Kell's left hand scrabbled around for something to use as a weapon but there was nothing in reach, just clumps of snow and ice. Balling up a handful he smashed it into the beast's face, aiming for its eyes. A shard of ice bit into the sensitive skin around its left eye and it yelped, pulling back slightly, easing its weight off his chest. Kell grabbed his dagger and jabbed it into the same eye. The maglau's vision hadn't cleared so it didn't see the blade coming. Kell buried it up to the hilt and then vainly held on as the creature pulled back screaming in agony.

It dropped the sword and danced a few paces back. Kell tried to follow but the bones in his side crunched together and he almost blacked out from the pain. Moving more slowly he eased himself to hands and knees, conscious that the fighting was still going on around him. The blinded maglau had tried to run but had only made a few paces before it had collapsed. Its sides were still heaving but it was out of the fight.

On his far right Bronwyn was not faring well against the largest beast. She was bleeding from a nasty gash on her arm and there was blood on her face as well. The beast was covered with half a dozen long cuts and it held one of its back feet slightly off the ground but neither of them was ready to back down. When she made a feint it tried to dash out of the way but instead it fell onto its rear. As Bronwyn went to press her advantage the maglau stopped pretending it was injured.

Pouncing forward, its blunt horns rammed Bronwyn in the midriff which sent her skidding back. Instead of falling over she stumbled to one knee putting her on the same level as the beast's muzzle. It charged forward again as she tried to hack its legs off. At the last moment, instead of biting her, it lowered its bony head which connected with her head and shoulder.

Bronwyn went sailing backwards. Her sword disappeared into the snow and she was left lying face down.

"No!" shouted Malomir who flew into a frenzy. His careful and precise motions became wilder and more intense. He was making mistakes and leaving openings but he was moving so quickly, the heavy scimitar swirling through the air, the maglau couldn't take advantage. Spinning on one foot, his head whipping around, Malomir's blade sliced across the face of his enemy, taking off part of its snout and both its upper and lower jaw. The creature went berserk as its teeth fell out and its tongue was severed. Malomir finished the beast with a heavy blow that severed its spine. Before the beast had even finished dying he was moving to help Bronwyn but there was no need.

Bellowing like a wounded bear she held the maglau that had attacked her off the ground with both arms. It was trying to rip off her face but her head was turned to one side and as her arms tightened Kell heard the beast's bones crack. Its teeth and horns snagged one of her ears and scored a line across her forehead but she refused to let go. Its howls of pain became even more high-pitched as Bronwyn's fingers came together around its back making her grip unbreakable.

Leaving her to finish the beast off Kell turned to help the others. Gerren seemed to be faring the worst and was bleeding from a cut on his leg. There was more blood on his face and his eyes were wide with terror. He'd picked up a long dagger from somewhere and now held it in one hand instead of his sword. When the maglau jumped forward he was too slow to move out of reach. Its jaws snagged one of the boy's feet and he fell backwards landing heavily. Its teeth bit into Gerren's calf and he screamed but still lashed out with the dagger stabbing it in the nose. Kell's sword bit into its flank and it finally released the boy's leg which was a savaged mess. Gerren's face had turned a sickly green and Kell thought he might pass out from blood loss. Screaming in defiance Gerren stabbed the maglau under its mouth, pinning its jaws together. The blade wasn't long enough to reach its brain but it had caught on something as the beast couldn't open its mouth.

Kell's sword took off one of its front legs and it dropped to the snow. Its back legs lashed out, its claws scoring cuts across his shins and a second kick knocked him over. Gerren had picked up his fallen sword and between each desperate breath Kell could hear him telling the beast to die as he stabbed it over and over. It gashed him across the chest and cut his stomach before its attacks began to slow. By this time Gerren was covered with blood up to his elbows as his sword came down again and again. Finally the beast stopped fighting and was still.

"Stop, stop," said Kell, waving at the lad who was still stabbing the beast. Kell had to pull him off the maglau which continued to bleed into the snow. Gerren collapsed beside Kell and his hands began to shake. He pulled Gerren close and held on to him tightly until it faded.

Bronwyn had broken the maglau's spine and now it lay dying in the snow while she and Malomir helped Vahli. With three of them surrounding the beast it should have run or been afraid. Instead it became even more vicious.

All of them were bleeding from their wounds and the beast's fur was matted with clumps of blood. When it lunged at Malomir the other two attacked, Bronwyn's sword severing a leg while Vahli buried another dagger in its side up to the hilt. The beast stumbled to one side as if drunk and then flopped down on its rear. Like a tired dog it lay down on its front paws and closed its eyes. The pool of red surrounding its body began to spread across the snow.

A peculiar whooping sound caught his attention and turning around Kell saw Willow wrestling with the last beast. They were rolling around together on the ground and standing out against the churned snow Kell saw spots of blue. It took him a while to realise it was the Alfár's blood. She had a cut on one arm and there was more blood staining her stomach. As its claws scrabbled to find flesh Willow began to keen as if in pain. With an inhuman surge of strength the Alfár seized the maglau by the bony frill and wrenched its head to one side snapping its neck. The beast didn't even have time to scream.

Staring at the broken bodies of the maglau Kell felt a surge of triumph. Everyone was injured but they'd survived another vicious attack from whatever power was set against them. He thought they'd done well until Bronwyn began to sway on her feet.

"What is it?" asked Malomir, trying to steady her.

Her eyes rolled back in her head and like a felled tree she toppled over backwards into the snow.

CHAPTER 26

Reverend Mother Britak, adorned in her finest ceremonial garments for the naming service, stared up at the high dome of the church with a sense of awe. It was not as impressive as the cathedral back home in Lorzi, the Holy City, but it was not far behind. She had been told the paintings on the ceiling had taken almost ten years to complete. After completing the mural the artist had declared it his greatest work and had laid down his brushes. Apparently he'd lived out the rest of his life as a farmer.

The glorious sprawling paintings portrayed all twelve pillars of her faith. They had been crafted in remarkable detail so that even a non-believer wouldn't need to ask what each represented. It was a suitable tribute to the Shepherd which renewed her belief that the King of Hundar was a worthy ally and, more importantly, a true believer.

"They're here, Reverend Mother," said Sallie, tugging on her sleeve.

"Thank you, dear," said Britak, turning her gaze towards the rear of the church. Her neck cracked alarmingly but she ignored both it and the pain shooting down her back.

She had been staring at the ceiling for too long. If anyone asked she would tell them she'd been lost in its majesty, which was partially true. She'd also lost track of time and had forgotten she wasn't alone in the church.

It was becoming increasingly difficult to focus her mind and the trip to the Hundarian capital city, Pynar, had not been kind on her ageing body. Britak took it as another reminder that life, much like the light of a candle, was finite and her time had almost run out. She needed to make certain that plans would continue in her absence which could be a lot sooner than she thought.

The church housed two thousand people in the pews alone. However, because it was such a special occasion, more had been allowed to stand around the edges, swelling the numbers. At the sound of heavy footsteps marching in time, all heads turned towards the rear of the church.

Armed Royal Hundarian guards were evenly spaced around the edge of the room, with more surrounding the main doors, but it was the dozen dressed in white, marching down the central aisle that everyone was watching. In gleaming conical helmets that covered most of their faces, silver breastplates and long cloaks made of the purest lambswool edged in gold, they were a marvellous sight. They reminded her of the ancient order of warrior monks who had once travelled across the Five Kingdoms bringing the glory of the Shepherd to all. It was a wonderful memory of the past and hopefully something that would come again. It was her greatest wish that in the future not a single village or remote settlement would miss out on the joy of the Book and its wonderful teachings.

Behind the ceremonial guards came the King and Queen of Hundar. The towering figure of King Elias was dressed in a silk outfit of royal blue and a cloak edged in fur that trailed across the tiled floor behind him. All Hundarians were tall but the King was head and shoulders above everyone in the church.

Elias was the one sovereign in the Five Kingdoms that she thought worthy of his position. He'd only inherited the crown from his father six years ago as he'd doggedly held on to the bitter end. Like every other nation Hundarians believed the throne could not simply be passed on when a King stepped down. It was only inherited upon the death of the previous King, which was why Elias was already approaching his fortieth year.

On his right arm came Queen Olenna, a slender willow of a woman not much shorter than her husband. Like all adults in Hundar her head was shaven and it gleamed in the reflected light from hundreds of candles around the room. Directly behind them, cradled against the significant bosom of the wet nurse, was the new royal heir, third in line to the throne, Prince Matteo. Britak had not been present for the naming service of their firstborn son and heir, so this was a lesser honour, but it still sent an important message.

For the next hour Britak focused only on the ritual. She'd seen it performed hundreds of times and had personally conducted it perhaps six times. It was a rare and special honour for the Reverend Mother to name a child.

After reading from the Book and blessing all of those present she called forth the witnesses. The King and Queen, plus four of their closest acquaintances, stepped forward, each pledging themselves to care for the child if the worst should happen to the parents. These days it was symbolic but in the past, during times of war, when parents left and never came home, it was a necessary rite to ensure children didn't end up on the streets. That way led to crime, drugs, prostitution, begging and other darker sins of the mind and body she didn't want to contemplate.

From their expressions she could see the King's friends thought this was nothing more than a jape until she impressed upon them the seriousness of the situation. Britak was certain they were heathens or casual believers but she would not tolerate a slapdash approach to the ritual.

"Will you care for this child until your dying breath?" she asked, looking each witness in the eye, one after another. The smiles slid away under the intensity of her glare and faces flushed with excitement paled into seriousness.

"Aye, I will," they intoned.

"Will you give everything you possess to ensure his survival and success?" she asked. In the old days being a witness was a curse not a blessing. It meant forsaking your own child and their needs for the changeling.

"Aye, I will," said each witness, now stony-faced as they realised what she and all of those present demanded of them. And if they failed in their obligation everyone would know of their transgression.

Once the swearing of the witnesses was complete they quickly stepped back, making way for the twelve soldiers dressed in white.

This part of the rite had not been performed in almost a hundred years. Some of Britak's predecessors had claimed it was barbaric and unrealistic but sometimes the old ways were still the best.

One soldier for each of the pillars of the one true faith. They lined up, forming a circle around the prince on the raised stone dais. As one they spoke making a promise in front of their King and Queen, thousands of witnesses and the Shepherd, to serve and protect the child. They would form the prince's Blood Guard, forsaking everything else in their life for him. They would take no husband or wife, bear no children, and abstain from alcohol and drugs. From this point forward only the Shepherd and the prince mattered. Each soldier had been carefully selected and from today they would become warriors of faith. Britak envied them. They would have little to worry about. Theirs would be a life free of distractions that sought to take them away from what was truly important. Family and their faith.

The naming rite had taken more out of her than she'd anticipated. Britak had to steady herself with one hand on the back of the plinth where no one could see. With the last sweep of her hand, blessing the assembled, it was done. Rapturous applause swelled the church, echoing off the walls, and despite her tiredness she couldn't help smiling. It was a good beginning.

Without being asked Sallie moved to her side, subtly shouldering some of her weight as they walked towards the priests' room. Britak gave the girl a gentle squeeze to show her appreciation as Sallie guided her down the corridor.

The private chapel was little more than a room with two pews and a gnarled statue of the Shepherd from two centuries past. One of his arms had broken off and his face had been ravaged by time creating an anonymous brooding figure of a hunched man. It was fitting. The sculptor had attempted to give the figure particular features but no one really knew the face of God. Each person had their own interpretation which was why all other statues had a robed figure in a hood.

Britak had barely changed out of her formal robes into something comfortable when she heard the rapid thump of boots coming down the corridor. Without looking around she knew who it was, especially as he wasn't alone. She'd thought he would at least wait until their official meeting at the palace.

"Wait here," said King Elias to his guards who took up their posts outside the chapel. Britak glanced over her shoulder and gestured Sallie towards the far side of the room where there was a jug of water. The King settled himself on the wooden bench beside her and took a moment to gather his thoughts.

"Thank you," said Britak, accepting water from the girl.

"No," said the King, flicking his hand at Sallie when she offered him a battered clay cup. "Leave us."

"The girl is a dullard. Just ignore her," she said. King Elias raised an eyebrow but then shrugged, dismissing the girl from his thoughts. Sallie wouldn't remember to get dressed unless someone told her each morning so it was unlikely she would recall what was said in the room.

"Close the door," said Britak. Sallie moved to comply then stood with her back against it, awaiting further instruction, a gormless expression on her face.

"Reverend Mother, can you please explain why there are nearly three thousand Choate camping on my land?"

She was impressed he'd kept his temper enough to use her title. If nothing else he was sincere in his devotion to the Shepherd. "I cannot, although the most likely explanation is to do with the blasphemer, Kell Kressia."

"I am tired of hearing that name," said Elias, picking some dust off his shirt. "I received your message, via my ambassador, and fifteen warriors were sent to deal with him. These were not mercenaries, Reverend Mother, but highly trained soldiers."

"And what happened to them?"

"They were last seen leaving Ruibeck in pursuit of Kell Kressia and his band of misfits. They disappeared shortly after."

The Choate were nothing but bloodthirsty savages who believed in some twisted story that put them above all others. Britak had only been exposed to the smallest amount of their dogma but had found it startling in its simplicity. It spoke to their barbaric cruel and brutal nature.

As much as she despised them for their heathen beliefs and sinful ways the Choate never left their homeland in significant numbers. There were a few of them dotted around the cities of the Five Kingdoms but there had not been such a large number of them outside their territory in almost two hundred years.

"Why get involved now?" asked Elias.

"I cannot say. Perhaps they believe in this nonsense about a new evil in the north. It would explain why they killed your soldiers."

"It's nothing but propaganda from that miserable old toad, Bledsoe. I just wish he would die. He's like my father." Elias had been willing his father to die for almost a decade but the old codger had stubbornly held on.

"The Choate are savages. Who can say what such inbred people believe?" said Britak. Elias was still clenching his jaw, angry about the murder of his warriors. "What are they doing? Are they preparing for war?" she asked, hoping this was not a precursor to another conflict.

"No. My spies report they're involved in some kind of contest. Games of physical strength and endurance. They're testing themselves against each other."

It tied in with their notion of being chosen and that only the strong deserved to survive. It also confirmed what Britak had long thought about the Choate and their tribal nature. They were probably competing for dominance although she would have expected more bloodshed rather than tests of skill. It didn't matter.

They were just another thorn in her side that would be dealt with when the time was right.

"Let Bledsoe play his games and try to win favour with the people. It's short-sighted and shows his ignorance. In a few years' time, it won't make any difference."

"And why is that?" asked Elias, calming down a little.

"His daughter, Princess Sigrid, is a true believer and not someone who is easily cowed. It will be her hand that guides the nation of Algany into the future. One where faith is paramount."

"That's good news. I'm relieved."

"My recent meeting with her went exceptionally well. I believe there will be a special partnership between Algany and the Holy City. Maybe even Hundar too," she speculated.

Elias relaxed at her good news. "We could do with an ally in the war to come."

Britak intended to win over the hearts and souls of all people living within the Five Kingdoms to the one true faith. She had no illusions. It would still be a difficult and widespread struggle. Trying to change the minds of adults was notoriously difficult and not all would willingly surrender to the Shepherd. It was far easier to set a person on the right path from an early age when their mind was malleable. Of course there would be some resistance but she was expecting it.

"Tell me, do you have any good news about the missionaries?"

The King relaxed and leaned back against the pew. "Ten days ago another ship carrying five hundred missionaries crossed the Narrow Sea."

The lands beyond Corvan were vast and untamed. There were huge swathes of fertile land that the primitive locals had been gradually converting into farmland. Fifty years ago the Corvanese had brought the notion of trade and money to them where before they had simply relied on a rudimentary barter system.

Now they were keen on acquiring tools and other possessions they couldn't produce themselves. In turn this had accelerated their agricultural efforts and built stronger ties with the Five

Kingdoms. It had been a logical and compassionate next step to raise them up out of the dirt. Devout missionaries had taken the Book and its holy gospel to their leaders and from there it was spreading like wildfire throughout the Untamed lands.

"Let the Choate play their games," said Britak, "and the heathens worship their false idols. It won't matter. By the time your first-born son comes of age and is ready to take his place on the throne of Hundar, Kell Kressia and all his ilk will be dust. If the savages cannot be tamed then they too will be cleansed from the Five Kingdoms."

"Glorious day," said Elias, his eyes alight with fervent passion.

"Do you have some good news for me?" she asked.

"Yes, Reverend Mother. The third compound in rural Hundar will be ready to open in the next few days. As we agreed, we will start small and adjust the education programme as required. Once we have the right system in place we can increase the numbers."

They both understood that building a holy army would take years, especially as they were trying to keep it secret from the other nations. In some cases the most challenging part would be shaping minds and re-educating those who had been led astray. Adult minds were like steel. You could apply pressure and bend them up to a point but if you pushed too hard they would snap. It was so much easier to mould young minds. Children were far more easier to control.

"While I'm here I'd very much like to visit one of the compounds," said Britak.

"I'll see to the arrangements," promised Elias. "Unfortunately the route there will have to be a little roundabout. There are spies from Kinnan everywhere."

"I wouldn't worry too much about King Lars," said Britak, with a smile. "He won't be a problem in the future."

"And why is there?"

"His son, Prince Meinhart, is getting a re-education at one of my monasteries."

King Elias raised an eyebrow. "Where?"

Britak shrugged. "It's better that you don't know. Suffice to say, Meinhart is learning about the importance of the Book. When he returns home he will be a true believer. In the meantime, I believe King Lars will do whatever we ask of him."

"Praise be," said the King.

"We're using similar methods to those at the compounds, but we have to move very slowly." She couldn't risk the Prince dying from being starved to death or having too many cold baths. That would put her plans back years and make the north even more intractable than at present. Slow and steady was the way forward. Eventually they'd break his mind and then rebuild it. Britak had no illusions about seeing her plan come to fruition but one day an army of devout followers would remake the Five Kingdoms. Then everyone would serve the Shepherd and a glorious future would emerge.

CHAPTER 27

Vahli had not received any training as a doctor but his knowledge of the body was better than most. A quick search of Bronwyn's injuries revealed the swelling on her head from where the maglau had struck her. The bard stitched and bandaged her other wounds to prevent infection and further blood loss, but it was the head injury that was the most worrying.

"I don't think her skull is broken," said Vahli, slowly walking his fingers over Bronwyn's scalp. "There's just this lump."

"Is she going to wake up?" asked Malomir. The Islander was so distressed he wouldn't sit down or let anyone tend to his injuries. He had a number of cuts, some of which looked severe, but he didn't care. Kell and the others had already been stitched up and slathered in foul-smelling poultices. Vahli had also confirmed Kell's suspicion. The maglau had cracked at least one of his ribs from where it had rammed him.

"I don't know when she'll wake up," said the bard. "But we need to keep it cold to reduce the swelling."

"We should make camp," said Malomir. "Until she's recovered."

"We can't stay here," said Kell, glancing at the bodies. The sled dogs had not been injured during the attack but they were distressed by the maglau. They shied away from the beasts and continued to pace back and forth in their harnesses. The spilled blood and bodies would attract scavengers and none of them were ready for another fight. All Kell wanted was to lie down and sleep but it was too dangerous to stay here.

Malomir didn't respond. He knelt down beside Bronwyn while the others gathered their belongings leaving the difficult conversation to Kell.

"We need to move," said Kell.

"I'm not leaving her," said Malomir.

Kell decided on a harder tack. "She'll freeze to death out here on the ice."

"Then I'll make camp."

"What if the smell attracts another sabre of maglau? Or a snow bear? You'll both be ripped apart." It was so strange to see Malomir morose and quiet. It was completely at odds with his normal temperament.

"Then I will fight."

Kell sighed and shook his head. "You're injured, bleeding and not at full strength. I'm sure you'll fight bravely but you'll still lose. Then you'll have to watch as she's killed and eaten in front of you." Malomir was in his face in the blink of an eye but Kell didn't fight back as the Islander's hands circled his throat. "Stay here and die, or come with us and live."

"What if moving her makes it worse?" asked Malomir, easing his hands away from Kell's neck.

"We'll be as gentle as we can," said Kell, resting a hand on his shoulder. "I promise."

"Do you believe in the Shepherd?" asked Malomir, looking at him with plaintive eyes.

"Yes I do." Kell didn't believe but he knew what Malomir was going to ask. There were no gods in the Summer Isles.

"Will you say a prayer for her?"

"I will," promised Kell. He knelt beside Bronwyn in the snow and searched his memories for a suitable blessing. As a boy he'd often heard his mother whispering a prayer before bed. It was always the same one. She'd wanted him to live a long and happy life and to become a great man. Kell muttered the prayer and much to his surprise found his face wet with tears. What would his mother say now if she could see him? Would she be proud of the man he'd become?

With great care they loaded Bronwyn onto one of the sleds, wrapping her in blankets to keep her warm. Malomir insisted on overseeing everything and only let them tend to his wounds once she was settled.

This time no one claimed a souvenir from the battle. They left the dead maglau where they'd fallen in the snow. The sled dogs were keen to put some distance between them and the dead beasts and they all felt the same way.

After about an hour they came to the edge of a frozen lake that stretched for miles in all directions. Kell searched for a suitable site to make camp and found a spot in the lee of two huge banks of snow that had formed from the wind.

When the dogs were comfortable and fed they seemed much calmer although a few were still skittish. Bronwyn had not woken up and her condition was unchanged as they pitched their tents. Despite her size, Willow picked up Bronwyn and carried her like a child before gently laying her down inside the tent. Malomir kept an ice cold cloth applied to the lump on her head but the swelling had not reduced.

As Kell dropped pieces of meat into the bubbling pot for their meal, Gerren voiced his worst fears. "What if she doesn't wake up?" he whispered.

"It's too early to tell," said Vahli. The lump was barely noticeable and so far there wasn't any bruising. The bard's reasoning was sound but when it came to head injuries it was difficult to know. There could be a lot more damage and even bleeding on the inside but there was no way to tell. Hopefully Bronwyn had a thick skull and the damage wasn't too severe but now came the worst part. The waiting.

Unfortunately their supplies were limited and they couldn't afford to camp in one spot for several days hoping that she would just wake up. They could fish to supplement their stores but it wouldn't be enough to feed both the dogs and them. Tomorrow they would have to cross the frozen lakes and continue north towards the castle. That was another difficult conversation he was not looking forward to having with Malomir. For the time being Kell focused on the task at hand; making a meal to replenish their energy.

Once they'd all eaten, including Malomir who had to be persuaded to leave Bronwyn's side, they boiled fresh water for a pot of tea. The peculiar herbs that Malomir added to the water stank but he insisted they were good for the blood and promoted healing. Once brewed the tea gave off a heady mix, similar to cinnamon and liquorice, but it was bright orange in colour. They carefully dribbled a small amount into Bronwyn's mouth but there was little else they could do except kept her warm. Everyone sipped their tea with little enthusiasm as it tasted foul despite the aroma.

A steady wind blew in from the north but thankfully they were sheltered by the snow banks. Nevertheless a scattering of flakes drifted down and soon everything in their camp was coated white. Normally after eating, everyone immediately sought out the comfort and warmth of their tents but today no one was in a hurry.

Sitting in companionable silence with the others Kell wondered if he would have been happy living abroad with a new name. Would his bad luck have continued or would it have ended the moment he left the Five Kingdoms? After thinking on it for a while he realised it didn't matter. It was just as he'd said to Gerren. Wherever he went, the memories would still be there. No distance would change that. It was the same as trying to outrun his fear. He couldn't escape his past and until this journey was over, one way or the other, he'd never be free.

As Kell sipped his tea he realised that during the fight with the maglau his hands hadn't shaken. Not once. The fear was still there, but he'd been so focused on trying to stay alive, he'd not dwelled on it.

The boy had done well too. His rudimentary technique was clumsy, and he'd nearly sliced off one of his own ears and stabbed Kell, but his will to survive had seen him through. Kell could see that he was now going over the fight in his mind while doing his best to control the shakes. The near misses and what-ifs would be going around in his head. At times like that it was difficult to ignore the voice of fear and feel gratitude at still being alive.

As the wind picked up a cold mist drifted in making it difficult to see far beyond their camp. Anything could be lurking out there in the endless white but right now Kell knew no one had the energy to fight. The temperature dropped and one by one the others drifted off into their tents until he was sat alone with Malomir. The mournful expression on the Islander's face was so foreign it was as if he'd been transformed into a completely different person. He was a far cry from the drunk they'd first met only a few days ago.

"You once asked me why I left the Summer Isles," said Malomir. Kell remembered his idyllic description. Even at the time he hadn't believed the reasons. "I didn't tell you the whole truth," he continued.

It was a neat way of saying that he'd lied. Kell waited in silence as he clearly had more to tell.

"At a distance the Summer Isles are perfect. They are a wonder to look at, green and glorious, but under the surface there is much that concerns me. People cling to old and dangerous traditions that are causing others harm. At the same time many young people are desperate to leave and find their fortune abroad, forgetting tradition and family. There is discord between the two ways of living and I fear it could lead to violence. The truth is, I am a coward."

It was the last thing Kell had expected him to say. "Why do you say that?"

"Because I want to be a popular King. The change that is needed will be difficult for some to accept and many of my people will hate me. They will call me a traitor to our ancestors. So instead of facing it head on, I came here, in search of adventure."

"What about all of those stories? Did you make them up?"

Malomir shook his head. "Fighting a beast is easy. It does not speak. It does not poke holes in your argument. It is kill or be killed. The problems at home require a different form of courage. One that is not eroded overnight. It would take months, perhaps years of struggle to save my people."

"And now? What do you want?" asked Kell.

Malomir glanced into his tent and then away into the snow. Somewhere in the distance Kell hear a faint whistling. "She is unique. In all my travels I've never met a woman like her. I never expected..." He trailed off and heaved a long sigh. "All I want is for her to wake up. That is the only thing that matters. When she is at my side I believe anything is possible."

"Then let's hope that–" Kell stopped as the whistling grew louder. At first he'd thought it was only the snow shifting in the breeze. It was easy to mistake such sounds for voices, like a rotting tree moaning as the wind moved through it. But as he listened Kell thought there was something familiar about it.

Through the whirling snow he saw a dark shape in the storm. Tall and slender it vaguely resembled a woman. It was there for a moment and then gone.

The wind had acquired a voice. It was feminine and the tone had a lilting, rhythm like a lullaby. There were no words but Kell was sure that if he concentrated the meaning would become apparent. It was just beyond the edges of his perception.

Malomir's expression changed from one of concern to surprise as he heard the voice. A question formed on his lips but Kell shook his head before he could ask. It couldn't be. He didn't want it to be true but, deep down in his soul, he knew.

Kell recognised the sound and was afraid for their lives.

The voice became stronger and deeper somehow, passing through Kell's body, rooting itself in his bones, making the hair stand up on the back of his neck. He turned his head, searching for the source, but the song was coming from all directions.

There was a disturbance in the tents as the others stumbled out, drawn from their rest by the peculiar sound. Gerren's eyes were already wide, a stupefied expression on his face as he became enthralled. Vahli and Willow were merely puzzled, unsure what had made them return to the cold seemingly against their will. It was their bewilderment that confirmed his worst fear.

"Don't listen to the voices," he shouted, waving his arms to attract their attention. "It's the Qalamieren."

Naming the danger had a dramatic effect on everyone except the Alfár. Vahli began to swear, something he'd never done before. Gerren's eyes widened in terror and Malomir drew his sword for all the good that it would do. The Qalamieren were not flesh and blood. They were spirits of ice and dark water. Malicious entities that drew a person's worst fears or greatest hopes to the surface of their mind. They taunted and teased, terrified and thrilled until their victim died from pleasure, pain or a combination of both. There was no shield against their power. Hearing their ethereal voices was merely the beginning.

They carried no steel and wore no armour. Their weapons came from within their victims. And while a person was forced to experience their worst or best, over and over again, the Qalamieren fed on the person's soul, slowly draining their energy until the victim was nothing more than a husk. And there the person would lay, unfeeling, unthinking, until they froze to death.

The Frostrunner clans feared nothing upon the ice except the Qalamieren. Even the most vicious of beasts were seen as a natural part of their frozen world, but the Qalamieren did not belong.

No one knew where they came from and no one had ever found a way to fight them. The only safe course of action was to run and keep running until their haunting voices were left far behind.

"Run. We need to run," said Gerren, scrabbling around for something that would help.

"It's too late," muttered Kell. The dogs were exhausted and the spirits were already too close.

Ten years ago he'd heard only the faintest echo of their

otherworldly voices but it had been enough. The heroes had urged the dogs to run and even then everyone had fallen into a stupor. If not for the sled dogs, he and the surviving heroes would have been consumed. They'd been lucky and Kell hadn't even caught a glimpse of them.

But now the Qalamieren were fully revealed in all of their terrifying glory. Kell thought about drawing his sword but not even its familiar weight would bring him any comfort. Five tall narrow shapes drew closer through the snow until they coalesced into beings that loosely resembled women dressed in rags. Their bare feet didn't touch the ground and they left no trail as they drifted through the air.

Graceful arms moved as if deep under water, twisting and turning their fingers into peculiar gestures he couldn't unravel. Stark black hair down to the waist of each wraith stood out in contrast against the pale corpse white of their flesh. They might once have been beautiful women but something had been taken from them. Hope. Love. Compassion. Or perhaps they simply lacked a soul.

The pale skin was so taut he thought a smile would split their faces in two. From their mouths came a skin-crawling sound. A harmonic mix of music and half-forgotten words in a language he almost recognised. The sound filled him with such deep longing that his heart ached.

Worse than their song was the eyes. They were deep green and they glowed with a cold inner fire like the beating heart of a living emerald. But there was no warmth or humanity in those eyes and Kell was powerless to turn away.

He hoped that one of the others had escaped but from his eye corner saw that all of them had been entranced, even the Alfár. Willow's head was cocked to one side and she was staring at the Qalamieren with a puzzled expression. The world around Kell faded away like smoke and he awoke in a familiar nightmare.

* * *

Gerren had never seen such a beautiful woman before in his entire life. Her rich black hair was so dark it was almost blue and in the warm sunlight it shimmered like flowing water. Her pale cocoa skin smelled of cinnamon and apples, although that could have been the pie she had set out on the table.

Gerren couldn't remember how he'd arrived at the Thirsty Ferret but he sat down at his usual table. A broad smile stretched across his face as she ignored the other patrons and made a beeline for his table. Hopeful smiles turned to envious glares as she sat down opposite clasping one of his hands in both of hers. Her smile warmed him inside in a way he struggled to describe. Gerren wanted to say her name aloud but whenever he tried it kept slipping away. She watched him struggle with an expectant smile and when she laughed his skin tingled all over.

There was no need for words. He belonged to her and she was his whole world. Nothing could change that. She threw down her apron and led him out the front door and down the street to his parents' house. No, it was his house. It was their home, together They'd lived here for years now.

As Gerren sat down in front of the fire she gently tugged off his boots, hung up his sword and massaged his weary feet. He wanted to thank her but found he had no voice. Something was restricting his mouth but nevertheless she seemed to understand. Her smile sent shivers of pleasure across his arms and chest.

The kettle began to whistle and she pulled it out of the fire, setting a pot of tea to brew while she finished making their evening meal. Tantalising smells of roasted meat and spices filled the room, flushing his senses with pleasure. The tingling had spread down Gerren's chest to his stomach now. There was a brief flash of pain but then it was gone.

Gerren scraped the last of the food from his plate while she watched him with a secretive smile. Even after all these years she was still the best cook he'd ever met. It must have been a long day because he was so tired and could barely keep his eyes open.

He was always amazed at her strength. With one arm over her

shoulders she helped him up the stairs as if he were an old man. She bore much of his weight but never complained. They laughed together as he tripped and fell face first onto the bed with her. She rolled towards him and Gerren's mirth faded as he saw the fire dancing in her green eyes. They weren't merry any more. She had something else in mind. Gerren felt himself stir and he groaned aloud as her fingers began to loosen his belt. The tingling spread across his groin, moving down his legs and now it was quite painful. It felt as if his nerves were on fire. His skin was flushed and sore. The pain in his head was spreading. The nerves inside his skull had become burning wires of agony.

Looking up Gerren realised that somehow they were both naked and she was astride him. He didn't remember getting undressed. As they moved together her beautiful face began to change, elongating until her jaws stretched wide enough to swallow his head. Her skin became transparent and he could see the bones moving in her face. Only the cold green eyes remained the same, without warmth or sympathy.

Gerren tried to move but his arms and legs wouldn't respond. She brought her full weight down on his crotch and he tried to scream, but there was something in his mouth, clawing its way down his throat, scrabbling into his stomach like a burrowing worm. The inside of Gerren's body was on fire while his skin remained icy cold. Throwing back her head she screamed in pleasure. The sound clawed into his brain like a host of hungry maggots that ripped him apart.

Kell watched them all die.

First his parents. His mother and then a father he barely remembered. Then it was the turn of everyone he knew back in Honaje. All those he could name and even familiar faces he often passed in the street. The heroes came next. Those he'd grown to like and those he'd hated from the beginning. Finally, those he now travelled with were subjected to the same torture.

They were butchered with sharp knives and cut up into meaty chunks. Bludgeoned to death with blunt instruments until they were flattened and bloody, their bones ground to dust. Torn open with meat hooks and their innards strewn about like dry rice at a wedding. Their pitiful cries for mercy and a release from their suffering tore at his ears. The horrors of their agony made him want to claw out his own eyes but the torture was just beginning.

Kell tried to turn his face away but found that he couldn't move. Someone had tied him to a stout wooden chair with leather straps around his wrists, ankles and neck. A second strap ran across his forehead preventing him from turning his head to one side. Closing his eyes didn't make a difference. There was no refuge in the dark. The images were just as bright with his eyes closed. He had to watch every single moment of their suffering.

It would have been a blessing if they could only die once. Perhaps the worst part was watching them all being put back together. It was not an instant thing. They were not made whole in the blink of an eye. Piece by piece their flesh and bones knit together and all the while they felt the pain. Screaming until their throats were sore, until their voices cracked, until they begged him for death. And then it began again. The knives, the hammer, the hooks.

Somewhere in the back of his mind a small voice was trying to catch his attention. A niggle of doubt ran through him that something was amiss. At first he ignored it but soon he realised he never saw who was responsible for the vicious assaults on his family and friends.

The innards were spilled. The screams were plentiful but who held the blades and saws? Looking across the room Kell realised the version of himself tied to the chair was a mirage. A figment of his imagination created to make this easier. He hands were free and so was his will. No one could force him to do anything. He had always been his own man.

That was when he felt the familiar weight of the bone saw in his hand. Kell's scream mixed with that of his victims as he cut into their flesh.

* * *

Malomir watched in terror as one by one his allies succumbed to the unseen powers of the wraiths. They crumpled into heaps on the ground and at first he thought they were dead. Relief surged through him as Malomir witnessed the slow blinking of their eyes. The Qalamieren had placed them under a spell of sorts. Powerful emotions gripped his friends as their bodies began to writhe and contort in pain. A wraith paused beside each, kneeling just above the snow while placing a hand against their cheek.

It was an imitation of care. A mockery of love and benediction as it bestowed pain and suffering upon the victim. Gerren's mouth stretched wide with pleasure, he began to pant as if engaging with a woman but soon he was screaming, his eyes rolling around, desperate for a reprieve. Vahli was weeping, begging someone for forgiveness while Kell's hands twitched as tears silently ran down his cheeks.

All of his friends were animated except for the Alfár. She lay utterly still and the wraith that hovered above Willow had a hand on both cheeks and an expression of rapt concentration. It was exerting more of its will than usual to contain their exotic friend.

And with each scream, every cry of pain or pleasure, the wraiths fed on wisps of bright green energy that drifted up from their victim's body like coloured smoke. The transparent flesh of the Qalamieren became more substantial with each pulse. Fattening the hollow cheeks. Filling in the bald patches on their mangled scalps. Smoothing the wrinkles from their sallow flesh.

While the others were engaging his friends the last wraith came towards him, bobbing through the air like a cork floating on water. The haunting beauty of the woman in front of him could not be denied. Her perfectly formed face. Her curvaceous body which had transformed to match his taste. The image of her tugged at him but he knew that it was poison designed to cripple him like the others. Although every fibre of his head told him not to do it, Malomir listened to his heart.

His sword whistled through the air heading directly for the wraith's torso. The blade passed through her body without any resistance but his actions made it pause. The wraith cocked one eyebrow, puzzled that he was not enthralled by his perfect woman. Malomir tried a few more casual swings but they had the same effect.

"You cannot touch me with steel," murmured a voice. It was a breathy, smouldering voice, designed to please him. Sheathing his sword Malomir looked around for another weapon. "Am I not what you dream about?" asked the wraith.

She was perfect. She was the ideal that he had unknowingly been seeking and had never dared voice aloud. The Qalamieren had reached into the deepest corners of his mind and moulded its flesh as if it were soft clay. The strength in her shoulders. The gentle curve of her neck. The brightness of her green eyes. The softness of her lips. She was what he desired. And yet the passion she stirred in him was nothing compared to his feelings for Bronwyn.

Bronwyn, who was too tall for him and whose strength exceeded his own. Who was loud and impatient, uncouth and proud of her scars. Who had a body that was hard in more places that he was used to on a woman. Who wielded a blade with such vicious brutality and recklessness it made him worry for her safety. A woman who was his equal in many things and surpassed him in others. She was a challenge that tested him every day.

There were so many things about her that he would never have said were attributes he valued. But in the short time they'd been together he had come to know her better than any other woman in his life. Their intimacy went beyond the physical which was always vigorous and exhausting. In the dark before sleep he found himself sharing secrets with her that he had told no other. When she wrapped him in her arms he felt at peace and fell asleep with ease. Troubling thoughts about the problems at home usually kept him awake long into the night.

The Qalamieren paused a short distance away. It was baffled but still determined to bring him under its spell. The illusion of his perfect woman faded and the decaying wraith returned. Instead the world around Malomir changed as the spirit faded from view.

The snowy landscape was replaced with a vision of home with its crystal blue water, golden sandy beaches and lush green forests bursting with life. All was peaceful until a plume of smoke began to rise from the trees. The fire quickly spread, consuming a huge swath of jungle while clusters of his people built bonfires on the sand. Struggling prisoners, with their wrists bound together, were thrown alive onto the blaze. The crowd cheered in celebration as their victims died while the forest turned black, the seas were poisoned and all the fish died.

Twisted effigies carved of wood were raised upon the sand. More victims were sacrificed, bent backwards over altars and their lives ripped away as if they were nothing.

Vision after vision of destruction rained down on him and while Malomir wept for what might happen to his people he did not succumb to the torment. The images began to flicker and through gaps, like holes punched in a curtain, he could see the snow. Doing his best to ignore the horrors he was witnessing, Malomir stumbled towards the sleds.

"There is nowhere to go," murmured the wraith, no longer speaking in a voice intended to seduce. "You cannot escape."

A desperate idea had formed in his mind. His efforts were made more difficult as screaming victims now surrounded him on all sides. In desperate voices they begged for his help and asked why he'd abandoned them. When his fingers closed around cold metal hope surged in Malomir's heart. He pulled out a shirt from his pack and wrapped it tightly around his sword. Breaking open the tin he spilled its contents over the material until it was soaked through.

The Qalamieren continued to force images upon him but now the holes in its waking nightmares were growing larger. He could see more sections of snow overlaying the jungle and beaches. Malomir's hands shook as he brought them together. Again and again he tried, trying to quell the ache in his heart, to ignore the hideous future he was being made to witness.

Finally there was a spark from the flint and tinder. The shirt, soaked in oil, caught fire with ease. With a whoosh the sword erupted into flames and holding it aloft Malomir swung his fiery blade at the Qalamieren. This time there was some resistance as the scimitar swept through the wraith's body. It screamed in agony and the illusions of his home vanished. Motes of fire lingered on its person, dancing across the remnants of its decaying dress like roaming fireflies. They left blazing tracks in their wake but these quickly faded until Malomir hit it again. Now the ends of its hair had caught fire and the other Qalamieren paused in their assault.

Screaming a battle cry Malomir went among them, slicing at each wraith with his blazing sword, forcing them away from his friends. Whenever his sword passed through one of their ethereal bodies a small portion of the fire snagged on the remnants of their clothing or flesh. The first wraith he'd set on fire was now screeching as all of its hair was alight, transforming it into a pillar of fire.

The flames turned green and blue as they spread while the wraith screamed and writhed in pain. Although all of the Qalamieren were now alight none of them gave off any heat. The fire was within the mind as much as the body.

Piece by piece the wraith that attacked him was being gobbled up. Bite-sized chunks of its body disappeared into nothingness. First its feet and hands, then its legs faded away. A hole appeared in its chest which quickly spread across its torso and up its neck. It gave a final shriek and then it was utterly consumed.

With terrified howls the remaining Qalamieren fled from the fire that sought to eat them up from the inside. Malomir thought about following but his friends were still lying on the ground. None of them were moving and he had no idea about the extent of their injuries.

Instead Malomir stood his ground, holding the now smouldering blade aloft as the last of his shirt was burnt up.

And the Qalamieren, ethereal wraiths of legend, ran scared for the first time in hundreds of years.

CHAPTER 28

Kell was drifting in darkness. It was warm and welcoming, without pain or screams. A blessed relief from the Qalamieren and their torture. Away. He needed to get away.

Sitting bolt upright Kell banged his head on the pole, nearly ripping the tent from its moorings.

"They're gone. You're safe," said Malomir. Kell's eyes were still adjusting to the gloom when he felt a warm hand squeeze his shoulder. Lying beside him, wrapped up in her blanket, was the Alfár. Willow was deep asleep but her whole body was tense.

"Malomir?"

"I'm here. Rest easy, Kell. You need to sleep." The Islander sounded weary but he wasn't panicked, which suggested the danger had passed. Kell tried to ask what had happened but he was so tired he didn't manage to say the words out loud. Malomir helped him lie down and before Kell had finished pulling up his blanket the darkness claimed him.

The next time he woke, the tent was empty. His stomach was gurgling and tight with hunger, suggesting quite a few hours had passed. Crawling outside with a blanket around his shoulders he found the others sat in a circle. A big pot of food was bubbling away and everyone was eating as if it had been days since their last meal. There was still no sight of Bronwyn.

"How long was I asleep?" asked Kell, as Malomir handed him a bowl and some bread.

"You all slept through the night and most of the morning." From the deep shadows under Malomir's eyes it looked as if he hadn't slept at all. Looking at the others Kell saw all of their faces were equally haggard despite having slept for so long. Gerren's eyes were red rimmed from crying and Vahli refused to make eye contact with anyone. Even the Alfár had been affected by the Qalamieren. Her yellow eyes were dull and she moved in a listless manner as if drunk.

It felt as if a great weight was pressing down on Kell's whole body. His limbs were heavy and it took a long time to form any thoughts. He ate all of the food in his bowl and scraped it clean but felt no better. Something was missing, or rather, had been taken by the wraiths.

"Bronwyn?"

"Still asleep," said Malomir. "She missed it all."

"The Qalamieren?" asked Kell. Vahli twitched at the name and Gerren moaned, covering his face with a hand.

"Gone. A story for another time," said Malomir, shaking his head. He didn't have the energy to talk about it and none of them were ready to hear it.

He could tell from the haunted look in their eyes that each of his friends had been forced to endure nightmares of their own creation. "We cannot continue like this," said the Islander.

Kell wasn't sure they had a choice. After the fight with the maglau he'd thought they would have a reprieve before the next attack. He didn't know if whatever was controlling the beasts could compel the Qalamieren but regardless their assault had been ill-timed. He was sure the wraiths had spelled their doom. They desperately needed time to rest before the icefields and whatever was waiting for them in the castle. Unfortunately in this desolate landscape there were no safe ports to shelter them.

A rhythmic tapping sound caught Kell's attention. At first he thought it was just the dogs' harnesses rattling in the wind but soon realised it was coming from elsewhere. The others had noticed too and were trying to ready themselves for another fight. On his third attempt Kell managed to stand up but then realised he had no idea where to find his sword.

The tapping was getting closer and in the distance he saw a dark shape amidst the endless white. Malomir drew his scimitar which was blackened in places as if it had been burned. The Alfár was standing but Kell could see she was leaning heavily on her weapon to stay upright. Malomir was the only one of them in any state to fight but he was on the verge of collapse.

The one shape became two and then ten but their features were still obscured by the whirling snow. Kell's heart sank as their numbers continued to grow. He stopped counting as thirty shadowy figures marched towards them. Whether it was the Qalamieren or something else they couldn't win against so many. They would fight bravely but in the end it wouldn't make a difference. But he would not run. Even if this had always been his fate he would not go willingly like a timid lamb. Kell drew a dagger from his belt and prepared to fight for his life.

All of the strangers stopped a short distance away and one came forward by itself into camp. When the snow cleared he saw the stranger's face and felt a huge surge of relief. Kell had been holding himself upright with sheer force of will but now he collapsed to one knee.

"You are far from home," said the Frostrunner, a stocky woman with a broad smiling face. She was dressed in traditional reindeer clothing – jacket, trousers, boots, hat and gloves – and looked quite warm despite the snow. There was a healthy glow to her rosy cheeks and her eyes twinkled with mirth. "Do you need help?"

Malomir was eyeing the clanswoman with suspicion, perhaps thinking it was another illusion of the Qalamieren, but Kell knew this was no trick. The others had never been this far north so they had no idea about the customs of the Frostrunners. Bold face lies or even just evading the truth, no matter how uncomfortable, was a grave insult. If they accepted the hospitality of the clan, Kell and his friends would be treated as if they were family for the duration of their stay.

With a grunt of effort he forced himself upright and slowly approached the woman with empty hands spread to either side. "My name is Kell Kressia and we have been tested by the Frozen North. We fought against the snow bears, the maglau and the Qalamieren." At mention of their name the clanswoman's smile faltered. "We are in desperate need of rest. We also have a friend who is severely injured."

"My name is Luopo," said the clanswoman, stepping close to Kell and peering up at him with her dark eyes. "I have heard of you from ten years hence. Strange company you keep," she said, glancing at the Alfár with a frown. Kell thought she wasn't going to offer them hospitality but then her smile returned. "We offer you food and shelter. Join us and be welcome."

"Thank you," said Kell, clasping hands with Luopo. Her fingers squeezed his through her gloves and Kell felt the strength in her grip. As the most senior she spoke for the clan but, like all of those who chose to live on the ice, she was as tough as old leather. The old woman lent him her strength as she guided him back towards his tent.

Gerren was trying his best not to fall asleep or stare in open-mouthed wonder but it was difficult on both counts. For the first time since they'd crossed onto the ice he was warm and safe. The Frostrunners had taken them back to their camp a short ride away where at least a dozen hide-covered yurts sat in a circle on the ice. Beyond the camp roamed a large herd of reindeer under the watchful eye of a few warriors.

Gerren had thought the Frostrunners lived in bare homes devoid of luxury but he was completely mistaken. Inside the yurt he shared with his friends the wooden floor was covered with layers of overlapping warm rugs. Lightweight cleverly built furniture, made from a material he didn't recognise, was dotted around the circular room, which made it feel homely. Thick fur-lined sleeping pouches had been laid out for all of them and light came from lanterns with yellow glass panels washing everything in a warm glow. Instead of candles or oil, the lanterns contained a swirling liquid that was constantly in motion.

Heat in the yurt came from covered braziers, apparently stuffed full of dried reindeer dung. Gerren had expected everything to stink but the air was clean and fresh with a faint floral odour. Kell had stressed that naked flames were strictly forbidden but he didn't have time to explain why.

Their host, a cheery man named Nieman, was sharing a pipe with Kell and Vahli. Gerren had not been offered it, perhaps because of his age, and he didn't ask. From the smell of the herbs it would only make him sick and he didn't want to offend anyone by vomiting on the rugs.

Currently Nieman was serving them warm cups of something that looked like milk. Gerren was going to turn it down but Kell indicated that he couldn't refuse. There seemed to be a lot of formality to the milk ceremony as Kell would only drink after their host had taken a sip. The milk tasted peculiar, spicy and yet sour as if it was fermented, but Gerren made sure he didn't show any displeasure. He drank the whole cup and stifled a burp with a cough.

Gerren was glad to see he wasn't the only one lost by the formality as the bard was equally reticent. Everyone was beyond the point of exhaustion from their encounter with Qalamieren but so far they'd not been left alone to sleep. Bronwyn had been taken to another yurt, where the clan's healer resided, and Malomir had gone with her. He refused to leave her side and Gerren didn't know if it was because Malomir didn't trust the Frostrunners or he couldn't bear to be apart from her.

With the milk ceremony complete Kell and Nieman exchanged a few pleasantries but neither of them spoke about their recent battles. He had the impression now was not the right time to talk about such an important events. The Frostrunners would want to know how they had survived and they were not the only ones.

Gerren didn't understand what had happened with the Qalamieren but the images from his nightmares were still fresh. He just wanted to sleep and find peace in the dark. He glanced at the sleeping form of the Alfár with envy. Willow seemed more affected than anyone else and had lain down to rest the moment they'd entered the yurt.

Finally Nieman retreated outside to be with his people.

"Later," said Kell, before Gerren could ask him any questions. "Sleep. It's safe here and they would protect us with their lives."

Vahli had been scribbling in his journal, probably making more notes for his grand saga, but he quickly curled up in one of the sleeping pouches. Gerren was afraid his whirling thoughts would keep him awake but he fell asleep moments after lying down.

Hours later when he awoke, feeling warm and rested, Gerren had a moment of panic. A face loomed over him and he thought it was the wraith again, come to torment him with its mix of pleasure and pain. He screamed and sat up, frantically searching for a weapon.

"Gerren, calm down," said a voice. "You're safe. It's over."

Was it? Was it really over? Then why did his body ache so badly? And why was his cock so hard that it hurt? There was also a deep and lingering pain in his groin as if he'd been kicked between the legs.

Gerren blinked and the vision of the Qalamicren faded. Slowly he recognised the familiar surroundings of the yurt. Willow was still asleep in her pouch but the others were empty. Vahli was standing a short distance away holding up two steaming bowls of food. Gerren's stomach gurgled but his heart was still pounding.

"You startled me," said Gerren. Vahli offered him a bowl which he accepted with a nod. It was some kind of meat stew swimming in thick black gravy. He spotted a carrot and what might have been a potato which was enough to set his stomach off again. The meat was rich and chewy which made him suspect it was reindeer but it didn't put him off. He needed something else to focus on to keep the images in his mind at bay.

"Do you want to talk about it?" asked Vahli, keeping his voice low so he didn't wake Willow.

Gerren studied the bard, noting the haggard eyes, the tight muscles in his hunched shoulders and the deep ridges in his forehead. "Do you?"

Vahli vehemently shook his head. Whatever he'd been forced to endure by the Qalamieren had taken a toll. Gerren wondered how his own face had been marked by the wraiths. Were his eyes just as haunted?

They all needed time to rest and try to come to terms with the visions. Gerren had questions about what had happened but those who could answer him were elsewhere. With his hunger sated for the time being he lay down to sleep again. Fear of what he might see in his dreams was at the forefront of his mind but his body still craved rest. He balanced on the knife-edge between wake and sleep for a time but mercifully fell into a dreamless void where no nightmares plagued him.

Malomir's knees ached from kneeling on the rug but he ignored the pain and bore it stoically. The Frostrunner healer, a gnarled walnut of a man, had carefully checked Bronwyn's head only to reach the same conclusion as Vahli. Her injuries were inside and there was nothing he could do for her. There had been a brief and frantic conversation in their native tongue between the healer and Luopo but neither had shared with him what the argument was about. All he knew was that they had sent for someone else to help Bronwyn and he was to remain with her.

A short time later Luopo returned with an ancient woman dressed in black whom he'd not seen before. All of the Frostrunners wore multiple layers of hide, trimmed or lined with fur for warmth, but the old woman didn't seem to feel the cold. Her hands and feet were bare and her long grey hair blew freely away from her face.

Dozens of charms had been woven into her braids and Malomir picked out pieces of bone, crystal chips, tattered pieces of colourful cloth and even what resembled a shrivelled, dead mouse.

Luopo was the leader of the clan but even she deferred to the old woman. Her face was lined with age but her dark eyes were clear and unmarred by her years.

"This is Ammarok, our spiritual healer," said Luopo.

The old woman ignored them both and immediately knelt down beside Bronwyn. Placing a thumb in the middle of Bronwyn's forehead Ammarok closed her eyes and began to mutter under her breath. Malomir was about to ask a question when Luopo shook her head forcing him to wait.

After a while Ammarok opened her eyes and stared directly at him. "Her body is very strong but this is a wound of the spirit. It wanders."

"Can you help her?" he asked.

Ammarok shrugged. "Perhaps."

"I will pay any price. Give you anything."

"You don't understand," said Luopo. "Ammarok has no magic. She will call upon the spirits for their help but then it will be up to your friend."

"I will seek a guide," said the old woman. "They will show her the way back to the flesh, but she must decide to return to this world by herself."

"Is there anything I can do to help her?" said Malomir, gripping Bronwyn's hand. The two clanswomen exchanged a look and Ammarok lifted one shoulder.

"Maybe," said Luopo. "But it is risky."

"You care deeply for her, yes?" said the healer.

"I do."

"Then you can be her anchor," said Ammarok. "But know this, if she chooses not to return, your spirit will also be lost. Your body will breathe for a time but then it will die."

Malomir considered the old woman's words carefully. He didn't know if he believed in spirit guides but his encounter with the

Qalamieren had opened his mind to the possibility. It was enough that they seemed convinced it could help Bronwyn. As traditional medicine had failed he was willing to give anything a try.

"Tell me what to do," he said.

A short time later he and Ammarok were sat on either side of Bronwyn in an ice-house. It was a crudely made temporary structure fashioned from blocks of ice packed with snow. It would stand for a few hours and then fall apart and be reclaimed by the land. Once they were inside, Malomir was surprised to see other members of the clan seal up the doorway. A small vent in the roof was left for air to escape but even so the inside quickly became unbearably warm.

He wasn't sure what he'd been expecting. A ritual. Perhaps a potion to soften the boundaries of the mind like some people at home drank to speak with their gods. Instead Ammarok ordered him to take off his clothes and sit naked on the ice. Bronwyn was allowed a thin blanket but it did not provide much protection from the cold.

"Shy?" asked the old woman with a grin. Malomir watched as she peeled out of her clothing without hesitation. The tan skin of her body was lined, the flesh sagging with age and her breasts hung flat against her round belly but she showed no embarrassment about her body. It wasn't embarrassment that made Malomir hesitate but shame, which he quickly put aside. Just as he knew little about Ammarok's beliefs, it was unlikely she knew much about his. He stripped off his jacket and shirt, revealing the jagged scar on his chest. He'd received the wound in his youth when he'd been arrogant. That day the beast had taught him a valuable lesson.

As he shrugged out of his trousers and boots Ammarok glanced at his body and raised an eyebrow. "You're a big one. You remind me of my second mate, but his was crooked."

Malomir tried not to wince as he sat down but the cold shooting through his legs and arse was intense. He hissed in pain and the old woman cackled at his discomfort.

"What happens now?"

"Now, we wait. Hold on to her hand and no matter what you see or hear, do not let go. And do not speak, not one word, until this is done," said Ammarok.

Malomir clasped one of Bronwyn's hands and Ammarok took the other before closing her eyes. He did the same and tried to ignore the growing pain and numbness in his legs, gritting his teeth against the discomfort. Another distraction was his balls which were trying to retract their way back inside his body.

Instead he focused on the sound of his breathing, trying to keep it slow and even. Water trickled nearby and Ammarok began to mutter something over and over in her guttural language. The rhythm suggested it was a litany but the meaning eluded him.

In such an empty space, cut off from the rest of the world, it became difficult to measure the passage of time. His only way was to count the number of breaths but that quickly became meaningless. Ammarok's voice seemed louder, or perhaps it was the lack of other sounds. Her words echoed in his skull like the rhythmic beating of a drum. His feet were completely numb and Malomir couldn't tell if wiggling his toes had any effect. Keeping his breathing even was becoming difficult as the pain continued to mount.

His teeth squeaked from clenching his jaw so tight. Ammarok's chanting filled his head. The words had become a painful sound that was burrowing into his mind, changing him, creating something new from his flesh and blood. His skin was tingling while everything below his waist was frozen and absent. Malomir felt something brush past his shoulder and his heart began to pound.

There was someone with them in the ice-house.

He sensed a presence. It was massive and filled the space, pressing down on his body, rooting him to the spot. Malomir tried to move his hands but his fingers wouldn't respond. It was also there in his mind, observing his thoughts, picking through his memories. He didn't know if its intentions were malicious but it had an inquisitive nature. Malomir couldn't help it. He opened his eyes.

He tried to scream but his throat was locked, his tongue frozen to the roof of his mouth. A small whimper was all that emerged. In Ammarok's place knelt the outline of a being made of blazing silver and blue light. All of the details were clear and yet Malomir could see through it like a pane of glass.

It was part man and part beast. A strange blending of the two that filled him with fear and awe. The shaggy creature loomed over Bronwyn, staring down at her face with a quizzical expression.

Growing from the top of its skull was a huge crown of antlers with sharp points. Its shoulders and chest were covered with russet brown fur which ended at the waist. Squatting down on cloven feet he saw huge genitals dangling between its legs. Long green hair fell to its waist and the six fingers on each hand ended in red tips as if they'd been dipped in fresh blood.

At the merest whisper of his voice its head whipped around. As Malomir stared into its eyes he felt the walls of his mind begin to crumble. It was too late to look away and now it had seized him on either side of his head with its massive hands. Pain blossomed in his skull but he couldn't escape. He felt its fingers pass through the skin and bone with ease. It penetrated his mind and everything was laid bare. Every memory. Every emotion. Every thought he'd ever had. A lifetime of choices that had brought him to this moment.

And in the whirlwind of his mind the image of Bronwyn emerged. She was sitting in the dark, alone and isolated from the world. He tried to reach out to her but he no longer had a body. Malomir had become an observer on a plane of reality he couldn't understand. The ice-house and everything was gone. At first there was only the endless dark and Bronwyn but then the landscape began to change.

She was huddled under a blanket inside a cave while outside a storm raged. Thick gusts of wind blew flurries of snow into the cave mouth forcing her to inch backwards. Malomir instinctively knew this was a mistake. To retreat into the cave was to leave behind the world and surrender to the dark. There was peace and serenity in that choice, but that had never been her way. Life meant struggle and sacrifice. It meant pain but also joy. The brightest memories obliterated the suffering, the despair and the failure. It made it all worthwhile.

The crowned man appeared at the mouth of the cave only this time he was whole, made of flesh instead of light. Bronwyn initially pulled back in fear but then her familiar steel returned. She searched for a weapon and finding none stood up to face him with her fists raised. He spoke to her but for Malomir the words were muffled as if coming from far away. All Malomir could pick out was the tone of his voice. The being raised a hand in surrender so as not to startle her. Malomir saw its mouth moving and Bronwyn answered. Back and forth they spoke while the wind raged outside, promising struggle and pain.

At one point Malomir was certain there was mention of his name. He felt it, like a trickle of ice water running down his back, there and gone a moment later. Bronwyn's eyes searched for him but he had no way to alert her of his presence. The wind blew harder, more snow poured into the cave but now Bronwyn stood her ground. Flurries whipped past the being's antlers but he gave no mind to the storm. He said one final thing to Bronwyn then turned and walked away, leaning into the wind. In less than a dozen paces he vanished, swallowed whole by the endless white.

For a long time Malomir watched Bronwyn struggle with her decision. She was balanced on the precipice between life and death. The guide had done as Ammarok had promised but now the choice was hers to make alone.

So many emotions surged across her face. Malomir wanted to reach out and comfort her but he was powerless. He knew she had much to live for but perhaps she was simply tired of the struggle. To be the strongest, the toughest, the best. It was not without reward but also isolating. He didn't know if she viewed the world as he did. There was still so much about her that he wanted to discover.

Finally, Bronwyn made her decision.

She cast one final glance into the quiet darkness of the cave before turning her back on it. The wind tried to force her inside but she leaned forward, braced herself against the storm, and took a step. Her jaw was clenched, her hands stretched out ahead and she refused to yield. Step by step she drove herself forward away from the darkness and into the eternal white.

Malomir felt someone squeezing his hand. He experienced a brief sensation of falling and then he was back in his flesh.

His heart was pounding, sweat ran down his naked body and the ice-house was full of trickling water. His legs were completely numb and when he tried to move bolts of pain lanced through his flesh. Ammarok was coming awake too, grunting in pain as she massaged the weary flesh of her thighs.

That was when he felt someone squeezing his hand again. Looking down he saw Bronwyn's eyes were open.

CHAPTER 29

It was still early but Kell was unable to sleep. He dressed quietly, wrapping up head to toe in warm clothing, and slipped out of the yurt he shared with the others.

It had been two days since Bronwyn had woken up. Apart from being tired and hungry she seemed to be in good health. If only everyone else was faring as well. Even after resting within the relative safety of the Frostrunners' camp they were still in a fragile state. The visions they'd been forced to endure haunted them awake or asleep. Gerren woke several times a night screaming. At other times, on the verge of sleep, Kell heard sobbing and didn't know if it was the boy or someone else.

Even the Alfár had been affected although it was more difficult to notice. Willow had never been verbose or particularly animated but there was a change. In a human Kell would have said they were brooding but Willow had become more introspective and unnaturally still. An hour or two could pass without the Alfár moving a muscle. He guessed she was re-examining the nightmares she had been shown like the rest of them. When Kell had tried asking Willow about what she had seen, the Alfár had ignored him.

Leaving his face uncovered Kell relished the cold air as it burned down his throat into his lungs. It made his chest ache in a good way. Without Malomir's help none of them would have been able to feel anything. In front of a rapt audience the Islander had told the clan leaders how he'd defeated, or at least driven off, the Qalamieren.

The idea of introducing a naked flame into the Frozen North, even as a weapon against the wraiths, was a dangerous idea. Although the results could not be contested the damage it could do to the landscape was significant. All sources of heat in the camp were carefully controlled and managed by the Frostrunners.

The brightness of a naked flame would attract unwanted attention. Any source of heat was covered and only ever used indoors. That way it slowly escaped from the yurts into the surrounding landscape. The only reasons the Frostrunners had survived in the north for so many generations was by maintaining a healthy respect from all of the predators and keeping their distance.

The temperature seemed static to Kell but it became clear from listening to the discussion that there were distinct seasons in the Frozen North. Even more surprising he learned that, like the temperature back home, the natural rhythms were already out of balance upon the ice.

Several of the clan instantly rejected using fire as a solution. They argued that the unfortunate few who were killed each year by the Qalamieren were a small price to pay to live here. Others were in favour of hunting down the wraiths until they were destroyed.

When they switched into their native language Kell left the clan to debate the issue among themselves. If the Qalamieren came after them again Kell and the others would not hesitate to wield fire against them. He was a visitor and a short burst of flame was likely to have minimal impact. It was up to the Frostrunners to decide about its use in the long term and the future of their land.

At the furthest point in camp away from the herd of reindeer Kell found the sled dogs. They were always happy to see him, in part because he fed them every morning, but also because of the prospect of a run. They had also benefitted from a rest and showed no lingering signs from their ordeal but he could see they were getting restless. Once again the dogs were full of energy and later today they would have their chance to get back on the ice.

"So this is where you go every morning," said Bronwyn, coming up behind him. She was still a little pale and there was a colourful bruise on one side of her face, but otherwise she acted as if she'd not been injured. In some ways Kell envied her injury as it had spared her from the nightmares.

"They're easily satisfied and they're happy." Kell threw one of the dogs another chunk of reindeer which it gobbled up in two bites. He wondered what it felt like to be truly happy. "When are you heading home?"

"Home?" said Bronwyn. "I'm not going home."

"I assumed that's what you came here to tell me."

Bronwyn shook her head. "This isn't over. I'm not going back. Not yet."

Kell dumped the last scraps of meat onto the ice and the dogs guzzled every bit. "No one would blame you, or Malomir."

"I would blame me," she said. "To give up now would be cowardice. I've been injured before and this was no different."

"Wasn't it?" said Kell, turning to face her. Bronwyn's bravado faltered and she looked away into the distance, unwilling to meet his gaze. "What did you see?" he asked.

Malomir had told him a little about his experience in the ice house but Kell didn't know how much had been real and how much imagined. He knew from experience that the mind was capable of conjuring powerful and convincing images when subjected to extreme pressures. The dead had stalked him for months after his return, standing in the shadows, their eyes full of accusation. Part of him still wasn't sure if they had just been hallucinations of a troubled mind.

"I saw a man, a being of light, with a crown of antlers," said Bronwyn, her brow furrowed in concentration. "The images keep slipping away, but they're so clear when I'm on the edge of sleep. He offered me a choice. I chose to come back. Just as I am choosing to see this through to the end. This isn't just about you, or even the Ice Lich, anymore. We all have our own reasons for being here."

He wasn't sure if he believed in the clan's beliefs about spirits of the land but ultimately it didn't matter. Bronwyn had recovered and she was still coming with them.

"We leave in an hour."

"I'll be ready," said Bronwyn.

As he stared out across the endless sea of white, Kell wondered if he was ready for what lay ahead. But it wasn't fate that had brought him to this moment. It wasn't the Shepherd or even a crowned spirit of ice and fire. He alone had made the decision to be here and, one way or another no matter the outcome, he had to finish it.

Kell needed answers, about the past, about the last ten years, and the only place he was going to find them was inside the ice castle. Good or bad, just as Bronwyn had said, he would see it through to the end.

Gerren watched as Kell thanked the leaders of the clan for their hospitality. It felt as if they'd just arrived. Part of him was aware of the last two days, but they had passed in a fugue. Gerren remembered sleeping, eating and talking to someone, but he couldn't remember who or what he'd said. Images from the Qalamieren still dominated his thoughts. With his eyes open or closed, awake or asleep, they taunted and shamed him. Gerren still felt aroused as he recalled the horror of being consumed by the wraith. It was still the closest thing he'd ever experienced to sex.

Two days wasn't enough time to recover. He wanted to stay longer and had been given the choice to remain. Kell had made the offer to everyone but no one else had asked to stay so he couldn't either.

The sense of belonging was all Gerren clung to as he'd packed his belongings onto the sled. All too soon Kell was shaking hands for a final time, thanking the Frostrunners for restocking their supplies, and then it was time to leave.

"Are you ready?" asked Vahli stepping up behind Gerren on the sled. Despite two days of sleep the bard's face was still drawn and pale, but there was a determined glint in his eyes. Unable to trust what he might say, in case he lost his nerve, Gerren just nodded and hunkered down on the sled. With barely a nudge from Vahli the sled dogs were off, eager for a chance to stretch their legs.

Gerren had thought that at some point he would get used to the cold but as they raced across the snow he began to shiver. The thin layer of cotton across his eyes shielded him from the worst of the sun's glare but occasionally he was still dazzled by the light. A kaleidoscope of colours flickered past his field of vision creating ghostly images and an army of moving black spots. He saw faces and frozen moments in time from the nightmares that continued to haunt him.

Desperate for a distraction Gerren studied his surroundings. The colour white wasn't something he'd spent much time thinking about before coming to the Frozen North. Now he realised there were endless shades tinted with blues, greys and purples. It was the same with snow. As they flew over one kind that crunched loudly at their passage, he heard the difference when it changed. The dogs continued to grunt and bark but the runners on the sled were almost silent.

Kell was gesturing at something ahead. Peering into the distance Gerren saw what he was pointing towards. The start of the ice fields. As if crossing over the Frozen Circle wasn't bad enough, with the constant threat of falling through into the water, now they were about to cross an area where the ice was at its thinnest.

Before setting off from the yurts Kell had told them that during what passed for summer in this desolate landscape the Frostrunners clans gathered by the ice fields. When the sun was at its warmest they cut through the ice to create fishing holes. The ice was still too thick to warrant fishing expeditions, however, that didn't make the area any less treacherous.

The ice fields were littered with numerous old fishing holes that might give way under the combined weight of a sled and two passengers.

Gerren and the others all leaned forward in their seats, watching for obstacles as they manoeuvred into single file. Kell and Willow led the way, then it was their turn, with Malomir and Bronwyn bringing up the rear. Vahli counted to twenty before following, increasing the distance between them and the sled in front. If the first sled got into any trouble hopefully they would have enough time to navigate around it. However, with the dogs running at their top speed they couldn't risk slowing down until they were clear of the thin ice. It was going to be a dangerous challenge.

The bard clicked his tongue urging the dogs to run as fast as possible. Just as the sled began to pick up speed Gerren heard the snow change beneath them. The silent whisper was replaced with a harsh grating sound like two pieces of metal scraping together. Ice chips flew up from either side of the runners as they cut twin channels into the surface. Gerren risked a glance down and was amazed to see the ice beneath them was a deep sapphire blue. He knew falling into the water would be deadly but there was something mesmerising about it. It would be quick. The cold would tear the breath from his body. It might even stop his heart. Surely it would be painless.

"Eyes forward," said Vahli, tapping him on the shoulder.

Gerren shook off his reverie and focused on the distant figure of Willow. When the Alfár moved to the left Gerren waved his left arm and Vahli adjusted their course. He had a brief moment to look at the fishing hole as they flew past and then it was gone. Despite being told the ice was thin at this time of year Gerren was surprised to see its depth was still almost the length of his legs.

The fishing holes became more frequent. Willow began to weave left and right faster than Gerren could follow. Instead they veered off to the left to find their own path across the ice. Malomir and Bronwyn steered to the far right giving each other plenty of space to manoeuvre.

Gerren had often seen farmers' fields blighted by moles, the surface pitted with mounds of earth, and this was no different. The fishing holes were scattered everywhere in a haphazard manner. Vahli was now using his own eyes to dodge around the holes. There was little that Gerren could do but hunker down and wait for it to be over. If they crept a little too close, or the bard missed something, he would shout but otherwise he'd been told to stay quiet to avoid distractions.

When the left runner caught on the edge of a partially hidden fishing hole their sled tilted slightly to one side. Gerren held on tighter and bit the inside of his mouth to stop himself from screaming. Vahli had never done this before and yet apart from that one slight mishap he navigated around the obstacles with remarkable dexterity.

As the wind whipped past his ears Gerren felt his heart begin to race. Despite the obvious danger part of him started to enjoy the thrilling ride.

Just as he was starting to feel more comfortable he experienced a creeping sense of dread. At first he thought it was just his imagination. He was getting carried away and a quick scan of the area showed nothing was wrong. There were more gaping holes up ahead but Vahli had seen already them. He tugged on the reins, giving the dogs plenty of time to veer to the left. But the fear sitting in the pit of his stomach wouldn't go away. If anything it became worse.

Gerren bit down harder on his cheek until he tasted blood, terrified by the idea of something he could feel but couldn't see. It was so close the hairs on the back of his neck stood up. That was when he looked down.

Beneath the ice, a massive black shape twice as long as their sled was shadowing them.

Gerren swallowed blood and shook his head, trying to dispel the illusion. It was just his imagination. Another waking nightmare. But the long sinewy shape refused to go away. He could just make out a tail that drove the beast through the water and a lumpy bulbous head, but few other details.

Turning around on the sled Gerren flapped a hand towards the ice. As Vahli caught sight of the shadow what little colour there was drained from his face.

"Garrow," he muttered.

That was when Gerren noticed several others swimming in formation to either side. A whole frenzy of horned sharks was keeping pace with them.

As fresh sweat froze against his skin Gerren began to shiver. There was nothing they could do but keep going. They were too far across the ice fields to risk turning back and the dogs were already running at full speed.

As his heart began to pound and his muscles clenched in fear Gerren waited for an inevitable attack. Nothing in the Frozen North had merely been curious about their presence. He didn't believe in coincidence and neither did Vahli judging from his clenched jaw. Gerren didn't know what use a sword or dagger would be against the garrow. Speed seemed to be the only thing that might save them. The horned sharks seemed to be waiting for something but he didn't know what.

When they suddenly swerved to one side and disappeared beneath the ice Gerren thought it was over but that was when he saw a cluster of fishing holes in the distance. Six or seven had been cut close together creating a communal fishing area. Something massive and black flew through the water beneath them, outpacing their sled, growing in size until it was just beneath the surface.

The first garrow swam up from the depths, striking the ice around the fishing holes with its horns. Gerren felt the impact through the sled in his bones. The ice tolled like an old church bell, deep and sonorous. Vahli was already steering to the left, keeping them well away from the cluster of fishing holes.

A moment later a second garrow struck the ice beside the first. Now that they were much closer to the point of impact it jolted Gerren on the sled. The dogs fell out of step with one another, stumbled but quickly recovered. A third and then a fourth garrow struck the ice almost in the same position.

The massive beasts were trying to breach the ice.

They were almost abreast with the fishing holes and still the surface showed no signs of breaking. Gerren grinned. Despite their efforts the garrow were too slow. They couldn't be out of the water for long and the sleds would be beyond their reach in moments. And yet they kept hitting the ice, over and over again like a hammer striking an anvil. It made no sense. What were they hoping to achieve?

Somewhere deep beneath his feet Gerren felt something shift. He couldn't see anything but he'd briefly felt an imbalance. With a huge sound, like clap of thunder, the ice began to crack.

One after another, now moving in a line away from the fishing holes, the garrow began to pound the ice from beneath. They weren't trying to create an opening. They were going to break the ice apart and drown them all before they reached the other side of the ice fields.

"Yah, yah," shouted Vahli, spurring the dogs to run faster. But they had nothing more to give. Their legs were flying across the ice, tongues lolling, hot air drifting from open mouths. Gerren felt Vahli lean forward, peering into the distance for more obstacles. Willow and Kell were far ahead and probably safe but they and Bronwyn's sled were still in danger.

Three garrow slammed into the ice almost at the same time. Each strike rattled Gerren's teeth, upset the dogs' rhythm and briefly slowed them down. There were no cracks on the surface but against such an onslaught it was only a matter of time.

"Faster, faster," muttered Gerren, willing the dogs to find some extra speed from somewhere. The dogs were aware of the danger, but with nowhere that was safe, they ran for their lives.

The garrow continued their assault and then it happened. The surface of the ice began to fracture.

Cracks appeared, running ahead of their sled, splitting and forking faster than the eye could follow. A deep grinding sound ran through the ice beneath them. It sounded as if the ice were alive, groaning in pain. Huge slabs pressing up against each other began to shift and squeak from the change in pressure.

On Gerren's left, water erupted into the air from a geyser. As it rained down, the water changed into hard slugs of ice, tinkling on the surface like pieces of glass.

Spurred on by the shifting of the ice the garrow continued with their devastating assault. The dull booming of bone striking the ice was muffled slightly by the pounding of Gerren's heart. It was so loud in his ears he thought he was dying.

The cracks continued to spread. The ice started to come apart and in the distance, something black appeared on the surface. It was there for only a moment but it was a sight Gerren knew he would never forget.

Although roughly shaped like other sharks, the black garrow had a crown of blunt white spurs across its nose. The garrow's mouth gaped open, revealing multiple rows of dagger-like teeth, before it sank beneath the surface.

As it disappeared Gerren caught sight of something that gave him a glimmer of hope. Willow and Kell had made it to the far side of the ice fields. They were standing beside their sled, weapons held at the ready while their eyes scanned the area.

Cracks continued to appear ahead of them. The grinding sound became louder and he felt their sled dip slightly to the right. The ice broke apart and huge chunks began to tilt at peculiar angles all around, throwing Gerren to one side and then the other. The dogs' feet skittered, struggled to find purchase and then they were running again. A second later Gerren felt his rear lift off the sled as the runners flew through empty space. It probably lasted barely a heartbeat but seemed to go on for a long time. He crashed down hard, scrambled to hold on, but missed the edge of the sled and toppled to one side. Something clipped him on the head, he flew upside down and then everything went quiet.

Someone was screaming his name. He could hear ice crunching all around. Opening his eyes Gerren saw black shapes moving beneath him. He was lying face down on the ice above a frenzy of garrow. Lifting his head Gerren saw Vahli and the sled hurtling away from him at speed. The bard had twisted around and was wrestling with the reins but the dogs wouldn't obey his commands. They were too scared and were running for their lives.

In the distance Willow and Kell were waving their arms. As he made it to his knees Gerren finally heard what Kell was shouting.

"Run!!!!"

Stumbling to his feet, aching and bruised, Gerren stared at the jumbled mass of broken ice standing between him and safety. The garrow were circling again, getting ready to strike. One false move and he could step into a fishing hole or fall through the broken ice into the freezing water. Would he die instantly? Or would he still be alive when the garrow ripped him into pieces?

He couldn't think like that. He wouldn't.

All of the sleds had now reached safety beyond the ice fields and the others were screaming at him as well. Gerren wanted to run but terror of what could happen rooted him in place. Maybe if he stood perfectly still they wouldn't know he was there. Surely they couldn't see or smell him?

The sharks swam deeper and then disappeared but all too soon they returned, slamming into the ice beneath his feet. The jolt of pain was enough to get him moving as his survival instinct kicked in. Screaming as he ran, Gerren's legs flew over the ice. From behind came a frenzy of sharks that quickly outpaced him. Like a line of falling dominoes they attacked the ice standing between him and the others. He was their last chance of a meal and the garrow were determined that he didn't escape.

As the ice cracked and then splintered in front, Gerren knew he was going to die.

CHAPTER 30

Pride swelled the chest of Reverend Mother Britak as she watched three hundred skinny Hundarian initiates running around outdoors. The assault course tested their physical strength, agility and endurance. They had to climb over a number of obstacles or crawl through the mud on their bellies to avoid sharp implements that hung down on ropes. All the while several large, and very loud, priests urged them on with words of encouragement.

"If you don't climb over that wall I swear to the Shepherd I will feed you to my dog!"

"Move, you lazy, slovenly arses!"

"Don't dawdle, this isn't a quilting circle!"

The priests' motivating banter made the initiatives run faster and try much harder.

The re-education compound was in a remote part of the Hundarian countryside, to keep it away from prying eyes, but also to dissuade anyone from trying to run away. The path to enlightenment was difficult. It required dedication and perseverance beyond what most people were used to. A few false starts were not unexpected but this way, without the distraction of family or temptations leading them astray, the initiates could remain on the right path.

If an initiate attempted to escape it was likely they would be eaten by a wild animal or starve to death before reaching the nearest village. In such a rigorous and demanding environment it was natural that some would not be up to the challenge. Thankfully there was plenty of woodland surrounding the compound to bury the bodies.

"How many initiates have you lost so far?" asked Britak.

"Seventeen," said Administrator Nikels, a gaunt Hundarian woman with sickly sweet breath. Britak had seen more meat on a stick of celery. "Seven died from malnutrition. Five attempted to escape. Four were eaten by the wildlife and one man almost made it to a nearby farm."

"What happened to him?" asked Britak, watching a woman struggle to climb over a wall. A burly priest shouted at the woman until she scrambled over, desperate to escape his bellowing voice.

"Don't worry, we caught him. He was hamstrung and left for the wolves."

"What did you tell the others?"

"The truth," said Nikels with disdain. "They were not worthy, so we released them."

"Good."

Adjusting the story meant that everyone else at the compound would fight for their position. They didn't need to know that there weren't a limited number of spots.

In another part of the compound were the classrooms where students were being drilled on the Book. Britak wasn't unreasonable. She didn't expect every person to be able to quote it, word for word, but they needed to have a thorough understanding and it needed to be at the forefront of their minds. Every encounter with a stranger was an opportunity to put them on the right path.

The initiates would never become priests but that was not their primary purpose.

In one classroom a teacher was walking up and down the line of desks with a long wooden cane in her hands.

"What is the seventh pillar?" she asked, stopping in front of a desk.

"Um—"

"Um is not one of the twelve pillars," shrieked the teacher. "Hands."

The student, a portly man in his forties, held out both hands in front of him. The cane came down across his open palms and he whimpered in pain. He was struck three more times before he found the right answer.

"Charity. The seventh pillar is charity," he said.

"Pain is a great motivator," said Nikels, sharing a satisfied nod with the teacher. Britak cast her discerning eye over the classroom. There were a few that didn't look up to the task ahead, but she had faith that the instructors would discover them.

Spies from other nations were another constant worry but Britak was confident the remote locations meant that, so far, no one knew about the compounds. It would be more of a problem as she increased the number of compounds. They just needed to stay secret long enough for her to build an army. One large enough that she could use it to apply pressure to uncooperative kingdoms.

"How long do you think it will take to complete a training cycle?"

Nikels grimaced. "A year, but no more than that."

Britak thought she was being extremely optimistic but she didn't say it out loud. Slightly different techniques were being used at each compound. Whichever produced the best and fastest results would then be adopted by the others.

Everything was going according to plan. In three or four years she would have a solid alternative to the introduction of compulsory lessons in all schools across the Five Kingdoms. If the carrot didn't work then her army would be used as the stick.

They moved on to another part of the facility where the initiates were learning to fight. Two rows of men and women carrying wooden swords and shields were battering each other on a large grassy field. They ran through a series of moves in unison while instructors marched around up and down the lines.

"Welcome, Administrator," said a red-faced instructor. "What do you think?"

Nikels wrinkled her nose at the sweaty man. "Adequate. Carry on."

Britak was not a martial arts expert but even she could see most of the initiates were fairly incompetent. The instructor said nothing but Britak was pleased when he bowed deeply to her before turning away.

It would take months before any of them developed even a modest level of skill. That wouldn't be enough to go up against soldiers who had been training for years. It was another reminder that there was a long road ahead and that she might not see all of her plans come to fruition. To highlight that fact Britak suddenly came over all dizzy and the strength ebbed from her legs. If not for her crozier she would have collapsed on the ground in a heap.

"Shall we move on, Reverend Mother?" asked Nikels.

"Give me a moment," said Britak, pretending that she was interested in the sword training. She took a number of deep breaths while she waited for the dizzy spell to pass. Her knuckles turned white on her staff from holding herself upright, mostly through sheer force of will. Gritting her teeth she waited until her legs felt strong enough to bear her weight again.

"Lead the way," she said, gesturing for Nikels to go ahead so that the administrator wouldn't see her first unsteady steps. Moving slowly and with caution her body eventually complied and her pace returned to a semblance of normality. At least her mind had not wandered off during part of the tour.

"Is there much more to see?" she asked.

Nikels gestured towards a long building with a smoking chimney. "I assumed you wanted to see the kitchens and dormitories."

"Not really. Unless there's something of particular interest to show me?" Britak was getting a little annoyed at the administrator's lack of respect. Not once had Nikels used her title and her tone was bordering on the peevish.

"The chambers of silence then," said Nikels. "They're my favourite."

Particularly difficult initiates were held in isolation in featureless rooms, without food or water, and only a bucket for company, until they became more accommodating. After a few days of not talking to anyone and being hungry, the gruel everyone ate would taste like nectar. Those who did well in their lessons were allowed better food but only after they had proven their loyalty beyond reproach.

A startled-looking rider came into the compound at a gallop. As soon as he spotted Britak he steered his horse towards her, slowing down at the last moment to avoid running her down.

The messenger slid from the saddle and dropped to a knee in front of her. "Reverend Mother," said the man, who stank of sweat and horse. "I have a message from King Elias."

"This is highly inappropriate," said Nikels, holding a hand against her face to try and minimise the smell. "You need to wash yourself, thoroughly, before you deliver your message."

"But–"

"Right now!" said Nikels, pointing towards the baths.

The messenger looked between them before focusing on Britak. "The King said it was rather urgent, and should be delivered in private."

"Come with me," said Britak ignoring the administrator's garbled protests. "Nikels, it seems to me that you need to work on your understanding of the first and eleventh pillars. In particular, your lack of humility needs some attention."

"Reverend Mother!" Nikels sounded appalled, which only confirmed Britak's concern. The power had gone to her head.

"You've obviously been so busy running the compound you've been unable to look after your own spiritual needs. We all need some time for self care. Therefore, I think a week in a chamber of silence should suffice," said Britak. "Or do you need longer?"

Nikels made a number of garbled sounds but didn't manage any actual words. Eventually she shook her head and hurried away before Britak extended her isolation.

"Speak," said Britak, turning to the now pale-faced messenger.

"There's been an incident at one of the monasteries."

A horrible sinking feeling developed in the pit of her stomach. "Which one?"

"The House of Silence and Serenity."

That was where she had ensconced Prince Meinhart of Kinnan. Only a handful of people knew where he'd been taken. She had purposely kept King Elias in the dark for his own protection. The only thing he'd known was that the prince was being re-educated in a remote monastery somewhere in his kingdom.

"What happened?"

"Most of the priests are dead and the prince is gone." The messenger spoke in a rush, trying to deliver all of the bad news at once. "Someone broke in during the night, when everyone was asleep. They attempted to sneak the prince out without being noticed, but they were caught in the act. There was a vicious fight and the assassin and prince cut a bloody path to the nearest exit. Several priests were killed in the fighting and four others later died of their injuries."

Britak took a deep breath to try and still the rage that was welling up from inside. She would say a prayer later for her faithful servants who had died in the service of the Shepherd. "Did anyone try to follow them?"

"Yes, Reverend Mother. Riders were sent but they didn't return."

"And how did King Elias find out about this?"

"Several horses, covered with blood, turned up at a nearby farm. The riders' bodies were later discovered."

It had to be King Lars. Somehow the northern king had discovered the location of his son and had orchestrated a rescue. It made her wonder if his network of spies was better than she thought, although it seemed unlikely. Britak didn't credit him with enough intelligence to have worked it out by himself. However, the alternative was more troubling. Either someone had helped King Lars or there was a mole within the church.

"Has there been any sign of the prince or the assassin?" she asked, even though she suspected what the answer would be.

"No, Reverend Mother. They seem to have disappeared."

It seemed as if she also needed to relearn the lessons of the twelve pillars. Everything had been going according to plan. Pride had made its way into her heart and now she was suffering the consequences. She would pay penance later, cleansing her mind and body, but right now she had more pressing concerns. If there was a mole within the church it made her wonder what other information they had leaked. Were the other kings already aware of her training compounds?

First things first. She needed to find if there was a leak within the church and if so, plug it with the traitor's body.

CHAPTER 31

"He's not going to make it," said Kell.

Turning away he ran to his sled while the others were shouting words of encouragement. The boy was running as fast as he could but the surface was uneven with fresh cracks appearing all the time. The garrow were hungry and after expending so much energy they wanted some fresh meat. He knew they were vicious beasts but even for them this wasn't typical behaviour. There was to be no reprieve until they reached the ice castle and faced whatever was lurking within.

"Here," he said, throwing one end of the rope at Bronwyn. "Tie this around your waist." Kell threw another rope to Willow who caught it and began to loop it around her body. He secured Bronwyn's rope around himself and kept the other in one hand. Kell slipped out of his armour and left his sword on the sled. It would be of no use against the garrow and would only slow him down.

The others wanted to go after Gerren with a sled but Kell knew it would be suicide. Even if, by some miracle, they could get the dogs to move towards danger the combined weight would be too much across the broken ice. The boy's only chance was if one of them went out there after him.

"It should be me," said the bard, holding out a hand for the rope. "I'm the lightest."

They probably thought he was being brave by volunteering to go after Gerren but if not for the sacrifice of another, Kell would have died ten years ago. He owed a debt and now it was time to pay.

In their own way all of the heroes had been flawed, broken men. Droshalla, often called the Beautiful, turned out to be cruel and selfish, showing that he cared for no one but himself, even those he'd called brothers for years. But as the days passed on the ice, without the need to primp and wash for his beloved audience, Droshalla began to change, becoming something worse. His callous attitude turned into spite and then hatred of the others.

It had been jealousy. Droshalla's legend paled in comparison to the rest. One night, while he'd been asleep, the others had cut off his famous golden locks. The bald angry man who woke up the next morning was nothing like the hero of legend.

Kell would have died on the ice fields if not for Droshalla. Whether it was a rare spark of compassion or an accident, he would never know, but the hateful man had shoved Kell to safety.

The garrow had bit clean through one of Droshalla's legs, taking his left foot. As his dagger plunged into its eye the beast swung its head about in pain. Its knife-like teeth clipped him across the chest, tearing his armour apart as if it were made of paper. The hero had been bleeding, missing one foot, but wasn't nearly finished. In a final fit of rage Droshalla had launched himself at the shark, stabbing it over and over. Even as it sank beneath the waves he'd held on, determined to kill the vicious beast.

A short time later they saw Droshalla's body beneath the ice. Beside him bobbed the bleeding corpse of the garrow, its side and head peppered with dozens of stab wounds. In death Droshalla's expression was no less bitter. In no time the water turned a deep red as his body, and that of the dead shark, were torn into pieces and gobbled up.

"I have to do this," said Kell, hefting the ice axe in one hand. "I owe a debt."

"You're too important," said Vahli.

"What does that mean?" he said. The bard looked as if he wanted to say more, but Kell didn't have time to wait for an explanation. "Once I secure the boy, pull us both in as fast as you can," he said.

Before he could change his mind Kell trotted out onto the ice, loping towards the boy with an uneven gait. With every step he tested the strength of the ice beneath his boots, using his full weight as a measure of its stability. This close to the edge there was very little movement but the further he went the more unsteady it became.

Gerren was already struggling to stay upright. Driven by fear of being eaten alive he wasn't thinking about where to place his feet. Several times his arms flailed about to help him regain his balance. He was stumbling forward at an erratic pace, dodging over blocks of ice and jumping across gaps that appeared. The garrow were always beneath and in front, destroying his path to safety. It had now become a race between Kell and the garrow to see who could reach the boy first.

Keeping his pace steady, Kell ran, almost hopping from foot to foot, testing the ice, adjusting his balance. He kept one eye on the boy, the other on the ground beneath him. There were minor cracks but more worrying were the swirling black shapes beneath the ice. A couple of garrow had already noticed him. The pair of sharks moved away from the others and began to shadow him. As if alert to the danger he represented they rejoined the others and redoubled their efforts.

Two garrow struck the ice almost simultaneously and a huge chunk of ice collapsed directly in front of Gerren. The crystal blue water looked so appealing despite being so deadly. The boy swerved around the hole but one of his feet clipped the edge and he tripped, skidding forward on his stomach.

Kell was closing the gap. He just needed the boy to hold on for a little bit longer. A garrow struck the ice directly beneath Gerren and he was lifted off the ground from the impact. Kell could hear him keening as he now crawled forward on hands and knees, scrambled to his feet and ran, only to trip a moment later. The ice beneath Gerren shifted again and then tilted to one side. His legs tangled together and he fell badly onto one hip, arms splayed out.

Beside him a garrow smashed into the ice and broke through in one motion, spraying the surface with lumps of ice. Its black bony head twisted around, trying to find Gerren but it only managed to graze his hand with its teeth, severing one of the boy's fingers. As fresh blood spattered across the ice and dripped into the water Kell's heart sank.

The garrow went into a frenzy.

Gerren reeled back, screaming in agony, cradling his damaged hand to his chest. Another beast erupted from the water through the same gap and half of its body breached into the air. Kell could see its gills working, its black eyes rolling around, huge jaws chomping as it searched for fresh meat. Reluctantly it slid backwards but not before chewing chunks out of the edge of the hole, making it wider.

Kell slid to a stop beside Gerren, ignoring his injury as he looped the rope around the boy's waist. Blood was spurting from his hand, soaking into the boy's clothes. Even though it was a risk Kell had to put down the ice axe to secure a knot. Two garrow rammed the ice beneath them and Kell felt it begin to break apart.

"I've got you," said Kell. "Hold on."

Gerren managed to grip the rope with both hands but he seemed unable to run any further.

Freezing cold water soaked into the knees of his trousers. Another garrow would breach any moment and try to take another bite out of them. His fingers were so numb he could barely move them. Finally the knot was done and as he grabbed the axe Kell saw the boy's eyes widen in terror.

With the ice axe in one hand Kell spun around, whipping it through the air with all his strength. The narrow metal blade bit into the side of the garrow's head, just behind one of its eyes. Despite the injury the garrow's momentum carried it forward towards them. Its gaping maw loomed large in his vision. As Kell saw its many rows of teeth he knew it was going to bite him in half.

In the infinite space between one heartbeat and the next Kell became aware of everything around him. Gerren cowering in terror. The garrow circling beneath him. The glittering of sunlight dancing across the ice. The spreading darkness as the beast's shadow fell across him. The defiant smile on his face as he smiled at death.

A tight band of pain formed across Kell's chest. It felt as if his heart was about to burst. As he began to move sideways the garrow's teeth snagged on his arm and a moment later he was yanked out of its reach. On the shore of the ice fields Bronwyn and Malomir were reeling him in, arm over arm, with the rope. He skidded and surfed across the ice, bumped and twisted before finally getting to his feet and running. Ahead of him Gerren was being dragged in on his side. Both hands were pressed to his chest which was now soaked with blood. His face was ashen and Kell didn't know if he was conscious. Despite being a dead weight Vahli and Willow were drawing him across the ice as fast as possible.

Kell was running to keep up. Blood trickled from the wound on his arm but he ignored it. All around he could feel the garrow. Their minds had been bent to the task at hand by something malicious. It forced them on beyond any semblance of sanity or self-preservation. They rammed into the ice so hard they began to break their bodies against it. Their blood now flowed in the water creating crimson tides.

His heart pounded in his ears. Feet skidding and slipping he ran, ignoring the pain burning in his side, the tightness in his chest, the freezing air searing his lungs. The ground bucked beneath his feet. Kell jumped, trusting the others to keep pulling him forward even as he lost his footing. He landed badly on one foot, twisted an ankle and went over again onto his hip.

Something black shattered the ice on his left but he was gone before it had a chance to reach him. Whipped away, dragged free, spinning around until he couldn't tell any more which was the sky and which the ground. It was all the same hazy white. Head whirling, fingers and toes throbbing from the cold. His whole body had become a mass of aching muscles, bruises and ice burns. The rope around his waist bit into him, blistering the skin but he had no breath to cry out.

Finally the forward motion stopped. Hands gripped Kell, lifting him from the ground, dragging him away, ankles leaving furrows in the snow. Looking back he saw the broken bodies of several garrow littering the surface of the ice fields. Their black bodies had been rent open, smashed flat in others, reforming them into lumpy creatures he barely recognised. Dozens of broken teeth were scattered like stray arrowheads. Geysers still erupted but now the water was tinged red, falling as strawberry-coloured hail.

The few survivors retreated to the deep, leaving the dead for scavengers. Normally they would eat the dead, even if it was decaying or frozen meat. But the remaining garrow knew that their kind had been tainted by something even they couldn't stomach.

"Madness," said Kell, trying to catch his breath.

Whatever was trying to stop them reaching the ice castle was becoming desperate.

CHAPTER 32

After a restless night Kell woke early the next morning, bruised and aching but thankful to be alive.

His injury from the garrow's teeth had been minor. Merely a dozen stitches compared to Gerren who had lost a finger and something else. His innocence. Until that moment, he'd seemed naïve. A child playing an adult's game. Now there was a hollow space inside him.

He knew that Gerren was desperate to belong. Desperate to give his life meaning with a defiant act of bravery. He'd shown courage against the vorans and the maglau. Kell had heard him crying in the night but Gerren had volunteered to stay even when he'd been given a final opportunity to turn back. He was alive because of others but also his own efforts.

After every fight he'd appeared to recover, on the surface at least. To find an inner strength and the will to keep going. Kell had been sure the Qalamieren would have broken him but something had made him stay. He'd thought it was courage but now wondered if it was pride. Echoes of the past continued to haunt Kell as the boy seemed intent on making the same mistakes as him.

Now when he looked in Gerren's eyes he didn't see a boy anymore. There was only pain, sadness and a terrible longing for what had been lost. For his home, the safety it represented, and the comforts he'd scorned. For the family he'd left behind. For the loss of ignorance, as knowing the true nature of horror that existed in the world was worse than fiction. If Gerren made it home would anyone recognise him? How many years would it take him to recover?

Willow stirred as Kell slipped out of her warm embrace. As he left the tent the Alfár rolled over and went back to sleep. As ever the dogs were happy to see him, particularly today because he was feeding them fresh reindeer. Even though his eyes were sandy from lack of sleep Kell knew he wouldn't get any more rest.

Today was the beginning of the end. Before what passed for night in this place they would reach the ice castle. It was something that had been preying on his mind. It was hard to know what they would face inside but last time the hallways had been a network of moving walls, pits lined with spikes and other death traps. The remaining heroes had died in those corridors leaving him alone to face the Ice Lich. Kell hoped that whatever they discovered he wouldn't be on his own again at the end.

Despite multiple layers of clothing to protect him from the biting cold, fear wormed its way through, flushing his skin with goosebumps. Kell's ears and the tip of his nose burned from the easterly wind. If he ever made it home Kell swore he would never complain about the cold in Algany. The worst day in winter was mild in comparison to this endless frigid wasteland. While he waited for the kettle to boil he stamped his feet to stay warm.

Overhead a thin layer of grey clouds obscured the sun but in some places it broke through. The dazzling pools of light suggested heat but there was none to be found, merely a change in light. A flicker of movement caught his attention. Kell was about to raise the alarm when he realised it was only a snow hare. It stared at him for a moment, flicked its nose and then disappeared. Kell didn't know whether it was a spy for whatever hunted them or just a curious animal. For once, he assumed it wasn't malicious and decided to take it as a good omen.

An hour later the others began to emerge from their tents in search of breakfast. After being in the same clothes for days without being able to wash they were all beginning to smell but that was the least of their worries. As they drank hot tea and chewed on salted fish and rice, Kell couldn't help smiling. A few months ago he couldn't have imagined being here again, beyond the Frozen Circle, surrounded by a strange group of people. It was familiar and yet he was no longer the naïve, arrogant boy searching for adventure.

Gerren was last to join them. Kell would have welcomed complaints about the cold, or his hand, but the boy remained silent and stony-faced. His dark eyes were haunted and empty.

When Vahli tried to lighten Gerren's mood, offering to give him the dramatic name of Gerren Ninefingers in the new saga, the boy didn't respond. Instead he just sat there, staring at nothing. The others were equally troubled by Gerren's change of demeanour but there was little to be done. The only thing to do was to keep going and hope the boy shook off his malaise.

They broke camp and headed north at a steady pace, keeping the dogs under control in case they needed a sudden burst of speed. Everyone was alert and watchful for danger. Kell constantly scanned the area ahead as Willow steered their sled. Sensitive to their moods the normally vocal dogs were quiet. The only sounds Kell could hear were the gentle whisk of the runners crossing the snow and the jingle of harnesses.

Towards midday, just before they were due to stop for a rest, Kell noticed the land beginning to change. The endless sea of white became speckled with black and grey. Frozen hills on the horizon came into view, their sides peppered with rock, and looming over them all was the Lich's castle.

Willow brought their sled to a stop and the others did the same without being asked. All eyes were drawn to the glittering monstrosity that shone with reflected light. The whole structure, towering walls and narrow spires shaped like needles, was a deep sapphire blue. At this distance its proportions deceived the eye. At first glance it simply appeared to be a vast building both in height and width. The castle dwarfed every palace and temple in the Five

Kingdoms by a significant margin but it didn't take the others long to notice what was wrong. The castle had been built on a scale to house something much larger than humans.

The doors were too tall and wide. Three men could stand on each other's shoulders and they still wouldn't reach the top. The spires that reached into the sky were impossibly high and narrow, scraping the clouds like accusing fingers. From where he was standing Kell could see a dozen towers and domes but he knew there were more.

Within its walls they would find a seemingly endless maze of corridors that stretched far into the distance. Getting inside had never been the issue. It was finding the enemy within that was the real challenge.

The weak sunlight, reflected over and over through the semi-transparent walls of the castle, made it difficult to look at without being dazzled. A rainbow of colours ran across Kell's face and even with his eyes closed he could still feel the movement of light. When he opened his eyes Kell found the others looking at him.

"I don't know who built it, or why it's so tall."

"Just look at the doors," said Malomir. "They're huge."

"And it's completely made of ice?" asked Vahli, frantically sketching the castle in his notebook.

"Every wall, turret and staircase. It's as if it was carved out of one huge block of ice," said Kell. He'd often wondered if the Ice Lich had created the castle or found it abandoned and claimed it for herself.

"This was not made by mortals," said Willow, surprising the others. She rarely joined in with their conversations unless asked a direct question. Kell had been hoping the Alfár had some insight into its origin as everyone else had only theories. People expected him to know more, being one of a handful of people to have seen it in person, but he was still as clueless as everyone else. "The castle was grown, not built," said the Alfár.

"Why do you say that?" asked Bronwyn.

"There are no marks, from hammers or chisels. No joints or

seams. It is made from one piece of ice, crafted in the mind and brought forth whole," said Willow.

They all knew what she was saying sounded impossible and yet Kell would also have said nothing could control the beasts of the Frozen North. Every day the extraordinary was becoming a little more commonplace.

"Do you know who made it?" asked Kell. "Or why it's here?"

Willow heard the questions but chose not to answer. Her unusual eyes remained on the castle, roaming over its walls and towers, searching for something. Kell waited, knowing that unanswered questions made her uncomfortable. He expected her to fidget but this time, much to his surprise, Willow ignored the questions. The others expected him to have an answer for her behaviour but all he could do was shrug. He'd thought they were becoming closer but perhaps he'd been expecting too much. Could a person ever truly know an Alfár?

"Willow?" said Kell, hoping for something. "Who made it?"

"Govhenna," muttered the Alfár, so quietly Kell thought he'd misheard. He waited, hoping for an explanation but Willow said nothing more.

"What does that mean?" asked Kell. There was no way to know if that was the name of a person or something else entirely.

"Someone waits," said Willow, ignoring the question and pointing towards the castle doors. Kell squinted but his eyesight wasn't as sharp. He could just make out a few black marks but then he caught sight of movement.

"What can you see?"

Willow squinted and tilted her head to one side. "Men. There are many figures."

The rasp of steel startled everyone as Gerren drew his sword. The boy's face had been expressionless but now it started to come alive. Fire was kindling behind Gerren's eyes and Kell didn't know if it was anger or fear. Everyone drew their weapons and then nudged the dogs into a walk.

Slowly they drew closer to the castle, constantly watching for trouble, eyes scanning for signs of a trap. Nothing stirred upon the ice and gradually the figures in front of the huge doorways came into focus. Kell counted at least a dozen warriors of varying height and size. Before he could see their faces Willow gasped in surprise. A short time later he realised what had startled the Alfár.

Kell recognised them. He recognised all of them.

"No, no, no," he said, over and over. It was impossible. It couldn't be true. They were dead. They were all dead.

Standing in front of the gates of the castle were the heroes of legend. Cardeas the Bold. Lowbren One Eye, Bron the Mighty and all of the others. Eleven dead heroes brought back to life.

At first he thought it was an illusion. A vision brought on by whatever dark force was conspiring against them. A second glance showed him there was something wrong with their faces. The skin was black and pitted like rotten fruit, full of gaping holes that showed the bones beneath. Strips and pieces of flesh were also missing from their arms, shoulders and necks, torn away by claws and teeth. Kell could see bite marks riddling their bodies from the time after their death when scavengers had feasted on their flesh. Despite their many differences all of the heroes' eyes were now identical. A cold blue like the heart of winter.

Disbelief continued to battle with what Kell could see for himself. It couldn't be them. The final straw came when he saw Bron. The greatest of them all. One of his arms was still missing from where they'd cut it off ten years ago. Kell could still hear his screams reaching out across the years.

Kursen the Hunter stepped forward. Raising one of his long arms in a salute he beckoned Kell forward.

It was them. Brought back from beyond the grave.

Kell's knees buckled and he sank to the snow. All thoughts fled as he stared at the walking dead. This was truly the end. He should have died with them. Here, at last, was his proof. They had been waiting for him, caught between two worlds, unable to join the Shepherd or whatever punishment awaited them. The last ten years living on the farm were nothing more than a hollow dream.

An imitation of life. Perhaps, once he was dead, they would finally be able to rest and he with them.

"Who is that?" asked Malomir.

"Don't you recognise them?" said Bronwyn in a taut voice.

"Yes, but who is that?" said Malomir, gesturing at one figure Kell hadn't noticed. He was standing close to the others towards the back of the group. It was a gangly Hundarian warrior, not as tall as Bron, with a square jaw and no ears.

Kell did a recount. There were more than eleven dead warriors guarding the doors.

He double-checked and came up with sixteen. After looking from face to face he realised two of the original eleven were missing. Droshalla, who had died under the ice and presumably been eaten by the garrow, was absent. The other was Pragor who had cracked under the pressure long before Kell had given up. They had barely crossed onto the ice when he'd died. Instead, a warrior of similar height stood towards the back to fill out their numbers.

"It's another trick," said Malomir.

"But it is them," said Kell, as his shock began to fade.

"Perhaps, but who are the others?"

Despite the decay Kell could see that the unknown warriors came from across the Five Kingdoms. They wore a mix of leather and padded armour in styles he didn't recognise. Any insignia or badge of rank had rotted away leaving him with few clues about their identities. To make it more difficult their flesh was in a much worse state than the others. He could see more bone and their bodies appeared to be held together by their clothing as much as sinew and what little flesh remained.

Their names were lost to history but perhaps they were warriors from ages past who had travelled here for another purpose. But who were they and why had they come?

Other than Kursen, whose hands continued to twitch, the dead remained immobile, apparently waiting for something. Then a hidden signal was given and all of the dead came to life, moving forward with purpose.

Instead of steel each dead warrior held a weapon made of ice in the mould of whatever they had favoured in life. Each sword, spear and axe glittered even in the weak sunlight, pulsing with some peculiar energy that made them shine.

"May the Shepherd protect me and give me strength," said Gerren. Kell hadn't heard the boy pray before today but now he called for aid. It was a testament to his fear. "May the Shepherd give me courage to do what's right."

There was no more time for talk. The dead moved towards them with surprisingly alacrity. Staring in the dead, empty eyes of what had once been Reeman, Kell saw nothing of the man he'd known in life. The face and height was the same but little else was familiar. Something else now inhabited his dead skin. The thing in front of him was silent and its mouth remained closed.

Rage he'd not felt in a long time began to well up. That something would use the flesh of Kursen and the others, defiling the dead as a weapon against them, was an insult he couldn't bear. At the end he may not have liked them but they were still heroes to many people. He had protected their legacy and to this day their names inspired others to be better. To see such legends reduced to this was an offence to the heart.

As the creature raised its weapon Kell attacked, swinging his sword at its torso with all of his strength. His blade cut through the remaining flesh, broke bones and then stopped just short of severing Reeman's body in two. Although there was no life in its eyes the body paused and its mouth gaped open revealing the black shrivelled remains of a tongue. His blow seemed to have had little effect. The dead man was unsteady but remained on his feet. Before its shock wore off Kell tried to yank his sword free. With a sickening crunch he ripped the blade from Reeman's body, spraying bones into the air, finally splitting him in two.

The two halves of Reeman lay on the snow still twitching even though they were no longer connected. Whatever dark power animated him was still at work. The dead man dragged his legs closer then positioned himself above his waist. The dead flesh and tendons began to stretch, trying to bind the two halves together. The repair was slow and imperfect but eventually the dead man would be able to stand again.

Kell's boot connected with Reeman's face, snapping his head backwards to an impossible angle. The broken neck didn't halt the regeneration so he tried again, kicking until the head came free of the body. Even then Reeman refused to die. With bile rising in his throat Kell brought his full weight down on the side of the dead man's head. Much to his surprise Kell's boot smashed Reeman's skull as if it had been an eggshell. Finally, whatever foreign energy had been animating the dead man fled as the scattered body parts became still.

Currently Bronwyn was hurling bodies left and right across the ice with her fists, scattering them like irate children. She was particularly angry and he would have said reckless, except that the dead warriors couldn't get near her.

Willow was faring just as well, severing limbs with ease with her axe. Vahli and the others were holding their own but every time a body fell it reassembled itself and came back.

"Go for the head," Kell shouted at the others. "It's the only way to stop them."

The Alfár cocked her head to one side, nodded at Kell and then flipped her weapon. The mace hammered into the head of its opponent, breaking the skull into dozens of pieces. The rest of the dead man dropped to the ice and was still.

A whisper of movement made Kell turn his head in time to see something coming towards his face. On instinct he swayed to one side. Instead of going through his eye the dagger scored a line across his cheek. Kell lashed out with his sword but something cold and hard punched him in the side. Stumbling back, swinging his weapon to keep his enemy at bay, Kell looked down to find the hilt of an ice dagger buried in his side. Rich, red blood soaked into his clothing and then began to drip onto the snow.

There was something familiar about the weapon. A narrow stiletto dagger, barely wider than a finger. As Kell's opponent came forward to finish the job he saw that it was Umbra the Quick. He couldn't be sure but Kell thought the dead man was grinning. The least famous of the eleven heroes, Umbra was regarded by many as a gallant warrior and stalwart companion. The truth was far less romantic.

Umbra had been a thief and an assassin. Whenever there was a dirty job that needed doing, one that the heroes couldn't be seen performing as it would sully their good names, they sent the Quick.

"Hello boy," hissed Umbra, hefting another dagger. "Fancy a fuck?"

CHAPTER 33

Gerren's heart was pounding. His hand was sweaty and despite the freezing temperature his eyes were stinging from running sweat. He'd always dreamed of meeting the heroes and now it had come true only not in the way he'd imagined.

Gerren slammed his sword into the dead man's head, over and over again, until the skull broke apart. He expected to see something peculiar inside and was disappointed when it was only grey mush. The dead man wasn't one that he recognised and his clothes looked ancient. It was difficult to tell but he didn't think he'd killed one of the legends. But if it wasn't one of them who else had travelled here? And for what reason?

Taking a moment to catch his breath Gerren saw all of the others were busy fighting the heroes. Malomir danced around them while they gawped and watched, lumbering after him like three-legged donkeys. Vahli was almost as light on his feet while the others hacked and slashed with brute force and stubbornness. Kell seemed to be struggling with his opponent, the two of them close enough to strangle one another, but at least he was still on his feet.

Rotting, held together with clumps of skin and tendon, the shambling dead were a mockery of the heroes he knew. Gerren had noticed they all had the same creepy blue eyes. It was like the freezing cold water he'd seen beneath the ice. Somehow the garrow could survive but it would kill him in a few heartbeats. Thinking of the bone-sharks made his missing finger ache. Right now he'd give anything to be somewhere safe and warm, not in the middle of another fight.

The shock of facing the living dead was starting to wear off and part of him simply accepted it. He was still anxious but was becoming numb to the impossible.

His wounded hand throbbed and when he made two fists he could still feel all ten fingers. How was that possible? His bladder was bloated and about ready to burst. Would anyone notice if he wet himself?

One of the dead men turned to face him and Gerren shivered at its unblinking stare. Most of the flesh on the warrior's face had been stripped away making him difficult to identify, but there was still something familiar. He wore a rusted chainmail vest over padded armour that was pitted with holes which exposed his innards. It was the remaining scraps of the golden cloak and the slightly curved sword that triggered a memory.

"Cardeas," whispered Gerren.

He wasn't the tallest, the strongest, the best with a blade or even the most handsome of the heroes. Nevertheless Cardeas the Bold had been their leader. His courage and willingness to charge headlong into the face of danger was one of the reasons the others had followed him. The other reason was that he always came back alive.

Whenever the odds were against them, whenever all hope seemed lost, Cardeas rose to the challenge. With a quick mind he could see a battle from all sides and find a winning outcome where others saw only a lost cause.

"Please," said Gerren, holding up his sword. "I don't want to fight you."

He wasn't sure he could. How could he win against someone who had already played through the scenario a hundred times in his head?

A terrible smile stretched across the dead face of Cardeas.

"I always win," he hissed, readying his sword. The movements were stiff which was the only reason Gerren clumsily blocked the first swing and then the second. Flipping his sword to his left hand Cardeas attacked again forcing Gerren to adapt. He had no choice but to give ground and stop his enemy from getting too close.

Gerren's foot caught on something and he nearly fell backwards but managed to regain his balance. The ground around the castle was littered with rocks, most of which were half buried in the snow which created treacherous footing. He would have to be extremely careful or else Cardeas would use the land against him. Perhaps that had always been his plan.

As Gerren continued to move with slow precise steps the dead man's smile faded and his cold eyes began to burn. Changing tactics he tried to rush forward but something snapped in one of his legs and Cardeas's left foot came off at the ankle. As he paused to assess the damage Gerren swung his sword in a huge arc. Cardeas's arm came up but the steel cut straight through severing it in two above the elbow. The momentum carried the blade into the dead man's body where it became wedged between Cardeas's ribs. No matter how hard he pulled it wouldn't come free.

"I see everything," said Cardeas. It was a phrase Gerren knew he'd often said when alive. Leaving his sword where it was, Gerren dove to the ground as something whistled overhead. He felt a sharp stab of pain on his crown and a moment later blood began to trickle down the sides of his face. Gerren stared in horror at the clump of his hair and scalp sitting on the ice. The pain was so intense he almost passed out as black spots danced in front of his eyes.

"Don't run boy, you'll only make it worse," said Cardeas.

He had been planning to run. To ask the others for help as without them Gerren knew he couldn't win. A quick glance showed everyone else was still struggling with multiple enemies of their own. Even Willow was under pressure as three heroes were attacking the Alfár at the same time. No one was coming to help him. Not this time.

The dead man shuffled forward, dragging his injured leg behind. Gerren's sword was hampering his balance so Cardeas wrenched it free and threw it away. He saw it sink into the snow but made a note of where it landed.

In need of a weapon Gerren considered using the dagger Vahli had given him but as his fingers crept towards it Cardeas just shook his head. He'd seen that as well and raised his sword in readiness. The searing pain in Gerren's skull was becoming unbearable and he was starting to feel light-headed. He needed to do something drastic or else he was going to faint. Grabbing a fist full of snow Gerren balled it up in his hand but instead of throwing it towards Cardeas he pressed it against the wound on his scalp.

Agonising pain lanced down Gerren's spine as if he'd been struck by lightning. The nerves in his arms and legs twitched and he howled as he squeezed the ice hard against his skull. It was so unexpected that Cardeas paused in surprise. The mocking smile on the dead man's face slipped to reveal an arrogant sneer beneath.

He was a man used to knowing everything that was about to happen. A man who liked the power it gave him over others. A man who hated to be surprised because it revealed an uncomfortable truth. The world didn't revolve around him and he couldn't control everyone and everything.

Cardeas was as human as any other man and that made him fallible. No one could know every outcome of every decision.

"Time's up," said Cardeas, raising his sword to end it. Gerren threw two balls of snow directly at the hero's face aiming for his eyes. Cardeas's blade cut one of them out of the air, spraying him with small pieces of snow but the second snowball hit him in the face. Gerren didn't wait to see what he did next. He rolled to his left and skidded across the snow towards his weapon.

Spluttering in surprise Cardeas couldn't see and yet he still swung with precision. The curved blade bit into the ground directly in front of where Gerren's sword lay half-buried in the snow. If Gerren had been going for his sword it would have been a killing blow.

Finding no resistance Cardeas was thrown off balance. He stumbled forward, slipped on his injured leg and fell to the ground. With only one arm it made it difficult for him to get up, giving Gerren all the time he needed to get in position.

Cardeas made it to his knees and kept swinging his sword in tight arcs, trying to keep Gerren back while his vision cleared. With only one arm he was forced to shake his head to get rid of the ice. Cardeas's head whipped to the left and right looking for him, but Gerren was nowhere in sight.

Before something else went wrong Gerren brought the rock down on the dead man's head with all of his strength. The rock crushed Cardeas's skull, smashing it to pieces while spraying brains everywhere. The dead man collapsed to the ground and the light faded from his eyes as blood oozed from his shattered skull.

With shaking limbs Gerren dropped to his knees. Grabbing more handfuls of snow he pressed them against his scalp to slow the bleeding. He still felt dangerously close to fainting and struggled to shake off the blackness that continually crept into his peripheral vision.

Not far away Gerren watched as Willow swung her peculiar weapon in a lethal arc. The axe neatly sliced through the neck of one enemy, severing the dead man's head from his body. Spinning on her heel the Alfár brought the mace end against another's man's knee which shattered like glass. It was then that the third hero struck, stabbing Willow in the side with a dagger. Hissing like a cornered cat the Alfár stomped on the severed head of one dead man, smashing it beneath her boot, while ramming the mace into the face of her attacker.

Pieces of the dead man's face fell to the ground but he came on undeterred. Within moments the hero was armed with another pair of daggers. Gerren watched in fascination as they formed out of thin air directly in the dead man's outstretched hands.

The man with one knee hobbled after Willow but the Alfár ignored him for now focusing her efforts on the other. Normally Willow's expression was difficult to read. Gerren had never seen her angry before but there was no mistaking the snarl that twisted her features. As Gerren stared at her outlandish face, catching only a glimpse of her rage, fear fluttered in his belly.

Before the hero could stab the Alfár again she brought her axe down with incredible speed towards the dead man's head. Even though the dead thing raised both of his weapons the strength of the blow shattered his daggers. The momentum was so great it split the dead man in two from his crown right down to the centre of his chest. The Alfár's weapon was buried in the hero's torso but Willow didn't seem to care. She grabbed the hobbling man in her bare hands and, raising the hero overhead, ripped him apart with an inhuman surge of strength. Bones and decaying flesh rained down on the Alfár while she glared at the scattered remains of her enemies.

Not wanting to meet her gaze Gerren turned his face away to focus on someone else. That was when he saw Bronwyn stood opposite a huge man with one arm. But instead of fighting she was talking and he seemed to be listening.

It wasn't over. The others were still fighting. Stumbling to his feet Gerren retrieved his sword but he could barely stand upright. Malomir and Vahli were now fighting back to back while Kell was on the ground being strangled by one of the dead men.

A scraping sound on his left caught Gerren's attention. As he turned to investigate, something punched him in the stomach driving the air from his body. White hot pain blossomed in his side and he felt something hot running down the inside of his trouser leg. He tried to breathe but there was something cold squeezing his chest. Somehow a scream was still torn out of his throat as his feet were lifted off the ground. The pain intensified and spread throughout his body until he was one mass of raw agony.

Just before he lost consciousness Gerren saw the familiar figure of Lowbren One-Eye. His colourful eyepatch had mostly rotted away revealing a flat plate of bone beneath instead of an eye socket. Most people thought Lowbren had lost the eye in a fight during his youth. A shameful act so bad he refused to tell anyone about it, even those closest to him. The truth was far more peculiar. There had never been an eye there to begin with. It was a mystery that no one had been able to answer until now.

Looking down Gerren saw the hero's sword was buried in his side up to the hilt. The dead man's cold blue eye watched with dispassion as blood ran from the wound turning the snow pink. Just before the darkness closed in Gerren wondered if the Shepherd was real.

Umbra refused to die. Kell had stabbed him at least a dozen times, once in the head, but the sneaky bastard just wouldn't stop. Whatever malicious power had resurrected the dead heroes it had also brought with it an echo of the person they'd been in life.

Umbra was even more grotesque and devious than before. To make matters worse he was constantly twisting out of Kell's grip and whenever he managed to disarm him another ice dagger appeared in the assassin's hand. One was still buried in Kell's side and he was afraid to look too closely at the wound.

Kell swung his sword at Umbra but the dead man dodged out of the way with incredible speed. He felt a brief moment of dizziness and then the world spun upside down as his legs were swept away. Landing hard on his back Kell had no time to recover as Umbra fell on top of him. They wrestled over the dagger in the hero's hand which Umbra was intent on driving through Kell's face.

"Just like old times," said Umbra, grinding his pelvis against Kell. The tip of the ice dagger inched towards Kell's cheek and Umbra laughed at him through his crooked set of teeth. The dead man's breath smelled of rot but his cold blue eyes were alive with a peculiar hunger.

The journey across the ice had taken a toll on Kell. Even though he struggled with all of his remaining strength and refused to give up, the dagger crept down, biting into his cheek. He screamed in pain and managed to keep it from plunging any deeper but his burning muscles couldn't force the dead man away. Kell tried rolling to one side but Umbra rolled with him, twisting around with serpentine grace until he was on top again. His full weight resettled on the dagger and Kell knew this was the end. So did Umbra as he began to pant as if they were having sex, delighting at the prospect of a kill.

With a howl of frustration Umbra was yanked backwards into the air. Kell watched in amazement as Kursen the Hunter wrapped the little man in his long arms and began to squeeze. The assassin was thrashing about so much he managed to get one arm free but before he could summon another dagger Kursen smashed his forehead into Umbra's face. Over and over he head-butted the little man until both of their skulls began to break apart. Kursen's arms tightened further and Kell heard the crack of bones as he crushed Umbra to his chest.

Screaming in pain Umbra dislocated his shoulder to get his arm free. It briefly flopped about before it popped back into place with a snap. A fresh dagger coalesced in his hand which he tried to plunge into Kursen's head. A final wrench broke more of Umbra's spine and he mistimed the blow. Instead his dagger punched Kursen in the face but it was enough to make him let go. Umbra dropped to the snow but could barely move as his legs wouldn't function. The two dead men lay side by side on the ice, dark blood trickling from multiple wounds.

A shadow fell over Umbra as Kell brought both of his boots down on the assassin's skull, flattening it like a coin. His body twitched once and then was still. The Hunter was still alive but Kell could see the hole that Umbra's dagger had made in his skull. One of the Hunter's eyes was gone but nevertheless he managed a smile.

"Good to see you, boy." The smile faded and he grimaced with distaste. "I was at peace. This is unnatural."

"I know," said Kell, gripping his sword with both hands. "I'm sorry."

"It's not your fault. Finish it," said Kursen.

Kell wanted to do it. He knew that the thing in front of him wasn't Kursen, not really, but still he hesitated.

"Kell, do it now, or it will only get worse." Kursen's fingers twitched and a weapon made of ice began to form in his hands. "I can't fight its influence much longer."

This mockery of life wasn't anything he'd wish on a friend or foe. To be brought back into a decaying body only to have your will supplanted by some malicious entity. Whatever power was behind this abuse of the dead it had to be destroyed.

Kell brought his sword down with all of his strength, driving the blade deep through Kursen's head into the ice. The cold light faded from the Hunter's eyes and he died for a second time.

Loud voices intruded and he saw Bronwyn facing off against one of the few remaining heroes. Even before Kell saw that the hero had only one arm he recognised the silhouette. There was no one taller or broader than Bron the Mighty. He was so large he even towered over Bronwyn. She had her sword held ready but was hesitating to attack.

"What are you waiting for?" said Malomir, struggling against his opponent. "Kill him."

"Is it really you?" asked Bronwyn. "Are you in there?"

The big man carried a huge longsword made of ice in one hand. In life he'd used a similar weapon and Kell had seen its devastating power. Bron had split his enemies in two and if Bronwyn didn't defend herself he would do the same to her.

"I am Bron," said the big man, although he didn't sound convinced.

"Then do you remember your country, Kinnan? And what about your city, Okeer?"

"I can see its narrow streets," said Bron, grimacing in pain. "And I can hear music, echoing through the corridors in the mountain. The rest is just darkness."

"Is there nothing else you remember about your home? Or your family?" said Bronwyn.

Bron dropped his sword and pressed a hand to his forehead as he struggled with his memory. "I remember I had a wife. I can see her face."

"What was she called?"

Bron went to answer but then stopped, his mouth agape. The strain on his face became intense. He seemed to fold in on himself, becoming smaller as he desperately tried to remember. "I know that we were married for twenty years, but I can't remember her name! Shepherd help me! Why can't I remember?"

"Her name was Rianne," said Bronwyn. "She was my mother."

The agony drained out of the big man's face. He straightened up and stared down at his daughter. "Little Winny?"

It was only now, as father and daughter were stood opposite one another, that Kell saw the likeness between them. Ten years ago, when her father had died, Bronwyn would have been just a child, but now she was a hero in her own right. As Bron stared at his daughter a smile briefly flickered across his face. It was as he took in their surroundings that it faded.

"I remember travelling here with the others. My arm. They had to cut off my arm," he said, weeping as memories of what had happened began to return. Kell saw a slow awakening behind his blue eyes that was full of pain and regret. "I died on the ice," said Bron, staring around at the other fallen heroes. "We all did."

"Not all," said Kell, stepping forward.

Kell wasn't sure how the big man would react at seeing him again but tears were the last thing he'd been expecting. Bron sank to his knees, broken, sobbing like a child.

"Forgive me, boy," he said. "Forgive me."

The lump in Kell's throat prevented him from speaking but he managed to nod. The big man smiled and Kell wiped at his face, surprised to find it was wet.

Suddenly Bron groaned in pain and his whole body spasmed. The burning light in his eyes flared and his spine bent backwards until he toppled over.

"Father!" said Bronwyn, rushing to his side.

"It writhes inside me," he gasped, thrashing about on the ground. "It wants me to kill."

Bronwyn knew what she had to do but like Kell she hesitated. "I can't."

Malomir started to step forward but Kell waved the Islander back. It had to be her. It wasn't really Bronwyn's father, merely a shadow of what he'd been, but in a way it was still her family. One of the reasons she must have come on this journey was to find her father's body. No one had expected to find a version of him that could talk.

"Hurry," said Bron, digging his hand into the ice as the muscles jumped in his arm. His eyes began to smoulder and the light behind them grew more intense. Bronwyn bent down beside the big man and whispered something which, even through the pain, made him smile. With a fierce cry she rammed her sword into Bron's head with all of her strength. His body spasmed and then stopped.

Looking around Kell realised the fight was over. Across the ice lay the scattered remains of the heroes they'd killed for a second time. Despite all that they'd done it pained Kell to see their bodies and spirits abused in such a manner.

"Did we win?" asked Malomir, helping Vahli to his feet. The bard had a hand pressed to his side but otherwise seemed to have avoided serious injury. Bronwyn wasn't badly wounded but her crying tore at Kell's ears as she wept beside the desecrated corpse of her father.

As Willow approached, Kell saw that she was carrying the limp form of Gerren in her arms. His clothing and face was covered in blood and from the waxy colour of his skin Kell knew the boy was already dead.

What a glorious, horrific victory.

CHAPTER 34

It was another cold and frosty day, far cooler than it should have been at this time of year. As Princess Sigrid stared at the grey sky overhead she wondered how much worse it would be next year. If Kell's quest to the Frozen North failed then it would mean another difficult one for farmers. As it stood this year would produce a lean harvest making it difficult to feed everyone.

Kell had been gone for many days now and although she was ready to give up on him, her father and Lukas were not.

"You have too much faith in him," said Sigrid, returning to the table where Lukas sat waiting. "We should start working on some alternative plans."

"Kell Kressia is tougher than you know," said Lukas. She waited for him to explain but, unusually, Lukas remained silent on the matter. Sigrid's intuition told her a lot more had happened to Kell during his first adventure than was recounted in the saga by Pax Medina.

"Then what do you want to do?"

"Give him a few more days," said Lukas. "You've seen the same reports that I have. He was seen leaving Meer and heading north with his companions."

"All right, but let's assume he doesn't return. What then?"

"I've already been making a few, subtle, enquiries," said Lukas. "There are one or two interesting people out there who might be up to the challenge."

"Do you think that will be enough?"

Lukas raised an eyebrow. "What do you mean?"

"The first time Kell went to the north there were twelve of them. This time there's half that number. Surely it's better to send more, not less."

"You have someone in mind," said Lukas.

"We should send the Raven," she said.

"Which ones?"

"All of them. They're the best warriors in Algany and they've been trained to fight together. Also, each one of them has additional skills that could prove useful. More than twelve and certain kings might get nervous and call it an invasion, but I'm sure a dozen shouldn't cause too many problems."

"And who would protect you and the king?" he asked. Lukas had not dismissed the idea outright which was surprising. It showed the level of desperation.

"There are plenty of soldiers in the city that are up to the task. Double the number in the palace if you're worried about our safety. This isn't a situation we can just ignore indefinitely."

"I know. It weighs heavily on my mind," said Lukas, showing his concern for the first time. "I look at my children and I wonder what kind of a future they will have if we fail."

The silence that filled the room was so loud Sigrid could hear the blood pounding in her ears. A rapid knocking at the door startled both of them from their reveries.

"Come," she said.

Sensing a tense atmosphere the servant delivered a letter and quickly scurried away. Sigrid read the contents twice before putting it down.

Glancing at the seal Lukas smiled. "Finally, some good news."

"Yes, King Lars of Kinnan thanking me personally for the rescue of his son." It hadn't been easy, finding the location of the monastery, but her father's most skilled spy had proven his worth. Prince Meinhart was back where he belonged with his family and the Reverend Mother no long had a hold over the northern king.

Even better, she still thought Sigrid was an ally and had alluded to some of her plans for the future. Spies in Hundar had confirmed the existence of the training compounds where Britak was training people to become zealots for a holy war. At the moment the numbers were small but Sigrid knew she would have to keep a close eye on them in the future.

Inevitably her mind returned to the present and her thoughts were dominated by Kell and his quest. The King's Steward was deep in thought, his eyes distant as he stared at the surface of the table.

"Will you tell me what really happened to him?"

Lukas looked up and offered her a wan smile. "One day. When he returns."

"Why do you believe in him so much?" asked Sigrid.

"If there's one thing I know about Kell Kressia, it's that he's a survivor. He watched eleven of the greatest heroes die in front of his eyes, and somehow he found the strength to keep going. He was utterly alone, but refused to give up. If there are answers to be had in the Frozen North, he will find them."

CHAPTER 35

Staring at Gerren's body Kell thought that he looked smaller. Maybe it was simpler than that. He was still a child, and in death, where there were no more masks, his true face was revealed.

When he was alive Gerren hid behind arrogance and ignorance, although the latter wasn't really his fault having never left home. In Meer he'd been given an opportunity to turn back but he'd chosen to travel north. Gerren had never shared why he'd chosen to stay. Kell just hoped that whatever the reason, it hadn't been about proving his worth to others.

He should have done more to prevent Gerren coming with them. He suspected that regret would haunt him for the rest of his life.

"What happened?" asked Kell, hoping that at least someone knew how Gerren had died.

"A man with one eye stabbed him from behind," said Willow. "I took his head but it was too late."

Lowbren One-Eye. One of the most revered of the heroes who had achieved greatness despite being born with only one eye.

The journey had never been easy, rarely comfortable and rife with danger. At the end had he thought it was worth it? Had Gerren been glad that his murderer was someone he admired? Kell doubted it. Dead was dead, no matter who held the blade.

The others were battered, bloody and bruised. Bronwyn's spirit had been broken. For the first time Malomir bore visible scars and the bard was spitting blood. Even the Alfár had a limp, and fresh blue blood on one arm. The wound in Kell's side was still painful but the frozen dagger was actually helping as it slowed the bleeding. Until it completely melted he had no way of knowing if it was serious.

None of that mattered. He had to finish this, even alone. He needed answers. Had Gerren's death closed the circle? Had he died in Kell's place alongside the heroes? More than anything, Kell needed to know who was responsible for all of this. What manner of creature had the power to turn the beasts of the Frozen North against them and raise the dead?

After retrieving the rope and ice axes from the sled Kell set off towards the castle.

"What are you doing?" asked Vahli.

"I can't turn back now," said Kell over his shoulder.

"We need to rest. Regain our strength," said Malomir.

"Whatever stands against us has been relentless. It won't stop now, especially with us so close. I have to finish it, otherwise all of this was meaningless," he said, gesturing at the dead heroes and Gerren. "I need to know."

If Kell survived he'd say a prayer to the Shepherd for Gerren and if not then hopefully someone would say one for him.

Without waiting to see if the others followed, Kell set off towards the huge double doors.

In spite of everything he couldn't help feeling amazed by the size of it. Whoever had created the castle, and for whatever purpose, he couldn't deny that it was beautiful. Even in weak sunlight every wall and surface sparkled with energy. Kell didn't know if it was the Lich's magic or just how the light refracted through the walls but he caught glimpses of colours he couldn't describe.

When he reached the top of the slope and stood in front of the doors Kell paused to catch his breath. In spite of everything the crunch of footsteps coming up behind made him smile. Willow was the first to join him. Kell detected what he thought was a sense of wonder in the Alfár's eyes as she looked at the castle. What did she see with her strange yellow eyes? Did she really view the world so differently to them?

With Bronwyn's arm over Malomir's shoulder and his arm around her waist, the couple followed. Her face was pale and stricken while his was scarred and bloody, perhaps for the first time in his life. Kell couldn't tell which of them was more shocked.

Lastly came Vahli, the bard. Even dressed head to toe in furs in the middle of an icy landscape there was something flamboyant about the man. Although his clothes were marked with blood, Vahli's makeup was still impeccable. Ignoring the weather the bard had discarded his woollen hat and thrown back his hood so that his long flowing hair blew around his face in the breeze. Kell was expecting a biting comment or perhaps criticism for leaving Gerren's body on the ice. Instead he was greeted with an unwavering stare and silence. The unforgiving landscape was stripping away all masks, revealing their true selves. There was a core of steel to the bard that he'd not seen before.

"Let's get this over with," he said.

Kell was about to push open the door when Willow knelt down and began to scrape away the snow. Barely a hand's breadth down, the Alfár found a thick layer of ice that formed the foundation of the castle. Willow moved to another spot and began to dig again.

"What are you looking for?" asked Kell. He peered down into the ice but couldn't see anything.

It was only when the Alfár moved a short distance away from the door that she found something. Pointing at the third hole she stood up and made room for the others. Vahli was the first to stare into the ice and he immediately stumbled away in shock.

"Sweet mercy," he muttered, falling backwards onto his arse. As Kell crowded around the hole with the others he felt a growing sense of unease.

Beneath the thin layer of snow, buried in the ice, were hundreds, perhaps thousands, of dead bodies. Kell was unable to count as there were so many and he could only see so far down into the ice. Warriors of all shapes and sizes from all nations, in every kind of armour he could imagine, had been laid to rest in front of the castle.

At first he thought it was an army but from the way the bodies had been posed he realised it was a graveyard. All of the warriors were lying flat on their backs and each had their weapons sat on their bodies or at their side. Some had both arms crossed over their chest and all of their faces were peaceful. The ice had slowed the decay but those closest to the surface were in the best condition. Many of the warriors had grey hair and beards while those further down showed more signs of decomposition. How long did it take for someone to rot if they were buried beneath the ice?

Someone had been burying people on this one spot for a long, long time.

"What is this?" asked Malomir, directing his question at Willow. "Why are they here?"

"It's a graveyard," said Kell, although he had no idea why they had been buried there.

"What if they all wake up?" said Bronwyn, asking the one question he'd not even considered.

The bodies closest to the surface were still quite far down, encased in dense ice, but it was possible they could dig their way out. They had barely held their own against a dozen undead heroes. It wouldn't take long for them to be overwhelmed by hundreds of undead warriors.

"We need to hurry," said Kell. "We need to get inside."

"You knew," said Vahli, glancing at the Alfár. "How did you know it was there?"

"Govhenna," said Willow.

"You've said that before. What does it mean?" asked Kell.

The Alfár actually shook her head. "Not now. I will tell you the story another time."

"I think they're all going to wake up," said Bronwyn, looking down at the dead warriors. There was a worrying tone to her voice. To Kell it sounded like longing and Malomir was staring at her with concern. He tried to pull her away from the hole but she refused to move.

"Let's go inside," said Kell.

Bronwyn finally relented and was led towards the front doors. Kell barely had to touch them before they began to open. Inside was a vast rotunda lined with icy columns five times the height of a man. Far above Kell's head he could see the first of the castle's many domes. Rather than an elegant curve the ceiling was angular, rising to a jagged point like a vast tooth scraping the sky.

Arrayed around the rear half of the rotunda were six identical doorways. All of them were unmarked and none of them showed any sign of recent activity. Like every other surface in the castle the floor of the rotunda was made of ice so there were no footprints to offer clues. Light came from an unknown source, filtering down through the walls until the interior of the castle glowed with pale white light. The air was cool but still considerably warmer than outside.

"Which way do we go?" asked Malomir, taking off his woolly hat and pushing down his hood.

They were all looking at him for answers but Kell was struggling to remember. Ten years ago he'd been in a daze and most of the heroes were dead. He'd wandered aimlessly through the halls for hours, maybe even a day. There had been no choice but to keep going forward in the vain hope that he'd find something. The remaining heroes must have died somewhere in the maze.

"I don't remember," he admitted.

"Then we split up to cover more ground," said Vahli, very matter of fact. "I'll go with Kell."

"We'll go together," said Bronwyn, glancing at Malomir.

They all looked at the Alfár, waiting to see how she responded. "I will travel alone," was all she said.

"Be careful of the floor, the walls, and even the ceiling," said Kell, passing some rope to Malomir and an ice axe to Bronwyn. "There are all sorts of traps, pits lined with stakes, tripwires. At some points the ceiling even caved in on me."

"Then how did you find your way out again?" asked the bard.

"It constantly rebuilds itself," said Willow, gently touching one of the walls. "Energy flows, changing the shape to confuse those who find their way inside."

Before anyone could ask how she knew Willow set off at a jog down the first opening on the right.

"Be safe," said Kell, before gesturing at the second corridor. He tied one end of the rope around his waist and secured the other end to the bard. Taking a deep breath he set off with Vahli a few steps behind.

Malomir waited until the others disappeared around a corner before turning to face Bronwyn.

"Shall we?" he said, gesturing at the third corridor. She secured the rope to them both and hefted the ice axe in one hand. Malomir could see that she was still shaken from what had happened with her father but he didn't mention it. Pushing Bronwyn to talk about her feelings, or her father, would only make it worse. So instead Malomir pretended that nothing had happened. When she was ready Bronwyn would share her thoughts with him.

All of the corridors were fairly narrow which meant there wouldn't be any room to swing a sword. The ice axe looked tiny in her fist but it was a lot more useful than a sword if the floor or a wall suddenly gave way. Bronwyn went first and he followed a moment later, keeping the rope loose between them.

As soon as they turned the first corner a strange hush filled the air. Somewhere in the distance he could just hear the wind and the rattle of ice but it quickly faded. Their breathing sounded loud in his ears and somewhere he expected to hear the trickle of water. But the castle was nothing like the crudely built ice-house that he and Ammarok had shared. There was much about his experience with the Frostrunners that still unsettled him. Malomir wasn't sure how much had been real and how much an hallucination brought on by the extreme cold. At least he wasn't freezing his balls off this time.

Bronwyn came to a sudden halt and he paused, cocking his head to one side to locate the cause of her alarm.

"Can you feel that?" she whispered.

Closing his eyes Malomir focused on his immediate environment, listening for anything that didn't belong, but the silence was absolute. There was no wind, not even a trickle of melting water behind the walls. He could see refracted light dancing across his eyelids but that wasn't a concern. There was a strained tension in the air. A sense of anticipation and something more. He felt as if they were being watched.

Malomir's eyes snapped open but the unseen watcher didn't fade. Whatever being was responsible for all they'd endured it was nearby and fully aware of their presence.

"We're coming for you," he whispered.

"What was that?"

"I was just thinking out loud," he said. "About the future."

"Is now really a good time?" asked Bronwyn.

"It's good to make plans. To consider tomorrow." She made a noncommittal grunt but he kept going. "Once all of this is over, I'd like you to come with me, back to the Summer Isles."

"I would like to visit your home. I've been almost everywhere else in the Five Kingdoms."

"No, not for a visit. To live there with me as my Queen," said Malomir, stopping in his tracks. Bronwyn took a few more steps before the words sunk in, then she stopped and walked back until they were standing face to face. Rather than looking excited, which he'd been hoping for, or even surprised, Bronwyn was distraught.

"Why would you say such a thing?" she demanded. It was badly timed, but the danger was unknown and he had no way of knowing how long they would live. It was only a few days ago that he'd almost lost her. Waiting another day to say what he felt could be too late.

A number of answers ran through Malomir's head before he decided on the truth so that hopefully, despite her pain, she would hear him.

"Because when you lay at death's door it felt as if I were being torn apart. Because I cannot imagine living the rest of my life without you. And because when I am with you I believe anything is possible."

Bronwyn held him by the shoulders, looking deep into his eyes. "You are a kind and brave man," she began, "and you know I feel the same way."

"Your words are sweet and yet I'm worried."

"We are about to face the Ice Lich, or whatever else is hiding at the heart of this maze," she said, gently placing a hand over his mouth to prevent further protests. "Now is not the right time to talk of such things."

Malomir eased her hand away, kissing the inside of her wrist. "You saw what happened to Gerren. If not now, then when?"

"Tomorrow. Ask me again tomorrow."

"But…" he began, but she silenced him with a fierce kiss until he was out of breath.

"Tomorrow."

Malomir sighed, knowing when he was beaten. "Tomorrow," he agreed.

Bronwyn offered him a smile as further recompense. "Although, I do like the sound of being a Queen."

CHAPTER 36

The maze was just as Kell remembered. An endless series of identical corridors many of which simply ended in a wall of ice. Each time it happened they were forced to retrace their steps to the previous junction.

It was monotonous but also exhausting as they couldn't relax, even for a moment. Twice he'd spotted a suspicious section of the floor moments before putting down his foot. The traps were subtle and numerous making Kell believe that last time he'd missed many of them by chance.

In such a repetitive place it was difficult to judge the passage of time but Kell thought they had been in the maze for at least a couple of hours.

"How did you find your way through the last time?" asked Vahli, voicing his frustration.

"I told you, I was in a daze. I don't know how long I wandered."

When he reached the next junction Kell turned left, as he'd been doing since the start. The corridor ended in another dead end and Vahli sighed.

"We should mark the entrance, so we don't come down here again," suggested the bard.

When they reached the previous junction Kell etched a small cross on the dead end to help them avoid it. He turned right instead, carefully shuffling his feet forward, watching for anything that didn't belong. The floor in this section of the maze was made of one clear piece of ice and it was so perfectly smooth it couldn't conceal any traps. Keeping his attention on the walls and ceiling should have helped but Kell's hand still caught on something protruding on the wall. There was a faint hissing sound, a distant click and then something heavy hit him in the middle of his back.

Kell was thrown forward to the ground, the air driven from his body, as a weight settled onto his back. He sensed something passing overhead and lifting his face he saw a series of ice darts slam into the opposite wall. If he'd been standing upright half a dozen darts would have penetrated his body from groin to throat.

Turning his head he saw it was Vahli who had knocked him down and was now lying on top of him. "Thank you."

Despite the cold the bard was pale and sweating. Being so close he could feel Vahli's heart pounding and looking into his eyes Kell was surprised by his level of worry.

The bard rolled away and slowly eased himself upright, placing his feet and hands with extreme care in case of further traps. Kell was about to follow suit when something made him pause. "How did you know?" he asked, taking a moment to catch his breath.

"I saw the wall begin to open," said Vahli, dusting the ice from his clothes.

"You look petrified."

"I thought you were about to die."

Kell shook his head. "No, there's something else. Something more."

"You flatter yourself," said the bard. "I would be equally worried if it were anyone else. Besides, Gerren just died. We can't afford to lose anyone else."

Some of what he said was true but something about the bard's words didn't sit right in his stomach, which triggered another memory.

"When I wanted to rescue Gerren from the garrow, you said I was too important. What did you mean?"

The bard had never hidden his reason for coming on this

journey. Since the beginning Kell had been sure it was for fame. Vahli wanted his saga to outshine the mediocre one created by modestly-talented, Pax Medina. Vahli's would be a superior first-hand account of events and if all went to plan his name would be remembered for hundreds of years. Medina would become nothing more than a footnote in history.

And because the bard had been so upfront Kell had never thought to question his motivation, but now he wondered. Bards were entertainers who loved being the centre of attention. They were not renowned for being adventurers.

"What?" asked Vahli, noting how Kell was staring at him.

The longer he looked the more he realised some of the pieces didn't quite fit. Without a doubt Vahli was a talented musician and someone skilled at commanding an audience, but where had he learned to fight so well? He moved with remarkable grace and athleticism. It was possible Vahli had been a soldier before taking up music but he lacked the rigid bearing and besides, he was still relatively young. He wasn't old enough to have done both to such a high level of proficiency.

Then there was the fact that Vahli seemed to have an endless supply of daggers and Kell had seen Gerren fighting with a blade given to him by the bard. The craftsmanship had been excellent, not something a modestly-famous musician would be able to just give away for free.

The bright clothing, the long hair, even the high-pitched voice. For the first time since they'd met Kell wondered how much of it was genuine and how much was a disguise.

"Who are you?" asked Kell. The question caught Vahli by surprise but he played it down. If it was all a facade Kell didn't see it crack, not even for a moment.

"What are you talking about? Did you bump your head?"

"Who are you?"

"Kell, you know who I am. Why are you asking me this now?"

Kell shook his head. "Why are you really here? And don't tell me it's all for a song."

"Get up. We need to keep moving," said Vahli, but the humour had drained from the bard's face. It was childish and his arse was getting a little cold from sitting on the ice but Kell folded his arms and refused to move.

"I want the truth, Vahli."

Much to his surprise the bard laughed and it was the same high-pitched cackle he'd heard in the past. Perhaps not all of it was a disguise, but he'd definitely hit a nerve. "No, dear boy, you don't. Ten years ago you discovered the truth about the heroes and look what that did to you."

This new version of Vahli was blunt and a little condescending. Kell dusted himself off and stood up, being careful not to touch the walls. "You knew about them?"

"Some," admitted Vahli. "The Medina saga plays well with the crowds but only a fool would believe it was all true. No one, not even the heroes, is without flaws."

"I thought I knew everyone, except for the Alfár, but once again I'm proven wrong."

Vahli sighed. "You're like a dog with a flea in its ear. You're not going to let this go, are you?"

"No," said Kell, folding his arms.

"Very well, I was sent to protect you."

"By who?" asked Kell. Vahli simply raised an eyebrow, waiting for him to work it out. "King Bledsoe."

The sly old bastard. It seemed peculiar that he'd been sent alone on the journey. Part of him had wondered if the King had wanted him to fail from the start.

"The King thought it would be prudent to have someone nearby to keep an eye on you in case you ran into trouble. You're an investment."

"What does that mean?" asked Kell.

"It means the King has a lot of enemies and despite the obvious ramifications, they want to see you fail."

"If we fail, everyone will freeze to death," said Kell. "That's madness."

Vahli shrugged. "It's politics."

If anything this was another reminder of why he'd refused to stay in the capital. Ten years ago King Bledsoe had offered him a position at court but he'd been in no fit state to accept the role. He had neither the mind nor the patience for the politicking, back-stabbing and constant one-upmanship games in court.

The peace of the farm had restored his mind and eased his spirit. If he'd stayed in the capital Kell suspected it would have driven him to madness or suicide.

"Your trip has been wasted. Beyond the Hundarians, no one has come after me."

Vahli laughed. "Actually, they have. Remember the red-handed Seith? She was an assassin. I persuaded her to leave you alone."

Kell shook his head. "Then all your talk of being more famous than Medina was a lie."

"Oh no, that's true. That cloth-eared idiot couldn't find his arse with both hands, never mind a tune in a bucket. The King's wishes merely aligned with my own."

"Let's just get this over with," said Kell, tiring of the bard. It appeared as if everyone had lied about why they'd come on the journey. "Can you continue?" he asked, gesturing at the fresh blood on the bard's clothing.

Vahli dismissed it. "It's nothing. The cold will keep it in check."

Kell was still afraid to look at the wound in his side. The pain had faded and the skin was numb but he had yet to study it. Putting it from his mind for now they pressed on with care, marking the walls at each junction.

When the ground changed from clear ice to snow Kell became even more cautious. At one point he placed a little weight on his front foot and immediately the ground gave way. Scrabbling backwards he shoved Vahli aside and toppled away from whatever was about to happen. Some hidden catch sprung open and the floor disappeared. Despite moving back down the corridor the edge of the chasm was still only a hand's breadth away from his feet. One leg dangled over the edge and peering down into the pit he saw that it was lined with rows of ice spikes.

"Now what?" asked Vahli. The whole section of the floor had given way. There was no lip around the edge on which to walk and the pit was too long to jump.

"We go back and pick another path," said Kell.

"We can't keep turning back endlessly."

"The maze is designed to wear you down. There is a way through. Just be patient," said Kell. He could see the bard wanted to argue but Kell had previously made it to the centre of the maze. With a florid bow the bard gestured for Kell to precede him back down the corridor.

When he reached the T-junction again Kell stopped so suddenly he felt the rope go taut as Vahli braced himself for trouble. Kell's heart sank. It was impossible.

"What is it?" asked Vahli, but when Kell didn't answer he moved closer and peered ahead. Shoving Kell aside the bard bent down to inspect the walls.

All of the corridors had been marked with a cross to indicate it was a dead end, including the one they'd just explored. "How? What does it mean?" he asked. There was only one explanation.

"The maze is changing as we explore it." Vahli opened his mouth to protest but the evidence was in front of them. The walls had reconfigured themselves around them.

"Let's go," said Vahli, trying to pull Kell to the right. He let the bard take the lead but after two short corridors, each ending in a left turn, they came to another dead end. When they returned to the T-junction only one of the walls was now marked with a cross. The maze had shifted again.

For a time they persisted, trying each new corridor, but every time it quickly dead-ended. By the time they returned to the next junction it too had morphed into something else. At one point there were four corridors to try, and Vahli suggested they split up and try two at the same time. It was dangerous but after what had to be several hours they were no further into the maze. Kell unhooked the rope from around his waist and cautiously explored the corridor. All too soon he came to a dead end and was forced to turn back. Vahli appeared a moment later looking equally annoyed.

"We should go back to the rotunda and tell the others what we've discovered," said Kell, admitting defeat for the time being. The others might have had better luck but if not perhaps one of them had an idea of how to find their way through if the walls were constantly moving.

"All right, let's head back," said Vahli.

Not willing to take any risks Kell retied the rope around his waist and took the lead, ice axe at the ready. He had barely walked a dozen paces when the corridor bent to the left. A dozen paces more and it bent to the right and then a sharp left.

"I don't believe it," he said, stepping into the rotunda. They had been walking for hours and yet after barely fifty paces they were back at the beginning. The maze had kept them from going too far but the moment they turned back it spat them out.

Malomir and Bronwyn were already there, sat against one of the walls, eating some of their supplies. "We wondered how long it would take you," said Bronwyn.

A short time later Willow emerged from the maze into the rotunda. Her surprise at seeing them quickly changed into a muted expression that Kell knew meant the Alfár was annoyed.

"Rest, eat, then we'll try again," said Kell. Instead the Alfár began to pace. He'd seen her angry before in the heat of battle but never so agitated. Willow had a personal connection to this place. She knew who had built the castle and about the dead warriors under the ice. Kell was surrounded by people with secrets.

"No more waiting. No more delays," said Willow.

"We need to plan how to get through the maze," said Kell, but the Alfár was already shaking her head.

"No. No more games." Her eyes were blazing but there was more than anger to her pained expression. He would never have said the Alfár was melancholic but now there was sorrow in her eyes. Something had wounded her deeply and Willow could not rest until it was done.

"Will you follow me?" asked Willow, hefting her weapon in one hand. Until now Kell had led because of experience. Being in charge didn't appeal to him and it was not something he'd ever sought. Part of him already felt like a failure because in spite of his best efforts Gerren had died. Letting someone else carry that burden of leadership for a while was a welcome reprieve.

"I will follow you," said Kell, feeling as if an immense weight had been lifted from his shoulders. A smile tugged at the corners of Willow's mouth as if she understood his relief. There was still so much that he didn't understand about the Alfár, or her people, but Kell knew that he could trust Willow with his life.

The Alfár's yellow eyes flicked past him. Glancing over his shoulder Kell saw the others had packed their belongings and were readying themselves as well.

"We go. Together," said Willow, studying each person in turn for a moment.

At first when the Alfár walked towards the front doors Kell wondered what she was doing. Spinning on one heel she sprinted across the rotunda and back down one of the corridors at full speed. Kell followed at a slow jog but soon had to quicken his pace as Willow outpaced him with her long legs. When she came to the first T-junction, instead of turning left or right, she ran straight towards the wall. The impact of the Alfár's mace was so loud in the confined space of the maze it sounded like a clap of thunder. As much as seeing it Kell felt the blow as vibrations ran through the floor.

Peering around the Alfár's body he saw a vast network of cracks running across the ice and at its centre a huge gaping hole. On the other side he could see another identical corridor but rather than being dismayed Willow whooped with glee. With a series of hard kicks the Alfár widened the hole until it was large enough to squeeze through. Kell followed on Willow's heels but as he was stepping through something snagged his boot. He stumbled to one knee and twisting around Kell noticed the hole was beginning to close up behind him.

Bronwyn's boot quickly stopped that, kicking huge chunks out of the wall, scattering ice across the floor. She and Malomir widened the gap until it was large enough for Vahli to step through. Using the ice axes and with repeated kicking, Kell and the bard managed to halt the repair long enough for the others to follow.

From the loud hammering coming from behind Kell could hear Willow had already started on the next wall. When they caught up the Alfár had broken through and was already making progress on a third wall. Looking over his shoulder Kell noticed there was no sign of where they'd come from. The wall behind them was completely smooth and even the broken chunks of ice on the ground had melted.

Ignoring whatever twists and turns the maze threw at them Willow was moving in a straight line towards the centre. They followed through two more walls before there was a change in the maze's defences. As Willow marched down the next corridor a section of the floor directly in front of her gave way. Kell was just behind and managed to grab the Alfár by the waist, pulling her backwards before she toppled into the trap.

Peering down he could see the stake-lined pit was half the length of the hallway and far too long to jump. Whoever was controlling the maze was doing their utmost to keep them away from the centre. Wasting no time Willow went to work on the wall beside them. Working together as a group with weapons and feet they created an opening in no time. Once everyone had stepped through Willow walked to the end of the corridor, estimated the length of the pit and then attacked the same wall returning them to the original corridor. The Alfár was relentless and would not be turned aside from her original path.

No matter what the maze threw at them with its traps, cave-ins, dead-ends and pits lined with frozen stakes, Willow led them in the same direction. At times they were forced to move incredibly slowly as every step seemed littered with pressure pads, but the Alfár refused to stop. Twice they were forced to rest and each time the walls directly around them moved, creating new corridors and dead-ends. Each time they set off again Kell was sure Willow had become spun around but somehow she had an internal compass that never led them astray.

When they burst through yet another wall and Willow stumbled, Kell thought their luck had finally run out. But as he lifted his eyes from the ground he realised they'd reached the heart of the maze.

Even though it had been ten years it looked exactly the same as when Kell had been here last. The vast domed chamber was built on an epic scale with four huge doorways at the principal points of the compass and four tall narrow windows at the intervals. Through some unseen and complex system of mirrors, beams of sunlight poured through the windows to converge on a central point. Eight golden shafts of sunlight also fell from windows in the roof to meet at the centre.

The floor of the vast room was empty apart from a wide dais at the far end which almost resembled a theatre stage. Extending almost the full width of the room the vast block of ice was twice as tall as Kell and would be difficult to scale if not for the crude steps that had been cut into its face. Compared to the smooth elegance they'd seen so far, the stairs had made by someone with little skill.

Perched on top of the stage, directly in the centre where the beams of sunlight met, sat a roughly hewn throne made of ice. Unlike the rest of the chamber it had been made to the correct scale for a normal human.

Even before he heard the intake of breath from the others Kell knew what they had seen. Resting on the throne, its blue eyes just as he remembered from his nightmares, was the Ice Lich.

CHAPTER 37

The Ice Lich, figure of legend and nightmares, peered down at them from its throne with unbridled hate.

Part of Kell had believed that whatever power had been opposing them was something that he'd not encountered before. The rest of him had known the truth from the start and finally here was proof that he'd been lying to himself.

Ten years of nightmares. Ten years of slowly rebuilding his life. Ten years of trying to forget and move on. All of it was erased in the blink of an eye and once more he was a bumbling seventeen year-old boy in over his head.

Even sat on the throne he could see that the Ice Lich was a tall woman. In other circumstances he would have said she came from Kinnan except that she had a wide Seith nose and a high forehead that wasn't common to any native of the Five Kingdoms. Even more unusual her skin was slate grey and what little hair she had clung to her balding skull in snowy white patches. The deep blue of her eyes was familiar, as they'd all seen the like staring out at them from the faces of the dead heroes.

The last time Kell had been here she'd been wearing a flowing silver dress that resembled chainmail but it had been made from hundreds of overlapping badges that he'd never been able to identify. He'd assumed they were nothing more than decoration but now he began to wonder if they'd been torn from the dead warriors they seen under the ice. Were all of them her victims? Had she torn a badge from each corpse and worn it as a grisly souvenir?

Now, instead of such a rich garment the Lich wore patchwork armour. It looked as if it had been cobbled together from salvaged pieces, none of which fit properly, and it would offer little in the way of real protection.

It was only then Kell realised something else was missing. There was no sign of the wound he'd inflicted upon her body.

The skin around her neck and shoulders was unblemished and there wasn't even a scar. Kell knew the others probably doubted what he'd done and looking at the smoothness of her skin he began to wonder himself. Had the Lich somehow tricked him and made him see what wasn't really there? Had he actually cut off her head all those years ago?

Everyone was stunned into silence and although the Lich had not used her power against them he could see they were frozen with indecision. Coming face to face with yet another figure from mythology was taking its toll. Kell watched as her eyes passed over each person in their group. Her expression never altered, even when she studied the Alfár, but when their eyes met Kell saw a spark of recognition. A smile spread across her face and the Lich held up one hand, gesturing at herself, whole and in one piece, mocking him.

A faint sound on the periphery of Kell's hearing quickly swelled until he realised that Willow was growling. The rumbling came from deep within her chest and it continued to build until it exploded from the Alfár's mouth in a loud bark. The sound echoed around the barren room, ricocheting off the walls and ceiling, repeating over and over again until it shook everyone from their reverie. If the Ice Lich was startled by Willow's outburst she showed no signs of distress. She focused her piercing gaze on the Alfár but Willow wasn't intimidated and showed no discomfort.

"Betrayer!" shouted Willow, surprising everyone with the vehemence in her voice. Much to Kell's surprise that word made the Ice Lich flinch as if she'd been slapped across the face. She squirmed in her chair and broke eye contact, turning her face away from Willow as if ashamed. "Oathbreaker." The word rang around the room as the Alfár stalked towards the throne.

Kell followed behind Willow at a distance, watching for trouble. The others were just as startled but they followed him towards the Ice Lich.

"You had a sacred duty, and worse than abandoning your post you defiled this place. You defiled the others and you defiled him," said Willow, spitting out each word. The Alfár had reached the first of the roughly made steps that led up to the throne. She glared up at the Ice Lich who shrank back in her seat. As Kell drew closer to the Lich he noticed a few details he'd previously missed.

The grey skin made it difficult to judge her age but he'd always thought of her as youthful. She also looked a lot more frail than he remembered from last time. Her hands were bony, the skin almost transparent and the backs spotted from age. There was a network of lines at the corners of her mouth and crow's feet around the eyes. He'd once described the light within her as so bright it was difficult to meet her gaze. Now, although her stare was no less intimidating, the power behind her eyes had dimmed.

"You speak as if you know what I endured," said the Ice Lich, talking directly to Willow. It was as if the rest of them no longer existed. "How many generations were supposed to sacrifice themselves? How many lives should be wasted?"

"Wasted?" shouted Willow. The word struck the Lich like the lash of a whip.

Kell didn't know what was going on between them but it was clear that she was weak. She must have expended an enormous amount of power to control the beasts, raise the dead and turn the maze against them. Her every effort had been to keep them out of this room which meant she was vulnerable.

If the Lich had any energy held in reserve she would have to use it quickly or risk losing her head a second time. Taking no chances in case he was wrong Kell kept his sword ready.

"After all that you were given, you still find cause to complain."
Willow was appalled by the Ice Lich. Kell had never heard her
speak with such raw emotion. Her harmonic voice always sounded
peculiar but now it wavered in a way he'd describe as human. He
couldn't tell if the Alfár was moments away from tears or an angry
outburst.

Willow took another step towards the throne and Kell saw the
Lich's eyes flick around the room as if searching for a means of
escape.

"I only took a little," said the Lich in a wheedling voice. It felt as
if she were an errant child apologising to an adult but Kell could
hear the lies. She had done more, so much more, to have angered
Willow.

With every step Kell waited for the hammer to fall. After all
that they'd endured he knew there would be one final trap. They
were probably walking straight into it but he just didn't care any
more.

For too many years he'd been living with the nightmares. For
too long he'd been carrying a huge weight on his shoulders. Guilt
still gnawed at him for surviving when all of the heroes had died.
Kell thought he'd moved past it and been made whole, but now
he felt fragile.

He needed it to be over. Looking at the faces of his friends he
knew they needed it too. They had nothing more to give.

"Your continued life is grotesque. A malignant theft," said
Willow, reaching the top of the platform. The Alfár moved to one
side and the rest followed creating a semi-circle around the throne.
Kell's muscles were so tense they were throbbing with unspent
energy. Malomir stood poised on the balls of his feet, ready to spin
and attack from any direction. Bronwyn was grinding her teeth
so hard Kell could see the blood pounding her temples. Vahli had
a dagger in each hand and his knuckles were white. They were
balanced on a knife's edge, at journey's end, but all of them knew
it wasn't over yet.

Willow seemed to have run out of words. The Alfár's hatred

for the Ice Lich was palpable and she shied away from Willow's intense stare.

"How are you alive?" asked Kell, struggling to speak past the lump in his throat. "I took your head, didn't I?"

The Lich turned its cold gaze on him but now her power to terrify him was gone. In every way she was a paltry shadow of her former self. A small part of him no longer cared if he died. At least he would be at peace. He just needed to know.

"Tell him!" shouted Willow and the Lich jumped. The sneer slid off her face and once more she became the misbehaving child. "He deserves to know."

"Was it real?" asked Kell. He had so many questions about her and the castle, but selfishly he put all of them aside.

"You did cut off my head," said the Lich adjusting her neck, but he could not see any sign of the injury. Despite her recovery a surge of relief ran through him. At least, after all the sacrifices that had been made, he'd actually done that much. He'd bought the Five Kingdoms ten years of relief from her power.

"Then how are you alive?" asked Malomir. Beside him Bronwyn's whole body was trembling with pent up anger. The grief about her father had given way to rage and now it was startling to boil over. Kell had a feeling she wouldn't be able to hold back for much longer. Vahli was aghast, staring at the Lich with huge eyes. He'd probably never thought that he'd end up here standing in front of her.

"There was a spark of life remaining in me." The Lich spoke with reluctance but with Willow glaring at her she couldn't remain silent. "I was able to regenerate my body."

Before Kell could ask how she'd done it Willow surprised everyone. Screaming with rage the Alfár swung her weapon at the Lich's head but the blow was deflected at the last second. An energy barrier sprang up around her and Willow was thrown backwards across the icy platform. Kell didn't hesitate and immediately lashed out, hacking at the Lich with his sword. There was a blinding flash as Slayer collided with something solid and then time slowed to a crawl.

Creeping cold, worse than any he'd experienced, coursed up his arm and then through his body before it sent Kell flying through the air. He landed in a heap but scrambled to his feet. His nerves felt as if they were on fire and his fingers spasmed uncontrollably.

The others were attacking the Lich on all sides but each time they were repelled by an egg-shaped sphere which encased her and the throne. Blue forks of energy, like localised lightning, lit up the room. Each time a weapon collided with her barrier it sparked, sending a jolt of energy into the person connecting with it.

Vahli and Malomir had been scattered but Bronwyn refused to budge even when the energy touched her. Her sword hammered against the barrier and a jolt of power ran down her arm, driving her to one knee, but she forced herself up and lashed out again. This time, gritting her teeth against the pain, she held on as more tongues of energy coalesced across her arm and body.

Howling a battle cry of her own Willow attacked from the other side. The feedback that struck the Alfár was almost as severe as that targeting Bronwyn, but now the strain was beginning to show. The Ice Lich was in distress.

Splitting her attention between two of them was proving to be a challenge as both refused to back down. With one arm raised to either side, energy leached from her body into the shield, keeping them at bay. But the cost was apparent as her flesh began to degrade. She couldn't keep them back forever. They just needed to hold on for a little while longer.

Kell charged in and added his own assault to the energy shield. For a brief moment there was a little give in the barrier but then all three of them were sent sprawling. Kell landed on his back, smoke rising from the centre of his chest. His heart was pounding in his ears and his arms twitched from the aftershocks. It took a while before he could sit up, by which time the energy inside his body had dissipated.

"Is that all you've got?" said Bronwyn. She was kneeling on the ice, holding herself upright with her sword. Everyone had been scattered and they were all lying on their backs. Malomir rolled over and struggled to his knees but Vahli was still. Kell didn't know if the bard was unconscious or dead. Willow had made it upright but the Alfár swayed on her feet.

With a grunt of effort Bronwyn stood and then spat at the Ice Lich's feet. Her armour had been blackened in places and the surface of her sword was pitted and uneven. As he reached for his sword Kell noticed Slayer was also riddled with marks. The energy barrier was eating away at the steel of their weapons.

"Get up," said Bronwyn, gesturing at everyone. She nudged Vahli with the toe of her boot and he groaned. With one hand under his armpit she helped him stand while Willow supported Malomir.

"Together," said Willow, who was struggling to stand upright. "We must all attack her together."

Three of them had nearly overwhelmed the barrier. Hopefully with all five attacking at once it would give way. This was the Lich's final line of defence. She was already weak and under pressure.

"Let's end this," said Kell, hefting his sword. Whatever happened next he would be at peace.

Summoning the last reserves of his energy Kell charged forward together with the others. Even before he reached the barrier a fork of energy shot through the air spearing him through the centre of his chest. His arms and legs began to convulse and his heart skipped a beat. His charge ground to a halt and then stopped, his arms dropping to his sides but he held on to his sword. The others were suffering just as badly, all of them caught like flies in a spider's web. Vahli had dropped to his knees and Malomir was bent over double. Somehow the others remained on their feet, unwilling to give in.

Gritting his teeth against the pain running through him Kell forced his left leg forward. It barely moved and he tried again, this time managing a small step. The flow of power running through him was starting to fall.

"Die! I want you to die!" screamed the Ice Lich.

On either side of the throne Bronwyn and Willow were doggedly shuffling forward one slow step at a time. When the Alfár raised her weapon in front of her face, some of the energy was absorbed as Willow's movements became easier. She ran forward the last few steps and slammed the mace into the barrier which tolled like a bell. Fractures ran across its surface and no further power ran into the Alfár. The flow of energy was further reduced and Kell could move more easily. Bronwyn had reached the shield and she too was hammering away at it with her sword. Kell reached it next, then Malomir and soon the four of them were pounding on it.

The Lich's body had decayed even further as her energy reserves ran dry. When Vahli jabbed his daggers into the shield it gave one final surge and then burst like a soap bubble.

The Alfár's axe was moving so quickly it became a silver streak that made a meaty sound as it bit deep into the Lich's body. The blade cleanly sliced the Lich's head from her body just above the shoulders. The power behind the axe was so great that it cracked the throne's headrest.

The whole room became silent and still. The Lich's body slumped down in the chair and sludgy black blood trickled from the wound in her neck. Her head had landed a short distance away and unluckily it was facing towards Kell. It took him a little while to realise that her eyes were still blinking.

"Why is she still alive?" said Kell, beseeching Willow.

The Alfár wrenched her weapon free from the throne and offered it towards Kell. "Like the others who were brought back, you must destroy the brain. End it, for all time."

He reached for the strange weapon but then hesitated. Kell looked towards Vahli but the bard just shook his head. "This isn't my story," he said, a little out of breath.

Malomir also refused. "I can't see them, but I know you still have scars. You must be the one to do this."

Kell turned to Bronwyn. If anyone had a right it was her but the anger seemed to have drained away. Now she looked exhausted and on the verge of collapse. Kell thought it was only sheer force of will that was keeping her upright.

"Finish it," she said, waving him towards the throne.

As Kell sheathed his sword he saw the Lich's body start to move. It reminded him of a headless chicken. The hands started to fumble around and on the ground the Lich's mouth was moving. A faint wheezing sound emerged as she tried to speak. There were words on her lips. Promises she would make to him or perhaps another curse.

Kell accepted Willow's weapon with reverence, marvelling at its weight. He had no idea how the Alfár swung it with ease. Each stumbling step he took towards the Lich's head seemed tougher than the last. He didn't know if she was working against him with her remaining power or if it was sheer exhaustion. Doggedly Kell forced himself forward, one step at a time, struggling to keep the two-headed weapon off the ground.

When he was standing above the Lich's severed head Kell closed his eyes and for a moment imagined what his life would have been like on a different path. One where he'd not been so arrogant and had turned back. Ten years was no time at all and yet also an eternity. It was a bridge he could not cross in his mind. The past and its dreams were fading like smoke on the wind.

Somewhere along the way the youth who'd set off on the journey had died. A broken man had ridden home in his place. Kell had tried to put the pieces back together but they'd never fit right. There was no going back. The past was immutable.

Screaming with fury Kell brought the mace down on the Lich's head smashing it to a pulp.

It was over.

CHAPTER 38

Kell stared at the puddle of blood that was spreading from the Lich's broken skull. He expected to feel relief at her death but nothing had changed. He still had questions and doubts. Had the curse been real? Had it been lifted with her death? If he was truly free of the past, what happened next?

"What is this place? Who built it? What is it for? Who was she?" asked Vahli in one breathless stream of words. Kell knew he had more questions, they all did, about what was really happening here. This went far beyond the Ice Lich and her manipulation of the seasons.

Even as the bard was asking his questions Vahli was studying the huge room around them. Kell could see his eyes were soaking up the details. No doubt it would feature heavily in his new saga.

They all turned towards Willow expectantly but the Alfár seemed to be waiting. With her head cocked to one side Kell realised Willow was listening intently for something in the distance. He couldn't hear anything, not even the wind outside, but then Willow smiled and the Alfár's eyes swung back into focus.

"Go, quickly," said Willow, gesturing for everyone to make their way down the crude stairs. As they went ahead Kell saw the Alfár kicking apart what remained of the throne before throwing the pieces to the floor below. With a touch bordering on reverence Willow brushed away any remaining chunks before following them down the stairs.

Kell was on the last step when he felt a peculiar shift beneath his feet. The others didn't notice but when he reached the floor of the room the sensation faded. Willow all but skidded down the steps before turning around to face the huge platform with an expectant look. Kell was about to ask what was happening but Willow shook her head and grabbed one of his hands with excitement. The Alfár squeezed and pointed to the eight beams of light in the ceiling.

While the Lich had sat on the throne all of the beams had been focused on her, creating a pool of light. Now, some unseen mechanism shifted, and the eight beams were spread along the top of the huge block of ice. Somehow the sunlight inside the ice was reflected over and over, bouncing around until the whole began to glow with pale yellow light. What had been nothing more than an immutable wall of ice started to take on a new appearance.

The crudely made steps started to disappear. The Lich must have carved them to allow her to reach the top but now that her influence was gone the castle was repairing itself. When the huge block of ice was whole again the light inside began to intensify. It became so bright that it was impossible to look at without being painful. Kell and the others were forced to shield their eyes but Willow didn't turn away.

"Look," said Willow, pointing again. "Look inside."

By peering through his fingers and squinting Kell managed a brief glimpse. The surface of the ice had become semi-transparent and at first Kell wasn't sure what he was looking at. Slowly the light faded until he could look at it without any pain. As his brain made sense of what he was seeing Kell stumbled and would've fallen over if not for Willow.

What they had assumed was nothing more than a stage for the Lich's throne was an enormous icy tomb. Lying flat on his back, almost the full width of the huge block of ice, was a giant man. They had been walking across his coffin.

The scale of the castle suddenly made sense. All of it had been made for him.

Kell couldn't place the giant's origins as he had no distinguishing features and his dusky skin was lighter than anywhere in the Five Kingdoms. Although not unattractive his rough blocky face meant you wouldn't notice him in a crowded room. In some ways the giant reminded him of a merchant's guard he'd shared drinks with at the Dancing Cricket.

The man was plainly spoken, happy to let others take charge and not one for philosophical discussion. He had a simple view on life and was content. The similarities continued as the giant's clothes were simply made, and the callouses on his hands suggested he'd been someone used to physical labour.

"Who is he?" asked Vahli, putting aside all other questions.

Bronwyn was swaying on her feet and Kell felt just as exhausted. Answers had to wait a little longer as they made a temporary camp a short distance away from the tomb. They only had a little food which they shared equally but mostly they needed to rest. Despite the leaden weight of his limbs Kell knew he wouldn't be able to sleep until he knew more about what was going on.

They sat in a loose circle around an imaginary fire and for once Willow was fully a part of their camp. The Alfár waited until everyone was settled before speaking in her harmonic voice. Even after all of this time, or perhaps it was because of where they were sitting and who lay sleeping behind them, Willow's voice was unnerving.

"It is Govhenna," said the Alfár, gesturing at the giant behind them. Vahli had his notebook open, pen poised above the page, but when Willow said nothing further he raised an eyebrow.

"We don't understand," said Kell. "Can you tell us more about Govhenna?"

Willow nodded and took a deep breath putting Kell in mind of bards that sometimes came to Honaje. "Many years ago, more than I know how to explain, what you call the Five Kingdoms was a different place. There were no kings, no countries, no cities. Your ancestors looked much the same but they were coarse, like fresh cut wood. They lived for the day. Hunt, eat, sleep and mate.

And then again and again," said Willow, spinning both hands in a cycling motion. "For many years it was this way. Sometimes tribes fought but always it was over land, for places rich with prey for good hunting.

"Slowly, over a long time, the people began to change. Your ancestors roamed as their numbers grew and they sought new lands. There were still no cities but instead of being nomads, some put down roots. Fire, simple metal-working, herding cattle and seeding the earth, these were known, but new skills grew from the minds of settlers. But always there was danger. Threats from others who wanted to steal. Then one day, Govhenna arrived and the tribes were changed."

The smile that tugged at the corners of Willow's mouth was almost a smirk. Kell sensed there was a lot more to Govhenna's arrival than Willow was telling them but today wasn't the time for that story. Kell recognised much of the tale, although no one had ever mentioned a giant man walking around in the version he knew about the history of the Five Kingdoms.

"Where did he come from?" asked Vahli, unwilling to let that detail slide.

Willow winced, uncomfortable with the question going unanswered. "Ask that question another day," suggested Kell. Vahli pursed his lips but eventually he nodded and Willow gave Kell a smile of thanks for intervening.

"Twelve. Twelve great things Govhenna taught to the people and these changed everything. Always he was there, working beside your ancestors in the fields, standing between the tribes to negotiate peace, showing them a way without war. His hands, deep in the earth, in the building of things," said Willow staring up at something far behind them in the distant past. "From him came many of the good things that you see today. Tribes began to change, their faces, their traditions, their favouring of one skill over another. Although there was much left to do, Govhenna's time had finally come. His remaining days were short. The people wept and begged but there was nothing to be done. This could not be changed. There is an end to all things, even one so mighty."

The Alfár bowed her head for a moment before carrying on in a voice thick with emotion. "Once more the tribes began to bicker, over where he would rest and who would watch over him. Govhenna had always treated all tribes equally and in this he was no different. Each would send warriors to protect him while he slept to show thanks. He came here to the Frozen North, so that no tribe could claim favour, and with his final breath he created the tomb that would protect him."

Willow's hands spread wide to take in the room but Kell realised more was meant by the gesture. The Alfár was talking about the entire castle that surrounded them.

"He made all of this?" said Kell. "With a thought?"

It had been difficult enough to imagine how anyone had built such a vast and complicated building in this climate. No one would ever believe that it had sprung into existence from a single thought.

"All of this is his tomb. The castle, the maze, the traps, the guards outside. It was meant to keep people out. To let him rest in peace." Willow spoke with such complete certainty that it was difficult to express doubt about her story.

How many generations had stood watch over the tomb in tribute?

"Then who was the Ice Lich?" asked Bronwyn.

Willow hissed like an angry cat, startling everyone. "She was one of the honoured, chosen by her tribe to stand guard, but unlike those before her she was ungrateful. She was not the only one to enter the tomb, but none made it to the heart. She was the first to stand before him. Although he is gone, even in death, Govhenna has power. To rebuild the ice, to change the maze, to keep himself safe. She was the first to realise that what little power remained in him could be stolen. She is the ice leech."

Kell was about to correct Willow when he wondered if they'd been using the wrong word. She hadn't named herself the Ice

Lich. In fact he struggled to recall who had first used the term to describe her.

"Many years passed, the tribes forgot their promise and no more warriors were sent to watch over his tomb, but she endured. She fed on him, drawing power, rebuilding her flesh, extending her life." Scorn for what she'd done dripped from Willow's every word. "Slowly she infected this place and then beyond. The beasts, the fallen heroes and the seasons, until even in the warm south, her presence was felt. All was off balance but then it stopped. I heard the story of Kell and thought it was over. The rest is known."

A heavy thoughtful silence filled the room as everyone mulled over the story. There were elements that sounded familiar from what he'd been told as a boy but much of the story sounded invented. And yet the Alfár knew a great deal about the castle and its surroundings.

Vahli had been furiously scribbling in his journal throughout Willow's story but now he'd paused. "I have just one more question," he said, knowing that asking Willow anything was difficult and most of the time you didn't get an answer. "Who is Govhenna?"

This time it was Willow's turn to look confused. "You know this. All of you," said the Alfár staring at each of them in turn. "Govhenna is not his name, this he shared with no one. Not even my people before. It is what he is, the title your people gave him long ago."

Puzzled faces surrounded Kell and he was still as baffled as the others. "Then, what does it mean?" he asked.

"In your language Govhenna means the Shepherd."

The Shepherd.

It was nonsense. It had to be, and yet, the more he thought about it the more what Willow had told them lined up with scripture. The Shepherd walking among the people. The twelve pillars of the faith. Bringing peace and prosperity to the Five Kingdoms. Raising the tribes from primitives into something greater. To Kell it had always been just a story, but now here was proof that it was true.

A heavy silence filled the room as everyone tried to make sense of it in their own mind. Malomir was the least affected and looked a little baffled at everyone's reaction. In the Summer Isles they had gods and customs of their own.

Kell had never really believed in the Shepherd but there were thousands who did. His mother had been devout and as a boy he'd often heard her whispering prayers at night, mostly for him to make something of his life. Many people used to make an annual pilgrimage to the Holy City of Lorzi. It was said the cathedral was built on the site of where the Shepherd had lived, but now he wondered. If he dug beneath the foundations would he find the remains of a vast home for Govhenna? Or was that another lie?

In the last twenty years there had been a steady decline in the number of faithful. People were busier than ever with family and other commitments. That was the reason he'd heard most often but those were just excuses. The truth was, believing in something abstract was difficult.

If the priests ever found out about Govhenna's tomb it would change everything. The castle would become a new site for pilgrims. Churches across the Five Kingdoms would be brimming to the rafters. There would always be doubters but even they would find it hard to disregard the giant man once they stood in his presence.

"We can't tell anyone about this place," said Kell, breaking the long silence.

"We must," said Vahli. "The truth must come out. Surely, you of all people, want that."

"For ten years a lie about the heroes has served the Five Kingdoms better than the truth," said Kell. It was one of the reasons that he'd sworn an oath to King Bledsoe never to tell the whole story. It had protected their legacy and ability to inspire others.

"No one must come here," said Willow, making a cutting motion with one hand. "Think of the damage one greedy warrior caused. It must end with her."

"Imagine if a priest came here. What do you think it would do to their faith?" asked Kell.

"I don't trust priests," said Malomir. "That's why we banned them in the Summer Isles. They do not listen to others."

"What if someone else finds a way to harness his power?" asked Bronwyn.

It was that thought more than any other which terrified Kell. It was one thing for an ancient warrior to abuse the Shepherd's power. In the hands of a zealot, the Five Kingdoms would be transformed into something unrecognisable. There would be no room for those who didn't believe. The rule of law would be replaced with the rule of faith. Kings would become powerless figureheads or simply disappear giving way to a new religious ruling class.

"Now that the leech is gone the balance is restored," said Willow. "All of Govhenna's remaining power will protect this place. No one will be able to reach him. Anyone who ventures inside will not return."

Kell would have to lie, again, about his journey to the Frozen North. With Vahli's help they would spin a story about a new menace, or perhaps mention the Lich, but the most important detail to stress would be her death and with it the destruction of the castle. If Vahli's song, like the Medina saga before it, was spread across the Five Kingdoms no one would ever have any reason to travel this far north. Only the Frostrunners were likely to stumble across the castle and any who dared go inside would not return.

"Let's go home," said Kell, struggling to stay awake.

Weary beyond any previous measure it took Kell three attempts before he managed to get to his feet. Everyone was exhausted but they all paused to study the Shepherd one final time before heading towards the door. Kell tried to record every detail in his mind, from the way the light filtered through the ice, to the angles of his broad face. It was a remarkable sight that few people had ever seen and one that no one would ever know about.

Before he'd taken a dozen steps Vahli collapsed to his knees. He spat blood and fell onto his side groaning in pain. Malomir reached him first and a quick search revealed a brutal stab wound in his side.

"Why didn't you say anything?" said Kell, but the bard just smiled.

"I didn't want to miss anything."

"How bad is it?" asked Kell.

Malomir's expression was grave and he refused to meet Kell's eyes. "Can you walk?" he asked, and Vahli nodded.

"Give him to me," said Bronwyn, passing her sword to Kell. Moving with care she lifted the bard in her arms, staggered once and then righted herself. "Let's go, before my stamina runs out."

When they reached the doorway Kell braced himself for another ordeal with the maze. Willow walked ahead of everyone down the corridor, scouting for traps, while Kell and the others inched along behind. Much to everyone's surprise after only a short walk they reached the rotunda without encountering a single obstacle. Peering over his shoulder Kell saw the walls begin to shift, once more obscuring the path to the heart.

When they reached the sleds the dogs were happy to see them after being on their own for so long. While Kell and Bronwyn tended to their needs Willow set up the tents. Once Vahli was warm and comfortable Malomir did his best to tend to the wound but when he emerged from the tent his expression was grave. Afterwards he tended to everyone's injuries with stitches and salves.

Kell didn't even jump when the needle bit into his skin. He'd been lucky. The icy dagger had missed his kidneys and leaving it in the wound to melt meant the bleeding hadn't been severe. The pain was mounting and Kell knew it would be worse tomorrow, but for now he was able to push it aside.

At first Kell just wanted to sleep but once he'd smelled the dogs' meat his stomach rumbled in an alarming way. They ate a hot meal in silence and then sought their beds as soon as they'd finished.

As he lay beside Willow in their tent, waiting for sleep to claim him, Kell's mind was whirling with questions. He expected them to keep him awake for hours but exhaustion pulled him into a dreamless sleep.

When he awoke the next morning, with sore muscles and in pain, it took him a long time to crawl outside. The others had already gathered but no one was talking. All eyes were turned towards Vahli's tent.

Peering inside, Kell saw Malomir pulling a blanket over the bard's head.

Vahli was dead.

CHAPTER 39

Back in the Meer, in the Lucky Fish tavern, Kell and the others made important decisions about their future.

Although they'd won, and the danger posed by the Ice Lich had finally been eliminated, it didn't feel like much of a victory. Gerren and Vahli's absence was keenly felt by all, particularly when they retrieved the bard's possessions and reclaimed their horses from Bomani.

That night in Meer, sleeping alone and in darkness for the first time in many nights, Kell's dreams had been troubled by strange images. Bordering on a nightmare he'd drifted through a twisted landscape where everything familiar had been transformed into a perverted version of itself. Trees became a tangled mass of scaly limbs that sought blood for nourishment instead of water. The dried out husks of animals hung from branches, their skins flapping in the breeze like sails.

The sky was a grisly shade of purple, run through with veins of black clouds that pulsed as if alive. Soaring through the air a flock of brightly coloured flying lizards suddenly dived towards a creature on the ground. He couldn't see their target but amidst the flurry of wings and sharp teeth he clearly heard tortured screams as the lizards ripped their prey apart. The whole world had been remade into something askew that tormented him throughout the night.

In the morning he awoke with a terrible sense of dread, the sheets tangled and wet with sweat. From their haggard expressions the others had slept no better, even Willow looked tired. Normally a few nights of rest would be a tonic for his weary body but from experience Kell knew he wouldn't sleep comfortably for some time. The only choice was to keep moving forward and wait for it to pass.

In the common room of the Lucky Fish he discovered that a man had died overnight, apparently from drinking too much. The odd thing was no one knew who he was or why he was there. Kell saw it as another bad omen.

In northern Kinnan they stopped off at a small settlement to bury Vahli and Gerren. No one had been willing to leave their bodies on the ice for the scavengers. They'd left the dead heroes where they had fallen outside the castle. Their decayed bodies wouldn't attract much interest and in a few days would soon be covered by snow and ice. It seemed fitting that eventually they would be entombed alongside the other warriors who had once protected Govhenna.

Kell had thought Bronwyn would want to retrieve her father's remains but she'd declined. Whatever shadow the Ice Lich had brought back to life it had not been the real Bron, just as it had not been his old friend, Kursen. They would both remember them as they had been in life.

Once their friends were buried, prayers were uttered and tears were shed they started drinking. It went on long into the night with each of them telling stories about their fallen friends. Willow barely spoke but Kell could see the Alfár was listening. Occasionally she gave one of those peculiar half smiles which he still found a little unsettling. Over whisky they laughed at Gerren's naivety but also his bravery in facing the maglau. Kell thought about telling them the truth about Vahli but in the end decided against it. It was better that they remembered him as a friend, not a spy sent by King Bledsoe. Besides, what was one more secret for him to carry?

The following morning Malomir and Bronwyn had their hands bound together in the traditional method by a grizzled priest of the Shepherd. Before making the journey none of them had really believed, but after what they'd learned about Govhenna, it became a moving ceremony. Kell watched with tears in his eyes as they made a sacred vow to care for one another. The vow wasn't needed. They'd already shown the depth of their feelings for each other.

Now that he had a future Kell wondered if he would ever find someone to share his life. If he was lucky there was still time for love and a family.

Malomir planned to return to the Summer Isles and with him went his new queen. There was much in the lush paradise that needed to change. Old ways that were no longer acceptable. It would be difficult and unpopular work that would take years but they were determined to see it through. Kell had faith in them. When the two of them were united nothing could stand in their way.

As a group they decided that as far as everyone in the Five Kingdoms knew, only Kell had survived on his second journey to the Frozen North.

Bronwyn had nothing more to prove. She had bested the most savage beasts in every land and whatever grievances she'd had with her absent father had been laid to rest with his body. Bron hadn't been the perfect husband, father or friend, but Kell still envied her. At least she'd had a chance to know her father.

In some ways Bronwyn's future would be ever more challenging than her past. She would be facing enemies that she couldn't simply beat into submission. Even as King and Queen it would them take years of careful negotiation and planning to slowly change the Summer Isles.

Before leaving the ice fields she'd hurled her necklace into a fishing hole where it was lost beneath the water. Malomir had followed suit, casting off much of what had come before. It was a fresh start for both of them.

Despite all of Malomir's accomplishments his name was not widely known in the Five Kingdoms so his absence wouldn't be noticed, making it easier to say that he had also died in the Frozen North.

As for Willow, most people didn't care. They knew almost nothing about the Alfár as a people and preferred not to think about them too much. They were oddities that existed on the fringes of society across the Five Kingdoms. Willow had no qualms about being excluded from what would no doubt become a popular new saga taken from Vahli's journal. In fact Willow preferred it that way and in return only asked for a favour.

"One day, I will need your help," said Willow.

"It's yours. Whatever you need. I swear it," said Kell without hesitation. The Alfár had saved his life, all of their lives, countless times. There was nothing he wouldn't do for her.

The newly wed couple left him and Willow on the road in Kinnan, riding east towards the city of Okeer. From the capital they would catch a ship south to the Summer Isles to begin their new life together. Kell was made to promise that one day, perhaps in a few years' time when circumstances had improved, he would cross the sea and pay them a visit. Part of him knew, as did they, that it was unlikely to happen but he appreciated the offer.

In the town of Liesh, just over the border into Hundar, he and Willow parted company. It had been a strange moment. Kell had hugged the others but with Willow he still struggled to know if such intimate contact would cause offence. In spite of the time they'd spent together and all that he'd learned about the Alfár and her people, it didn't come close to bridging the gap between them. There was still so much he didn't understand. Perhaps one day, if Willow returned to take him up on his promise, Kell would learn a little more.

Deciding that caution was better than leaving on a sour note Kell had offered Willow his hand. The Alfár had smiled, touched him on the lips with two fingers and whispered something in her native tongue. Before he could respond Willow walked away with her familiar loping gait. After that it was just him and Misty on the road south.

Their party had been recognised but the people there were a different breed. Kell could imagine them in years to come listening to the Vahli saga with a secret smile. A few might try to expose the lie and claim that the others were still alive, but he didn't think it would make a difference. He knew that speaking out against heroes, especially those who'd sacrificed themselves for others, was never a good idea. Those who did were rarely believed, just as Gerren had been ignored by the others.

Less than an hour south of town Kell found a group of people waiting for him beside the road. The half dozen Choate were sat in plain sight beside their horses, playing bones to pass the time. As he approached they packed away their belongings and one of the men stepped forward.

"I am Gar Darvan."

"I remember you," said Kell, getting down from his horse.

"Your quest went well?" asked the Choate, glancing at the sky. There hadn't been a significant change but Kell knew it was happening. It would take some time for the seasons to fall back into alignment. It would still mean a difficult year ahead with a poor harvest but if they could make it through the winter next year would be better.

"The threat is gone," he said. "So you can tell whoever sent you that it's done."

"You can tell them yourself," said Darvan. "He would like to meet you."

Kell followed the Choate west towards the distant Breach mountains. Even at this distance they filled the horizon like an impenetrable barrier. Some of the peaks were hidden in the clouds and many were dusted with snow. It was easy to see why people used to believe they were the edge of the world.

Kell noticed they were not far from where he and the others had been attacked by the Hundarians. The Choate must have been waiting the entire time he was in the north, although he didn't know why. After a short ride he saw something in the distance that made his stomach tighten with fear.

An army of Choate had assembled for war.

Hundreds of tattooed warriors were gathered together and had made camp in Hundar. As they rode closer he saw countless tents and signs that the Choate had been here for some time. There were dozens of cooking fires, pens for sheep and goats, several huge paddocks for the horses, clothes drying on washing lines and children running around at play. The air was alive with the burble of a foreign language and his nose was overwhelmed by the smell of cooking meat.

A temporary arena had been created with tiered wooden benches focused around a flat area that had been cleared of trees and scrub. Although he couldn't see past the screaming crowds that were on their feet, he could hear the clash of weapons. A contest of some kind was underway but he didn't ask about its purpose.

Kell knew little about the Choate but he was still able to pick out differences between various groups suggesting they were from different tribes. Some of the warriors had tattoos across the bridge of their nose, whereas others had symbols on the right side of their face. Some had tattoos on their neck and back of their hands but nothing on their faces. Most of the warriors, men and women, carried swords and axes, but he also noticed a few dressed in dusky red leather armour walking around with spears. Each had a single tattoo across their foreheads and he spotted a number of them patrolling the area, keeping the peace. Regardless of tribe Kell saw that everyone gave way before them.

"Not what you were expecting?" said Darvan, with a lop–sided smile.

Kell shrugged, not willing to say anything until he had a better idea of what was happening.

They left their horses tied to a post and approached the arena. The Choate weren't surprised to see him and more peculiar was when several of them waved or hailed him as if they were old friends. Kell returned the greetings and smiled at everyone but despite their apparent friendliness the gnawing fear in the pit of his stomach wouldn't go away.

The noise of the crowd swelled as they reached the seating area where hundreds of Choate were cheering at the current match. In the centre of the arena was a pit of sand that was ringed with a thick rope. Inside, stripped to the waist, two burly Choate warriors were wrestling, trying to trip or throw the other outside the circle. It was a lot less bloodthirsty than he'd been anticipating. He was surprised to see there were dozens of children and families cheering in the crowd.

Darvan moved away to speak with one of the armoured guards leaving Kell to watch the match. One of the wrestlers, a bald ,middle-aged man with a tidy beard, seemed to be flagging while his younger opponent was still fresh. He tried to throw the older man who stumbled back and fell to one knee. The younger man rushed in to finish him off but it had been a trap. The veteran grabbed his opponent by the wrists, rolled backwards and flipped him overhead out of the ring. The crowd roared and a wave of noise rolled over Kell. It was so intense he swayed on his feet but someone's hand on his back kept him upright. When he turned to see who had come to his aid Kell's mouth fell open.

It was Dos Mohan.

The crowd was now cheering the victor's name making it impossible to talk. Mohan gestured for Kell to follow him and they walked a short distance away from the arena until the noise had subsided.

"What are you doing here?" said Kell. It was only as he asked the question that he noticed the way the other Choate deferred to his old barber. He'd assumed the six warriors were there to guard him but now he could see they were protecting Mohan. "Who are you?"

"That is a long story," said the old Choate, giving him a toothy smile.

"Is this an invasion? Are you going to war with the Five Kingdoms?"

"No, no, you misunderstand. Come with me," said Mohan, guiding him towards a spacious tent which was open at the front. There were more guards around the perimeter and inside he found lots of sheepskin rugs piled on the ground to create a soft area for lounging. Brightly coloured cushions were scattered around the tent and on top of a wooden travelling chest there was a small wooden barrel and some glasses.

Mohan slipped off his boots and then poured two beers before gesturing for Kell to sit down. Kell slowly lowered himself to the rugs, accepted the beer and waited for an explanation.

"I know who built the ice castle and why," said Dos Mohan, raising a hand before Kell could say a word to deny it or otherwise. "All Choate know, but we don't know his name, only his title. Govhenna."

"How?" said Kell, taking a gulp of beer to wet his throat which was suddenly very dry. Willow wasn't the only one who had been keeping secrets.

"What do you know about the Shepherd's Book?"

"Not much. Just a bit about the twelve pillars. Charity, love, compassion. That sort of thing. My mother was devout but I never paid much attention. Now, after what I've seen, I wonder how much of it is true."

"More than you might think. However, the Book was created much later because the real story was more difficult to understand. We only have fragments but we know they buried the truth about why Govhenna came to the Five Kingdoms. Did you see warriors buried beneath the ice?" asked Mohan.

"There were more than I could count. Hundreds, maybe thousands, had been laid to rest."

"An unbroken line of warriors were sent to guard his final resting place. Once, long ago, we also sent people north. But with the invention of the Shepherd's Book, the other tribes turned away from their oath. It wasn't long before they believed the priests and the words in the Book alone. The truth, passed down from their elders, was ignored. We were shunned and outcast for our apparent heathen beliefs, so we withdrew from the other tribes. To my shame, my ancestors also stopped sending warriors to the north."

"So why are you all here?" asked Kell, gesturing at the vast camp around them.

"You have powerful enemies, Kell. People who wanted to see you fail. King Elias of Hundar is one of them. He has strong ties with the Holy City and the Reverend Mother. Her power is not what it once was but they're working together to change that. You represented a threat to their plans, so we had to ensure you made it as far as Kinnan. The King in the North has no time for their religion."

"Why would King Elias send warriors to assassinate me?"

"Imagine what would happen if you were to reveal the truth about Govhenna. It would split the church in two. Over the last ten years the Medina saga has given the church a lot of headaches. It implies that the supernatural and magic are real which is against the teachings of the church."

"Well, whatever their plans were, it doesn't matter. No one in the Five Kingdoms can know the whole truth about what I found," said Kell. "The risk is too great."

The Vahli saga would clearly state that the ice castle had crumbled to dust upon the death of whatever menace they invented this time. It was the only way to ensure that no one ventured north to find it. Anyone foolish enough to try would not get beyond the maze. It angered him to think that his silence would serve those who'd tried to kill him but they'd all agreed on this course of action.

"I'm pleased to hear that," said Mohan, sipping his beer. It was so strange to see him in these surroundings and yet Kell still felt at ease in his presence. "Two hundred years ago the Choate tried to bring the truth to the Five Kingdoms and it resulted in a bloody and pointless war."

"Then it's over. They'll leave me alone."

Mohan sighed and rubbed at his face. He looked tired and for the first time Kell thought the tribesman seemed old. "No, I don't think they will."

"Why?"

"Because the Reverend Mother is ambitious and you're still dangerous to her. Your stories serve as a constant reminder that there's something else out there beyond her god. She wants everyone in the Five Kingdoms to pray to the Shepherd. One day, there will be another holy war where she'll try to get rid of all the heathens. I just pray it's not in your lifetime."

"Do you think she'll try to send someone else to kill me?" asked Kell.

"Maybe."

"Is that why you were in Honaje all these years? Protecting me from assassins?"

"One of the reasons, yes. Once we heard about your quest to the north it seemed prudent to have someone nearby to keep an eye on you. Over the years my wife and I buried at least a dozen bodies in the woods beyond old Grover's farm."

"A dozen?" said Kell, struggling to take it all in. "Why else were you in Algany?"

Mohan looked out of the tent at the other Choate moving about in the camp. When he turned back Kell saw there were unshed tears in his eyes. "Long ago, when I was a young man, I made a promise to your mother. I swore to stay away, but after her death, and then what happened to you, I had to protect my family."

Kell didn't remember his father very well. He'd died when Kell had been three or four years old and no one ever talked about him, not even his mother. Whenever Kell had asked, the only thing she'd say was that his father had been a great man. Mohan was someone important to the Choate. In a perverse way everything fit together perfectly.

As he stared at his old barber Kell could definitely see a bit of a family resemblance, particularly around the eyes and mouth.

"Kell, I'm not your father," said Mohan. "That was Javeed, my younger brother. He died in a skirmish shortly after you were born. I offered to take care of you and your mother, but she made me swear to stay away. She married a local man but then he died a few years later when you were still young."

Kell could see that Mohan was saddened about the death of his brother but he struggled to feel anything. He'd never known his real father but, for the first time in many years, he had a family.

"So tell me, uncle, who are you really? Are you their King?" asked Kell, gesturing at the gathered horde of Choate.

Mohan smiled and some of the pain faded from his eyes. "No, that's my older brother. I'm their War General, or I was, ten years ago."

"Does that mean one day I could inherit the throne?"

Dos Mohan laughed and it almost felt as if they were sat together in his tent back in Honaje. "You are about twenty-third in line, so I wouldn't get too excited."

A comfortable silence filled the tent and for the first time some of the horrors of the last few weeks faded.

"So what happens now?" said Kell.

"Now, you should go home and tell that old goat, King Bledsoe, your story. After that you deserve some peace. Go back to the farm. Find yourself a wife, maybe start a family."

"That's all I want," said Kell. "Are you returning to Honaje?"

"No. I'll be going home, but don't worry, someone will keep an eye on you in my absence," said Mohan with a wink.

CHAPTER 40

This time when Kell entered the capital city of Thune he was relieved when no one even gave him a second glance. To them he was just another weary rider passing through the gates. It also helped that a steady rain was falling. A lot of people were hurrying about their business with eyes downcast to avoid the puddles.

Kell's cloak was dripping wet and he was soaked through but after the cold of the Frozen North it didn't bother him.

Since leaving the Choate back in Hundar he'd spent a lot of time thinking about the past and his future. No matter what the King offered he planned to turn it down. The others had all moved on and started a new chapter of their life. It was time for him to do the same.

Going back to Honaje would be strange but he hoped that in time the ghosts that had haunted him would be laid to rest. He'd considered selling the farm and moving somewhere new to start afresh but now, no matter where he went, people would know his name and face. At least in Honaje for the most part people left him alone.

Last time when he'd returned to Thune he'd been hoping for a glorious welcome with people lining the streets cheering his name. This time he preferred the anonymity despite feeling that, once again, he was sneaking into the city like a thief.

When he reached the palace gates it took a while for Kell to persuade the guards of his identity. He didn't blame them for not recognising him in such a bedraggled state but eventually he was let inside while a servant was sent to fetch Lukas.

When the King's Steward arrived he barely glanced at Kell before he started barking orders. Lukas's voice lashed the guards and lingering servants alike, sending them into a flurry of activity. Misty, his faithful horse, was led away to the stables where Lukas promised she would be treated with the utmost care. Another servant took Kell's weapons and belongings ahead to his room while two young girls sprinted away to carry out additional orders. He and Lukas followed behind at a more sedate pace with Kell's boots squelching every step of the way down the corridors.

By the time Kell arrived at his room his belongings had been unpacked, fresh clothes had been laid out and a fire was blazing in the hearth.

"You look frozen half to death. We'll speak once you're more comfortable," promised Lukas.

This time when he entered the bathhouse Kell wasn't greeted by the burly matron who'd previously offered to wash him. The water was gloriously hot and, although he was still sore and healing, the bath eased the aches from his weary muscles. He was pleased to find that all of his toes had survived his second trip to the Frozen North.

Once he was dry and dressed in ill-fitting uncomfortable clothing Kell was primped again by a barber, who tidied up his beard and hair. Staring at himself in the mirror was an uncomfortable experience and he didn't focus on his reflection for long. The death of Gerren still weighed on him. Making the journey south by himself meant his thoughts were his only company. He went over every conversation and moment with the boy thinking about what he could have done differently. Despite the protests of the others Kell knew the guilt would be with him for a long time.

The other reason he didn't linger on his reflection was the revelations made by his uncle, Dos Mohan. He regretted not spending more time with him and asking more questions. Most of all he wondered how his mother had met and fallen in love with one of the Choate. It was an unusual pairing so their first meeting must have been special.

He needed time alone. To think. To make sense of it all and find a new version of normal, whatever that was. Today he was still performing, playing the role of a richly dressed man who'd come to court to speak with the King. He needed the peace of the farm and its isolation. Just one more day of this farce and then he would be free to ride home.

Kell was expecting an audience with the King but instead a servant led him to a private room where Lukas was waiting. A modest feast had been laid out but only the two of them were dining together. Never one to stand on ceremony the King's Steward gestured for him to eat and Kell didn't need a second invitation. It felt like a long time ago since they'd previously eaten together.

After a plate of braised beef and stewed vegetables, buttered bread and tangy cheese, Kell felt ready to burst. He nursed a third mug of black ale and idly watched the flames dancing in the fireplace. Lukas had not yet asked him anything about the journey. Instead he'd filled the air with news about events in Algany and abroad. The idiot king in the Holy City was banging the drum again about the importance of faith in schools. He wanted every child to learn about the Shepherd from an early age. Normally such news would have made Kell roll his eyes. Now that he knew about the Reverend Mother's plans he listened intently and wondered if Lukas was aware.

In Seithland a disagreement between two of the most prominent families had turned into a bloody feud. Such arguments were disrupting trade which affected everyone, especially with a poor harvest on the horizon. As a neutral party a delegation from Algany had been sent to try to prevent further loss of life.

In northern Algany people had started complaining about the Choate. More tribal people wanted to settle on this side of the Breach mountains and the locals didn't like it. They wanted to restrict the numbers of Choate in each settlement which sounded like a fool's errand. A few paranoid people were confident this trickle would turn into a flood and that it was the first step towards an invasion. Now that he knew more about them Kell didn't believe that was their intention but he didn't share his insight.

Eventually Lukas ran out of stories and a heavy silence, broken only by the crackling of the fire, settled on the room.

"So. What happened?" asked the Steward.

Instead of answering, Kell tossed Vahli's journal on the table between them. He'd been unable to read the other journal, as it was written in code, but Kell was determined to decipher its contents.

"That is a fair and accurate accounting of events, more or less, written by the bard, Vahli. I can tell you what happened after your spy died." Lukas's eyes widened in surprise but he didn't deny it.

"We wanted to make sure you returned safely," said Lukas by way of explanation.

"So you didn't set me up to fail?" asked Kell.

"No, of course not," he said, but Kell wasn't sure he was telling the truth. "I'll read the journal later, but can you tell me in your own words what happened? Was it… her?"

Kell smiled at his unwillingness to name the Ice Lich, or Leech, as he'd come to think of her. Over the course of a few hours, drinking only to wet his throat, Kell told Lukas his story, sparing few details.

Ten years ago he'd told Lukas the whole story about his journey and the truth about the heroes. At the time it had been the Steward who'd implied not all of the facts would make it into the saga. Back then Kell hadn't really understood. The legacy of the eleven heroes, and what they represented, needed to be protected and so Pax Medina had conveniently missed out some information. The song painted them as glorious warriors and a close-knit brotherhood of friends who were generous teachers to an errant young boy.

When he reached the last part of his story Kell lied for the first time in his recounting. He said nothing of Govhenna and the countless warriors buried beneath the ice. He said nothing about the tomb at the centre of the maze or the real purpose of the castle. Just as they had agreed, he told Lukas that everyone else in his party, apart from Willow, had died.

Kell could almost see Lukas dismissing the Alfár from his mind the moment she was mentioned. He suspected details about Willow in the new saga would be few and far between, if she wasn't just removed altogether. The story was far more powerful if Kell was the sole survivor of this legendary quest.

Once in a lifetime was extraordinary, twice was a miracle. It would inspire countless others to greatness, just like Gerren, who had wanted to be like him.

"And you're sure she's gone this time? For good?"

"I smashed her skull to a pulp to make sure. The moment she was dead the castle began to crumble. I ran for my life and barely escaped before the whole building collapsed. You can't imagine the noise it made," said Kell, shaking his head and feigning a smile.

"Then it's truly over," said Lukas, sitting back in his chair. His relief was palpable and Kell realised the Steward had been holding back. Lukas had barely drunk from his mug but now he drained it in two long gulps. "You must be tired from your journey. You should rest."

Kell was ready to fall asleep but he stubbornly fought it a while longer. "I want to see it this time, before you send it out," he insisted.

"See what?"

"The new saga by Roe Vahli," said Kell. He still wasn't sure if the bard Pax Medina existed or if it was merely a persona that Lukas had created with the help of others. Then again, the person he'd known as Vahli had been a mask. Lukas studied him for a while but Kell didn't look away. He'd stared into the eyes of savage beasts far more terrifying than the King's Steward.

Lukas grunted and actually smiled as if he were pleased by

Kell's stubbornness. "I think that's fair. Get some rest and we'll talk again in the morning."

Satisfied that the song wouldn't be concocted overnight in his absence Kell returned to his room. Moments after he closed his eyes he fell into a long and dreamless sleep.

Princess Sigrid waited until the sound of Kell's footsteps had receded down the hallway before entering the dining room. Lukas was adding more wood to the fire but he didn't turn around as she sat down. He knew that she'd been eavesdropping on their conversation the entire night.

A few days ago Lukas had finally told her the whole truth about Kell's first adventure to the Frozen North. At the time some of it had sounded far-fetched, but after listening to what had happened to him this time, she didn't doubt a single word.

"He's changed," said Lukas when he'd finished tending to the fire.

"I'm not surprised, having survived all that, but it won't be enough for what's to come."

"No, but it's a good start," said Lukas. "That resilience will help. Last time he was purely focused on reward. Did you notice he didn't ask about the job or the money I promised him?"

Sigrid shrugged. "Maybe he's just tired."

"Perhaps," said Lukas. He always said that when he thought someone was wrong but didn't want to say it outright. Lukas had known Kell for many years so she was willing to concede to his knowledge of the man's character.

"Why didn't you tell him?"

Lukas shrugged. "It's his first night back. I think he deserves a reprieve before we overwhelm him, don't you?"

Sigrid grunted. "Well, the least you could've done was introduce us. I haven't even met him face to face, never mind spoken to the man."

"There will be plenty of time for talking and more," said Lukas, ignoring her frown. They both knew what he was implying. "It's not as if he's going anywhere."

She had been preparing for this day her entire life, but Kell had no idea what was about to happen. A part of her couldn't help feeling sorry for him.

In some ways Sigrid still felt as if she were trapped. She hated the idea of not being in control of her own destiny. However, much as she railed against the idea of a tradition, founded on superstition, she understood that it wouldn't change without the support of others. At the moment she was the sole voice complaining about it. The best way to bring about lasting change was from the inside.

"At least you could have told him about my father," said Sigrid.

"Tomorrow," promised Lukas. "Let him rest."

Even though it was over a week since her father's death the pain was still intense. She felt raw, as if her insides had been jumbled up and badly reordered. Most days Sigrid woke up thinking that he was still alive. Whenever she entered a room in the palace she expected to see him reading at his desk, dozing by the fire or studying the sky out a window. He'd done a lot more of that in the last few months. Never one for long ponderous thoughts on the nature of life or death, he'd recently become philosophical.

People told her that, eventually, the pain would fade. That one day she'd wake up and it would hurt a little less. Sigrid noted that no one had promised it would ever go away. At some point she would have a normal day. She had no idea if that was possible, as everything in her life was about to change.

With the death of her father she would become Queen of Algany. Normally such a role carried no real power, but she would not be someone's puppet or silent companion. They would rule together. She had the experience and her new husband had the fame and respect of the people for his grand accomplishments. After all, he was Kell Kressia, slayer of the Ice Lich and saviour of the Five Kingdoms.

ACKNOWLEDGMENTS

With every book the list of people I need to thank grows longer. Some people, without even knowing, have carried me when I felt like I couldn't move forward, so I wanted to take a moment to thank them.

First, I need to thank my agent, Juliet. Starting a brand new series in a new world is exciting but also daunting and scary and she always believed in this book.

Second, I need to thank my family, for their unwavering love and support.

Third, to my seven brothers from very different mothers, yeah, you know who you are. I can't wait to return to the Barn, hopefully, next year.

I also need to thank the many authors that I talk to on an almost daily basis via social media and email. There are too many individuals to name, but sharing in the ups and down of writing is incredibly cathartic and I look forward to seeing you all in person in the future.

Big thanks to Tom Parker. He is the wizard who created an amazing map from the scribble I sent him.

I also want to thank everyone on the team who has worked on this book at Angry Robot. This includes Eleanor, Gemma, Caroline, Sam, Brittany and Daniel and no doubt other people I've forgotten.

Finally I want to thank you, the readers, for coming with me on a new journey to a new land. I hope you enjoyed it and that you'll come with me on more adventures in the future.

Fancy a sneak peak at the second book in the Quest for Heroes series?
Gotcha covered!

Read on for Chapter One of The Warrior by Stephen Aryan

CHAPTER ONE

Kell Kressia, King of Algany, and two time saviour of the Five Kingdoms, cursed as his opponent's sword clipped his fingers. He managed to hold on to the wooden practise blade, but only just. His opponent today was the same as yesterday and every day before that for months.

Odd Heinla was a member of the Raven, one of twelve elite warriors, who were his sworn protectors. Each of the Raven would throw themselves in front of a sword, sacrificing their life to save his, only not today. Today he and Odd were just two men, stripped to the waist, sparring with wooden blades.

Kell's torso was dotted with fresh purple bruises, a few green and two yellow from a few days ago. There were scrapes and cuts on his shoulders and now the fingers on his right hand were starting to swell up like fat sausages. Amazingly, he was getting better with a sword. Six months ago he would have been one giant walking bruise. Now he managed to parry half of the attacks.

Odd was the best swordsman in Algany and also an incredibly private person, which perfectly suited Kell. Odd barely spoke, didn't comment or offer his opinion on current affairs unless asked, and he never gossiped. After two years of sparring the only things Kell knew about the man was that he was lethal with a blade and was respected by his peers. Even among the Raven he was regarded as the best of the best. Odd wasn't a fawning sycophant or someone who let him win because he was King. He was relentless and utterly focused. Every time they set foot in the circle, each man fought as if their life depended on it.

"Again," said Odd, swinging his arms to loosen his shoulders. "You're too tight," he said, gesturing for Kell to do the same.

Kell tried to relax his body, to anticipate Odd's next move and not stare at his feet. Even after all of this time there was still so much to remember. It was coming, gradually, and he was developing muscle memory, but it still wasn't easy. Part of Kell had hoped that by now his skill would have overshadowed the famous heroes he'd admired in his youth. For all of their faults, of which there had been many, they had been talented fighters. These days he didn't hold them in such high regard, but he did respect their ability.

As always, he and Odd were in a private courtyard in the palace, far away from prying eyes. They were just two anonymous men fight one another in a chalk circle.

Kell signalled that he was ready and then moved to meet Odd in the middle before he was driven backwards. The man was so damn quick, Kell barely saw his blade coming. He sensed it, managed a rough parry and quickly lunged, trying to maintain his balance. He missed, of course. Odd wasn't there anymore but Kell didn't overextend. When Odd riposted, Kell was able to shift his weight and adapt, blocking a series of blows. But he still had no time to go on the offensive. He barely had enough time to breathe.

His lungs were burning, his shoulders ached and his swollen hand screamed at him to drop the blade. Kell grimly held on, blocked on his left and then felt something thwack him across the ribs on his right. The blow left him winded and a little light-headed.

Odd stepped back, waiting for Kell to catch his breath before they continued. The man was barely breathing hard but his dark skin glistened in the noonday sun. At least Kell had managed to make him sweat.

"Your Majesty, I'm sorry to intrude, but there's urgent court business," said a wheedling voice. It was Follis. If there was a more annoying person in the Five Kingdoms, Kell had yet to meet them.

Follis dressed in garish colours that sometimes made him think of his old friend, Vahli. Sadly Follis had none of the charm or wit of the bard. Vahli was gone and so were all of the others. As far as everyone else knew, they were dead and once again Kell had returned as the sole survivor from the Frozen North.

He'd paid close attention to the new saga that had been written about his quest. This time, if anything, there was a lot more at stake. He had to protect his friends and the huge secret about what they had actually found in the castle beyond the Frozen Circle.

As he had anticipated, the new Vahli saga had been an enormous success. In every tavern and bar, bards across the Five Kingdoms had been singing about his adventure, much to the annoyance of certain people in the church. Kell's only wish was that Vahli was still alive to see it. His new saga was more popular than the old one, written by Pax Medina, which had been inferior in every way.

All of that seemed like a long time ago and part of another life. For two years he had been King of Algany. After all that time Kell was still getting used to the idea of it. Sometimes it still felt like a joke. He almost expected someone to tell him there had been a terrible mix up. Then take away the crown and put someone else on the throne instead of him. In fact, he hoped for it most days.

Damn that cunning old bastard, King Bledsoe. He'd trapped Kell into this new life. Kell had wanted fame and fortune only to realise what he'd really yearned for was the peace and isolation of his farm. He still missed his old life. These days he was surrounded by people and rarely had a moment to himself. Follis was one of many unctuous aides that had been foisted on him since becoming King.

"Can't the Queen deal with it?" asked Kell. Sigrid was more than happy to look after the day-to-day issues of running the kingdom on his behalf. He didn't enjoy the responsibility, didn't want it and hadn't been born for it. Unlike her. She'd been training for it her entire life.

"I'm afraid this task is not suitable for Her Majesty," said Follis. He didn't want to be here either. They both knew he would rather be dealing with the Queen. She knew her way around court etiquette. Kell tended to blunder along and apologise after he inevitably made a mistake. It was a dance far more intricate than fighting with a sword, and one he had no desire to master.

Follis knew better than to intrude on his private time. That meant it was serious. If Kell didn't attend to whatever it was, Follis would keep interrupting and there would be no way to concentrate.

"We're done for today," said Kell, saluting Odd with his blade.

"Majesty," said Odd, giving him a short bow.

"Any improvement?" asked Kell, hoping for something.

Odd see-sawed a hand. "Maybe."

At least he wasn't getting any worse. "See you tomorrow then."

Kell poured a jug of water over his head, letting it run down his chest, then dried his body with a towel. He scrubbed most of the water from his short-cropped hair and left the rest to drip dry. Turning up slightly dishevelled would annoy his wife, but it couldn't be helped. It seemed that there were few things about him that, for some reason, didn't annoy her.

These days Kell didn't bother trying for a kingly facade and dealt with everyone as himself. It was simpler and more honest. The Honest King of Algany. That what some had taken to calling him. There were far worse monikers in the history books.

It wasn't Kell's fault that the Queen's late father had chosen him as heir to the throne. It also wasn't his fault that tradition in the Five Kingdoms dictated that only a boy could inherit the throne. As an only child, Sigrid had been forced to marry him in order to become queen. It also wasn't his fault that their daughter had died at three months old of a rare disease. Not that it mattered. She blamed him for that too. It had been the final blow which sent their house of cards tumbling down around them.

Now they slept in separate rooms and did their best to avoid each other as much as possible. Unfortunately, despite the size of the palace, it wasn't always that easy.

It was a far cry from Kell's little farm in Honaje. Most days he still missed it. The peace and serenity. It had been hard physical labour with long hours but at least it had been honest work. Worthwhile. He didn't know if anything he did these days actually made a difference to the lives of others.

When he'd finished dressing in his uncomfortable royal finery, he gestured for Follis to lead the way. Kell's boots echoed along the corridors of the palace. It was nice and quiet in this part of the building. It was far away from the noise and daily bustle. There were always so many visitors in the palace with people coming and going.

Every day he tried to find a little time for himself, away from his responsibilities and duties as King. It was difficult but he always managed. Without it, he became cranky and impatient. More so than usual.

Over the last two years everyone around Kell had learned about his need for solitude. They didn't understand it, but they made an allowance. Some people found peace in prayer; for him, it used to be the farm. These days Kell found it honing his skill with a blade. It allowed him to block out everything and focus only on the moment. To forget everything that existed outside the chalk circle. It made the rest of his life bearable.

By the time he reached the heart of the palace, Kell had settled into the mantle of his new role. He smiled and nodded when people greeted him. He paused to shake hands and make small talk with those he knew had influence and power in Algany and beyond. As far as anyone outside the palace knew, he was a happy and enthusiastic king. Over time he'd become adept at putting on a mask and playing to the audience. If he were still alive, Vahli would have been proud.

As ever there would also be a line of ordinary people waiting to have their grievance settled by someone in authority. Kell diverted from the most direct to the throne room so that he could speak with the petitioners. Sigrid hated it when he did this, so it was a good thing she wasn't around. Follis tutted at the minor delay but held his tongue.

Today there were thirty people standing or sitting in a line. All of them could have been one of his old neighbours; farmers, labourers, craftspeople and a few merchants. Their faces lit up with genuine warmth as he approached. Such an honest reaction was missing from his daily affairs.

Kell shook hands, listened to a few stories, traded a couple of jokes and was disappointed when someone tugged on his sleeve.

"Majesty, we must be going," insisted Follis.

The atmosphere changed. The people stepped back as if he was someone special. For a brief moment he'd been one of them again. An ordinary man talking with his neighbours about their daily struggles. Now they were looking at him in a way he didn't like.

Kell quickly turned away so he didn't have to see the adoration and awe. It was the kind of look he'd dreamed about receiving as a young lad. One reserved for heroes and figures from legend. Now, it made him feel sick.

What's wrong, hero? whispered a voice in his head. If Kell squinted he could almost see Vahli, striding down the corridors. He would have loved being a member of the royal court. All of that power and influence. All of the political wrangling and verbal sparring that hid people's real agenda. Maybe Kell could have appointed him as the Royal Bard and forced him to perform the Medina saga out of spite. How he would have hated that!

"Something amusing, your Majesty?" asked Follis.

"No. Nothing," said Kell, noting the worry on the little man's face.

Two members of the Raven were on duty guarding the doors to the throne room. Normally they were stoic and Kell had never seen one of them lose their temper. Today, both guards were visibly unsettled. A strange form of relief washed over their faces as Kell approached. Before he could ask what was going on they pulled open the doors and practically shoved him inside.

The room had been cleared of all non-essential people making it feel cavernous. With only five people inside, Kell had never seen it so quiet. Queen Sigrid was sat on her throne and lurking off to one side was Lukas, the King's Steward. Two more members of the Raven were on duty inside the room.

As Kell entered, Sigrid rose from her seat. Much to his surprise she was also pleased to see him. Her eyes flicked to the stranger in the room and then back. There was a question in her eyes as if, somehow, she expected him to have the answer. As if he'd known this day was coming.

Even before the figure turned around, Kell knew who it was. There was no mistaking the pale blue-grey skin, the long bony limbs, the white hair and tapered head. It was an Alfár. It was Willow.

Many times in his dreams Kell had seen her yellow on black eyes but it was still a shock to see them again in person.

As they stared at one another across the throne room his mind was flooded with memories from their journey together. His return to the Frozen North. Their battle with deranged beasts and evil spirits upon the ice. The ever-changing maze inside the huge castle and the second death of the Ice Lich. Inevitably, he thought about the friends who had accompanied them, all of who were now dead or elsewhere.

Kell had liked to imagine that when he was really old, and had only a few teeth, they would have met up again and talked about the good old days. Now, he wondered if anything like that would ever happen.

Willow's presence and the urgency of the summons had put everyone on edge. Since the time of Kell's grandfather, everyone had heard stories but few had seen an Alfár in the flesh. There had been no sightings for two years. Willow's return was an ominous portent of bad tidings.

"Hello," said Kell, maintaining eye contact as he approached. Unlike the others, he wasn't afraid. Willow had saved his life many times over. He trusted her, but today Kell sensed there was something between them. An uncomfortable pressure. A question she wanted him to ask. "Are you well?"

Willow tilted her head, not avoiding the question, but visibly agitated in her own way. She never shouted or screamed. She had all of the same emotions as him but the physical tells were small and slight. He tried to think what might be upsetting his old friend and then it came to him.

Vahli's famous saga about Kell's second adventure to the north barely mentioned the Alfár. As far as most people knew, Willow had died in the north along with the others. All heroism in the story had been laid solely at his feet, which in turn, had led to great fortune for the kingdom of Algany.

The modified version was easier for people to understand. No one really knew what to make of the Alfár and, as a result, didn't care about them. Kell understood the reasons for the omission but he didn't like it.

Willow didn't care about fame or even a reward. Her exclusion from the saga had cost him little. Only a promise that one day, in the future, if she needed his help Kell would give it with no questions asked.

"I made you a promise," said Kell, crossing the room and gripping one of her hands. Her skin was just as warm as he remembered. "Do you need my help?"

It was the right question. Relief showed in every angle of her body and a smile touched the corners of her mouth. Willow squeezed his hand in thanks.

Regardless of what Willow's visit meant for the future, Kell was pleased to see her. It was a reminder of who he used to be. A person that, over time, he had grown to like and better understand.

"My people are in danger," said Willow. It had been a long time since he had heard the Alfár's peculiar sing-song voice, but it was not something he would ever forget. The others in the room were already shocked but now they looked worried about what was unfolding. Even Lukas, the King's Steward, who was rarely lost for words, was off balance. There was no formal court etiquette for dealing with a situation like this. It was unknown territory for all of them, except Kell. Her echoing voice was still unsettling but nonetheless Kell had missed hearing it.

"What do you need me to do?" asked Kell.

"Come with me to my homeland," said Willow.

"Can you tell me what's happened?" said Kell, hoping for more details, although it was a risk. Often Willow didn't feel comfortable talking about personal matters in front of strangers. Thankfully, for once, she was willing to share.

"Do you remember how the beasts of the Frozen North had been altered?" asked Willow.

"How could I forget?" said Kell.

The Ice Lich had used her stolen powers to change their nature, forcing them to behave unnaturally. Some had been driven into a frenzied rage so severe that the beasts had maimed themselves in their attempt to kill him and the others. Sometimes, in his nightmares, he ran across the ice fields trying to escape the beasts. The ice broke beneath his feet and he sank into freezing cold water only to be torn apart by the savage bone sharks.

"Maybe we shouldn't be talking about this here," said Lukas, but Kell ignored him. The Raven could keep a secret. The truth about what had happened wouldn't leave the room. Now wasn't the time for delays and political niceties. Willow hated being enclosed by a city. She wouldn't have made this journey if it wasn't important.

On her throne, Sigrid was staring at Kell as if he was a stranger. From the beginning, he had told her the truth about his journey to the Frozen North. He didn't understand why any of this was a surprise. Maybe a small part of her had thought he'd made it up. Or maybe, like everyone else, she'd just never seen an Alfár.

A side door opened and Odd came into the room, dressed once more in his Raven uniform. He observed the strange tableau but said nothing and took up his post beside the throne. If he was rattled, it didn't show on his face. He was as expressive as Willow with little on the outside.

"I remember that the beasts were driven berserk," said Kell, turning back to Willow. "It was the Lich's influence."

"At first I thought it was something else. It's why I've been here for so many cycles," said Willow, turning both hands in a tumbling circle. Kell didn't know if she meant months or years. "My kinsman, Ravvi, and I came here, searching for the Malice."

"What is that?"

Willow tilted her head back and made an awful keening sound. The Raven were immediately on edge, drawing their weapons but Kell waved them back. It was a cry of anguish and suffering. When the echo had faded Willow stared at Kell again, her eyes burning with intense fury.

"A long time ago, my homeland became infected. At first the changes were small and no one noticed. It trickled through the soil, slept beneath the sand, the bark of trees and even our skin. Over time it showed in the plants and then the animals. We named the blight the Malice for the twisted versions that it produced were cruel. Beasts driven into a rage, consuming their own and taking glee in savagery that was not in their nature. Plants that trick and trap their prey. Poisoned fruit that created madness and horrors in the mind. The Malice consumes and remakes all that it touches. It is relentless and all of our attempts to stop it have failed. Ravvi and I came to your Five Kingdoms in search of a cure. When I heard of the changes here, in the weather, in the beasts, I feared the Malice had spread."

"Is it here?" asked Sigrid. Her face was pale and Kell knew that her first thought concerned the safety of their son.

"No. It was the Lich," said the Alfár, tilting her head to one side, regarding the Queen at an angle. "It is not here. I was worried we had brought it with us, but it cannot pass through the doorway. The Five Kingdoms are safe."

Kell could understand why Willow might have thought the Malice was in the Five Kingdoms. The changes had also been slight to begin with but over time they had built until they couldn't be ignored and had threatened the lives of everyone.

"What happens if your people can't stop it?" asked Sigrid.

Kell's thoughts immediately turned to the Ice Lich and the spreading cold. If she had not been stopped then everyone in the Five Kingdoms would have starved or frozen to death.

Willow didn't need to say it. He could see the answer in her eyes. If left unchecked the Malice would consume the Alfár's homeland and then continue to spread.

"Our search for aid has been long and difficult. Ravvi has lost hope. He clings to an idea of a cure from a dark ritual." Willow turned her head to one side and spat on the floor. He'd never seen such a visceral response of disgust from her. Kell was certain he didn't want to know the details of the ritual. "It will fail and could even make it worse. He must be stopped."

Kell didn't hesitate. "When do we leave?"

Some of the anguish eased from Willow's features and her half smile returned. Perhaps, when he knew about the danger, she had thought he would change his mind.

"Now," said Willow, gesturing across the room to where her belongings and strange double headed weapon had been confiscated.

"I'm ready," said Kell.

For more great title recommendations,
check out the Angry Robot website and
social channels

www.angryrobotbooks.com
@angryrobotbook

Science Fiction, Fantasy and WTF?!

@angryrobotbooks

We are Angry Robot

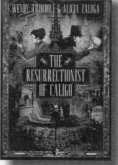

angryrobotbooks.com

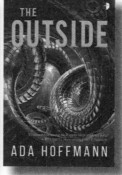